KHYVEN THE UNKILLABLE

LEGACY OF SHADOWS

TODD FAHNESTOCK

Khyven the Unkillable

The characters and events portrayed in this book are fictitious. Any similarity to real persons, living or dead, is coincidental and not intended by the author.

Trade Paperback Edition

ISBN 13: 978-1-952699-45-0

Cover design: Rashed AlAkroka

Cover Art by:
Rashed AlAkroka

Cover Design by:
Rashed AlAkroka, Sean Olsen, Melissa Gay & Quincy J. Allen

Map Design by:
Sean Stallings

Dedication

To all the dedicated fans of high fantasy. I see you online. I see you in your colorful costumes at the cons I attend. You inspire me. You keep me writing.

This one is for you.

The Chronicler

Khyven the Unkillable

The man in the stocks had been there for longer than anyone could guess.

The stocks were made of crude, pitted iron with a riveted latch on the right side secured by a lock as old as the ruined city behind him. The man's only accouterment was a dazzling ruby ring on the middle finger of his right hand.

He ate when gawkers brought him food. He drank when they brought him water. But he appeared to need none of this. From what the astonished denizens of Strawford could tell, he could not die.

The nearby villagers had discovered the man in the stocks a year ago when one of their hunters had stumbled across the ruins of the ancient city barely more than a mile from their newly established hamlet. The man stood on a rise before a valley that contained broken buildings, collapsed walls, and a single metal tower. The ancient city had been abandoned in another age, and its absent keepers had left nothing behind besides that single tower....

And the man in the stocks.

Of course, they'd tried to free him. They had clothed him. They had broken saws and prybars on that immovable latch, to no avail. They had even shattered the head of a sledgehammer on it. During the night, a few thieves had tried to remove his ring, one going so far as to try to cut the finger from the man's hand.

But the man's finger was as indestructible as the latch. Magic.

Soon, they had come to consider the man as unchangeable and immovable as a mountain.

He stood there, bent over, gnarled hands and gray-haired head stuffed through the holes of the stocks during the heat of the summer. He stood there during the snows of winter.

And he told his story.

He told it to whoever would listen: The story of the Second

War of the Giants. Of Khyven the Unkillable. Of the Guardian Rellen back when he was a mortal man. Of Ora and the Dragons. Of Queen Mikaela of the volcanoes. He told of how they had made the world safe from the Giants. A myth that, of course, everyone knew. But the man in the stocks seemed to have details that even scholars did not.

He drew a crowd every day. Sometimes it was only a few children who had escaped their parents to come see the eternal man. Sometimes it was an entire crowd of travelers who had heard the tales of the man who could not die. Sometimes it was those same scholars who came to fill in the patches from history that their books had not captured.

"Do you know the story of the Second War of the Giants…?" the old man said. "Most people think they know about the war. Some say it was what opened the Thuroi and connected the five continents of Eldros.

"Some believe the war began on the continent of Daemanon when the coyote men attacked Pelinon. Some say it began in Drakanon, when the dragons took flight. Some say it began right here in Noksonon when the army of bloodsuckers emerged from the Great Noktum.

"They are all of them wrong. In the writing of history, it is always the big battles that are given the credit. But it was the first battles, those fought in the shadows long before the strife ever came into the light, that tell the true tale.

"How do I know? Oh, I know, little one. I know because I was there.

"I was there the day Queen Rhenn of Usara turned the tide of darkness. I was there when the great wizard Slayter Wheskone outwitted an elder dragon at his own game. And I was there during the rise of the one they call Unkillable…

"When you think of the war, you think of King Rellen's sacrifice at the Elder Portal. Or the charge of the bat army of Pyranon.

"But the seeds of victory began with a young gladiator named Khyven, a selfish man. He had no interest in anything except his own desires, and certainly he had no idea that he would come to be the man that stood between us all and oblivion.

"But I'm going to tell you his story, the true story of the man who saved the world...."

MAPS

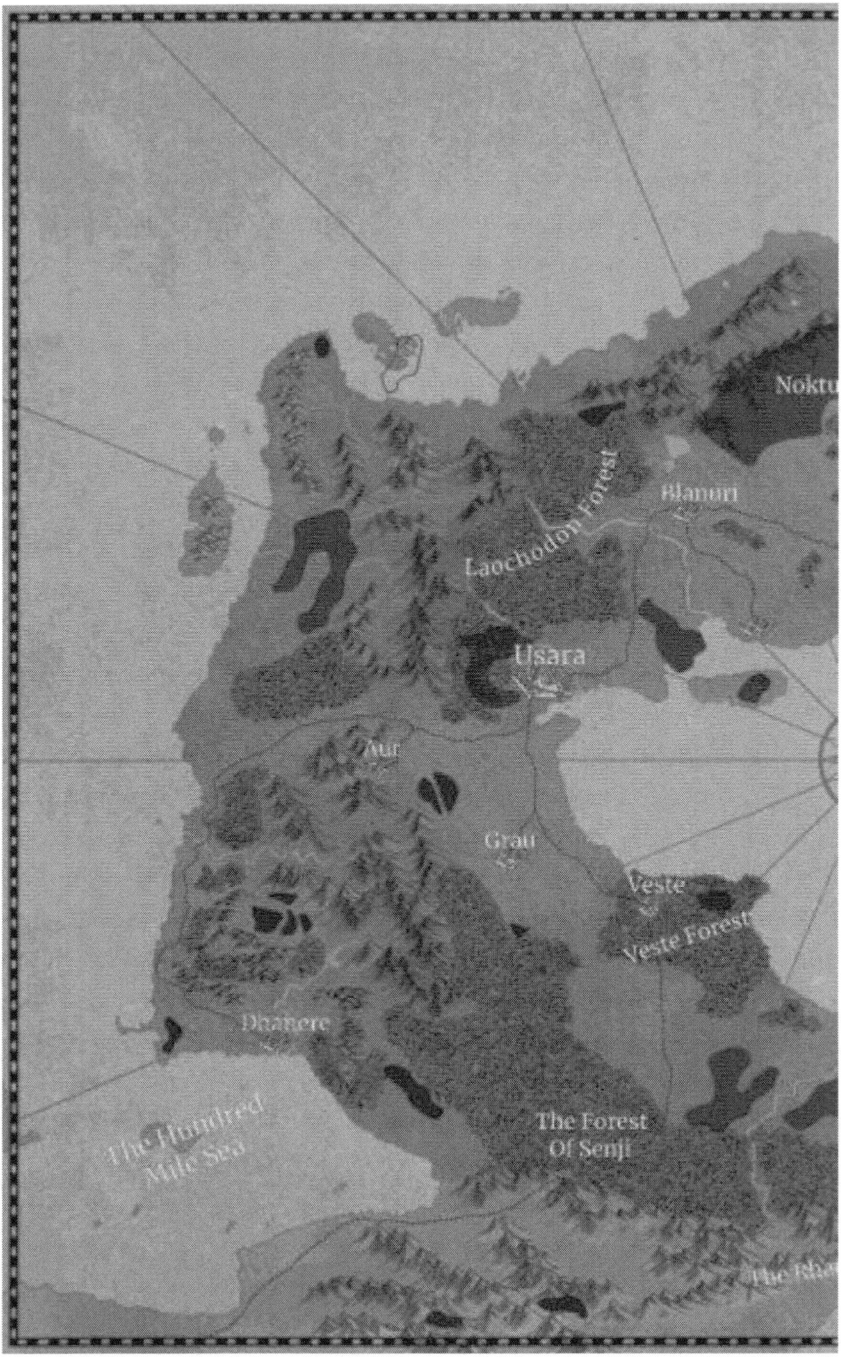

Noktu
Blanuri
Laochodon Forest
Usara
Aur
Grau
Veste
Veste Forest
Dhanere
The Hundred Mile Sea
The Forest Of Senji
The Rha

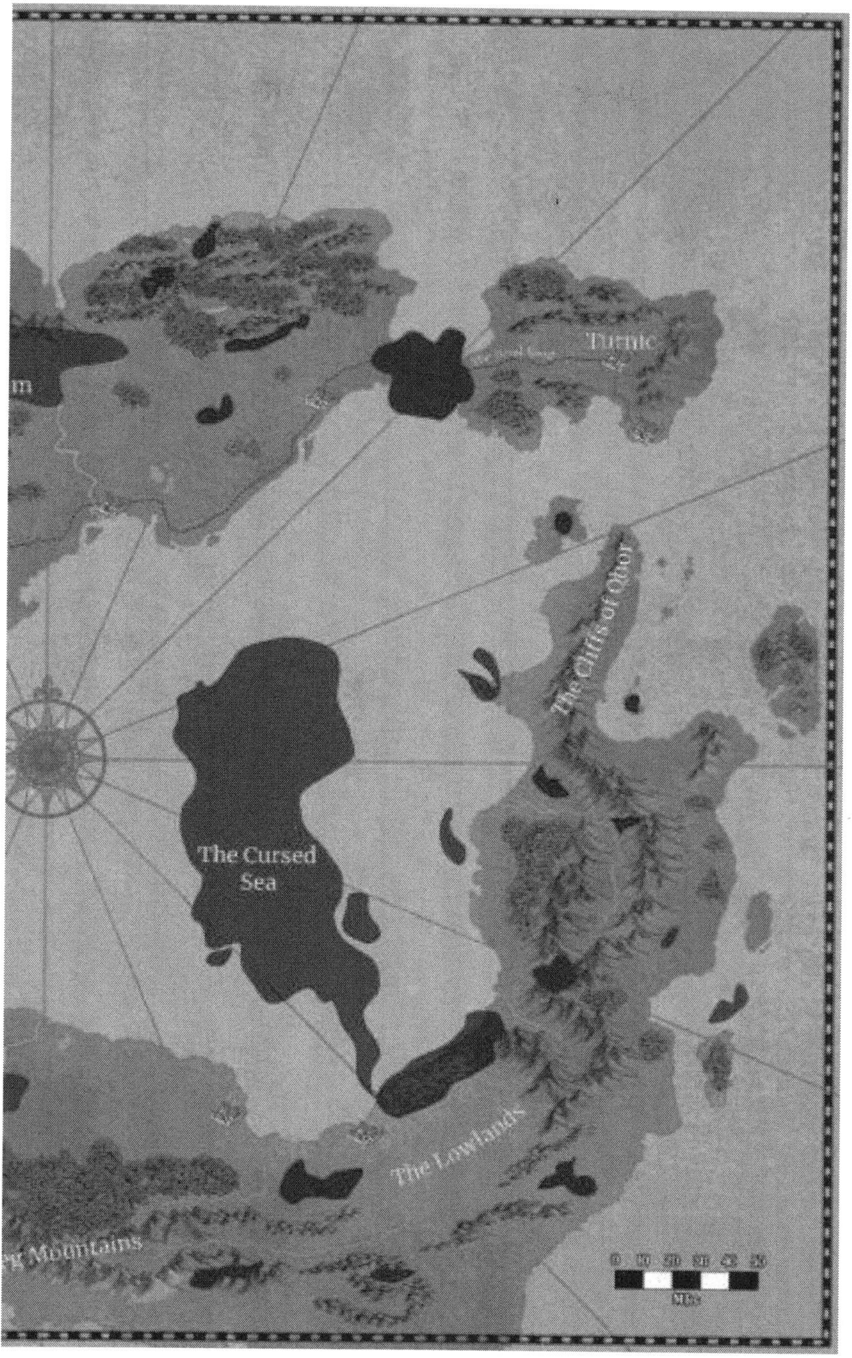

Turnic

The Cliffs of Qdor

The Cursed Sea

The Lowlands

Mountains

PROLOGUE

VAMRETH

Ten Years Ago...

The coup began long before Vamreth's fighters poured through the palace gates that night, but the bribe was the key. Vamreth would always remember that. What would come to be known as the Purge of Usara took a year of planning, secrecy, the expert counsel of the mysterious and chilling Tovos, and a hundred swordsmen. But in the end, a bag of gold coins pushed into the hands of two guardsmen brought the Laochodon reign crashing down.

Once the bribed guards let Vamreth and his fighters through the gates, the loyalists fell quickly, surprised and unprepared for his single-minded onslaught. Vamreth's force cut through the palace like a scythe.

If the king's guards had possessed even another few minutes to rally, the battle would have gone differently. But they didn't, and Vamreth did not delay. Tovos had counseled him not to hesitate, even for a second, and to show no mercy.

Once inside, blood on their blades, Vamreth's mage cast her

spell and located the king. By the time the alarm had raced throughout the palace, Vamreth burst through the door to the royal bedchamber.

In his night clothes, the king spun to face the armed men and women.

A veteran of the Triadan Wars and no stranger to swordplay, King Laochodon went for his blade, perched on iron hooks embedded in the marble wall. He attacked and Vamreth leapt to meet the king.

Steel rang as Vamreth and the king crossed swords. They exchanged a flurry of blows while Vamreth's cohort respectfully stood back. Parry, riposte, lunge, retreat. Vamreth had hoped the king would be caught by surprise, that his worry for his queen—for his entire kingdom—would distract him and sour his swordplay. It didn't.

The king and Vamreth were evenly matched.

"No," Vamreth finally said, winded. He leapt toward the safety of his fighters. "It's taking too long. Kill him."

"Coward!" Laochodon snarled, lunging. But Vamreth's men rushed forward and a dozen swords pierced the king at once. Laochodon collapsed, gurgling his last breath.

The queen screamed.

At a nod from Vamreth, his men charged the queen.

She screamed again and leapt off the bed, but not before a pair of blades stabbed her. She fell to the floor, crying, gasping, crawling toward her dead husband.

Vamreth stood over her. In sight of a dozen of his fighters, his mage Halenza, and her ten-year-old apprentice, he ended the queen's life with one brutal thrust.

He waited until her body went still before pulling out his sword.

"Where are the children?" he asked.

"They are being dealt with," Vamreth's captain said over the screams coming up the hall.

"No survivors," Vamreth said. "Not one."

"And the servants?" the captain asked. "The tutors?"

"Kill them all. When the guards arrive, I want nothing left but the blood of the dead. Let the Laochodon loyalists feel my presence. Let them know that carnage and despair comes for them if they stand in my way."

"Yes, sir." The captain hurried away.

More screams echoed down the hall as Laochodon's children and servants were put to the sword. The captain returned, bloody blade in hand.

"She wasn't in her room," the captain reported.

"Who?"

"The youngest princess. Rhennaria."

"Did you search it? If she's hiding under the bed—"

"Every inch. She wasn't there. The Luminent girl is missing, too."

A queasy feeling spread through Vamreth's gut. He heard Tovos's voice in his mind, the last thing the frightening man had said: *Be quick, for Fate will attempt to thwart you. Kill them all. Not a single can remain.*

There had been a family of Luminents living in the royal wing, honored guests of Laochodon. A father, mother, and a girl the same age as the now-missing princess.

"What of the Luminent girl's parents?" Vamreth growled.

"Dead," the captain replied.

Vamreth turned to his mage. "Find the princess."

Halenza's eyes were already closed as she concentrated. Her young apprentice, a boy named Slayter, stared down the hallway, his brow furrowed like he was working through a mathematical problem. Halenza had insisted on bringing him, said it was part of his training. To Vamreth's surprise, the boy was bearing up well. He hadn't gasped or flinched; he'd just held that intense expression the entire time. Vamreth wasn't sure if he should be impressed or cautious. The boy was certainly odd.

Halenza drew a symbol on the air. It burned like fire then vanished.

"Down the stairs," she said. "The Luminent girl is with her."

Vamreth cursed. "How did she get past us? If she reaches a

bastion of loyalists and they spirit her out the gates—"

"I do not believe that is her goal, Your Majesty."

Vamreth's head came up at the use of the title. It was the first time someone had called him that. With a smile, he nodded. "What, then, is her goal?"

"I think she is heading for the noktum."

"What?" Vamreth said incredulously. "In the Night Ring?" That was half a mile away.

"Actually, Your Majesty, there is a doorway to the noktum in the bowels of the palace," the mage clarified. "Barred and locked. It could be their destination."

"Why would that be their destination?"

"They are children, sire. Perhaps they think it is an escape."

"Show us," Vamreth said. "We find her. We kill her. Not even one of Laochodon's progeny can live."

The mage spun, her robes flowing around her. She ran quickly down the hallway, her soft red boots tapping the stones. Slayter hurried to follow, as did Vamreth and his force. The screams in the royal wing had ceased and booted feet could be heard clearly in the eerie silence.

Halenza entered the king's study. She crossed to a larger-than-life painting of Laochodon that stretched from the floor to the ceiling. Only when she put her hands on the frame did Vamreth see it was hanging away from the wall. Halenza pulled and the painting swung open on hinges. Behind it was a narrow wooden door, banded in steel and carved with ornate images of Giants and dragons. It, too, was ajar. Halenza threw it open and ducked inside. Her young apprentice was right behind her.

"What is this?" Vamreth had to twist sideways to fit into the tiny passage. The narrow hallway immediately turned into a spiral stone staircase so tight that Vamreth's armored shoulders scraped on both walls. It was blacker than a moonless night and the light from the doorway only illuminated the first turn.

"Halenza!" he called into the darkness.

As if in response, a light swelled before him. One of Halenza's magical symbols burned in the air, seemingly balanced on the tip of a finger and Vamreth could suddenly see quite well.

The stairway was polished stone the black of a charred log, a sharp contrast to the white marble in the rest of the palace. Also, these blocks were perfectly wrought and fitted without mortar... just like the Night Ring arena.

Vamreth's men followed, and the stairway was soon filled with the thumping of many boots.

Vamreth felt like a hunting dog forced to chase a weasel down its hole. In the bobbing, flickering light, he saw snatches of carvings on the walls depicting some never-ending battle. Men and women, armor and shields, spears and swords. A dragon. A ship. He passed an iron sconce, but it held no torch.

What is this place?

It seemed to descend forever. Around and around and around. The stairs were so steep and so small that only half of his boot fit on each. Each step could easily turn into a slip. One slip might send him sliding down, out of control.

His thighs burned with fatigue and he called out again when it seemed they must have descended all four stories of the palace and another few, deep into the ground beneath.

"Halenza!"

"We are close," she shouted up the stairwell.

With a muttered curse, Vamreth forced his weary legs to keep going.

Suddenly, the stairway opened onto a flat floor and Vamreth felt pushed into the ground. He stumbled and almost went to a knee before he was able to stand upright.

Halenza's light illuminated a cavernous space, constructed from the same black stone. Vamreth stood awestruck in the center of the perfectly circular room. Walls curved to his right and to his left. The six-foot-wide column of perfectly fitted stones containing the circular stairway had plunged down from the high ceiling right into the middle of this place.

Vamreth nearly gaped, but he managed to keep his mouth shut. The hairs on the back of his neck and arms prickled. This place hadn't been made by Human hands. He didn't know how he knew, but a chill of dreadful certainty rippled through him.

Halenza's ghostly blue light showed the curved, bare walls, a bare floor, and two archways in addition to the archway of the staircase.

Vamreth's gaze was drawn to the largest archway, which was at least fifteen feet tall and ten feet wide. It had a thick, elaborate facade carved with the same figures from the same endless battle he'd glimpsed in the cramped stairwell.

At first he thought it was the gateway to the noktum, but as he stared at it, he realized it couldn't be. There was no darkness beyond. No passageway. It was just an infinite depth of shifting colors.

He shook his head, thinking the lack of light was playing tricks on his eyes. He could swear the colors were glowing, but they cast no illumination. Azure blue transformed to amber, then to green, then to red, then to charcoal black, then back to blue…

"What is this place?" he finally said, his gaze stuck to the huge archway.

"Your Majesty!" Halenza's urgency snapped his attention away from the mesmerizing colors to the smaller, normal-sized archway. It was plainly built. A rough, banded-iron gate had been bolted into place over the opening and fixed with a lock. He ran to stand beside Halenza and her apprentice as his fighters spilled into the room.

Beyond the locked gate stood the princess and her Luminent friend. The slender elf girl's hair shone, as though each strand was filled with a bright, buttery light. It was said the hair of a Luminent glowed when they experienced extreme emotions.

And the girls looked terrified.

Both had tear streaks on their dirty faces. The Luminent's mouth was open, her huge eyes wide as she stood behind the princess, a hand on her shoulder.

Princess Rhennaria was closest to the gate, frowning, her eyebrows creased as she tried to put on a brave face. She had a dagger in one hand and a large key in the other; that was how they'd passed the gate. And the princess—smart girl—had had the presence of mind to lock the gate.

Behind the girls was the noktum, a shifting mass of utter

blackness that filled the hallway some twenty paces beyond. Thick, black tentacles reached out, blindly questing for something to grab. It was just like the noktum doorways in the Night Ring. If the girls got close enough—if they even touched one of those amorphous tentacles—it would wrap around them and pull them into the noktum. And that would be the end of them.

What could have possessed them to think this was an escape?

If that had been their intent, they had clearly reconsidered. They cringed away from the questing tentacles, which forced them to stand just a few paces from the iron gate.

"Open it," Vamreth said to Halenza.

"It is... bound," she said.

"Bound?" Vamreth was confused. He had seen her perform magic miracles far more impressive than picking a lock.

"The key is the only way," she said. "This lock cannot be picked and it cannot be forced by any spells I possess."

"Then what good are you?" Vamreth snarled. He looked over his shoulder at the dozen men who had entered the room. All of them were looking around, obviously having similar experiences to Vamreth's. "Crossbow!"

Halenza looked downright bloodthirsty as she gazed at the children, but the rest of Vamreth's fighters hesitated. He wasn't sure if it was the noktum that had weakened their spines or if they were having a collective attack of conscience.

Vamreth rolled his eyes. "Senji's Teeth, get yourselves together. Somebody give me a crossbow."

Armor clinked and creaked as the men turned and a crossbow was passed forward. Vamreth took it and the three offered bolts. The string had already been ratcheted back. He fitted a bolt and turned to the girls.

His confidence grew, and he tasted victory on his tongue like the sweet sting of fine Triadan whiskey. These children were already dead, really. They'd died upstairs with their parents. They were the last barrier between him and the kingdom of Usara, and that barrier had to be shattered.

"You're in a bit of a spot, aren't you?" he said conversationally.

The Luminent began crying, looking between Vamreth and the noktum's tentacles. Princess Rhennaria clenched her teeth. A quiet keening sound leaked from her like steam from a kettle.

"You—" she said, choking on the words. "My parents—"

"Are dead." He carefully put the tip of the arrow between the slats of the gate and leveled the crossbow at the girl.

"Nnnnno! Nnnnno!" the Luminent sobbed. Her hair brightened, pushing back the shadows like a miniature sun. Vamreth squinted against the light but he kept his eye on his target. He always kept his eye on his target.

He pulled the trigger.

"No!" the Luminent girl cried, jerking the princess backward. The arrow, intended for Rhennaria's heart, struck her left arm instead and she screamed.

The girls stumbled back—

—and into one of the tentacles. It twitched, then several shot forward. Black tentacles coiled around the girls, over and over, and pulled them into the gulf of utter blackness.

The Luminent's hair winked out.

They were gone.

Blinking against the sudden darkness, Vamreth lowered the crossbow.

"Remarkable," Halenza said, her eyes sparkling with interest.

"Well," Vamreth said. "That is that." He tossed the crossbow to the nearest fighter, who barely caught it.

Vamreth glanced at Slayter, the young mage apprentice, who stared past the gate into the noktum, where the girls had vanished. He still had the look of concentration on his face.

"You don't see that every day, do you?" Vamreth said to the boy.

Slayter turned his focus to Vamreth, like a judgment. Then Slayter smiled a wooden smile. "You don't see it every day. It is remarkable," he repeated.

Vamreth nodded. The first part of his plan—the hardest part—was finished, but there were still many things to do. Toppling a king was one thing, taking the reins of the kingdom was entirely different.

"We have work to do," Vamreth said. He returned to the stairway and his men parted for him. He stopped at the entrance.

"Halenza! I need your light."

"Of course, Your Majesty." Halenza glided past him into the stairway, her little floating symbol burning in front of her.

Vamreth looked past his men to the giant archway with its shifting colors. That was a mystery he'd have to explore later.

He turned on his heel and started up the steps, following the light.

Chapter One

KHYVEN

Two knights threw open the door of the tavern, and the scent of last night's rain blew in with them. Khyven heard their boots thump on the rough planks, heard the creak of leather and clink of chainmail as they shifted. He sat with his back to them, but he didn't need to see them to know where they were.

The room went silent. This dockside drinking hole didn't see knights very often, and their appearance had rendered the entire place speechless. That was respect. That was what being a knight meant in the kingdom of Usara.

They paused just inside the threshold, perhaps hoping to spook the fearful, but Khyven wasn't a jumper. He had more in common with the newcomers than those who fled from them.

Ayla, the pretty barmaid sitting across from him, looked past Khyven, her eyes wide. She had been a lively conversationalist a moment ago and he'd been daydreaming about what it would be like to kiss those lips.

Now she looked like an alley cat who'd spotted an alley dog. Reflexively, she stood up, the wooden stool scraping loudly on the floor. She froze, perhaps realizing belatedly that when the powerful—the predators—were in the room, it was best not to draw attention to yourself.

Khyven heard the metallic rustle of the fighters' chain mail and Ayla's face drained of color. He envisioned the alley dogs turning at the sound, focusing on her.

She needn't have worried. They weren't here for her or any other patron of the Mariner's Rest. They were here for Khyven.

He had killed a man in the Night Ring two days ago, and not just any man—a duke's son. The entitled whelp had actually been a talented swordsman, but his ambition had outstripped his skill. And the Night Ring was an unforgiving place to discover such a weakness.

After Khyven had run the boy through, Duke Bericourt had sworn revenge. No doubt he had been waiting for an opportunity to find Khyven alone, vulnerable, to send in his butcher knights.

Men like these, sent to enforce a lord's will or show his displeasure, were called butcher knights. Usually of the lowest caste—Knights of the Steel—butcher knights didn't chase glory on the battlefield or renown in the Night Ring. They were sent to do bloody, back-alley work at their lord's bidding.

Khyven took a deep breath of the smoky air, sipped from the glass of Triadan whiskey, and enjoyed the fading burn down his throat.

The booted feet thumped to a stop next to his table.

"Khyven the Unkillable?" One of the men spoke, using Khyven's ringer name—the flamboyant moniker the crowd had laid upon him.

Khyven glanced over his shoulder. Indeed. He had guessed right. The pair were Knights of the Steel.

There were three castes of knights in Usara: Knights of the Sun, Knights of the Dark, and Knights of the Steel, which was the lowest caste and the only one available to most lords. The pair wore chainmail shirts instead of full plate, conical steel caps with nose guards instead of full helms, and leather greaves and bracers.

As predicted, they wore Duke Bericourt's crest on their left shoulders.

There was a code of honor among knights—even butcher knights. Except in cases of war, civility was required before gutting a man, especially when there were onlookers. Often a knight would give a flowery speech—including the offense he'd been sent to address—before drawing weapons. This was enough to justify murder.

Sometimes there was no flowery speech, but a knight would always at least say their victim's name. If the victim acknowledged their name, that was all it took to bring out the blades.

Khyven didn't give them the satisfaction. He took another sip of his whiskey and said nothing.

"Did you hear me?" the knight demanded, his hand touching his sword hilt.

If Khyven had been a normal ringer—a caged slave thrown into the Night Ring to slay or be slain for the sport of the crowd—these men would probably have forgone their code of honor and drawn their swords already.

But Khyven wasn't just any ringer. He was the Champion of the Night Ring, and the king had afforded him special privileges because of that fact, like a room at the palace. Khyven had survived forty-eight bouts, the longest string of victories since…

Well, since Vex the Victorious had claimed fifty, won a knighthood and become the king's personal bodyguard.

Steel scraped on steel, bringing Khyven back to the present. The second knight drew his dagger and placed it against Khyven's throat.

Ayla gasped and backed away.

"You think you're protected," the second knight growled in Khyven's ear. "You're not."

Of course, if Khyven didn't acknowledge his name, there were other ways for the butcher knights to start the fight. If Khyven attacked them, for example, they could retaliate. The powerful could always push a victim into a corner when they needed to. That's what the powerful did. Khyven had learned that long ago.

That was why, when Khyven had won his fortieth bout and his freedom from the Night Ring, he'd continued fighting, risking his life in every bloody bout. For the prize at the end of ten more bouts. For the power that would come with it.

When Khyven won his fiftieth bout, he would be elevated to knighthood, just like Vex the Victorious. And no one would look at him as a victim again.

The blade broke the skin, just barely, and a bead of blood trickled down Khyven's neck. His pulse quickened. The familiar euphoria filled him, the rush of pleasure that came with the threat of death.

The euphoria brought vision, and Khyven saw with new eyes, his battle eyes. He saw his foe's strengths and weaknesses as a swirling, blue-colored wind.

"You are Khyven the Unkillable," the man breathed in his ear.

Khyven chuckled.

The second knight's face turned red. He slashed—

But Khyven was already moving.

He shoved his palm against the man's fist, arresting the strike. The blade nicked Khyven's neck, but that wasn't enough. That wasn't nearly enough.

Khyven twisted his assailant's fist and the man grunted in pain. The dagger fell into Khyven's right hand.

The euphoria sang through him and he saw how this fight would go. The blue wind would show him where he must strike, where his enemies would *try* to strike.

Khyven shoved the dagger's flat, steel pommel under the knight's nose-guard. The heavy steel jammed into that painful spot just below the man's nose, right above his teeth.

Bone crunched. The knight stumbled back with a cry, hands flying to his face and knocking his helm askew. His legs wobbled and gave out while Khyven delicately pinched the pommel of the falling man's sheathed sword between two fingers, lifting it from its scabbard.

With an outraged cry, the first knight pulled his blade and lunged. He was fast, but the blue wind swirled, showing Khyven where he needed to be. He danced with it—one step ahead of it—exploiting the man's weaknesses.

Khyven's new opponent was left-handed, which gave him an advantage against those who didn't expect it. Also, he was fast. Those were his strengths, but he leaned on them like a crutch, and that in itself was a weakness.

The man thrust at Khyven: a clean, straight strike. Khyven twisted, let the blade come within an inch of him. It licked past his chest like a snake's tongue as he slid inside the man's guard. This close, swordsmanship didn't matter. Belly-to-belly with the stunned knight, Khyven wrapped his arm around his foe's sword arm and wrenched upward.

The man gasped, jumping onto his tiptoes to escape the joint lock. His sword clanged to the ground.

Khyven kneed him in the groin.

The knight doubled over with a grunt and backed up. The agony of a groin strike always came with a delay, but the realization came immediately. He gave Khyven a wide-eyed look of disbelief… then the pain hit him.

With a shuddering gag, he slid to his knees. To his credit, he pulled his dagger, but the hilt clacked on the wood floor as he fell on all fours, gasping for breath, twisting and hoping for some position that would ease the pain. Unfortunately for him, no such position existed.

The first knight collapsed onto his side, groaning pitifully.

Khyven picked up the man's sword and added it to his collection.

By this time, the second knight had staggered to his feet, helmet lopsided, nose broken, blood pouring down his chin. He blinked one eye and then the other like he was trying to get at least one of them to work correctly.

Khyven tossed the dagger hilt-first at Broken-Nose, who yelped and dodged. The dagger hit the bar and thunked to the floor.

"Well done," Khyven said. "Try again." He offered the man's sword next, hilt-first. Broken-Nose stared at it like it was a rainbow-colored snake. Khyven raised an eyebrow. "Yes? No? Would you like it back?"

The knight took the sword with a shaking hand. Khyven dropped the other blade next to Kneed-in-the-Groin, who was still doubled-up, hands cradling his jewels.

The euphoria faded, the blue wind vanished, and Khyven let out a breath. He walked back to the stool, sat down, picked up his glass of Triadan whiskey, and winked at Ayla.

Khyven was always surrounded by enemies, but that was a good thing. If you remembered everyone was your enemy, you were never surprised when they attacked.

A shuffling step behind him told him Broken-Nose had regained some of his courage and, just maybe, was thinking about jumping back into the fray.

"Come at me again," Khyven said darkly, "and I'll pretend we're in the Night Ring."

The shuffling step stopped.

"Go back to Duke Bericourt and tell him his son chose his path, and that he fought well. The duke shouldn't sully that with back-alley theatrics."

Khyven paused for a breathless moment, the whiskey halfway to his lips as he listened for what choice the knight would make. There were several awkward thumps as Kneed-in-the-Groin got painfully to his feet but Broken-Nose didn't come any closer. They were afraid of him now.

That is power, Khyven thought. *It's the only thing that ensures safety. The only thing that really matters, in the end.*

He downed the rest of his whiskey and stood. A smile had begun on Ayla's pretty face. He nodded to her. Much as he'd like to explore what that smile might avail him it was time for bout forty-nine. It was time for Khyven to do what he did best.

"Gentlemen," he said to the butcher knights as he stepped around them and walked to the door.

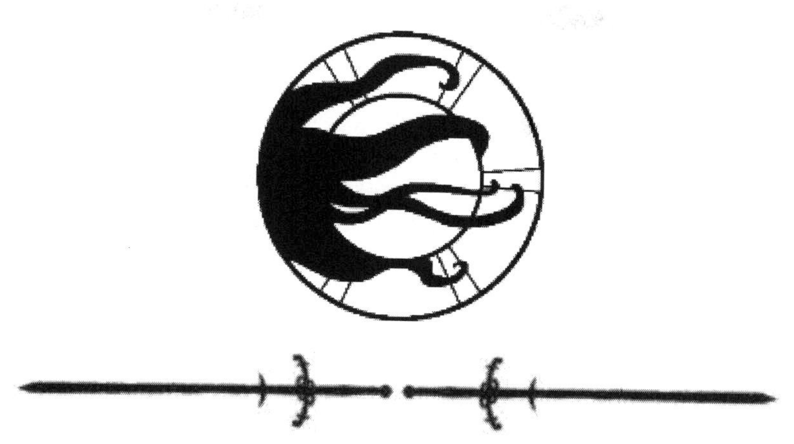

Chapter Two

VAMRETH

King Vamreth pulled his breeches on, lacing them up as he walked to the window overlooking his city. His gaze lingered on the mighty Night Ring, the largest building in Usara save the palace. The afternoon sun touched the top of the dark pentagonal walls, orange and yellow flaring behind it like a portent of death. Though hundreds of people visited that place every day, it was still forbidding to look upon at first glance. The scalp-prickling sensation faded quickly, but that first glance…

That made him think of Tovos, and an involuntary chill went up Vamreth's back. Vamreth had faced many challenges in his life, had faced death over and over, but Tovos made his blood turn cold. Every time he was in the presence of that aberration, he fought the fear, but Vamreth supposed that's what any creature felt standing in the shadow of a predator. Tovos would be coming tonight. Always in the dead of night. Vamreth would be alone, then suddenly Tovos would be standing there, in whatever room Vamreth occupied. No alarm given. No guards the wiser.

Vamreth shivered.

"Your Majesty?"

He turned to view the beautiful Shalure, half-clothed. She'd donned her burgundy dress, but the laces in the back were in disarray from where he'd torn at them in his haste. The dress's tight shape leaned off-kilter on her young body.

"You had better hurry," he said, glancing at the falling sun. "Khyven fights within the hour." Shalure had to be dressed, presentable, and seated at the Night Ring when he did.

"My point exactly," she said, giving that charming smile that had drawn him to her in the first place. She held up the ends of each sagging lace. "Some assistance, perhaps, would speed me on my way, Your Majesty."

Vamreth frowned. He didn't have time for this. He had tired of Shalure already. Her very voice annoyed him, let alone her disguised demands. She assumed the allure of her youth would overcome a man's good sense, and it probably worked with most men. She did have a fair mind for manipulation, but she was a novice compared to him. He understood well how power shifted, even if a person acceded to small demands, and he wasn't about to give her the advantage.

Shalure was the daughter of an inconsequential baron far to the north and she had come to the heart of the Usaran Kingdom looking for a landed husband, a union that would keep her among the nobility. She was ravishingly attractive, with a quick wit and an impeccable sense of fashion. She would be a fine match for any noble if her family wasn't so poor as well as politically irrelevant. As nobles went, her father barely qualified. Shalure was acutely aware of this.

Her beauty had caught Vamreth's eye months ago, lucky for her. He had come to find that this waif had brought barely enough coin to keep herself fed and housed for a week. Without his assistance, she'd have been begging for food by now.

After he'd first bedded her, she'd had the temerity to suggest they marry, that she become the Queen of Usara. Her allure had been so fresh at the time he'd found her impudence invigorating.

No longer. If she dared to suggest such a thing now, he would probably have her whipped.

"It will give you the chance to put your hands on me again," she murmured seductively, holding up the laces.

"I can put my hands on you whenever I wish," Vamreth said shortly. "I'm not a chambermaid. Lace yourself."

Shalure's sexy smile faded, but she managed to keep her composure. "Of course, Your Majesty," she said warmly, as though she'd expected him to say that. She straightened the front of her dress and began sorting the tangle at the back, pulling the laces tight. He had to give her credit, she did have a talent for courtly graces: when to shut her mouth and when to smile. How she'd learned that in her father's swampy holdings, he'd never know.

"I was thinking, Your Majesty, that I should have more than one servant when I go to the Night Ring today. This is his forty-ninth. Don't you think it would be more appropriate to secure his interest by showing that—"

"If you haven't secured his interest yet, Shalure, then you're not who I thought you were. Khyven knows what you are, where you come from. I daresay he knows what you want. Do you think he will not question why Baron Turnic's poor daughter suddenly has more servants?"

"I think it will impress him, Your Majesty, show him that I am more than a suitable match for him—"

"He knows you are more than a suitable match. Mere months ago, he was a slave. If you wore a burlap sack and walked about barefoot, he would know you are more than a suitable match. Because of your poverty, he views you as within his grasp. It makes the lure legitimate. I will not disrupt my plan for your petty vanities. What will he think if you suddenly have an unexplained influx of wealth? Do you think he will simply overlook it? Do you think he is stupid? Because if you do, you're of no use to me." He fixed her with a narrow stare. "Did I err in choosing you, Shalure?"

Her hesitation lasted the perfect amount of time, then she flashed a winsome smile. "It doesn't hurt for a girl to ask." She switched faces smoothly and despite his annoyance he grudgingly admitted to himself that it was charmingly done.

"I have given you as much as I am inclined to give until you pay something back, pretty Shalure."

Her smile stiffened at that. No doubt she considered their recent lovemaking a gift to him. As though Vamreth couldn't have any woman in the city.

Shalure quietly managed the laces by herself; she obviously had practice dressing alone. A good deal of practice. As poor as her father was, it was possible she'd never even had a chambermaid.

In a short time, she looked tidy and presentable, except for her tousled hair. Senji's breasts, the woman would look stunning in anything. Barefoot in a burlap sack, indeed!

Shalure slipped on her boots and sat in the cushioned chair by his wardrobe to lace them up.

"I want to make sure we are clear, Shalure," Vamreth said. "Khyven is important to me. He is my next Vex the Victorious and I want him by my side. If your charms are not a sufficient lure, well..."

She stood as though she hadn't heard—or didn't fear—the threat. She swung her head back and forth, shaking out her mane of auburn hair, then quickly worked two braids at each temple. She picked up her little leather tie from the table and secured the braids at the back of her head like a crown, creating a lovely effect.

"I understand your wishes, Your Majesty. It is in hand."

"Good."

She went to the door. Watching her fluid movements, a flicker of desire rose within him again. She was such a graceful creature.

"Use the back stairway," he told her.

"Of course, Your Majesty."

"And Shalure..."

With a hand on the door handle, she turned to look at him. "Yes, Your Majesty?"

"This is ended." He gestured to the bed. "Do not come here again."

Her eyes flashed over a smile. He had ordered her to come here today, of course, but she prudently didn't say it. Instead, she curtseyed low, giving him a long view of her bosom.

"Of course, my liege. As you command."

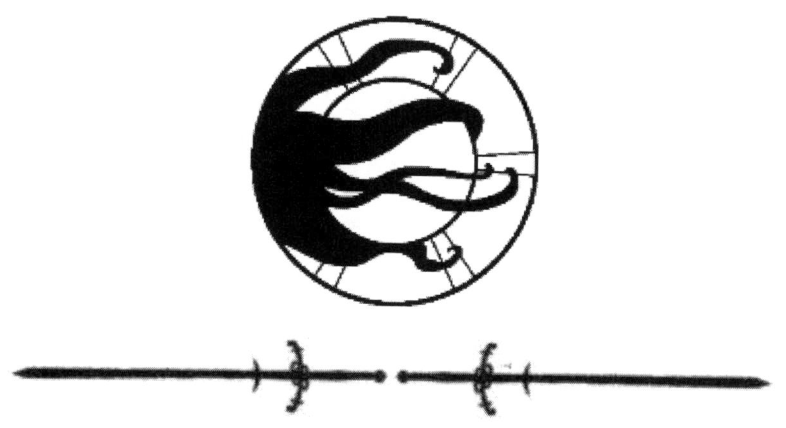

Chapter Three

KHYVEN

Khyven strode through the streets of Usara as the sun shone down. Last night's rainwater glimmered between the cobblestones and along the clay shingled rooflines. A formation of King Vamreth's fighters marched up the wide street. There had to be a hundred of them, part of the army Vamreth continued to grow, month after month. It was said the king's standing army was a thousand strong, and that he always accepted young recruits.

Khyven watched them go by. That was one way to enter the king's service, but it was rare that a fighter in the army distinguished himself enough to become a knight.

He turned back to the task at hand, and the nervousness began to rise in his belly. Despite how often he had walked this street, no matter how many times he passed beneath the shadow of the Night Ring's high, black walls, he always remembered the first time. He always felt it like it was happening all over again.

He remembered every detail of that day, because it was the day a group of knights had killed Nhevaz, the old man, and Khyven's other adopted brothers. No matter the years that had gone by, Khyven could still see the broken hut, the bodies of Roahl and Farsin laying in the dirt, long streaks of blood trailing away from them. Khyven could still see Nhevaz, fighting Vex the Victorious. Three other knights had stood by, laughing and watching like it was a bout in the Night Ring.

Khyven had rushed to help, to come to Nhevaz's defense, but someone had struck him from behind. The last thing he'd seen before blacking out had been Vex's sword thrusting into Nhevaz's back.

When Khyven had awoken, he'd been in a caged wagon rolling down this very street toward the Night Ring. He'd looked up at those dark walls, taller than any building he'd ever seen before, and that's when the hard realization had slammed home: the only family he could remember was dead—and Khyven was next. Even living in the woods with the old man he had heard of the Night Ring. It was where King Vamreth threw traitors to fight and die for the pleasure of the crowd.

Those who went into the Night Ring didn't come out.

Khyven shook off the haunting memory and looked up at the massive edifice that had been his home and his hell for the last two years.

It was said the Night Ring was a remnant from the time of the Giants, a time before Humans could even build thatched huts let alone cities of stone. Its presence could be felt throughout the city, as though every shop and every house had been built with eyes on the Night Ring. Even the palace, three times the size of the Night Ring, seemed to look across the city in fear.

Khyven could hear the distant roar of the crowd as he approached the western archway. A bout was already in progress, of course. It was late in the day. The sun was almost down and, as champion, Khyven's bout would come last.

He passed under the arch of black stone and the bright sunlight fell away like it had been cut by a headsman's axe. He blinked three times and his eyes adjusted. He had trained himself to do this, to adapt quickly to sudden darkness or light. The masters of the Night Ring liked to throw a ringer off balance. Sometimes, they held mirrors at the edge of the arena, reflected sunlight into a ringer's eyes during a bout. Once, they had pushed Khyven from a dark antechamber into full sunlight with an opponent's sword ready to strike. Another time, they'd kept Khyven in a brightly lit antechamber, then thrust him into a night bout.

If a ringer was going to survive in the Night Ring, he had to cope with cruelty. He had to thrive on it. No situation—and no other person—could be trusted. The masters? Never. Other ringers? A bad bet. Alliances were sometimes made in the heat of battle, but they never lasted.

Some ringers put their faith in the highborns of Usara, nobles who favored them, just as the king now favored Khyven. It was a popular practice for nobles to sponsor a given ringer, to even take them into their households and lavish them with luxuries. Khyven had seen many a ringer lose their edge by indulging in this highborn pastime, thinking it elevated them past danger.

But sweet promises spoken by perfumed ladies or bright-eyed lords meant nothing in the end. Every single ringer favored by a highborn had still died in the arena, just the same as the rest of them. Every single ringer, of course, except for Vex the Victorious.

All that mattered in the Night Ring was the next bout and whether or not you won. Until that fortieth bout that bought a ringer his freedom.

Or that fiftieth bout—for Khyven at least—that would win him the station of knighthood. The other ringers had said he was mad to tempt Senji's wrath, throwing himself back into the Night Ring after he'd gained his freedom. The warrior goddess only protected the righteous, warriors who slew with noble purpose, not those who slew for personal gain.

"Senji don't protect cutthroats."

"Goddess'll leave you to bleed."

"She'll have your sword, Khyven. She'll turn it around and shove it

through your guts."

They'd said he was arrogant. They'd said the goddess would curse him. They'd said he was doomed. That had been eight bouts ago. They weren't saying it now.

Now they called him Khyven the Unkillable.

Khyven had only two more bouts before his ultimate prize, and each would be harder than the last, he was sure. For Vex's fiftieth, they'd loosed a Kyolar from the hellish noktum itself. Two thousand pounds of muscle, midnight fur, gnashing teeth and ripping claws; a man-killing supernatural cat. Vex had slain it, of course, and it was rumored he'd mounted the head on his wall.

After, Vex had been proclaimed a Knight of the Sun and placed at the king's right hand. The legend told that the king had given Vex a full suit of plate mail armor after that final victory.

That, however, was a lie. King Vamreth had not given Vex that armor. Vex had taken it from Nhevaz's hut. After Vex had killed Khyven's brother, he'd taken everything of value, including his suit of armor.

Vex wore it all the time now. Never took it off, it seemed. It was said no one had seen Vex's face for two years, only that polished, glimmering visor.

Khyven had hated Vex in the beginning. But in the end, Khyven appreciated him. After Khyven's first six months of near-death scrapes in the arena, he realized that Vex, rather than destroying his life, had taught him the most valuable lesson there was: every man stands alone. Family could die, so they could only make you vulnerable. They could only make you weak.

Khyven turned left, walked down the vaulted corridor, turned right down another corridor. There were a hundred rooms squirreled away in the walls surrounding the Night Ring, connected by a maze of corridors. Khyven had memorized them all.

He approached one of the antechamber doors along the curved hallway and stopped before it. A spearman with leather armor and a leather helm stood before the door. Most ringers were slaves, kept in cages in the antechambers just off the arena. Khyven was, currently, the only free man who fought in the arena.

Well, there had been Duke Bericourt's son, but that hadn't lasted long…

"Khyven," the spearman said, nodding his head. When Khyven had been a slave, this man had been one of his jailers. With Khyven now a free man, they were essentially equals. But soon, if Khyven survived, this spearman would have to defer to him.

The spearman fumbled with his keys and unlocked the door. Khyven stepped through and the spearman slammed it behind him. He twisted the key and the lock ground home.

Strangely, that sound reassured Khyven. Despite the cruelty and death of this place, it had become his home. Here, he knew all the rules and had mastered them. In this place, Khyven was already a lord.

The antechamber smelled of oiled steel, dust, and Human fear. Khyven's heart beat faster.

A dozen other ringers poked hands out of cages on either side of him. He walked past them and began to prepare himself for the fight to come.

The roar of the crowd outside came in through the high, barred windows set in the east wall. Beyond those windows, when the crowd quieted, Khyven could hear the quick shuffle of feet and the clash of steel as the current bout continued. Up there, men struggled in earnest, strove to escape death or to give it.

Khyven sensed the direction of the bout just from the sound of it, the eager advances of the ringer who would win. The frantic retreat of the one who wouldn't.

Khyven counted his own heartbeats—one… two… three—as he walked down the aisle between the cages. This particular antechamber had six cages, three on each side of the aisle which opened up to a larger room—the weapon room—where swords, hammers, clubs, daggers and scraps of armor rested on racks or on hooks hammered into the walls.

Beyond the weapon room was a ramp of steel-banded, rough wooden planks that led up to a blinding square of light. Four spearmen stood there, watching the bout, ensuring a ringer couldn't flee back into the antechamber.

Khyven had a flashback of his first time ascending that ramp, urged by spears at his back. The gibbering man next to him had been barefoot because the guards had taken his rich leather boots. He'd hissed when a thick sliver drove into his heel and had begun whining about how he couldn't be expected to fight without his boots. It was unfair. Didn't they want a good fight? He'd blubbered and hobbled all the way up the ramp toward the blinding square of light—

And flashing steel had sliced out of the brightness as the ringer waiting on the arena floor struck. With a gasp, the blubbering man stopped blubbering and started screaming as his guts spilled out onto the ramp…

Khyven let the memory go as he walked down the aisle and ran his fingers along the bars of the cages. The caged ringers clamored, trying to get his attention. All of them had something to say. Naïfs pleaded with him to open their cages. A few old hands wished him good luck and asked for a blessing in return—the blessing of the Unkillable. There were curses, too, from those who wished death upon him. There were more than a few ringers who'd been injured by Khyven in the past.

He ignored them all.

Instead, he concentrated on the cool bars, smooth under his fingers. The chill of steel, the smell of it, the feel of it… These things prepared him for what was to come.

He reached the weapon room and looked lazily into the harsh daylight above the ramp, a practice he'd adopted after that first time, after he'd emerged blind into the arena. It had only been Fate's blind luck that day that death had taken the blubbering man instead of Khyven.

While his eyes were seared, prepared, his attention went inward to the calm place the old man had taught him to create. The old man had called it meditation, a practice he claimed he'd learned from a Luminent.

A Luminent…

The old man had loved regaling Khyven with ancient legends

of Giants and heroes, Luminents and Taur-Els, gossamer tales of magic. It had been the best thing about him—

"You're Khyven the Unkillable," someone said from behind him.

Khyven didn't know why he heard that voice above all the others vying for his attention, why that voice alone broke him from his trance. Maybe it was the calm tone, so out of place here. Maybe it was the odd timbre, a throatiness that wasn't quite Human.

Khyven turned and looked for the voice's owner inside the nearest cage.

A creature huddled against the back wall of that closest cell, almost touching the bars. He had pulled his legs up to his chest, toes avoiding the shaft of light that cut across his cell. The creature's midnight black body was almost invisible in the shadows. Only his milk-white horns shone in the dark, practically glowing. They curved up from his forehead, sloped back along his scalp, then curled inward again, pointing at the top of his head.

"Senji's Teeth, you're a Shadowvar," Khyven blurted.

He'd never seen a Shadowvar in person, had only heard stories from the old man of the magical demons that lived far to the south, beyond the known lands, beyond the Rhaeg Mountains and even beyond the far-away kingdom of Triada.

The old man had said there used to be Shadowvar in Usara before King Vamreth took the throne. Shadowvar used to walk the streets like Humans. Shadowvar and Luminents and even Taur-Els, the huge bullheaded men who had supposedly descended from the mythical Giants themselves.

But the king didn't like outsiders. He'd run them all out.

"What are you doing here?" Khyven asked, suddenly off balance.

"What are *you* doing here?" the Shadowvar snapped back as though Khyven had done something unforgivable.

For a moment, Khyven didn't know what to say. So many people hated him. It was part of living in a world full of enemies. He hadn't been affected by another's anger for a very long time, but something about this Shadowvar's rage hit him hard.

"I'm the Champion of the Night Ring," Khyven said.

"Champion..." The Shadowvar sneered. "You are no champion."

Heat rose in Khyven's face. No wonder the king had run these creatures out of the kingdom.

"This is my forty-ninth bout," Khyven said. "Only Vex the Victorious has done better."

"Vex the Victorious," the Shadowvar said in the same way he'd said champion, as though he was spitting on the ground. "You're referring to the beast who stands next to the king?"

Khyven clenched his teeth. Vex the Victorious was the greatest fighter in Usara, the greatest ringer in history, and Khyven was about to tie the man's record. This irreverent little Shadowvar didn't get to say these things.

"I could kill you right now and the king would thank me for it," Khyven said in a lethal tone. He pointed at the rack of sharpened weapons—everything from axes to spears to swords—behind him.

"While I'm huddled in a cell, weaponless?" the Shadowvar replied. "I'm sure you could. Moreover, I'm sure you *would.* That sounds like the kind of champion you are."

The Shadowvar didn't seem to fear this place or Khyven. Was he just stupid?

The Shadowvar smiled, and his teeth were as straight and flat as Khyven's own except for two sharply pointed eye-teeth.

"Answer my question or I *will* kill you," Khyven said. "Who are you and how did you get here?"

"I don't go where the spear pokes me, ringer. And I don't whore myself out for the promises of a fiend."

Khyven was so flummoxed by the Shadowvar's brazen attitude that he looked around for one of the masters. Was this a test? Had someone planted this sharp-tongued, irreverent Shadowvar to throw Khyven off his stride?

But he saw no masters in the antechamber.

"They found him plotting against the king," one of the naïfs in the cage across the aisle said eagerly. "Brought him in with a new group of traitors."

"Traitor," the Shadowvar repeated carefully and stared at Khyven, as though redirecting the word. The little demon's gaze dropped slowly and deliberately to Khyven's neck, then came back up. "You're the traitor, Khyven the *Unkillable.* To wear what you wear yet do what you do."

Khyven caught the gaze and glanced down at the amulet his brother Nhevaz had given to him before he'd died. He'd called it the Amulet of Noksonon.

The amulet was a circle surrounding a sun, wrought in gold and connected by five symmetrical rays of sunlight. The golden rays extended out from the sun to the amulet's top, bottom, and right edge. But the left edge of the amulet, where a sixth ray might have been, was blotted out by a darker, jet black metal that slithered from left to right, over the face of the golden sun, black tentacles grasping for more, trying to consume the orb and its remaining five rays.

The craftsmanship was peerless and it was the only thing Khyven had left of his brother, of his other life. It was, in fact, the only thing Khyven owned that was sacred to him, and yet the amulet was a complete mystery. Nhevaz had died the day after he'd given it to Khyven. He'd never had a chance to ask Nhevaz any questions about it. Where it came from. What the symbol meant.

But the Shadowvar seemed to know something about it.

Khyven pinched the amulet between thumb and forefinger. "Do you recognize this? What do you know about it…?" His voice trailed off and the breath went from his lungs. The Shadowvar was wearing the same necklace. He had an Amulet of Noksonon!

All possessions were taken from ringers when they were thrown into the cages. Khyven's necklace had been taken away when he'd been brought here, but apparently the king had kept it. He'd given it back when Khyven had won his fortieth bout. Or at least, that's what Khyven had always assumed. It had been placed on his pillow when he'd been given a room at the palace the day he'd won his freedom.

"Where did you get that?" Khyven demanded, grabbing the bars.

The Shadowvar pressed his lips together in a line and his eyes narrowed. "You serve a liar and a killer, *champion*." He spat the word. "I would ask you the same question."

"Khyven!" one of the spear guards shouted down the ramp. "It's time."

The roar of the crowd above had changed from the random cheers and shouts of a bout in progress into an expectant, thunderous chant.

"KHY-ven! KHY-ven! KHY-ven!"

"Your master awaits," the Shadowvar said, gesturing to the bright square of light leading into the arena. "Please him well."

"Who are you?" Khyven demanded.

The Shadowvar wrinkled his nose as though Khyven stank, leaned back, and vanished into the shadows.

"Khyven!" one of the spearmen shouted, impatient.

Off balance, Khyven turned to face his fate.

Chapter Four

KHYVEN

hyven was rattled. He hadn't started a bout this ill-prepared in more than a year. Entering the Night Ring without focus was more dangerous than any single opponent Khyven could think of.

Usually, he took time to armor himself, to strap a single shoulder plate on his left side, perhaps a buckler or bracers on his arms, if he felt like brawling. He didn't like heavy armor, preferred uninhibited movement to a clumsy, general protection because a talented swordsman could pick armor apart.

He also usually had time to select a weapon. A sword was his natural fallback. He was the best blade in the Night Ring—and arguably the kingdom—but he was proficient with every weapon. Morning stars and flails, war hammers and maces, even a crude club or a rock. Leaning on one weapon could become a crutch, so he'd learned them all. Knowing how to use whatever came to hand could make the difference between life and death.

But the Shadowvar had thrown him off, used up his precious time. The spearmen looked like they were about to piss in their breeches, but Khyven still couldn't get his head straight.

It was the amulet. The Shadowvar's damned necklace. Was it real? Was it a fake? The only other Amulet of Noksonon that existed, so far as Khyven knew, was the one around his brother's neck when he died. How could a non-Human from a far land have the same necklace?

"Pick a weapon or go without, ringer," one of the spearman said. They'd all been exceptionally polite up to this point because of who Khyven was, but they were obviously done with that. "They're pulling out a Kyolar and I'm not standing here when that monster hits the ring."

A Kyolar! That was the nearly impossible challenge they'd given Vex the Victorious for his *final* bout. They were giving it to Khyven on his second-to-last. Again, Khyven felt the cruelty, felt the weight of knowing that everyone was against him. They hoped he'd fail. They *planned* for him to fail. If this was his forty-ninth bout, what would his fiftieth look like? They had never intended to make him a knight....

He clenched his teeth and fought to master himself.

No.

This was the game. This was what they tried to do, get into his head and throw him off balance. They must have planted the Shadowvar, made a replica of his amulet. The masters wanted him to fear. They wanted him to make mistakes.

He shook his head, shook the doubts clear.

He could handle it. He had trained himself to handle it.

He let the malicious intent, the cruelty, and his fear of the Kyolar flow into him and through him. He turned it into steel inside, strong and flexible. They wanted to scare him. He would only use it to make himself stronger.

"Go now or forfeit the bout!" the spearman said. The other three had their hands on the gate, ready to pull it down and lock it into place.

The spearmen were frightened of the Kyolar getting loose in the arena because a Kyolar didn't care if it killed a ringer or the spearmen standing in an antechamber gateway. Meat was meat and the more the better. The spearmen wanted to slam that thick, wooden gate shut before the Kyolar emerged and began hunting. If they did, Khyven forfeited the bout, and a ringer's life was forfeit if he committed to a bout and then didn't enter the ring, slave or free man.

Khyven chuckled.

"Relax, gentlemen," he said, walking to the weapons stand. His hand hovered over a beautifully balanced longsword. He'd used that one before, but he paused and didn't grasp it.

Next to it stood a rack of a dozen hardwood practice swords. He could hear the old man's voice in his head.

Never do what the enemy expects...

He laughed louder and snatched a pair of practice swords instead. The ring masters expected him to be afraid. Everyone expected him to be afraid. He had to be the opposite.

"Khyven," one of the spearmen said, stunned. "It's a Kyolar. You're going to use wooden swords?"

"Has anyone ever killed a Kyolar with a wooden sword?" Khyven asked, looking down the length of the practice blade speculatively, like it was real steel.

"You're insane," another spearmen growled.

Khyven looked over his shoulder at the Shadowvar, but only its white horns shone in the darkness. Khyven sent a defiant glare at the invisible face below those horns, then turned to the bright sunlight, swinging his wooden swords as he headed up the ramp.

The chant of Khyven's name metamorphosed into a roar of excitement as he emerged. He swung his swords, one in each hand. The roar faltered, then fell into hushed murmurs as they realized his swords were made of wood.

That stunned silence lingered for a second, then the crowd screamed in approval. The roar shook the entire Night Ring.

The arena was pentagonal, like the building of the Night Ring itself. Surrounded by tall walls, the arena was three hundred feet across one side to the other, large enough to run, but only for a little while. Especially if your pursuer was faster than you.

Black sand covered the floor, making it seem like solid ground, but that was an illusion. Beneath that half foot of sand lay wood flooring, and there were numerous trap doors that could be opened, suddenly bringing forth animals, other fighters, or sometimes simply creating a hole beneath the unsuspecting foot. A ringer had to be careful.

The walls bordering the arena were two stories tall, and behind them were the screaming, fist-pumping common folk of Usara. Each of the walls had a fifteen-foot-tall archway set between the two smaller seven-foot-tall gateways of the antechambers. The larger archways were what gave the Night Ring its name. Each was a doorway to a lethal, mystical noktum.

The noktums were scattered all over the kingdom of Usara—eldritch worlds of inky darkness that consumed the landscape at seemingly random places. A noktum could be ten feet across or a hundred miles. It could rise hundreds of feet into the air or bury itself underground. It was not inhibited by forests or mountains or seas.

The borders of noktums went straight up from the ground like the folds of a curtain. Along that dark curtain, inky tentacles reached out a dozen feet, writhing, questing, always seeking the warm flesh of the living.

Mysteries abounded about the noktums. Why they were there? What had created them? What lived within them? Whether a person could breathe inside a noktum or if a person suffocated instantly after being dragged inside. Whether a person pulled into a noktum changed into the monsters who resided there.

The one good thing about the noktums was that they were predictable. Except for their questing tentacles—which only had a range of about twelve feet—they did not move. A noktum did not grow or shrink. Charted and laid out on countless maps, all the noktums in Usara hadn't altered in a thousand years.

Each of the tall arches within the Night Ring led into a noktum, and each had a different name engraved on the stone, along with a different symbol, at the top of the arch: The Fire Way, The Dragon Pass, The Demon Portal, The Night Door, and The Lore Gate.

They also had thick, cross-woven iron gates as tall as a house. During the daytime, the gates were kept open as part of the thrill and danger to the ringers. But they were locked tight and triple-checked before the sun fell. There were legends—from centuries ago—about a massacre in Usara, an army of nightmare creatures that emerged from the noktums. Hundreds of people in the city had died. Creatures beyond imagining had emerged, slaying and eating everyone they found.

A dozen feet inside the tunnel of each arch roiled the noktum itself, a shifting blob of utter blackness that sent its tentacles out, poking a few feet into the arena, trying to grab whosoever might foolishly come close enough. All ringers knew to stay away from those archways when the gates were open. Once the tentacles got hold of a ringer, they pulled him into the darkness and swallowed him.

No one who had ever gone into a noktum had ever returned.

Not Humans, anyway. Sometimes, if tempted by fresh blood, a creature of the noktum would stalk into the world of Humans. Khyven had only ever seen a Kyolar emerge from that blackness, but it was said that horrors even larger than Kyolars lived within the noktum.

A Kyolar was the horror the masters had conjured today for Khyven's bout. It was a midnight black lion-like monster, as tall as a horse with the thickly muscled body of a feline predator. It crouched over the carcass of the deer they'd used to lure it, tearing into the meat and bone with hungry abandon.

A dozen men standing atop the wall used long poles with hooks to slam the Night Door shut behind the Kyolar. The gates on the other archways had already been shut, locking the Kyolar in the arena with Khyven.

Creatures of the noktum didn't just emerge into the daylight for no reason. They despised sunlight, and Khyven was pretty sure it hurt them. They would not emerge unless there was fresh blood right before their archway. Khyven surmised they could only last so long in daylight before retreating to the protection of their benighted homeland. If the king's men didn't close the gates before the fight began, the Kyolar would try to escape back into the noktum.

The antechamber gate slammed shut behind Khyven, locking him in with the monster, and he heard the old man's words in his head again.

"Embrace death before a fight. See yourself dead already and the fear of death diminishes."

The giant cat, jaws bloody, jerked its head up at the slamming of the antechamber gate, and it fixed its baleful gaze on Khyven.

Khyven began jogging toward the monstrous cat. "It is time for us to dance," he murmured, his heart racing.

The thing spun to face him, its muscled back legs bunching as it crouched. It screamed at him.

The familiar, thrilling euphoria burst into Khyven and the blue wind formed. He saw it coiling around the twitching tail of the cat, encircling its body, flowing forward from its bared teeth, from its claws. A ribbon of blue, like a pennant snapping, preceded the cat as it charged.

That blue color flowed directly at Khyven, and he spun to the side, narrowly dodging it. A split second later, the cat's claw slashed past his back, narrowly missing his flesh.

The crowd roared.

Khyven turned and the cat spun, its claws digging into the sand and wood below. Black sand flew. Khyven was aware of the huge beast, but he focused on the blue wind. As long as he stayed ahead of the blue wind, he would stay ahead of the cat. Blue swirled around the Kyolar, lashed out at Khyven again. He dodged it, and the cat's claw swiped the air a second time.

Khyven backpedaled quickly as a swirling ball of wind—roughly the same shape as the cat's head—rolled by him.

Half a second later, the cat's teeth snapped to the right of Khyven's chest, so close it could have disemboweled him. Khyven steeled himself, kept himself from running away in panic, waiting for his opportunity.

A swirling funnel of blue wind appeared. The first weakness he'd seen. That was Khyven's target, and he stabbed his sword into it.

The cat was far stronger and faster than Khyven. Pound for pound, Khyven was ridiculously outclassed, but the Kyolar couldn't see what Khyven could see. It didn't see Khyven's weaknesses before they appeared, didn't see his moves a second before he made them.

Khyven stabbed his wooden sword into the swirling blue funnel—just as the Kyolar drove its own head into Khyven's sword.

The impact knocked Khyven back and the Kyolar snapped its jaws on air a second time.

Khyven used his momentum, staying with the euphoria, dancing with the blue wind. He moved faster than he ever had in his life.

In a blur, Khyven leapt, locked his stance, delivered his blow. The cat lunged, biting the air where Khyven had been and he rammed the wooden sword into the cat's open ear with all the force he could deliver.

The cat howled and withdrew, but Khyven followed the trails of blue wind, staying close to the cat. If he let even the smallest wisp of blue touch him, it meant the cat would touch him half a second later.

Three more funnels of blue—each a different size—appeared as the cat retreated. Khyven attacked.

Each funnel was a different severity based on its size. The smallest funnel would hurt the cat. The medium-sized funnel would temporarily paralyze the cat. The largest would knock it unconscious.

Khyven struck at all three.

He jumped as the Kyolar swiped a massive paw at his legs. Its claws sliced the air beneath Khyven's feet as he brought his sword down on its left eye.

It howled and backed away, but Khyven stayed with it, landing and lunging, stabbing at the second funnel. The cat moved directly into the thrust and the point of the sword connected with the beast's neck just below the skull. Half of the cat's body went limp. Khyven jumped again, over another swirl of blue. Time seemed to slow as Khyven hovered before the cat's wide, angry face…

He whipped both swords around with all his might, striking the cat in each temple. A crack resounded throughout the arena and the right-hand sword snapped in two.

The Kyolar crumpled to the ground. Khyven landed on the black sands in front of the cat's great head and stumbled to the side. The blue wind fell, swirling low against the body of the cat.

He huffed, breathing hard, his swords at the ready…

But it was over. The beast was unconscious, its tongue lolling out of its mouth, its breath coming in little huffs. The blue wind circled, forming a swirling funnel over the beast's right eye. This funnel was thick, dark blue, dense.

A killing strike.

Khyven's mind hovered in a weightless space. In every other fight, when the death strike appeared, he always took it. He had never hesitated.

With the Kyolar unconscious, he would simply have to stab with the jagged, broken sword. With Khyven's strength, even a wooden sword would find the great cat's brain.

He stood there, ready to do it…

But he didn't.

The euphoria faded. The blue wind that no one else could see swirled around the cat one last time, dimming from a dark blue to a light blue and finally to a wisp that was barely blue at all. Then it was gone.

Khyven turned his back to the cat and thrust his arms into the air, crossing the broken and unbroken swords over his head.

The crowd screamed with pleasure.

Chapter Five

KHYVEN

A dozen spearmen of the Night Ring emerged from the antechambers, even as another dozen workmen emerged with axes to chop up the Kyolar.

"Don't," Khyven said as they approached. Sweat dripped down his face and chest. The fight had been so quick he'd barely had time to draw a breath, but his fierce exertion had caught up with him all at once.

The workmen looked confused, and they paused with their axes. "Don't kill it, m'lord?" one of them said, mistakenly using an honorific that didn't belong to Khyven yet. "Won't it wake up?"

The spearmen milled uncertainly.

"It is my victory," Khyven said. "This Kyolar belongs to me."

"You're going to keep it?" one of the spearmen asked. "It'll rip your throat out when it wakes."

"I'm not going to keep it; you're going to throw it back into the noktum."

Nobody moved.

"By right of combat," he shouted, letting his voice carry to the crowd and to the royal box where King Vamreth sat with

Vex the Victorious looming behind him. "This is my Kyolar! And I say let the noktum fear Khyven the Unkillable! Let whatever monsters reside within know that I am *their* nightmare. Let this Kyolar spread the word. Let my name be known to those who threaten Usara."

It was ludicrous, of course. A Kyolar was an animal. It couldn't speak, couldn't spread a word about anything. But Khyven had built the drama with his actions, and the words barely mattered. This was the kind of story that would create a legend and the crowd loved it. They began chanting his name again.

"KHY-ven! KHY-ven! KHY-ven!"

The workmen's hesitation vanished and they began nodding, caught up in the fervor of the crowd. They slipped their axes into their belts and took hold of the Kyolar, six men to each back leg. Quicker than Khyven would have thought possible, they dragged the heavy Kyolar to the nearest noktum gate—the Night Door. Those who had opened the Night Door to let the Kyolar out scrambled to unlock and lift the grate with their hooked poles. The spearmen quickly lined the cat up, careful to stay away from the questing noktum tentacles, then rolled the cat beneath the archway. The hungry, black tentacles shot forward, wrapped around the Kyolar, and pulled it in. It vanished without a trace.

The workmen backed away and the spearmen, with their hooked poles, pushed the gate back down with a *clang* and locked it.

The crowd went mad, cheering and chanting. Flowers and scarves and envelopes of paper rained down on Khyven. People pressed against the edge of the barrier twenty-five feet up, leaning over, whooping and holding their fists in the air.

He looked past them, searching for Shalure. With the surging crowd, he couldn't find her.

The spearmen escorted Khyven from the Night Ring, through the mazelike hallways and out into the city. The streets had begun to fill with the dispersing audience, but Khyven's guards—a half dozen spearmen—steered him up the street to King Vamreth's palace.

The sprawling, four-story building made entirely of white marble, shone gold in the sunset. Most of the buildings in Usara were made of plain gray granite or midnight granite, like the Night Ring. Only the palace was white, and it seemed like a light source in itself, casting its light onto all the smaller shops and houses nearby. The tall, white wall that surrounded it enhanced the effect, a circle that radiated outward from its core.

The spearmen took Khyven through the gates and up the wide, shallow steps to the three tall archways before passing beneath the center arch.

The grand foyer had a few people milling about. A pair of middle-aged nobles in their fine clothes regarded one of the sculptures lining the hall. A cook, in her gray and white dress, hurtled toward the doorway to the kitchens beyond the grand stairway. A young lady with long blonde hair marched across the width of the foyer, an angry expression on her face. A well-dressed young man chased after her, hands up in supplication.

Khyven's gaze fell on a man in crimson robes standing in the shadows of one of the eight archways of the main foyer. The man stepped forward, as though about to approach Khyven, but he stopped. Khyven got a good look at him. He wore robes tailored to fit his thin frame, with long, dagged sleeves that came together in front of his waist, hiding his hands. The cuffs and hem of the robes were embroidered with strange symbols.

A mage! He had to be. Khyven had never seen one before, but he'd heard tell that the king had a dozen living in secret passages within the palace, men who could manipulate the elements, could bring fire from the air, make a tree grow from solid stone, or enslave a man's mind.

Khyven had always envisioned mages to be old, with long beards, wrinkled faces, and gnarled fingers. This one was incredibly young, perhaps even younger than Khyven. The mage's wavy copper hair was slicked back from his face and his green eyes watched Khyven intently.

The spearmen guided Khyven to the right. The mage passed out of sight when a column blocked Khyven's view, and a chill went up his spine. The way the mage had stepped into the light. The way he had watched Khyven, as if with a special kind of recognition.

The spearmen escorted Khyven to his rooms some fifty feet away from the main foyer.

His apartment was lavish compared to anywhere Khyven had ever lived, complete with a bedroom and a sitting room almost as large as an entire Night Ring antechamber, all white marble with a copper tub beneath the wide window.

Khyven stopped short as he closed the door.

Two attractive women stood near the copper bath wearing sleeveless white shifts, ready with soap and towels.

When Khyven had first been given a room at the palace, the assigned bathers who had greeted him on his first night had been a wonderful surprise. He had thrown himself into the experience with hearty abandon. It had been a tantalizing taste of his future life, as one of the powerful, he remembered thinking at the time.

But even after his death-defying performance with the Kyolar, even after the adoration of the crowd, his encounter with the Shadowvar resurfaced. The little creature had somehow stolen the joy from his victory. Khyven should be giddy, but all he could think about was that damned, smug little Shadowvar.

No, he didn't want companionship tonight. He needed solitude.

"Thank you," he said. "I can manage on my own."

Both the women looked surprised.

"Are you certain, milord?" the woman on left asked, the one with luxurious blonde curls. She tilted her head and raised her eyebrows. She had helped him with his bath once before.

"I…" He hesitated. "I am certain. Thank you."

"Very good, milord," the second woman said, standing up and setting her washcloth on the side of the tub.

"If you're certain," said the blonde.

"I am."

"We'll just be on our way then," the second said.

"Thank you."

They both bobbed curtseys and left.

Stripping out of his clothes—which stank of sweat, smoke, and whiskey—he settled into the hot water and exhaled.

He tried to relax into the bath, tried to let all of the events of the day float away…

But the smug face of that insufferable Shadowvar rose in his mind. The creature and his words, his very presence, had become a sliver underneath Khyven's fingernail. How did that Shadowvar have the Amulet of Noksonon? Was it Nhevaz's? Had the creature stolen it from Nhevaz's corpse?

No. He wasn't going to be able to relax. He had to go back there, question the Shadowvar until he told Khyven everything.

He washed himself quickly, stood up, dried off, and dressed.

No sooner had he buckled on his tunic than someone rapped on the door. Surprised, Khyven went over and opened it.

"I present the Honorable Shalure Insela Chadrone," the spearman intoned officially, then stepped aside.

Radiant, Shalure stood in the hallway just behind the spearman. Two braids of her long, auburn hair encircled her head like a crown and the rest fell in tumbling curls to her shoulders. Her floor-length burgundy dress was low-cut, with two embroidered bands following the neckline, crossing the center of her chest, and continuing until they disappeared around either side of her waist. Embroidered bands of the same design encircled her delicate wrists, and the sleeves were made of a diaphanous, smoky cloth, shadowing her bare arms all the way to her shoulders. It was a daring dress for a lady of the court, but then, Shalure was a daring sort.

She entered, her head held high. "Leave us," she told the spearman.

"Of course, milady," the spearman said and closed the door.

Shalure turned back to Khyven and smiled, creating the tiniest curlicue on each side of her red lips.

Their dance began again.

Shalure had entered his life mere months ago, and just one look at her made his face grow warm. His thoughts drifted back to his bath, daydreaming that Shalure had come to help him bathe instead of the two servant girls. That was an invitation he would have accepted.

She glided across the room and leaned against the window, which suddenly seemed to exist only to frame her.

"You were magnificent today," she breathed, lifting her chin a little. She knew how much he loved her long, pale neck. She always gave him ample opportunities to appreciate it.

"You were there?" he asked.

"Khyven," she said. "Miss your forty-ninth? What must you think of me?" She put a delicate hand to her neckline.

When Khyven had first met Shalure, he'd thought she was like the other noble ladies at court who took an interest in the Night Ring, perhaps interested in being his patroness. It was a popular practice to pay for the privilege of having a famous ringer brought to one's household. The highborns saw it as a sign of status and daring. Usually stripped down to a loincloth and chained to the wall, the ringer would be forced to stand in a noblewoman's sitting room like some kind of wild tiger while the ladies drank tea and gossiped about the latest scandal.

Shalure had never done this, though. Instead, she had orchestrated passing visits, capturing Khyven with a coquettish glance or offering him a compliment about his bouts. She'd met him outside the Night Ring twice, flirting and then gliding away with her servant. She had stopped him twice with a quick word inside the palace as well. Every meeting had been in passing. All save one…

She'd actually visited him in the Night Ring antechamber right before a bout. That was not something nobles did, men or women. In his two years as a ringer, Khyven had never seen a noble brave the tunnels below the Night Ring, let alone lock themselves inside an antechamber. It was dangerous. There were weapons in those rooms, and ringers were desperate people, most of whom would do anything to escape their fate. They wouldn't hesitate to grab a dagger and hold it against the throat of a baron's daughter if they thought there was even a chance, no matter how remote, to use their hostage to escape.

Still, Shalure had come alone. She'd shut herself into the antechamber with him and, lucky for her, just him. The other ringers had been locked in their cages.

Her audacity had left him speechless. He'd gaped as she'd crossed to him, pressed her lithe body against his, and kissed him like they were lovers.

And oh, what a kiss. He could still feel the press of her soft lips, a thrilling promise. He could still feel her bosom against his chest. He could still feel her fingers push into his hair, gentle at first, then urgent, grasping, pulling like an animal intent on devouring him.

She had whispered, "Good luck, warrior. I will be watching you."

That one kiss had been the most erotic thing Khyven had ever experienced. It was like she'd cast a spell upon him.

And, of course, it made him instantly suspicious.

If Shalure had hired him to stand half naked in her sitting room while she chatted with other ladies, he would have thought nothing of it. That was part of the game, part of the normal rules between nobles and ringers.

But that kiss had birthed a mystery.

A highborn lady didn't brave a Night Ring antechamber to kiss a ringer. If she'd wanted the thrill of a kiss, she'd have paid the fee, brought him to her house, and bribed his guards to look the other way while she kissed him.

So why kiss him in a dirty Night Ring antechamber?

Nobles didn't do things without a reason. And if Khyven didn't know the reason, it meant he was being manipulated.

Possible motives had loomed large in his mind after the kiss. Shalure was highborn. Khyven had recently been a slave. It was like she was enacting some play to make it appear as though they were courting each other. But why? He could only imagine the sneers Shalure must endure from other highborns by flaunting her association with him in public. Why put on this act?

He'd have thought she was crazy if it wasn't for her eyes. The woman seemed to know exactly what she was doing. She was… calculating.

But Khyven could calculate as well.

He'd first started compiling information about her by memorizing the family crest embroidered on the bosom of the dress she had worn the day she'd kissed him.

Unlike most ringers, Khyven could read. It was a rare leftover from the part of his childhood he couldn't remember, before the old man and Nhevaz. So Khyven had gone in search of Shalure's family's history. He'd managed to procure a volume on the various titles and symbols of the nobility and discovered that Shalure was the daughter of the Baron of Turnic, master of a minor holding so distant from Usara that Khyven had never heard of it before.

Apparently, Shalure was the sixth daughter of this barely known baron. With some carefully couched questions to the librarian of the palace library, as well as the knowledge in the book, he'd discovered a thing or two about the daughters of barons in general.

Strangely, they didn't have their own titles. Apparently, a baron's daughter was referred to as "honorable" when introduced, but not as "Lady Shalure." Her current station was wrapped up in her father's holdings. Her future station would depend on her marriage. If she married a lord, she would become a lady. If she married a peasant, a peasant she would be.

After a long afternoon of poring over that book, Khyven understood Shalure's plan: She had come to Usara to find a husband, and she'd decided Khyven was to be that man.

At first glance, it made no sense. What lady would stoop so low as to marry a ringer?

But if Shalure was a romantic—not to mention a gambling woman—marrying a ringer on the verge of winning his fiftieth bout could be quite appealing. If Khyven won through, he would be a knight in service to the king, a worthy consort for the sixth daughter of an obscure baron. If Shalure married Khyven the knight, she would be Lady Shalure. If Khyven died in the attempt, Shalure lost little. She could explain away the affair as a racy dalliance.

Shalure was jockeying for power, which was something Khyven understood well. The mystery was solved and their dance continued.

After understanding his part in her story, Khyven began to understand other things about her, like the fact that she only ever traveled with one servant, and that servant was never the same. Not only that, but these rotating servants always wore poor clothing that did not bear Shalure's family's crest. Most nobles traveled with two or more servants who wore the family livery.

Shalure used hired servants. It suddenly became clear why she hadn't paid the fee to bring Khyven to her house. She couldn't afford it. In fact, it was possible she had no house within the walls of Usara. She could be living off the generosity of the crown, living at the palace.

The idea of a desperate noble had seemed impossible to Khyven at first, but he slowly began to entertain the idea.

Shalure meant to dazzle Khyven while he was just a ringer, freshly emancipated, capture his interest while his life and future was still uncertain so she could claim him once he came into his prize.

He'd once wondered if her kiss had been the prelude to an epic love story, a song for the minstrels. That fantasy had been a weakness and he'd almost fallen prey to it.

As he looked at her leaning against the windowsill, her breasts pushed up by the tight dress, its folds draping the curves of her hips and legs, his desire flared. Yes, he would dance with her. Then, when he became a knight, he would take her to wife, just like she wanted. After all, it would benefit them both. He could only grow in social standing by marrying the legitimate daughter of a baron.

"Such a long pause," Shalure said. "Cat got your tongue?"

He smiled. He liked that she was clever.

"It tried, but I managed to keep all of my pieces, my lady."

She preened when he used the word "lady" to refer to her. She may know what he liked, but he was learning what she liked, too. Two could play the game.

She made the little curlicues appear and his heart beat faster.

"Are all ringers so gallant?" she asked.

"Just me," he said.

That made her smile wider. "Tell me, dashing Khyven, what were you thinking about? Was it me?"

"It's always you. A ringer has to stay alert for dangers," he said. "Inside and outside the arena."

Her curlicues vanished. "A danger? Me?"

"You."

"By the Dark, you defeated a Kyolar today. How can you think I am a danger?"

"Hidden claws are the deadliest," he said.

"You don't trust me," she said, pouting.

He grinned and shook his head. "Trust isn't really what you want from me, is it?"

"Of course, it is, my love," she said.

"Your love…" he said pensively. "Am I?"

"Did I not show you my heart when I pressed my lips to yours?"

"I think you showed me your plan."

"It was your bravery that drew me, sir," she said, stiffening. "Would you drive me away?" But he'd already seen past her wounded look—just for a second—and there was a feral animal there, threatened that he *had* uncovered her plan, looking for the words that would make him do what she wanted him to do.

Just like the masters.

"Perhaps we could be honest with one another," he said. "Our dance might be more… fluid if we were. Just because you want to use me doesn't mean I won't let you."

"I have been honest with you, my love," she protested.

"Shalure—"

"What you need"—she slid from the windowsill and crossed to him, putting a hand on his chest and another on his cheek—"is to trust me." She caressed his chest with one delicate hand. "Trust in me, Khyven the Unkillable, and all you want will be yours."

His body responded to her nearness and she saw it. Her eyes glittered like she had set the trap and he'd chomped the bait.

"Think of us together," she murmured.

"I do."

"Good." She stood on her tiptoes, bringing her face to his. He prepared for another earth-shaking kiss, but at the last second, she turned, touching her lips lightly to the corner of his mouth.

She drew back coyly, spun in a swirl of dress, and opened the door.

"Soon, my love," she said, "we will be together."

She closed the door.

Chapter Six

KHYVEN

The sun vanished behind the rooftops of Usara bringing the darkness and Khyven lay awake. He should have been exhausted. He'd fought a Kyolar, for Senji's sake. Everything he'd worked so hard to accomplish was coming to fruition. He'd done what only one man in a thousand had ever accomplished. He was revered by the common folk of Usara. He was living in the palace. The king was sending him beautiful women to bathe him. The daughter of a baron wanted to marry him.

He should be exultant…

The powerless part of his life was nearly over. He was no longer a slave, no longer beholden to others for his welfare. Even the masters seemed to have left off with their torture. If he survived the bout tomorrow, all would be forced to defer to him, save the nobility: the dukes and earls and barons. He would have everything he wanted. He should be able to rest.

But his mind turned over and over.

It's the Shadowvar, he thought. *The damned Shadowvar with Nhevaz's necklace.*

It didn't matter. It shouldn't matter. Nhevaz had been weak, and the old man's teachings, in the end, hadn't saved them. Vex and the knights had killed them all, had taken Nhevaz's armor.

Now some Shadowvar had stolen Nhevaz's necklace. Why should Khyven care?

He glanced out the window. The moon hung low in the sky. He got out of bed, dressed, and pushed through the door. The hallway was empty and dark. He moved quietly up the hallway, encountering no one until he walked out the front archways. Two palace guards stood there, one on either side, but while they looked at him, they didn't stop him.

Khyven descended the wide, sweeping stairs to the courtyard, and went to the gate at the wall. More guards, but after a quick exchange, they opened the gates for him like he was a noble.

A rush of power flowed through him.

He peered into the shadows of the houses and shops as he walked down the street. He saw a wretched beggar with a broken leg that smelled like rot leaning against an alley wall. He saw a couple of urchins vanish into the darkness.

Khyven slipped through the streets. Close to the Night Ring, a pair of thugs emerged from the shadows, cudgels in hand. They were obviously intent on violence, ready to thump Khyven and take whatever of value he might carry, but when they emerged into the moonlight they saw him better and hesitated. Khyven was well over six feet tall, wide-shouldered and well-muscled, honed by his years in the arena. If these thugs were looking for easy prey, Khyven did not fit the description.

Khyven locked gazes with the leader and shook his head. The thugs glanced at each other, thought better of it, and faded back into the shadows to wait for someone else.

The guards at the Night Ring knew Khyven and they let him in. He wended his way through the tunnels to the Shadowvar's antechamber.

At Khyven's request, the spearman guarding the antechamber opened the door. He handed Khyven one of two lanterns that hung on either side of the door and let him in, then locked the door behind him.

Flickering orange lamplight glinted off the bars and the bodies of the prone captives in the cages. Most of the dozen or so ringers were asleep, either recovering from their own bouts of the day or marshaling their strength for tomorrow.

One of the naïfs was awake and he instantly recognized Khyven. He jumped to the bars and whispered, "Khyven! Khyven the Unkillable! Let me out!"

"Shut up and sit down," Khyven hissed. He didn't want everyone awake and clamoring for his attention. Naïfs. They all thought Khyven would just let them out.

Naïfs always asked the question, "How do I escape?"

The standard ringer response was always the same. For the experienced ringers, it was a mantra. There were three ways to escape the Night Ring: *Up, down, or through the night.*

Either rise to knighthood, as Vex the Victorious had done, fall down dead on the arena floor, or jump through one of the arches into a noktum.

Khyven went to the last cage and around to the side. He looked for the Shadowvar and managed to spot him. The creature was awake, watching Khyven's approach. Even in the ruddy light of the lantern, the little demon was almost invisible.

"Where did you get it?" Khyven demanded.

"I saw you fight the Kyolar," the Shadowvar replied, ignoring the question.

"I'm not fooling with you," Khyven growled. He went to the rack of spears, selected one, and brought it back to the cage. He thumped the butt of the spear against the ground. "I've come to kill you or get answers. Your choice."

"You let it live," the Shadowvar said, still unnervingly calm.

"I—What?"

"The Kyolar. You let it live."

"I'm not talking about the Kyolar. I want to know—"

"Why?" the Shadowvar interrupted, but the derision in his voice was gone. He seemed genuinely curious, and Khyven hesitated.

"I was playing to the crowd," he said.

The Shadowvar narrowed his eyes. "Tell me what—"

"Senji's Boots," Khyven cursed, banging the bars with the spear. "You don't get it, do you?" The entire antechamber started to wake. Ringers were light sleepers. "I'm interrogating you. It's not the other way around. Did you take that necklace from a dead man?"

The Shadowvar cocked his head like that surprised him. "I did, in fact."

"My brother!"

The Shadowvar narrowed his eyes and said with absolute certainty, "No."

"How do you know what my brother looks like?"

"It was not your brother," the Shadowvar repeated. "How did you come to be here, Khyven the Unkillable? Where did *you* get *that* necklace?"

Khyven clenched the haft of the spear. Why wasn't the little bastard afraid?

"These necklaces belonged to my brother," Khyven said. "They belonged to his family. There were only two. He gave this one to me."

"His family?"

"Yes."

"The Amulets of Noksonon were made by Giants long ago. Was your brother a Giant?"

Khyven couldn't think of what to say to that ludicrous statement. Giants were myths. People invoked their name to explain the inexplicable. Where did that storm come from? The Giants sent it. How did the architects build the Night Ring? The Giants. What made the noktums? Giants.

"Giants?" Khyven blurted.

The Shadowvar looked pensive. He stood and walked to the bars. He was a thin little thing with scarecrow arms and a gaunt face, five feet tall if he was an inch. They'd stripped him down to the usual loin cloth naïfs were given. He stopped an inch from the bars.

"Listen to me, Khyven the Unkillable," the Shadowvar said. "This King Vamreth is a blight upon Usara. He stole his throne. He is a liar and a murderer. When I first met you, I assumed you were the same. A preening, sycophantic thug, and I have no use for such a person, but"—he glanced at the necklace—"perhaps you are something else, and if that is so, I can help you."

"Help *me*? You're the one in the cage."

"I'm not the one in danger, *ringer*," he said. "If you serve this man, it will drain whatever is left of your soul. You should serve the Queen-in-Exile."

"I should—" Khyven blinked and then barked a laugh. "You're a *queener*?" For a moment, he'd thought this Shadowvar was a mysterious, mystic creature, but he was a Senji-be-damned queener!

The Queen-in-Exile was a myth dreamed up by desperate naïfs who wanted to believe in something. Someone to come save them. Queeners thought the daughter of King Laochodon, long dead these past ten years, was hidden somewhere in the Royal Woods gathering her forces. This mythical queen was always on the verge of storming the walls of Usara and pulling King Vamreth down from his throne.

And of course, when she did this, she would free all the ringers.

"I suppose the Queen-in-Exile gave you that amulet," Khyven said.

The Shadowvar smiled thinly. "After I'm dead tomorrow," he said, "find her. Ask her."

"You don't seem to care much about dying."

"Everyone dies, Khyven the Unkillable," the Shadowvar said. "Few live a worthy life. Is yours worthy? It's the only question worth asking, and knowing the answer can save your soul. It's the only thing that can."

"And you've lived a worthy life, have you?" Khyven asked.

The Shadowvar just watched him. "Have you?"

A memory of the old man and Nhevaz flickered through Khyven's mind. What would they have thought of Khyven's vocation these past two years? Would they have approved of the killing, the lives Khyven had taken to save his own? Would they have approved of Khyven becoming a knight in King Vamreth's court?

He banished the troublesome thoughts. It didn't matter what Nhevaz or the old man thought. They were dead. Their advice hadn't saved them; it wouldn't save Khyven.

He was one of the few ringers who could claim he'd escaped the Night Ring by going up instead of down. *That* was worthy. Khyven had been a slave. He'd become a free man by his own hand. And tomorrow, he was going to become a knight.

"Your words mean nothing. They're taunts."

"They are," the Shadowvar agreed. "That they sting you… well, it means you *might* be worth saving."

"Go to hell, Shadowvar!"

"Find the queen," the Shadowvar said. He went back to the wall and sat down, disappearing into the darkness except for his white horns.

Khyven waited an interminable moment, gripping the spear, on the verge of thrusting it between the bars and killing the little demon.

Arms rigid, he cast the spear across the floor, stalked down the aisle, past the cages, and banged on the door. He didn't look back at the Shadowvar, but he could feel the creature's gaze on him.

This trip had been a waste of time. The creature wasn't giving up any secrets. Khyven had looked into the eyes of enough foes to know the Shadowvar would die with the secret of the necklace still behind his teeth.

The guard eventually opened the door and Khyven left the Night Ring. He suddenly couldn't get away fast enough. His belly twisted with emotions he didn't understand. What the little demon had said shouldn't bother him so much. It didn't make sense. *He* didn't matter. Nothing mattered anymore except the next bout. Khyven's new life was on the other side of that. He shouldn't be thinking about the arrogant little Shadowvar, or Nhevaz and the old man, for that matter.

But he did.

As he strode out of the Night Ring into the dark streets of Usara, up the streets and back to the palace, his mind floated back to the last lesson the old man had ever taught him, the lesson of the blue wind….

Chapter Seven

KHYVEN

Rubbish," the old man said.

Khyven barely heard the criticism. The old man's voice warbled as though Khyven's ears had been shaken and hadn't stopped moving yet. The coppery taste of blood filled his mouth, dripped down his lip, and dotted the dirt in front of his face. He tried to lift his head, but half of his body was limp. The other half seemed poked by a hundred needles. Nhevaz had practically paralyzed him with that last hit. A sweltering pain lit up his skull where Nhevaz had whacked him with the practice sword.

He had to get up. He had to regain his senses. Nhevaz's politeness would last a moment, but only a moment. Every time he knocked Khyven down he would wait for a count of ten and if Khyven didn't get up Nhevaz would move in for the final strike. Khyven had been knocked unconscious two times this week already.

"You aren't feeling it," the old man's voice warbled in Khyven's ears. He would have ignored the comment, but experience had taught him that doing so only brought more suffering. If it seemed like Khyven wasn't paying attention, if his focus faltered for even an instant, the old man made sure the fight went badly.

Ears ringing, mouth bleeding, arms and legs feeling like sacks of sand, Khyven tried to understand what the old man was on about.

Split lip, ears ringing, vision fuzzy, body afire with pain, blood running down my chin… How am I not *feeling it?*

Nhevaz circled Khyven, stalking like a mountain lion preparing for the kill. It was a signal his patience was almost up.

"Your hesitation limits you," the old man said. "You think he has no weaknesses, but he does. You must find them."

Khyven gritted his teeth and pushed to his knees. His right arm seemed to be working again; it had lost that numb feeling. Nhevaz had hit him with a double strike, one to the neck that had nearly paralyzed him and one to the head that had dropped him.

Get up, he thought. *Get up, get up!*

"You could be a champion," the old man said. "You could be something this world needs, but until you feel it you're just another stupid boy with a sword in his hand and his face in the dirt. Until you feel it, you're nothing."

As if that was his cue, Nhevaz came for Khyven.

Khyven fought the pain, the confusion, and the frustration that he didn't understand what the old man was saying. He focused on Nhevaz, though there was no reason to believe the outcome of this fight would be any different from the last dozen times. Nhevaz was the superior fighter in all ways; his swordplay was far more advanced. Khyven was big, strong, and fast, but Nhevaz was bigger, stronger, faster. While Khyven had triumphed over Roahl and Farsin long ago, he'd never beaten Nhevaz. Not once.

And Nhevaz was going to knock him unconscious again. Khyven was certain of it, and so was Nhevaz.

So was Nhevaz…

A flicker of wisdom lit Khyven's mind, like a tiny candle at the bottom of a well. Nhevaz knew he was the superior fighter. He counted on it.

And that was it. That was his weakness. The old man had said many times that an overconfident opponent was like an inverted pyramid. Intimidating, but precarious.

Every battle can be won. Every battle, no matter how unlikely. A fighter who believes he cannot lose has lost sight of the truth.

It wasn't much, but perhaps Khyven could do something with it. He sucked a breath through his bloody mouth and put one foot on the ground, tensing as if to thrust himself upright. Nhevaz charged.

Once Khyven imagined the weakness, he felt his brother's confidence. He *felt* it rather than just knowing it, and it formed in the air like a blue wisp of wind that enveloped Nhevaz's body, swirled up the edge of his sword and preceded its sweeping path toward Khyven, showing him exactly where it was going.

Khyven moved, grasping the spear of blue wind with his hands.

He caught Nhevaz's blade.

The blue wind flickered as if Nhevaz's confidence had wavered.

Khyven yanked with all his strength and fell onto his back. With a surprised grunt, Nhevaz stumbled atop Khyven. Khyven jammed his boots into Nhevaz's belly and shoved.

Nhevaz flew over him with a startled cry, letting go of his wooden sword. Khyven continued his roll and stood up. He spun in time to see Nhevaz twist in mid-air and land on his feet like a cat. Khyven had hoped for a crashing tumble, but Nhevaz was simply too good.

A euphoria rushed through Khyven, a confidence he'd never felt before. It was like he had sucked Nhevaz's confidence into himself with that blue wind.

He charged, whipped his sword up from below, and swung Nhevaz's sword from the side, hoping to catch Nhevaz under the chin or in the side of the head, or, if he was lucky, both at the same time.

Nhevaz spun and ducked and both of Khyven's strikes

missed. His euphoria faltered. The blue wind vanished. Nhevaz lashed out with a kick, catching the back of Khyven's bent knee, and Khyven went down. He rolled to his feet, sword in each hand, but Nhevaz was simply too fast.

Nhevaz punched at Khyven's face. Khyven winced, ready for the pain—

But Nhevaz stopped his fist an inch from Khyven's nose.

"Well done," he said.

Nhevaz uncoiled his lean body as he stood upright, signaling the end of the fight. For a moment, Khyven almost pounced. Nhevaz was weaponless and Khyven had two. The odds were in his favor.

But the unspoken rule of the old man's practice yard was that the combatant who had the clear strike and relinquished that strike called an end to that fight. That or a yield were the only two ways to end the fight unless one of the combatants was rendered unconscious.

Just when I've got the advantage, Khyven thought. *He calls an end to it. Coward.*

Nhevaz watched Khyven with glittering black eyes as though he could hear the unkind thoughts.

Breathing hard, head still ringing, Khyven mastered his temper and rose from his crouch. He tossed the wooden swords to the ground, more to avoid using them than to signify he was fine with stopping.

Nhevaz's face was expressionless as he looked down at Khyven. "Well done, little brother," he said in his deep voice. He rarely spoke, and he almost never gave praise.

"Well, well, well…" the old man said, peering with his one good eye at Khyven. "Perhaps you aren't a waste of time after all." His tone was just as harsh as ever, even if his words were not. It was the closest thing to praise Khyven had ever received from the old man.

Khyven's battle rage settled and curiosity replaced his anger. For a moment, it was as though he could predict what Nhevaz was going to do. That ephemeral blue wind superimposed over

Nhevaz's body....

"What happened?" Khyven asked. "I saw... something."

The old man grunted. "So you did."

"What was it?"

The old man nodded to himself as though he'd been waiting for this. He glanced at Nhevaz, but Khyven's brother was looking over both their heads, south as though he could see something coming, though there was nothing but a breeze.

Finally, Nhevaz caught the old man's gaze, nodded once, turned, and walked away.

"What was it?" Khyven asked the old man, watching Nhevaz retreat. "What happened?"

"Tomorrow," the old man said and he almost sounded sad.

"Why not tell me today?"

"Because tomorrow is better," the old man snapped, sounding more like himself.

"I want to know now. What was the blue wind?"

The old man raised an eyebrow over his single eye, the other invisible behind a black eyepatch. The old man paused, then said, "Those are your instincts, Khyven. I thought maybe you didn't have any, but apparently you do." The old man began walking back toward the hut where Khyven's two other brothers slept. "No more training today. Go find Nhevaz, then find us some dinner."

Khyven had been given all the hunting duties for the last month. Even after his grueling workout, he was expected to find food. Anger rose within him again and he wanted to lash out at the old man. Just once, couldn't the old man tell Khyven what he wanted to know?

Khyven considered attacking the old man. But while the old man only had one eye, he seemed to have a pair of invisible ones in the back of his head.

Khyven had lived here for eight years, close to the forbidding noktum that swallowed most of the forest. In the early days, he had tried over and over to catch the old man off guard, but he had never succeeded. Every time he charged, the old man bent over, leaving a leg out for Khyven to trip on, or turned just in time to catch Khyven in the nose with an elbow. Every time, it had seemed unintentional, an accident. After the first few attempts, Khyven had been spooked by the old man, like he was surrounded by an unknown force that kept him from harm.

But now, on the cusp of this new knowledge, a knowledge that had almost allowed him to defeat Nhevaz, Khyven felt that original fury again. The old man knew so much, but he shared so little.

The old man wasn't even related to Khyven. Khyven couldn't remember his real parents, couldn't remember if he'd had any siblings. Whatever had happened to him before the old man had taken Khyven in at age ten was a giant blank spot on his memory. The only thing he could recall was flames and screams. Great flames licking up walls he couldn't quite see. The screams of one person, maybe two, maybe half a dozen.

Khyven had always suspected that the old man knew about Khyven's past, but if so, it was one of the many things the old man kept secret.

Khyven let out a breath and went to the second hut, where he and Nhevaz slept, to get his bow and arrows. The woods were full of game if one didn't walk too close to the noktum. It wound through the forest with its questing tentacles and gave Khyven the shivers. The old man said the noktum swallowed boys who were unwary, and Khyven believed it wholeheartedly.

Of course, when Khyven had asked the old man what was inside the noktum, his predictably cryptic answer had been: "Monsters larger and hungrier than you are."

Khyven batted aside the leather flap and entered the hut. He drew up short, surprised to find his brother standing there, head slightly bowed beneath the low ceiling.

"Nhevaz," Khyven said.

"That was well done," Nhevaz said. "The old man had his doubts. I did not."

"Doubts about what?" Khyven asked. "What did I see? The

old man won't tell me. Will you?"

Instead of answering, Nhevaz held his fist forward. An amulet dangled from it, a stylized golden sun with black tentacles slithering over it.

"What is that?" Khyven asked softly, his previous question suddenly forgotten. There were no riches in the old man's little camp, just weapons for fighting, bows for hunting, pots and implements for cooking, and clothes. "That—Those tentacles look like the noktum."

Nhevaz reached into the neck of his tunic and pulled out a duplicate amulet. Khyven hadn't known Nhevaz wore jewelry of any kind.

"Where did you…?" Khyven was going to ask him where he'd kept it but stopped himself. He refused to ask another question that was simply going to be ignored.

"This is the Amulet of Noksonon. We are brothers now," Nhevaz said. "Forever."

"There is so much I need to learn," Khyven said.

Nhevaz nodded. "You will."

"I want to be as good a fighter as you," Khyven said, feeling heat in his cheeks at the admission. He had long since surpassed his other two brothers, but Nhevaz seemed always a step ahead of him.

"Nhevaz, will you show me how? And this amulet… Will you tell me what it is?"

"It is time for you to hunt," he said, and his voice sounded… odd. Nhevaz was a man of few words, but those words were usually emotionless. This time there was… what? Was that affection? Sadness? Khyven couldn't be sure.

Khyven snatched up his bow and quiver of arrows, trying not to be angry. He went to the hut's flap, but Nhevaz's words stopped him.

"Wear it always," Nhevaz said, nodding at the amulet still in Khyven's fist. "Around your neck. Against your skin. Always."

Khyven lifted it and put the chain around his neck. "You're going to tell me more about this, brother. We're going to have a conversation when I get back."

Nhevaz gave a ghost of a smile.

Khyven let the flap swing back into place.

He hunted and found a huge buck that came too close to their camp. He stalked it until he took it down. By the time Khyven returned to camp, the beast slung over his shoulders, he had lost his anger. Today had been an extraordinary day.

Tomorrow will be even better, he thought. *A day of great—*

The clash of steel on steel caused Khyven to stop in his tracks. He waited, the cool breeze tickling his ear. Had he heard what he thought he'd heard? That was the sound of swords. Real swords—?

The sound came again and a chill went up Khyven's back. The old man didn't allow practice with steel. Not yet.

A scream rose in the distance. Khyven threw the buck from his shoulders and sprinted through the trees.

He burst into the clearing. There was blood everywhere. The bodies of Roahl and Farsin lay in the dirt, sword wounds punched through them and dark stains on the dirt below them. The side of Nhevaz's hut was broken and Nhevaz was battling four knights: three in full plate mail armor, one in chainmail, and he was keeping them at bay, blocking, riposting, driving them back just enough to keep them from skewering him.

The old man was nowhere to be seen and a sick feeling settled into Khyven's gut. If the old man wasn't here fighting it could only mean one thing.

"Bastards!" Khyven shouted at them. The knights swiveled their helmeted heads his direction.

"I've got this one," the single knight in chainmail said. "The rest of you get the boy."

"You're certain, Vex?" one of the plate mail knights asked.

"Consider it my fifty-first bout," the man called Vex said. He had a brutish face with a wide chin and close-set, beady black eyes. His big, red nose looked like it had been whacked with a mallet over and over, but the way he held his sword—the way he deflected Nhevaz's strikes—it was obvious he knew how to use it. Vex was a master. Even Khyven could see that.

The three knights in plate mail started toward Khyven.

He had to get a sword. His eyes darted frantically about the camp, but only wooden swords lay in the dust next to the bodies of his brothers.

Khyven drew his dagger and ran for the old man's hut. There were steel weapons in there. If he could just get one of them, he could help Nhevaz.

But the knights were faster. They blocked his path, steel bristling in his direction.

"Easy, boy. Don't make the same mistake your brothers did. Drop the blade. If you attack, we *will* kill you."

Khyven froze, dagger held before him. Steel clashed to his right as Vex and Nhevaz fought.

He readied himself. He'd just have to try to get one of the knights' swords. If he could wrest one away in time, spinning and using the knight's metal body as a shield, maybe he could—

Khyven heard the noise behind him a second before something hard and heavy thudded into the back of his skull. His legs turned to butter. Stars burst in his vision and he fell to his knees.

Everything turned sideways as he fell, his vision blurred. He tried to shake it off, tried to get up, but his limbs wouldn't work. Rough, steel-encased arms grabbed him, pinned his hands behind his back. They bound him with thick rope.

When he was trussed up tight so he couldn't move, two of the knights wrenched him upright to watch the fight between Nhevaz and Vex.

"Watch the master at work," the knight holding Khyven said.

"You got him, Vex!" said another knight.

Steel rang as Vex and Nhevaz strove against one another. Khyven thought the knights were stupid to let their underling fight Nhevaz one-on-one. He'd cut the man to ribbons.

Khyven's vision cleared and he saw the battle. Nhevaz's sword defended again and again, but… there was something lacking. Khyven had seen him fight better than this.

Nhevaz's gaze went past Vex and locked on Khyven.

Vex's sword slipped past Nhevaz's guard and plunged to the hilt in his belly.

"No!" Khyven screamed.

With a victory cry, Vex ripped the blade out. Nhevaz fell to his knees, then onto his face. Vex stepped on his neck and drove his sword through Nhevaz's back.

"I'll kill you!" Khyven screamed. "I'll kill—"

Hard steel slammed into the back of Khyven's head again, and this time darkness took him.

Chapter Eight

KHYVEN

The sunlight woke Khyven the next morning, lightly touching his eyelids. His mind rose to consciousness.

I'm in the palace, he thought. *My fiftieth bout is today. Today I fulfill the old man's prediction. Today I become a champion. A knight.*

During his early days in the Night Ring, when terror had slowly transformed into confidence, he had dreamed about this moment, but he hadn't ever really believed he'd reach it, not then. In the cages, hope could make a man go insane. Worse still, it could make a ringer lose his focus.

That hope had recently resurfaced. He was so close to knighthood—to real power—that he could taste it.

He tried to focus his mind on what they would throw at him today. This was the quiet before the storm.

As though Senji the Warrior Goddess was listening, one of the guards rapped on his door, then opened it without waiting for Khyven to respond.

Four Knights of the Sun, in gleaming plate mail, stood in the hall in perfect formation. They stared forward and did not move.

Their breastplates, helmets, shoulder plates, and scabbards were wrought with curving designs inlaid in pure gold. King Vamreth's crest was engraved upon their chests, a sun with six strong rays lancing outward to the edges of the circle. It reminded Khyven of the Amulet of Noksonon, except there were no tentacles of dark creeping over the sun. Only the king's elite guard bore that symbol.

The king's elite were well-known for their fighting prowess—and their short tempers. They sometimes killed those who offended them, often with little provocation.

"Khyven the Unkillable," a sonorous voice said from behind one of the impassive visors. "Come with us."

The four elite guards stamped their feet in unison, then moved to flank him.

Khyven's heart began to race. It was a group of four just like this who had killed Nhevaz.

When the elite guard marched, Khyven followed. They took him up the grand, sweeping stairway to the second level, guiding him to the right, around the rail toward the next staircase.

To Khyven's left, paintings of historical battles hung on the walls, bordered in elaborate, golden frames. He and his escort climbed a narrower stairway from the second floor to the third. The granite balustrades bore carved patterns, depictions of dragons and Giants.

On the next landing, instead of paintings, marble sculptures of knights and dragons, as well as Giants, stood in shallow alcoves along the wall.

As they ascended the next staircase to the fourth floor, the stairs became a gentle spiral that wound around in the open air. Higher up, a wrought-iron chandelier hung from the ceiling. There had to be a hundred candles on that intricate spidery thing. As they climbed higher, they reached the chandelier, and Khyven had the feeling he was walking too high. There was something odd with the world when a man walked above a chandelier.

On the fourth story landing, the marble of the floor had been polished so meticulously it was as smooth as glass. He hesitated before putting his booted foot upon it. That floor was cleaner than most tables.

Khyven couldn't help but feel intimidated, even though he was sure that was the emotion this grandeur was meant to elicit.

The guards took him to a room not far from the stairwell, where the doors were reminiscent of the towering archways of the Night Ring.

The doors were made of pure gold and they swung open as Khyven and his escort approached. The granite floor gave way to black and white checkered marble, like in the throne room two stories below. There was no throne here, but a carved mahogany table stood in the center of the room.

On the far side of the table sat King Vamreth in an impressively carved, high-back chair made of the same mahogany. He was drinking what looked like dark, purple brandy from a crystal glass.

To the king's left sat two young women wearing the skimpy, diaphanous clothing of dancers. To the king's right was another dancer, similarly dressed. Each of the women had thin, glittering collars around their necks and they sat upright, hands together on the table as though their wrists were cuffed.

Behind the table and to the king's right stood the baby-faced mage Khyven had seen in the foyer of the palace yesterday. The mage's crimson robes looked like a slash of blood across white sheets. He had his cowl thrown back and he watched Khyven with that same peculiar intensity.

Vex the Victorious towered behind the king's chair and to the left, imposing in Nhevaz's shining plate mail. The very light seemed to bend around Vex, like he was at the center of a funnel and the entire room wanted to swirl toward him.

Even with the king sitting in front of Vex, wearing a bejeweled crown and a cloak bordered in ermine, Vex drew Khyven's gaze. The knight faced forward, the dark eye slits of his visor seeming to stare balefully at Khyven.

Khyven stared back, trying see past the armor, to learn more about the greatest ringer who'd ever lived. Nhevaz had been the best swordsman Khyven had ever fought and this man had killed him.

But that had been before Khyven had fought for his life every day, day after day, for two years. That had been before Vex had spent two years as a knight, supping off the luxury that came with his station.

Khyven stared at Vex and he couldn't help but wonder who the better swordsman was now. With just one touch, blade on blade, Khyven would know the answer to that question. The euphoria would flow through him and he would see Vex's weaknesses. Khyven would *know* his chances in a fight.

"Your Majesty," Sir Cantoy, the leader of the elites, said. Armor creaked and clinked as all the elites descended to one knee at the same time. Half a heartbeat slower, Khyven did the same.

"I present Khyven the Unkillable," the leader said, his head bowed.

The elites abruptly stood, turned as one, walked back to the door, and took up posts by twos on either side.

"Khyven the Unkillable," the king said, drawing out the word unkillable. On the table before the king lay three pewter plates filled with an array of succulent delights: sliced apples and raspberries, steaming chicken wings, and cubed steak in a brown sauce. The king, holding his brandy in one hand and a fork in the other, stabbed the steak plate and lifted a steaming morsel to his mouth.

"Your Majesty," Khyven bowed his head, wondering if he was supposed to stand now. He almost did but decided against it.

The king chewed a while and considered Khyven. The mage also watched him. The dancers remained upright, their backs stick-straight, their hands on the table, but their eyes shifted back and forth, glancing surreptitiously at each other. The meeting room was so quiet that a dropped coin would have rung like a gong.

"You're a knight now, Khyven," the king said.

Khyven's heart skipped a beat.

"Well..." The king chuckled, "almost a knight. One more bout and it's done."

"I'm grateful, Your Majesty. I look forward to it."

"Let's talk about that." King Vamreth sat back in his chair, shoving the plate away. Chunks of steak tumbled onto the table amidst a splash of sauce. One of the dancers twitched, then swallowed and held herself perfectly still. Khyven watched a small blush touch her cheeks. She was terrified; he surmised she wasn't supposed to have moved like that.

The king swirled the purple liquor in his glass then sipped it.

"Your Majesty?" Khyven said.

"Your performance was inspired, Khyven. With the Kyolar. By the Fates, wooden swords? Even I thought that thing was going to kill you." The king chuckled, slammed an open palm on the table. This time, none of the dancers jumped, but their rigid stillness at the loud noise was even more eerie. The king took a deep, satisfied breath. "You had us on the edge of our seats."

"Thank you, Your Majesty."

"And that last little bit, where you didn't kill the thing, where you spared its life..." The king leaned forward, eyes glittering. "Mercy? Really? For a monster?" He sighed and leaned back. "I confess I was disappointed but then"—the king took another sip—"you turned it around."

He raised his glass, saluting Khyven. The brandy sloshed about but didn't spill. "Senji's sake, you turned that little show into a legend. The crowd will be talking about it for years. A warning to the creatures of the noktum? Where did you come up with that? Brilliant. You obviously understand your audience, Khyven. You captured their imagination. You gave them something unexpected."

"Thank you, Your Majesty," Khyven said.

"For old Vex here"—the king jerked a finger over his left shoulder—"we built him up to the most difficult bout we could imagine. But you've surpassed his victory with flair, my son. With wooden swords and *mercy*, of all things."

"Thank you, Your Majesty."

The king's mirth eased and he looked pensive. "It got me to thinking. Because the next question is, of course, how do we top that? What can we possibly do to Khyven the Unkillable that will be more impressive than besting a Kyolar with a wooden sword?"

"As you say, Your Majesty."

"We need something surprising, something that will make the crowd roar."

"Yes, Your Majesty."

The king went silent and watched Khyven steadily. "Truth be told, I don't think you need a fiftieth bout. As far as I'm concerned you've proven your prowess. I'd like to make you one of my knights today and begin using you for other things."

Khyven said nothing. He held his excitement under rigid control.

"But the Night Ring is important," the king said. "It pacifies the commoners, and they're anticipating your fiftieth. So, I thought, why not do both at the same time?" The king leaned forward and grinned. His teeth were crooked but bright white, and he seemed to be waiting for an answer.

"That sounds brilliant, Your Majesty. But..." Khyven trailed off.

"But how? How do we do that?" the king finished for him. "Make you a knight and have a fiftieth bout at the same time?" The king leaned back, looking smug, like he knew the answer to that question. He fell silent and regarded Khyven with a half-smile. Finally, he said, "Slayter tells me you visited the Night Ring last night."

Surprised, Khyven shot a quick look at the mage. No one had followed him last night. Khyven was sure of it!

Vamreth chuckled. "It's creepy what they can do, isn't it?" he said, seeming to read Khyven's thoughts. "Mages. They can make fire appear out of thin air. Listen through walls. Follow a ringer through the streets without him knowing it. And of course, they shroud themselves in mystery on purpose just to spook us, don't they? The cowled robes. The long, droopy sleeves. So much showmanship. Mages want us to believe they're all-powerful, to believe they're demi-gods. I tell you, Khyven, I've had mages claim they could turn the sun black or teleport themselves from here to Nokte-Shaddark in the blink of an eye. Slayter himself claims he has a bottle of Giant's blood in his laboratory. Actual Giant's blood! Isn't that right, Slayter?" Vamreth cast the question toward the mage, but Slayter said nothing. Finally, Vamreth rolled his head toward Slayter. "That bottle's got to be, what, a thousand years old?"

"About two thousand, Your Majesty," Slayter said.

"Two thousand years...." Vamreth marveled. "The kingdom of Usara didn't even exist that long ago. How could a bottle of Giant's blood last two thousand years? Wouldn't it just... dissolve away in all that time? Doesn't glass turn back into sand after two centuries?"

Slayter cleared his throat. "No, Your Majesty."

Vamreth looked at Slayter with an amused half-smile. "Oh, I've upset him. Did you see that, Khyven?" Vamreth shook his head. "Don't try to pull back the curtain with mages, Khyven. Never try to do that." Vamreth waved a pacifying hand at Slayter. "My apologies. My apologies." He faced Khyven again. "Slayter here is the most talented mage in all of Usara—in all three of the northern kingdoms, I'd wager. I shouldn't tease. If he says it's actual Giant's blood, then when he drips it out onto a metal pan and grows a Giant for us, I suppose I shouldn't be surprised."

"Yes, Your Majesty," Khyven said.

"What *did* surprise me, though," the king continued. "Was your trip to the Night Ring last night." The king tapped his cup lightly on the table as he regarded Khyven. "When you left the palace, I thought for certain you'd head back to that comely wench at that dockside tavern. The... uh..." He snapped his fingers, looking for the name. "What was it called?"

"The Mariner's Rest, Your Majesty," Slayter supplied.

"Yes, of course. The Mariner's Rest," the king repeated, still watching Khyven. "But you didn't. You went to talk with that Shadowvar."

Khyven's scalp prickled. There had been no one in the Night Ring when Khyven had entered, not in the hallway or the antechamber. None save ringers in cages. Khyven had searched the shadows. The mage must have really listened through walls! Or had he turned himself invisible. Otherwise, how could he possibly have heard that conversation?

"And you know what?" The king tapped a fork on the table. "It's perfect."

"It's… perfect?" Khyven asked, confused.

"Khyven, it's as though you anticipate my needs before I even know them." The king stood up, pushed his chair back and walked around the table. The dancers held rigidly still.

"Follow me," the king said affably. Khyven rose to his feet and fell in step behind the king as he walked toward one of the wide windows at the back of the room. The king leaned forward, putting a hand on the wide marble windowsill. "Look," the king said, pointing out over the grand view. The city sprawled below them. The buildings looked so small they might have been models. The king glanced back, realized Khyven had stayed a respectful distance away, and beckoned him again. The king patted the windowsill. "Come here. Come stand here."

Khyven joined the king and stood shoulder to shoulder with him.

"It looks peaceful, doesn't it?" the king said.

"Yes, Your Majesty."

The king went silent and the back of Khyven's neck prickled. He thought of Vex the Victorious and the elites standing behind him. But then, if the king had wanted him dead, Khyven would be dead. He tried to relax the tight muscles between his shoulders.

"Out there," the king said softly, "rebellion festers. Conspirators gather."

He was talking about the same thing the Shadowvar had. The conspiracy of the queeners.

The king gave Khyven a sidelong glance. "Surely you've heard of the rebels who lurk in the Royal Forest? Followers of the so-called Queen-in-Exile?" he said. "These lying traitors have tempted two of my nobles over to their side."

"The old king's children," Khyven said. "I thought they were all dead."

"They are," the king said. "They claim Laochodon's daughter leads them when I know that is impossible. The girl got swallowed by a noktum. I saw it. She's dead, but that doesn't stop the gullible from believing."

"So… who is this woman?"

"Probably nobody. I doubt if there even is a woman. Or if there is, she's a face to spin into the legend. Real or imaginary, whoever she is—whoever is propping her up—they're as cunning as rats. My men can't seem to root them out of those woods. We've caught a couple of them, but they never speak before they die."

Khyven thought of the smug, close-lipped Shadowvar, and he believed it.

"Does this impostor exist?" the king ruminated. "Is it a cabal of traitors inventing a story? These are worthy questions, Khyven." The king turned to face him. "And I want you to find those answers."

Khyven's heart skipped a beat. "Me?"

"Yes, you."

"I… I don't see how I—"

"Slayter followed you last night. He heard your conversation with the Shadowvar. That creature is obviously in league with this group of traitors and he just as obviously wants to recruit you. So, we're going to let him. I want you to join the rebellion."

The king hadn't mentioned the Amulet of Noksonon, that link between himself and the Shadowvar. Was that on purpose?

Khyven fought the urge to look at Slayter, suddenly wondering if the mage hadn't heard the entire conversation or if he just hadn't *told* the king the entire conversation.

The pitfalls of courtly life suddenly seemed deadlier than the Night Ring itself. Khyven considered telling the king about the amulet. After all, it was Vamreth who had returned it to him in the first place, had placed it on Khyven's pillow as a reward for his fortieth bout.

Hadn't he?

Khyven was so lost in his own thoughts that he missed the first part of what the king was saying. He quickly turned his focus back where it belonged.

"… fiftieth bout will be different from anything we've seen before. You're going to escape, Khyven, and you're going to take that Shadowvar with you."

"Escape?"

"You will join me in the royal box for today's bout, an honor for your triumph yesterday. We will watch the final bout of the day together. Twelve traitors against three ringers. We'll make a fight of it. When the fight is at its most tense, you will enter the fray. You will slide down from the box, run through the crowd, and leap into the arena. We'll make sure there's a gate hook for you. Just hook it into the edge of the wall and slide down."

"Your Majesty?"

"You will then make a flowery speech about my tyranny. You'll finish off whatever ringers are still fighting the traitors and you'll escape through the northwestern gate—I will make sure it is open and thinly guarded. You'll have to kill a few spearmen, of course, but that will make it look real. It will give your escape authenticity. I'll leave two horses at the entrance to the Night Ring, the gates of the city will be open at that time of day. I will have my elites stand in for its normal guards; they will not oppose you."

Khyven fixed a blank expression on his face. "You want me to escape with the Shadowvar?" he said.

"Your fiftieth bout will not be inside the ring, but beyond the gates of the city," the king said pointing past the city wall toward the forest. "Follow the Shadowvar back to this impostor's camp. Become one of them. Get the intelligence I need."

"You want me to become a spy."

"You lead me to the impostor's camp and I will raise you up," the king said. "I will make you a baron, not a knight. You will have lands and titles and a legend that lasts forever. The slave who became a noble. What do you think of that?"

Khyven could barely believe his ears. "That is… generous, Your Majesty."

The king returned to the table and sat down. "I daresay it will impress even the Honorable Shalure Chadrone," he said.

Khyven didn't know what to say. He hadn't realized the king had taken any interest in his love life. Silently, he followed the king and took up his place in front of the table.

"She's a beauty, isn't she?" the king said. "Do this for me and she is yours. I will approve the match and we shall have a lavish wedding."

"This is… I don't know what to say, Your Majesty."

"Say that we understand each other."

"We understand each other, Your Majesty."

The king smiled and picked up his glass. "I'm going to be honest with you, Khyven." He sipped the brandy. "I like your style. Your daring. Your gift for speeches to the crowd. You will need that silver tongue and all of your courage for this test. Do not fail me."

"I won't, Your Majesty."

"Trust in me, Khyven, and everything you want will be yours," the king said, echoing Shalure's words from the previous day.

"Yes, Your Majesty," he said.

"You get to their hidden camp. Slayter and I will do the rest."

"The rest, Your Majesty?" Khyven glanced at the mage. His youthful face remained expressionless.

"In a manner of speaking. Slayter?" The king glanced over his shoulder. Slayter brought his hand out from one of his sleeves and flicked a coin to Khyven. It flipped end over end and Khyven caught it.

Except it wasn't a coin. It was the same size, the same thickness, but it wasn't made of bronze, copper, silver, or gold. It wasn't made of any metal at all. It felt like hardened clay, and it bore a symbol, a single line crossing over itself many times to create a symmetrical shape. Khyven had never seen anything like it. An eerie chill went up his back.

Magic.

"What is it?" he asked.

"When you reach their camp," Slayter said, "complete the symbol."

"Complete it?"

"The symbol is missing a line. When you complete that line, you complete the spell. It will show me where you are."

Khyven looked closely at the clay coin and saw that the mage was right. The entire, intricate symbol was carefully rendered but for one small line that was missing.

"A sharp rock. The tip of a dagger," Slayter said. "Anything will work, but the line must be precise and straight. If you scratch through existing lines or make a sloppy connection, it won't work." He tossed a bit of metal to Khyven, who snatched it from the air. "I use this," Slayter said.

At first glance, the item looked like some kind of writing device, a stylus maybe, but it was more of a scratching device. It was three smooth sticks of metal twisted together like a braid, straight and pointed on one side and braided into a loop on the other.

"One other thing," Slayter added. "Keep it safe. As you can see the disk is fragile, if it breaks, the spell breaks."

Khyven looked down at the scratching device and the clay disk. "I am to keep this during the bout?" he asked.

"You are," the king replied. "You'll escape directly from the arena. No time to run back to your room to grab what you've left behind."

"That… may be difficult," Khyven said. "If I'd had this during the fight with the Kyolar, I'd have certainly crushed it."

"You'll only be fighting people this time," the king said. "No Kyolars. It should be easy. Or have I chosen the wrong man?"

"No, Your Majesty," Khyven said. He tucked the clay disk carefully into his tunic.

The king nodded approvingly. "Together, we'll do away with this annoyance of a rebellion."

"Yes, Your Majesty," Khyven said.

"Good." He raised his glass, saluted Khyven, then waved a dismissive hand. "Now, go away from me."

The four elite guards stamped their feet in unison and approached Khyven, forming up on either side of him.

He bowed deeply toward the king, who was already ignoring him in favor of fondling the chin of one of the dancers.

Khyven followed the guards as they led him through the tall, golden doors.

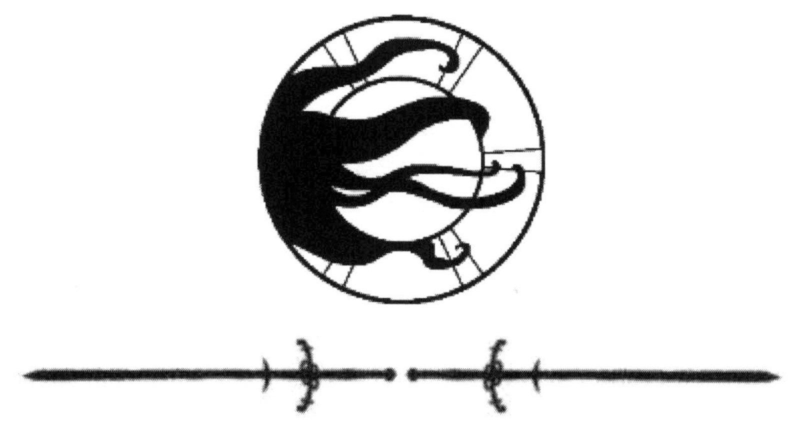

Chapter Nine

KHYVEN

Khyven returned to his room and found a beautiful steel sword on the chest of drawers, complete with a sheath and belt. It had been lined up next to the broken and intact wooden swords he'd brought back from the arena after his bout.

He ran his fingers along the beautifully wrought sheath of his new sword. There were no gems set upon it, thankfully. He'd seen many highborns' scabbards so decorated and he'd never liked it. Swords were for fighting and, sometimes, killing. Turning them into jewelry seemed sacrilegious somehow. But the scrollwork on the sheath was beautiful.

He drew the longsword, felt its perfect balance. It was finer than any of the blades he'd ever fought with in the arena. It reminded him of the old man's sword, the one he'd hung in his hut as a testament to what Khyven and his brothers might one day wield, if they were worthy.

One night, when the old man wasn't around, Khyven had taken that sword off the hut's wall, had felt its perfect balance, had dreamed of one day wielding it. Of course, the old man had caught him. Nothing ever happened in the old man's camp that he didn't know about. He'd made Khyven pay for his trespass. The old man had worked Khyven until he'd thrown up, then he'd made Khyven get up and work more.

But this sword belonged to Khyven, a testament to how he had grown beyond the old man's teachings and influence.

He laid the sword down, went to his soft bed, and fell upon it. He thought of grabbing the decanter of wine from the table near the door, but he left it. Instead, he dreamed of Shalure and how she might feel lying next to him.

He was still daydreaming an hour later when the spearmen knocked on his door to take him to the Night Ring.

In addition to the new sword, a russet-colored tunic with laces at the cuffs and sleeves, black breeches, and new black boots had been left for him as well. It wasn't exactly knightly attire, but then he wasn't a knight. Yet.

He dressed quickly, making sure to put the clay coin—and the braided steel scratcher Slayter had given him—carefully in his pouch. Finally, he strapped on the sword. It felt good. Then—he didn't know why—he took the intact practice sword and slid it through the belt next to the other.

The spearmen escorted him to the Night Ring. Khyven felt an odd sensation as he walked beneath the arch of the Night Ring, as he heard the roar of the crowd, the smell of sweat and oiled steel. It had always felt like he was coming home, but this time he felt an air of finality. After today, he would never have to come here again if he didn't want to.

Butterflies fluttered in his belly as he ascended the steps. Khyven had never been a spy before. He wondered just how good of a liar he could be, if pressed.

They came out of the covered stairway and the cheers of the crowd multiplied as they stepped into the open air. The spearmen escorted him to the royal box which, of course, had a prime view of the fight below.

Two chariots pulled by pamants—the giant desert birds the distant Sandrunners used to cross the Eternal Desert—were fighting a dozen naïfs with spears. The chariot riders had an arsenal of steel weapons in their chariots—swords, lances, morning stars, bows and arrows—and, of course, they had the pamants themselves. The eight-foot-tall creatures could spear a man with their sharp beaks, and while they were normally docile, these had been trained to attack.

Khyven had fought pamants before. They were tricky. In short, the naïfs didn't stand a chance.

Bloodthirsty cries went up from the crowd as naïf after naïf was cut down while the chariots took their passes, back and forth.

The spearmen left as Khyven closed the half-door to the royal box behind him. The king sat on an ornate chair in the center of the box, some fifteen feet away from Khyven, with a pair of the scantily clad dancers at his feet. To his left and right stood Vex and Slayter, of course, and beyond that, radiating out in order of standing and importance, Khyven supposed, were the other nobles of the court.

For a moment, Khyven hoped he'd see Shalure, but of course she wasn't there. She wasn't anywhere close to being important enough to sit with the king.

But Slayter was there, and so was Vex the Victorious. Khyven forced his gaze away from the big man, away from that plate mail armor that had belonged to Nhevaz, and Khyven's gaze fell upon the king.

Vamreth glanced over, then beckoned Khyven forward.

"Khyven the Unkillable," he said loudly. "You honor us with your presence. Yesterday was quite a show. Quite a show…" He beckoned again. "Come, sit here." He indicated a spot on the steps where the dancing girls lounged.

Khyven hesitated, feeling like a dog called to the hearth, then he did as he was bid.

The battle below wrapped up, with the chariot riders the clear victors. The crowd cheered. Spearmen and workers came out to clear the bodies.

Butterflies danced in Khyven's belly and he surveyed the arena. He saw that, as promised, the northwestern antechamber gate was open, as were all the gates to the noktums, since it was daytime, to heighten the tension. Tentacles of midnight writhed, endlessly searching, reaching just outside the archways. It was a crowd favorite when someone got snatched by the noktum. The screams as they got pulled into darkness were always drowned out by the approving roar of the crowd.

Khyven glanced at the top of the wall a few dozen feet below the royal box. The king had been true to his word. One of the long, hooked bars that the workers used to pull the noktum doors open from above lay there, as though forgotten.

The announcer called the next bout, a demonstration of knights versus traitors. Three men in chainmail, leather armor, and conical helmets entered the arena. They looked like actual butcher knights, Knights of the Steel, and they didn't play to the crowd like experienced ringers would. Khyven suddenly wondered if they were real knights. Perhaps they had displeased King Vamreth.

The southeastern antechamber door opened and a dozen naïfs came out with wooden spears without metal heads, daggers, and cudgels, weapons far inferior to those the knights held. Not one of the naïfs had a steel sword. None had armor or shields.

Khyven saw the Shadowvar walk up the ramp amidst the crowd, squinting, his white horns glowing in the bright light. He had a dagger in his hand, but he held it at arm's length like he was considering whether or not to drop it.

"What do you think, Khyven the Unkillable?" the king asked.

"I think the knights will win through," he said in a monotone.

The king smiled as though that was exactly what he'd wanted Khyven to say.

The announcer blew the horn to start the bout. Khyven craned his neck and found the king glancing expectantly down at him.

Below, half of the naïfs backed away from the knights while the other half tried to convince them that the only way to survive was to make a coordinated attack.

Khyven's heart beat faster, but the euphoria didn't come.

Six of the naïfs charged the knights and the fight began. The little Shadowvar, meanwhile, drifted toward the northwestern gate, almost as though he already knew the plan.

Khyven stood up and one of the dancers drew a sharp breath. Two nearby elites came to life, swords out, barring his way toward the king, but Khyven lunged in the other direction, vaulting over the short wall of the box and into the crowd below.

He deftly landed between two spectators, who cried out and threw themselves to the side. He darted for the stairway, then flew down the steps, toward the hook with the rope tied around it. Shouts went up behind him as nearby spectators turned their attention from the fight below to Khyven in the stands.

His local disruption became arena-wide when he grabbed the hook—a fifteen-foot-long pole with a hook at one end—secured it on the top of the wall, and flung himself over.

The sharp hook scraped to the edge of the wall, but it didn't come free. He slid down the pole and landed softly on the black sands.

The crowd went wild, roaring their approval.

The six naïfs were actually doing well against the knights, encircling them and driving them back with spears while the knights took up a defensive posture. Their bold attack had even strengthened the spines of a few of the other naïfs who were running to join the fight.

Now there were only three holding back from the battle. One stood, dumbstruck, gripping a cudgel like he didn't know what to do with it. One had fallen to his knees and was praying, the third was the Shadowvar. He'd been sidling ever closer to the northwestern gate, but he had stopped right in front of the Night Door's archway when he saw Khyven running toward him. He stood before the yawning archway of the noktum, tentacles reaching outward some ten feet behind him.

"Come on," Khyven said. "I'm getting you out of here."

But the Shadowvar didn't move. He looked at Khyven, stunned, and he thought he saw a flicker of hope in the Shadowvar's eyes.

"They'll kill you, Khyven," he said. "What about your fiftieth?"

"Forget the fiftieth. You're right." He pointed at the king. "That man is a villain. I'm through fighting for his pleasure."

Khyven turned to the crowd, drew a deep breath, and bellowed his next words. "King Vamreth is a usurper! He stole the throne from the rightful king. He doesn't deserve to rule here." Khyven thrust his gleaming sword into the air. "Overthrow the usurper! Long live the Queen-in-Exile!"

The entire arena fell silent. The cheers faded. Even the battle between the naïfs and the knights paused.

Khyven turned and grabbed the Shadowvar's hand. "Come on. The northwestern gate is open. If we're fast enough, we can get out of the city."

But the Shadowvar hauled back, breaking his grip. A grim smile had spread across his face. "Well done, Khyven. Well done."

"Yes. Thank you, but let's shut our mouths and escape first, yes?"

Several spearmen gathered against the closed gates of at least three different antechambers. It wouldn't be long before they opened those gates and emerged to keep the bout from getting out of hand.

Khyven grabbed the Shadowvar by his thin arm again.

"My thoughts exactly," the Shadowvar said, again dislodging his arm, "but you are going the wrong way."

"What are you—"

"I admire your bravery, and you might even be able to cut your way through those spearmen. You just might at that," the Shadowvar said. This time, the Shadowvar grabbed Khyven's arm and pulled him toward the yawning darkness of the Night Door. Inside that hall of blackness, the noktum roiled. As though sensing the Shadowvar's intention, the tentacles stretched out to their limit, seeking.

Khyven balked. "You're joking."

The Shadowvar pointed at Khyven's neck. "Did you think that was just a pretty piece of jewelry? It protects you, Khyven. From the noktum. That is its purpose."

Khyven glanced at the amulet, then back at the Shadowvar.

"You're insane."

"It is true," the Shadowvar said, and he held out his hand. "Do you trust me?"

No, thought Khyven, but he didn't say it.

"Sometimes, a leap of faith is required," the Shadowvar said. He backed into the archway of the Night Door, toward the tentacles.

"Don't!" Khyven said. "We can make it. We can escape." The Shadowvar was crazy. Nothing survived the noktum.

The tentacles sensed the Shadowvar's approach. They flailed faster, reaching eagerly for him, only a foot away.

"Don't be stupid!" Khyven said.

"You have the power, Khyven. You've had it all along." The Shadowvar tapped his own amulet. "Trust."

Khyven lunged for him, but the Shadowvar stepped back. The tentacles wrapped around him and pulled him out of Khyven's reach.

"No!"

The Shadowvar vanished, swallowed by the dark.

"Senji's teeth!" Khyven cursed. He whirled around, looking for a solution. The fight between the knights and the naïfs had begun again. One knight was limping, but two of the naïfs were dead. The crowd, however, wasn't even watching that fight. They were all watching him, including the king, who had stood up, his fists clenched at his sides. He was over two hundred feet away, but it was obvious the man was furious.

There was no help there. No understanding. Khyven had lost the Shadowvar. His mission was a failure. There would be no barony for him. Not even a knighthood. And there would be no second chance. This *was* his chance.

Khyven looked to the northwestern gate. Could he still fight through and prevail? Escape on his own? But if just Khyven escaped, all the things the king had promised would evaporate. The few spearmen in the tunnels would turn into twenty. And even if Khyven managed to fight his way past them, the elites at the gate would do their best to kill him.

Khyven cursed again. He was trapped. Forty-nine bouts and

now this. He'd avoided death and he'd avoided the tentacles of the noktums. Forty-nine times, and now there was no way out. He slowly looked at the writhing tentacles.

Unconsciously, he reached up and touched the amulet. It was just a necklace. Just a pretty disk of metal.

Unless it was actually magical.

A cold sweat broke out on his forehead. Whenever he fought he felt the euphoria, but there was no euphoria for this. The blue wind could not come to his aid.

His gut twisted.

He glanced back up at the king and saw Vex and the elites had sprung into action. They had jumped from the box and were running toward the hook Khyven had used to slide into the arena. They'd seen his indecision. They saw his desperation. They were coming for him.

You have the power, Khyven. You've had it all the time....

Vex landed on the black sands and sprinted toward Khyven. A rage at the injustice of this whole situation flared inside him and, for a moment, he wanted that fight. If he was going to die, he could die fighting Vex. Against Vex alone, Khyven might have a chance, but not against Vex, four Knights of the Sun, and every spearman who would soon pour into the arena. It would be a legendary fight, a legendary end…

But he'd still be dead.

"Senji's Blood…" Khyven said.

He turned and ran into the tentacles.

Chapter Ten
KHYVEN

Khyven wanted to scream when the tentacles grabbed him. Maybe he did. At first, they felt cold, like he was being wrapped in cool sheets, but he would later wonder if that was only his imagination. The bright sun of the arena vanished, plunging him into absolute blackness. He lost all sense of location or the pull of the ground. He could have been falling through the night sky for all he knew.

He reoriented, felt that his toes actually were scraping along the ground, but he could see nothing.

Was he dead? Was this what it was like to die? Voices filled his mind.

"Say that we understand each other," King Vamreth's words returned to him.

"I showed you my heart when I pressed my lips to yours..." Shalure murmured, and images accompanied her voice, her mysterious smile, curlicues at the edges of her mouth.

"Concentrate!" The old man's voice came next, shattering Shalure's beautiful face. *"Some day you will need this and you'll wish you'd paid more attention."* And Khyven recalled the lessons with a

blindfold. The old man had taught him how to fight blind, how to use his other senses in a fight.

Khyven felt the ground and he put his feet against it. He drew his sword, crouched, and used his other senses. He listened, but it was nearly impossible to hear anything over the pounding of his heart, the roar in his ears, and his own heavy breathing.

"Well, you do surprise..." The Shadowvar's voice came out of the darkness. "I honestly didn't think you'd follow. I didn't think you had it in you."

Khyven swallowed, panted, and tried to see the Shadowvar, tried to see anything.

"You are brave, Khyven the Unkillable. I'll give you that."

"We're not...?" Khyven almost finished the sentence, but he stopped himself.

"Dead?" the Shadowvar finished for him. "No. When I promise something, I don't lie."

"But... how?"

"We'd best get moving. It doesn't last long."

"What doesn't last?"

"The necklaces."

Khyven gulped and tried to get his racing heart under control. "And what... happens then?"

"Just about everything you've heard. Everything you've imagined in your worst nightmares. Everything you thought was going to happen the moment you stepped into the noktum," the Shadowvar said. "Now, if you're quite recovered, we should get moving."

"Where...?" Khyven clenched his teeth and told himself to stop acting like a naïf. "How can we go anywhere if we can't see?"

Dark light welled out from the Shadowvar's chest. The Shadowvar had a finger on the amulet, stroking it in a clockwise direction.

The sun in the center of his amulet, the one that peeked out from the edge of the five little tentacles of black, glowed, but it wasn't like any light Khyven had ever seen. It didn't fill the world with brightness and color. It wasn't even really light. It was as if, suddenly, the world around the amulet was slowly being revealed, like a watercolor painting, starting at the Shadowvar's amulet and working outward, revealing his skinny chest, his face and horns, the dark granite walls behind him.

"Senji's Boots…" Khyven murmured.

"Go ahead," the Shadowvar said, nodding at Khyven's amulet.

Khyven reached up and traced his finger around the edge of the medallion. Nothing seemed to happen until Khyven looked at everything around him and realized the dark shapes had coalesced into vivid details. The ground below looked like the black sands of the arena. The cave walls were dark black. Everything in the world was rendered in shades of charcoal black.

He turned—

—and cried out, whipping his sword up. A massive Kyolar crouched behind him, close enough to touch. Its glistening black eyes fixed hungrily on Khyven.

He kept his sword between them, pointed at the giant cat. He imagined the moment he'd first crossed into this place. For all he knew, he might have fallen at the feet of that thing. It could have breathed on him, an inch way from his head this whole time. "The amulet is keeping it back?"

"It keeps them all back."

"All of them?" Khyven spared a quick glance away from the Kyolar to look at the Shadowvar. The little demon nodded his chin upward. Khyven followed his gaze and cringed. Barely a few feet overhead, giant, otter-like creatures slithered through the air.

The beasts had sleek, furry bodies, short legs, and serpentine tails, and they swam through the air like it was water. Thin tusks protruded from their upper lips, long as daggers. The otters moved back and forth, obviously drawn to Khyven and the Shadowvar, and just as obviously kept at bay.

"What if we take the amulets off?" Khyven asked.

"Don't do that," the Shadowvar said. "I'm not joking. Take

it off and you're dead. Come on, let's hurry before it stops."

"How long do we have?"

"An hour perhaps. The smarter ones will begin to gather when the amulet's power wanes."

"There are smarter ones?" he asked.

"The Noksonoi left many things behind and almost all of them live in the noktums. Some of them are smarter than you, ringer."

"What's a Noksonoi?"

The Shadowvar shook his head and started down the tunnel. It sloped precipitously downward, away from the archway. It was so steep Khyven had to fight to keep his footing. "We can give you a lesson in Giant history later," he said. "Assuming the queen doesn't decide to kill you."

"There actually *is* a queen?"

The Shadowvar frowned over his shoulder. "I've not once lied to you, ringer. For that, look to Vamreth."

After a long descent, the path evened out and the tunnel went on for a while. Then, the path started upward again and finally opened into a forest of dark pines.

Again, the world seemed to be rendered in charcoal water-colors. A path bordered in black stones meandered away from the tunnel's entrance. Beyond the path, black weeds grew to the edge of black bushes and a line of tall black pine trees grew to the left and right, all the way to the horizon, as far as he could see.

The light from the amulet wasn't like the light of a torch. It didn't only illuminate a range of twenty feet or so. It illuminated… everything. Or maybe it just made it so Khyven could see in this dark world. The sky was a lighter shade of dark and there were no stars overhead. The mountains in the distance were a dark charcoal as were the trees that poked up into the sky. It was as though the color had been leeched from this world, but Khyven could see… all of it.

The Kyolar paced them. Another loped from the woods and joined it. The fanged otters slithered overhead, but none of the creatures moved to attack.

"Let's jog," the Shadowvar said, and he started a light run.

Khyven scrambled to keep up. "Can you run for an hour, Khyven the Unkillable?"

"I've fought men to the death for an hour before."

"Understand that if you fall here, you'll never emerge."

"So, we will come out of this eventually?"

The Shadowvar didn't answer.

The path wended back and forth a little but stayed mostly true. Khyven tried to get a sense of direction in this benighted place, but he couldn't.

Two more Kyolars joined the throng, muscles bunching and relaxing as they walked along, easily keeping pace. The sky overhead was now a slithering mass of fanged otters. Khyven forced himself not to think about what would happen if the power of the amulets suddenly failed. He kept looking for the end of the noktum, some wall that would tell him its border, but he couldn't see it.

The trees cleared and they ran across a wide, flat expanse. A castle emerged on their left, far away. The thing was huge. He squinted, trying to make out details. A dozen towers thrust into the air, many crumbled at the tops. The wall around the castle was jagged, broken in too many places to count. The thing was a ruin.

"What is that?"

The Shadowvar, breathing heavily, glanced to the left. He grunted and nodded. "Nuraghi," he said, as though that explained it.

Khyven clenched his teeth. Noksonoi. Nuraghi.

"What," he asked, "is a nuraghi?"

"Stronghold of the Giants," the Shadowvar said. "Abandoned when Humans were still wearing loincloths and running around with wooden spears. Remember those intelligent monsters I mentioned? That's where they live. Seems the closer you come to the nuraghi, the smarter the creatures become."

"How do you know that?"

"Save your breath, ringer. Run," the Shadowvar huffed.

Time passed and Khyven followed the Shadowvar. It was

impossible to tell time in this place, but he soon began to get nervous. A crowd of Kyolars paced them now and their eagerness had increased. Drool dripped from their jaws in anticipation, like they knew the power of the amulets was failing. The sky overhead was completely blotted out by the twisting, writhing mass of the fanged otters.

The very air seemed to press in on him. With every step, he felt more and more that this wasn't a place Humans were supposed to be, that the very fact of their survival was an offense in this place. The protection of the amulet was a thin, fragile barrier, and each of the monsters that hovered around them knew it. They were simply waiting for a little crack, and then they could devour them.

"Can't you run any faster?" Khyven asked of the short-legged Shadowvar. "Where is the exit?"

"You're welcome… to run on ahead," the Shadowvar huffed.

Khyven wanted to tell the demon what he could do with his humor, but he refrained. The little Shadowvar held Khyven's life in his hands.

A moment later, though, the Shadowvar said, "We're close. But they won't give up until we get there."

Khyven hated the fact that the Shadowvar's words flooded him with relief, like the Shadowvar was a father who had just reassured his child.

After a few more moments, Khyven noticed that he couldn't see the horizon anymore. The mountains in the distance were gone, like the black sun had set on this dark world. Even the distant castle was blurry now, and Khyven realized that the "light" from the amulets was beginning to fade.

A low, throaty growl began in the throats of all the Kyolars. They sensed it, too.

"Shadowvar!" Khyven said.

"Keep running, ringer," the Shadowvar said, but there was a bite to his words, a fear that hadn't been there before.

By Senji, he thought. *It's over. We're done.*

Ahead, the bordered path curved to the right around a giant boulder and ended, as if at a wall of darkness.

One of the Kyolars snapped at Khyven. It didn't bite him, but it was as though the creature was testing his protection.

"Go ringer! Go!" the Shadowvar said.

"Where?"

"Into the wall! Follow the path!"

Khyven grabbed the Shadowvar and threw him over his back. Khyven's scalp prickled with cold sweat, and he ran for his life.

The Kyolars keened, snapped at Khyven, but they all hissed and withdrew, as though something burned them. The fanged otters overhead went crazy, crossing over each other again and again until they looked like a mass of flying black worms.

As Khyven shot toward the end of the path, he saw other figures emerge from the hazy darkness. There was nothing in the distance now, as though the amulets finally *were* torches now, only showing the terrain directly around them.

Tall, birdlike creatures hopped into the sphere of "light." They looked like pamants, except far more deadly. Where pamants had blunted beaks these had the viciously hooked beaks of raptors and they were twice as large, creatures of nightmare with large, blinking eyes fixed on Khyven.

Unlike the slavering hunger of the Kyolars or the fanged otters, the nightmare pamants seemed more curious about Khyven and his Shadowvar burden.

"Go, ringer!" the Shadowvar said, panic in his tone.

The Kyolars screamed in frustration, snapping at the air, getting closer to flesh each time.

Khyven dove into the wall of black before him.

Light exploded around him, blinding him. Something—a root perhaps—tripped him and he tumbled to the ground. The Shadowvar was flung from his back and Khyven rolled.

He blinked against the brightness, trying to force his eyes to adjust.

Trees and tents resolved, dozens of them standing in the

midst of a huge glade, as well as portions of encroaching trees, all surrounded by a hundred-foot wall of noktum darkness, except it was smooth, without tentacles. The sun shone down through the huge hole directly overhead. More than a hundred people stood nearby, an army of ragtag men and women armed with swords, spears, and cudgels. Mixed among the people were a few huge, thick hunting dogs. All of them—including the dogs—faced Khyven.

The Shadowvar pushed himself to his feet, breathing hard.

Khyven backed up, but the dark, smooth wall of the noktum rose behind him. He was caught. He wasn't going back into that damned noktum, but by the looks of the hostile crowd before him, he didn't want to be here, either.

A young woman stepped forward from the group. She wore a fighter's leather armor and a wide strip of red cloth tied around her head. A mop of unruly brunette hair tumbled past her shoulders. She'd drawn her sword and she waved it lazily before her like a snake's tongue testing the air.

She grinned.

"Well, well, well… What did you bring us, Vohn?"

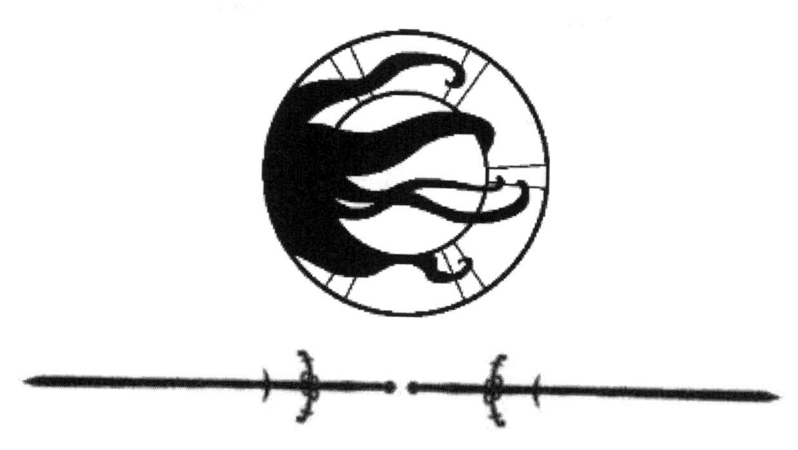

CHAPTER ELEVEN

KHYVEN

"This," the Shadowvar—apparently his name was Vohn—said, still breathing hard, "is Khyven the Unkillable."

"Khyven the Unkillable?" the woman said, raising her dark eyebrows. "The ringer?"

"The same."

"I've heard of you." She turned to the crowd behind her. "Have we heard of Khyven the Unkillable?"

The crowd cheered, but they still looked ready to attack.

She turned back to Khyven.

"You should be flattered. Out here, we don't get to see the Night Ring bouts. But even we've heard of the great Khyven the Unkillable. You have what we call renown. Do you know what renown is?"

Khyven searched the woman's eyes. Was this some kind of test to see if he was a blithering idiot?

Her eyes glittered with mischief. She was toying with him.

"Re-known," he said, mispronouncing it intentionally. "Doesn't that mean you knew something and then you know it again?"

The woman raised an eyebrow.

"He's playing stupid," Vohn said.

"Really?" the woman said sarcastically.

"But he's not stupid; I suspect he even knows how to read," Vohn said.

"What a treat."

"He had an amulet," Vohn said. "I don't know why. He says his brother made it."

"*Made* it?" Now both her eyebrows lifted. "I thought you said he wasn't stupid."

"Ignorance isn't *necessarily* stupidity." Vohn rubbed his neck self-consciously.

"Did you see your brother make it, Khyven the Unkillable?" the woman asked.

Khyven kept his back to the implacable black wall, beyond which he imagined the Kyolars were just sitting, waiting. He wondered why they didn't leap through and snatch him. Kyolars could cross the barrier into the Human world. They did when the masters of the Night Ring put fresh meat in front of the archways. Why not now?

He glanced left and right. This was the only place he'd ever seen the wall of a noktum be smooth, without tentacles. Surely it had something to do with that. He noticed a post sticking out of the ground to his left, right at the edge of the noktum. Atop the post was some kind of trinket, a small statue, and it was glowing with a dark light.

Magic.

He only got a quick glance, but somehow it reassured him that the Kyolar wasn't going to come charging out and wrap him in its claws. He turned his full attention to the woman.

She glanced at Khyven's sword hilt, cocked her head, and appraised him, her gaze roving up and down his entire body.

"He's pretty," she said. "I haven't seen many pretty ringers."

Vohn rolled his eyes.

"Don't you think, Lorelle?" the woman said, looking over her shoulder, but Khyven couldn't tell which of the crowd she was speaking to.

The warrior woman sauntered closer. She was so close

now—with that sword waving in front of her—that Khyven didn't take his eyes off her.

"Do you know who I am?" the woman asked.

"I'm guessing you're the Queen-in-Exile," Khyven said.

"A point for the ringer." She raised her sword in salute. "So, are you going to draw that blade, Khyven the Unkillable? Or do I have to keep waving my sword in your face?"

"I'll draw if I have to," he said.

She chuckled. "Trained to look death in the face, are you?"

"Vohn invited me to join your rebellion."

"I'm sure."

"And now I'm not welcome?" he asked. He glanced at Vohn. The Shadowvar raised his hands helplessly.

"We only have two types of people who come here," the Queen-in-Exile said. "New recruits and spies. The question is: which are you?"

He forced himself not to swallow.

"Recruit," he said.

She nodded but didn't look like she believed him. "Very well. New recruits must face a trial by combat. Usually, we have them face Basant." The crowd laughed and the Queen-in-Exile gestured toward a very fat man in grimy leathers and a waist-apron that might once have been white but was now smeared with all manner of grease and food juices. Basant looked up and grinned a toothless grin. "Would you like to fight Basant to establish your spot within our little clan of rebels?"

Khyven didn't answer. That was obviously a trap.

That seemed to amuse the Queen-in-Exile. She chuckled. "No?"

"I'll fight whoever you put in front of me," Khyven said.

"I bet you would. I bet you would. The vaunted Khyven the Unkillable will kill anyone the usurper throws in front of him, won't he?"

Again, Khyven said nothing.

The Queen-in-Exile seemed to like hearing her own voice, and she obviously liked playing to her audience. "Well, I'm not going to make you fight Basant the Mighty."

The crowd laughed.

"We'll make it easier on you." Her blue eyes flashed. "You'll just have to fight me, pretty boy."

The crowd laughed again.

"And who do I fight after that?" Khyven asked.

The mob whooped at his temerity.

The Queen-in-Exile pointed at him with her sword. "Oh, I like you, Khyven the Pretty. No, just me. You win, and you're one of us. You lose, and…" She shrugged and held her free hand up helplessly.

"Real swords or practice?" He tapped the wooden sword stuffed through his belt.

She threw a glance at the crowd. "Do we use practice swords here, my worthies?"

The mob hissed and booed.

Khyven saw the trap. If he fought her with a real blade and lost, he'd be dead. If he fought her with a real blade and won, she'd be dead. And, of course, the mob wouldn't leave him alive after that.

"I don't think they'll let me join if I kill you," Khyven said.

She winked. "You won't have to worry about that, Khyven the Pretty." She lowered her blade and pointed it at his heart.

He glanced at Vohn, but he couldn't read anything on the Shadowvar's dark face. Khyven glanced at the mob. Their cheerful demeanor had fled. The game was over. The time for action had come.

Khyven flicked his gaze back to the Queen-in-Exile. The moment he made an aggressive move, the duel would begin.

Slowly, carefully, he drew the wooden sword from his belt.

The Queen-in-Exile raised an eyebrow. "Cocky bastard, aren't you?" she asked.

"Part of the job."

She chuckled. "Be a shame to kill you."

"Maybe you shouldn't," he said.

"Maybe you should show us if you live up to your legend," she said.

So, this was happening.

"Be sure that's the weapon you want, Khyven the Pretty," she said. "You won't get the chance to draw another."

"I'm sure." He might not know about the inside of the noktum or the magic of his amulet, but he knew fighting, and this fight was a practice bout. He would measure her skill, then take her out.

He smiled as she circled him. The blue wind, of course, did not show up. It wouldn't come unless he felt threatened, and he had this in hand.

She lunged, slashing downward.

He sidestepped, almost giving her his shoulder. She was fast; her sword whispered within an inch of flesh. He spun and faced her again.

With his wooden sword, he was going to be at a constant disadvantage. She could deflect his blade at will. The Queen-in-Exile could cut at him from any direction and every strike would be deadly. If he blocked her at the wrong angle, she'd crack his wooden sword, perhaps even shear it in half.

Khyven, on the other hand, would have to land a perfect blow to stop her.

He'd have to end the fight quickly. He didn't want her getting used to the idea that she was facing a non-lethal weapon. He'd draw her in and attack so quickly she'd react instinctively, treating his sword as a real blade for a split second, and that would be all the time he'd need.

She struck again. He sidestepped, moving his body as he angled his sword correctly to block. Her chop chipped the wood but skittered down its length and away. Khyven whipped his sword around to the other side, going for a quick strike to her neck. Once she was down, it would send a message to her mob that—

His blade clacked against the leather gauntlet of her free hand.

"Wooden sword." She winked.

A thrill of uncertainty ran up Khyven's spine. Instinctively, a combatant would never be so foolish as to block a steel edge with a leather gauntlet, it would have cut right through her arm.

But this woman had reacted correctly. She knew swordplay, knew when to use her instincts and when to replace them. She obviously had real life experience.

His plan to strike fast, flummox her instincts, and make her act like she was facing a real blade had failed.

The Queen-in-Exile kicked him in the chest.

The kick jarred him, knocked him off balance. He went down, but he used the momentum, rolled over his shoulder and came to his feet.

She followed him, and her thrust was already on its way when his head came up. He threw himself to the side and barely dodged.

That had nearly skewered his eye!

With a grunt, his thighs burning at the effort, he lunged forward, inside her guard, and slugged her in the gut. Her leather chest plate blunted the strike, but Khyven was a big man who outweighed her by a hundred pounds. The punch lifted her off the ground.

A gasp went up from the crowd.

Like a battering ram, he drove forward, keeping his legs churning. He shoved her backward and brought his forearm up to slam an elbow into her face—

She blocked him with her bracer again and kneed him in the groin.

He twisted at the last second, so she only connected with the inside of his thigh.

Senji's Sword, the woman was a brawler, too?

Khyven leapt backward, disengaging.

The Queen-in-Exile didn't press the attack. Instead, she sauntered in a half-circle around him, resting her sword on her shoulder. He'd seen the tactic before. After a savage attack, an experienced fighter might give a show of relaxed confidence to unnerve an opponent.

The Queen-in-Exile glanced at the real sword at Khyven's hip and raised an eyebrow. He heard the unspoken question.

You sure you don't want to switch?

Khyven narrowed his eyes. Very well. He'd underestimated her skill. Time to get serious.

He charged.

Instead of defending or stepping back, she struck like a coiled snake, closing the distance and thrusting her sword at his face. He blocked it with barely an inch to spare.

By Senji, she's fast!

Following his sword with his free hand, he batted the flat of her blade away and whipped his sword around with a strike to the side of her knee.

She twisted. He hit the back of her leg instead, but it dropped her to her knees—

He hissed as her blade sliced into his side. He spun away, getting out of her range. She popped up and began sauntering again, sword resting lazily on her shoulder, this time with a fleck of his blood on it. She seemed no worse for wear for having her knees knocked out from under her.

Khyven, on the other hand, was bleeding. It was little more than a scratch, but this obviously wasn't working. She wasn't just better than he'd thought, she'd surprised him. He hadn't expected that thrust. As she'd fallen, she'd sneaked the strike not only past his guard, but past his notice. That was chilling.

For the first time, he realized he wasn't in control of this fight. She was. And if he couldn't get control, she was going to kill him.

His heart began to race and the euphoria came with it. The blue wind took shape, swirling around her as she cocked her head and assessed him.

"I think you ought to draw that sword, Khyven the Pretty," the Queen-in-Exile said. "Stop insulting me and maybe I'll let you live."

"Your Majesty is too kind," Khyven said, watching the swirls of ephemeral blue around her. "But I don't go back on decisions once I make them."

"Pretty talk. Is it worth your life?"

"Let's find out."

Khyven saw the blue wind swirl into a point, straight at him, and he leapt into motion, spinning around it. Her sword whistled past his head, but this time he was dancing with the blue. He saw the swirling funnels, one at her clavicle, one just above her hip. He thrust at the second one.

She huffed as his blade snuck just beneath her leather armor plate and hit soft flesh. The blue wind rushed at his legs. He jumped just as her sword cut beneath him. A blue funnel opened at the side of her head, and he swung at it, delivering a glancing blow.

She stumbled and he pursued. Blue funnels opened up all over her now—her neck, her gut again, her knees, her forearm, her sword hand—and no sharp points of blue came at him to warn of attack. She was reeling.

He took the advantage and struck her open wrist, just above her bracer. She made a tight gasping sound and her sword fell from nerveless fingers. He whipped around in a tight, high arc and found the target he was searching for: the side of her neck.

Her other arm came up, but this time it was just a fraction of a second too slow, and he whacked the artery in her neck, hard.

The Queen-in-Exile dropped to her knees, then fell forward onto her good hand. The strike should have knocked her out, but she fought for consciousness.

Something stung the back of Khyven's neck like a wasp bite. He slapped it and his hand came away with a dart. He jerked his head around and saw a tall, slender woman standing behind him, lowering a blowgun. Two tall, pointed ears split her golden river of hair, which had three thin asymmetrical braids that framed her face. Her lips were pressed together in a flat line and her large brown eyes seemed to swallow him.

Pointed ears?

Her face blurred, as did the trees behind her, and the noktum behind those. He saw her, then he saw the crowd, then her, and he realized the world was spinning.

He hit the ground, his head bouncing off the spongy grass, but he barely felt it. The ground rocked like a ship on the sea. Next to him, the Queen-in-Exile was still on her hands and knees. Khyven tried to rise, but his legs and arms did absolutely nothing. It was like they weren't even there.

"You let him hit you," the tall woman said, her voice a husky lilt that sent tingles through Khyven. She knelt gracefully, almost like she was floating and coming down for a soft landing. She took hold of the queen and pulled her to her feet.

"Did you see how fast he moved, Lorelle?" the queen asked. "I've never seen anyone move that fast."

Lorelle… The tall, graceful woman with the pointed ears… Her name was Lorelle. Why were her ears pointed?

Lorelle shook her head in disapproval.

"He could be useful," the queen mused.

"He hit you in the neck, Rhenn. Someone hits you in the neck, we kill them."

"I baited him," Rhenn said.

"You're the queen."

"You worry too much."

Lorelle gave a terse shake of her golden head.

"Hey," Rhenn said, her gaze falling on Khyven. "He's still awake."

Lorelle turned like a tree swaying in the wind. Her smooth brow wrinkled as she looked down at Khyven.

"I thought that was your knock-em-out poison," Rhenn said.

"It is." Lorelle raised her blowgun to her lips. Her cheeks puffed. Khyven didn't feel the sting this time.

The world went black.

Chapter Twelve

Lorelle

Lorelle held the tent flap open for Rhenn, but it always took the queen forever to leave the group. She thrived amidst her subjects. Despite the horrors of her childhood, Rhenn actually liked and trusted people. She managed to find something good in every single person she met. Lorelle had never known someone so full of hope.

The sun was going down, giving their little band of rebels their short sunset before it vanished behind the ever-present wall of the noktum, and Lorelle took a wistful moment to remember a normal sunset. In this place, they didn't get to see the sun spread fiery wings over the mountains, or light the tops of the trees with gold.

This safe little cove had been integral to Rhenn forming her modest army, but it was eerie living inside a ring of midnight all the time. It preyed upon the mind. People weren't meant to live like that. The noktum had been created by the Giants thousands of years ago, and she suspected only those ancient beings could feel comfortable in its eldritch embrace. If not for Rhenn's limited discoveries about Giant magic, that darkness would swallow them. It *longed* to swallow them. Living here was like living inside the open jaws of a sleeping monster. At any moment, the monster might wake and snap its teeth shut.

Lorelle closed her eyes, smelled the fragrant forest breeze that still managed to climb the walls and blow through this place. She inhaled the scent of pine sap and oak leaves, the vibrant earthiness of rich soil and long grass. She imagined a house where she could live with her friends Vohn, Rhenn, Boh Mal, Saneera, and the others. Not a castle or a keep or a protected hideaway to fend off enemies, just a house with her friends on a safe and sunny mountain where there were no grand schemes, no dire consequences, no frothing murderers bent on their destruction. What would it be like, Lorelle wondered, simply to live?

She opened her eyes to find Rhenn still chatting, though she was moving toward the tent. She talked with Vohn, who followed her.

"… saved a Kyolar," Vohn was saying.

"Saved it?" Rhenn said.

"In the Ring. Didn't kill it. Beat it with a pair of those wooden swords."

Rhenn whistled. "Well, he's good with them, that's for sure."

"I don't know who he is," Vohn said.

"An assassin?" Rhenn replied with a wry smile.

"I don't think so," Vohn said.

Rhenn chuckled. "I love your trusting mind, Vohn. Do they teach you that in Nokte-Shaddark? Do Shadowvar train to be trusting?"

"Rhenn…" Vohn said in his serious voice. He didn't like when she mocked him. He hadn't been with her long enough to know that Rhenn's whimsy covered her fear. When something spooked her, she laughed. When the odds were steeply against her, she gave that wry grin, a grin that said she was more than a match for anything.

Rhenn likely knew a great deal about Khyven the Unkillable, even if she acted otherwise. She knew about every single noble who followed Vamreth, every knight who swore fealty to him, and every upstart who wanted to swear fealty to him.

"Truss him up. Search him," Rhenn said.

"He could be useful to us," Vohn replied.

Rhenn shrugged like she didn't buy it, but Lorelle could see through that act even if Vohn couldn't. He took everything at face-value and tended to miss it even when Rhenn was being intentionally annoying.

"He could be an asset," Vohn pushed. "If he—"

"I'll think about it," Rhenn said. "Mark my words. You search him, you'll find something an assassin would carry."

"What does an assassin carry?" Vohn asked.

"Lock pick kit. A hidden knife. A disarming personality."

Vohn frowned.

Rhenn chuckled fondly and put a hand on Vohn's shoulder. "We'll talk about it tomorrow. But for today—for tonight—we celebrate your return. We thought we'd have to break you out of the Night Ring and then, *fzzatch!*" she said, "you appeared through the noktum. You got big nuts, Vohn."

"Rhenn…" Vohn looked distinctly vexed.

"I'm just saying." Rhenn cupped her hands like she was carrying something heavy. Vohn cut her off by pushing her wrist down.

"You're impossible to talk to when you're like this. Good night, Your Majesty." He bowed formally.

"I'll talk to you in the morning," she said cheerily as he stalked away. She turned, saw Lorelle holding the flap, and strode over.

"I love Vohn," Rhenn said, "but sometimes he needs to get drunk, you know? Just a little?" Rhenn gestured with her hand as she approached, indicating Lorelle should precede her into the tent. "Go ahead."

Lorelle didn't move. "My queen." She bowed at the waist and indicated that Rhenn should go first.

"Senji's Rolling Eyes," Rhenn said, rolling her *own* eyes. She went into the tent and Lorelle followed, letting the flap fall shut. "You're doing the formal thing. I've made you angry. How did I do it this time?"

"You let him hit you," Lorelle said, her pulse quickening. She breathed and put her emotions in their place. Her parents had taught her breathing techniques to control her emotions since she was old enough to walk.

"I actually did everything to *keep* him from hitting me. Weren't you watching?"

"You know what I mean."

"I know if you had your way, I'd sit on my wooden throne and send everyone else into harm's way."

"You are the queen—"

"Not that way. Not like him." For the first time, Rhenn lost her smile.

Lorelle knew better than to say anything. They both had deep scars from Vamreth. He'd murdered everyone they'd loved, and those wounds would always be fresh. There was no joking where Vamreth was concerned.

But just because Rhenn didn't want to rule like that lying murderer didn't mean she should take dangerous chances. Especially unnecessary ones. Khyven *was* most likely an assassin. Giving him an opportunity to get that close to Rhenn—to swing a blade at her, wooden or otherwise—had been ridiculously stupid.

This was the worst thing about Rhenn, that she refused to act like a queen. It was also the best thing about her. It made her subjects love her.

Rhenn threw herself into a padded wooden chair—her "wooden throne" as she called it. She pulled her Amulet of Noksonon from beneath her tunic, and the other necklace she wore came out at the same time, half tangled with the amulet. The other necklace was a smooth steel chain that held the iron key that had saved their lives, had given them the opportunity to escape from Vamreth when they were children. Rhenn never took it off. She slept with it, bathed with it. So far as Lorelle knew, Rhenn hadn't removed the key in ten years.

She untangled the key from the Amulet of Noksonon, pulled

the amulet over her head, and hung it over the back of the throne. Absently, she tucked the iron key back into her tunic.

Sighing as though removing the amulet had lifted a burden, she rolled her head from side to side and shrugged her shoulders to loosen her muscles. She touched the long red mark on her neck, which was slowly turning to a purple bruise, where Khyven's wooden sword had hit her.

"He did get me good," she said as she grabbed a pewter pitcher of beer from the table. She cast about and snagged a mug, then poured herself some beer.

"That beer is flat," Lorelle said, but only after Rhenn took a sip.

"Mmmm…" Rhenn enthusiastically licked her lips. Lorelle rolled her eyes. Obviously Rhenn wasn't going to talk about Khyven anymore, at least not why she'd let him strike her.

"So I played prudent with Vohn." Rhenn changed the subject. "Because, you know, it's fun to see him twitch, but he has a point."

"About the assassin?"

"About him maybe not being an assassin."

"He *is* an assassin."

"We don't know that," Rhenn said.

Lorelle sighed. "Rhenn…"

"What?"

"Don't do that."

"Do what?"

"See what you want to see, instead of what is there."

"Being a queen means having vision," Rhenn said.

"Unfounded expectation is not vision—"

"He's damned good with a blade," Rhenn interjected. "Did you see?"

"What an odd skill for an assassin to have."

Rhenn chuckled and took another drink of the flat beer. "If he'd wanted to kill me, he could have."

"You think too little of my aim," Lorelle said.

Still grinning, Rhenn pointed at Lorelle. "What I'm saying is that Vohn may be right. We don't have so many assets that we can just throw one away."

"We have plenty who are skilled with a blade."

"As good as he was?"

"Yes," Lorelle said quickly, trying to end this conversation. She was getting that sinking feeling she always got when Rhenn latched on to a crazy idea.

Rhenn arched an eyebrow. "Name one of our knights—any of our people—who could best me."

Lorelle hesitated. "Well… Lord Harpinjur," she said, trying to sound confident.

"Lord—?" Rhenn raised her eyebrows and then laughed. "Lorelle, Lord Harpinjur is a good man. I grant you that, and he is an invaluable political ally, but—"

"He is a renowned swordsman."

"*Was* a renowned swordsman. That was twenty years ago!" Rhenn said. "Lorelle, this ringer beat me with a wooden sword. A wooden sword! I can only imagine what he could do with steel." She shook her head.

The sinking feeling got worse. "Tell me this isn't going somewhere," Lorelle said. Rhenn was formulating one of her crazy ideas.

"He's the one," Rhenn said.

"What one? The one for—?" Lorelle's eyes went wide. She shook her head. "No."

"I'm thinking he might be the one," Rhenn said.

"There is no 'one.' We discarded the Sandrunner idea," Lorelle said.

"Now we're picking it up again. This is perfect."

"Perfect? There are so many reasons this is *not* perfect."

"Do you think he could beat their Champion of the Sun?"

"No."

"You said that too quickly."

"It's not going to happen. We already decided."

"When it was me," Rhenn said. "With me fighting."

"So you'll replace yourself with him. Let him ride beside you into the Burzagi's camp? What message will that send? Why don't you just bed him and give him the crown?"

"Maybe I will." Rhenn grinned.

"You can't get the Sandrunners to do what you want them to do." Lorelle shook her head. "They hate women."

"All of them hate women?"

"The Sandrunner culture hates women."

"How can a culture hate women?" Rhenn said.

"That's the dumbest thing you've ever said to me."

Rhenn held her hands up in surrender. "Very well. But I'm not talking about hate. I'm talking about honor. Sandrunner culture revolves around honor. If they make a bargain, they'll stick to it."

"They won't even talk to you."

"They'll talk to me if I have a male champion. We stick Khyven out front, make him earn his keep."

"His keep?"

"Whatever. We don't kill him; he does this favor for us."

"A queen doesn't ask for a favors—"

"She most certainly does." Rhenn rolled her eyes. "That's the one lesson I *have* learned being queen."

"It doesn't matter. The Sandrunners won't turn to our cause," Lorelle said.

"They don't have to. They just have to obey their own laws."

"You're thinking only of the prize, Rhenn, about what happens if we succeed.

"Let us say that you *do* convince Khyven to fight for you, let us say that the Sandrunners *do* agree to follow their own 'laws' and let you pull off this trick, and let's say we actually reach the point where we get to put Khyven in the fight. The Champion of the Sun isn't some scrappy ringer. He is a monster, the absolute best the Sandrunners have. It isn't just possible, it's *likely* Khyven will lose. And then what? You've made yourself a slave of women-haters."

"They're not going to ask me to become their slave."

Lorelle rolled her eyes. "Nobody *asks* you to become a slave,

Rhenn. If you lose, they're not going to let you go!"

"Then we do it smart."

The woman simply would not relent. She never had, even as a child. Lorelle clenched her fist. "It is the quickest way to suicide without using a dagger."

Rhenn shrugged. "It's the only way—"

"It's not!"

Rhenn held out her hands helplessly, her charming smile in place. "We're caught between the stone and the Giant's fist," Rhenn said. "We can't overcome Vamreth with what we have. It's the Sandrunners or it's Triada."

"You're not marrying Alfric, either." The wily king of Triada—who had no love for Vamreth—had sent his second son Alfric to woo Rhenn in the woods. He was out there with her subjects right now, a part of Rhenn's camp, and he'd been making doe eyes at her every night for the last two weeks. Rhenn had strung him along like the consummate diplomat she was, but he would only be put off for so long before he'd need an answer.

"I could appeal to the king of Imprevar," Rhenn said.

"I don't think you're funny," Lorelle said.

"You don't think anything is funny," Rhenn said, filling her mug again with the flat ale. Vamreth had just announced his betrothal to the princess of Imprevar; the wedding would occur in a matter of weeks. So now the king of Imprevar was almost as interested in killing Rhenn as Vamreth was.

"What we need to do is—"

"You say I cannot marry Alfric," Rhenn said. "You say I cannot brave the Rites of the Sandrunners. Shall I just sit here and hope that Senji herself descends from on high to unseat Vamreth?" She waved toward the tent walls. "We need more fighters, Lorelle."

Lorelle paused. She thought again of that house, that imaginary safe place where they could all go, where there would be no battles. "Rhenn… I just don't want…" She trailed off and silence fell in the tent.

"I know." Rhenn rose to her feet and crossed to Lorelle.

"Sister of my heart… I know. But you can't protect me from everything."

Lorelle swallowed the lump in her throat. "Why not?"

"Because we don't get to have safety," Rhenn said softly. "Because we were doomed to that fate the moment he killed our families." She put her hands on Lorelle's shoulders. "And we have one slim chance to bring justice to him. That, we have. But not safety."

Lorelle's hair began to glimmer, a sign that her tight grip on her emotions had slipped. She swallowed hard and tried to shove her emotions down. She was a Luminent and she couldn't just fling her emotions around like a Human. Not at her age, not until she was bonded. *But damn it…*

"If I lose you…" she said.

"Look at me." Rhenn thumped her own belly with a fist. "Hold it in and look at me."

Lorelle gazed down at Rhenn, her sister in this life and every other. Rhenn knew better than anyone the dangers Lorelle faced if she felt something too strongly, especially if her best friend was feeling it, too. Those steady blue eyes held Lorelle's. Lorelle took a deep breath, using the techniques her parents had taught her. Slowly, the overwhelming sadness and fear became controllable. She pushed her emotions back into place, where they had to stay, locked behind a thick door in her heart. Her hair lost its glimmer and settled into its normal sandy blond color.

"Yes?" Rhenn asked.

"I am all right."

"Very well."

Silence fell between them, but they didn't break their gaze. Staring into Rhenn's eyes comforted Lorelle. They had held each others' hands when they'd fled through the noktum as children. They'd held hands as they'd made their way through the woods, as they'd carved out a life among the trees. When they'd grown too old to hold hands, that connection had stayed through their gazes. Looking at Rhenn always made Lorelle feel as safe as they would ever be.

"Lorelle," Rhenn said softly.

"I know," she said.

"I have to lead," Rhenn said.

"I know."

"And that means risk. We have to run the gauntlet. We shouldn't even be alive, so we have to use it. We do what we must in every moment and that's all we can do. Right now, we're vulnerable, and that's my fault. We need more fighters. I have to get them any way I can."

"Many have rallied to your banner," Lorelle said. "More will come."

"Not fast enough," Rhenn said. "I have reports that say Vamreth is attempting to explore the noktum. We are out of time."

"Let him brave the noktum," Lorelle said coolly. "It will devour him, and whatever makes it through, we cut it to pieces."

"He'll learn to navigate it like we did," Rhenn said. "We aren't the only ones with magic."

Rhenn hugged Lorelle, and she hugged her sister back, though she did not allow her emotions to leak out again.

Rhenn ended the embrace and squeezed Lorelle's arms. "Cheer up. We could die long before Vamreth finds us."

"How comforting. Your subjects will appreciate your strategic—"

"My queen!" Vohn shouted from outside the tent.

Rhenn hung her head and chuckled. "I knew he wasn't going to wait until tomorrow."

She started for the tent flap, but Lorelle stopped her with a gentle hand. "Allow me, my queen."

Rhenn frowned at the formality. "You have to stop that," she said.

"No, you have to start that," Lorelle corrected. "Go. Sit."

With a heavy sigh, Rhenn went back to her throne and sat in it, rebelliously cocking one leg over the arm of the chair as she picked up her mug.

Lorelle opened the tent flap and Vohn rushed in, anger plain on his face. He held up a coin between two fingers.

"I am ashamed, my queen. You were right. He is an assassin."

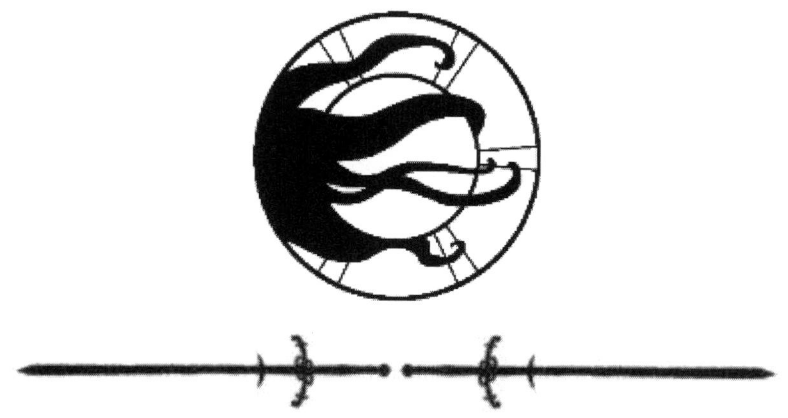

Chapter Thirteen

KHYVEN

hyven heard voices first. He knew he should be able to understand them, but it was as though they were speaking a different language.

Next, he felt his arms. His head and his chest had, apparently, woken first, and the rest of his body was slowly following, coming alive with a sensation of pins everywhere, spreading out from his chest to his stomach to his legs and toes, to his arms and fingertips.

That's when his neck began to ache like he'd been swung around by the head. The voices resolved into something he could understand.

"The water isn't necessary," a woman said, her voice husky, melodic. It sent a tingle through Khyven that rivaled the pins.

Sharp, cold water splashed onto his face, and he gasped. He blinked and opened his eyes. It was dim, and his first thought was that he was in the cages of the Night Ring.

Then it all came back. He was in the Queen-in-Exile's camp, in some kind of tent.

Vohn's angry face came into focus. He was gripping a

dripping, empty wooden bowl. Standing behind him was the wild-haired Queen-in-Exile, Rhenn, with a wry smile on her face. To Vohn's left stood the stunning pointy-eared woman, the one who'd shot him with a poison dart, who moved like she was floating. Lorelle... Her face was expressionless except for her eyebrows, which sloped down ever so slightly over her huge brown eyes.

Khyven sat up.

"Go slowly," Rhenn warned even as two women and two men in chainmail moved forward, daggers in hand. A long, purple bruise had formed on the side of her throat where his wooden sword had struck her. "Move too fast and we'll end your trip right now, Khyven the Pretty."

"It was all a plan, wasn't it?" Vohn growled, holding up Slayter's clay coin.

Khyven swallowed his panic. By the look on Vohn's face, the Shadowvar knew what the coin was. There would be no feigning ignorance, claiming it was some kind of good luck charm.

"It's Line Magic," Vohn said, as though reading Khyven's mind. "This is an inert spell. See this missing line?" He waved the coin as though everyone could see the intricate detail in the dim light. "Complete that line and whatever spell that symbol represents will activate." He threw the wooden bowl aside and produced the metal device Slayter had given him along with the coin, made for scratching that last line. "See?"

And suddenly it was like the Night Ring all over again. Everyone was an enemy. Death hovered in this room, waiting, and if this group decided he was a spy—which Vohn already seemed to have done—they'd haul him out and stick him with a hundred swords.

Or the beautiful woman with the pointed ears would stick him with another dart, except this time coated with something deadly.

Khyven needed to think and think fast.

"It was planned, wasn't it?" Vohn asked again. He looked

betrayed, even angrier than when Khyven had first met him. The Shadowvar's black brow was wrinkled so deeply the golden lantern light glimmered off a half dozen furrows. "Vamreth sent you into the arena to 'save me,' didn't he?" Vohn produced a dagger from the folds of his tunic. "Except I jumped into the noktum instead. You didn't expect that, did you, you feckless—"

"Vohn." Rhenn put a gentle hand on his shoulder.

"My queen, he's here to kill you, to kill all of us!"

"We don't execute someone just because we suspect him of ill deeds," Rhenn said lightly. "That's what Vamreth does." She held out her hand to Vohn. He looked at it, then at the items he held. Reluctantly, he passed them over.

"Crush it," he said. "You break that clay, you break the spell."

"All in good time," Rhenn said.

"Your Majesty—"

She held up a pacifying hand and Vohn settled into a reluctant silence.

Her wry smile never wavered. "Tell us, Khyven," she said. "Does Vohn have the right of it?" Her blue eyes glittered, and he realized this casual queen was waiting to hear the timbre of his words, to assess the truth in them. His life hung on his next response.

The room was as taut as a loaded crossbow. They wanted him dead. It was only Rhenn who kept the rest of them from tearing him apart.

His gaze flicked from the four guards to Vohn to Lorelle to Rhenn, assessing his chances of fighting his way out. Rhenn was nearly as good a swordsman as he was, and she had a sword; he didn't. The four guards were an unknown quantity. For all Khyven knew, they were as talented as Rhenn. Lorelle stood with her blowgun in her slender hands.

It was an impossible fight.

And even if by some lucky chance he spun past them, dodging and weaving his way through the gauntlet, outside this tent were two hundred people and a wall of noktum. And they'd taken his amulet. He was trapped.

"Yes," Khyven said. "Vamreth sent me."

Rhenn's eyes narrowed almost imperceptibly. If Khyven hadn't been holding her gaze, if he hadn't been trained by half a hundred battles where life and death hung on what he could see in a man's eyes, he'd have missed it. She'd made a decision about him, right then, but nothing changed on her face except the intensity of her eyes.

"That's a brazen thing to admit," she said. "We're going to kill you for it, you know."

"You're going to kill me anyway," Khyven said.

She raised an eyebrow.

"It's the same thing they told me every morning in the Night Ring," he said. "'Today you die.' They told me that forty-nine times, to be exact."

Rhenn chuckled, glanced over her shoulder at the impassive Lorelle. "Is he bragging? I feel like he's bragging."

Lorelle said nothing. Her gaze stayed on Khyven's face.

Rhenn turned back to him. "This isn't the arena. I'm not Vamreth."

"What's the difference?" Khyven asked.

Rhenn held her hands out like she was helpless to stop Khyven from saying stupid things. "He's got a spine," she said to Vohn, who looked like he was snarling without the noise. "You've got to give him that."

No one said anything, but she didn't seem interested in an answer.

"The difference, Khyven the Pretty, is that Vamreth would now be trotting you out as a spectacle. He'd devise a way to make your death two things, painful for you and useful to him. We don't do that. We'll just kill you for treason, quick and clean. So here's my question: is there a reason we shouldn't?"

"Is there a reason you haven't?"

Her eyes glittered and her smile widened. She glanced over her shoulder at Lorelle again. The tall woman didn't react, didn't even glance at Rhenn, but Khyven learned two things in that instant.

First, of all the people in this room, Lorelle was most important to the queen. The queen always sought Lorelle's counsel first. Second, Lorelle's absolute lack of reaction meant she'd seen this kind of performance before. This was the queen's way; she was putting on a show. This wasn't an interrogation to deduce Khyven's guilt. She *knew* he was guilty. This was something else. The queen didn't want to kill him, otherwise he'd be dead. So why keep him alive unless…

Unless she needed him for something.

Somehow, Khyven had value here. He had something the queen wanted.

"I don't believe in wasting assets," Rhenn said, confirming his guess.

Vohn jolted like he'd been stuck with an arrow. He craned his neck, disbelieving. "My queen—"

She made the barest of gestures and Vohn stopped talking.

"I'm an asset?" Khyven asked.

"That depends," Rhenn said.

"You want me to fight someone," he guessed. He had nothing of value except his sword arm and the amulet they'd already taken from him.

"Maybe," Rhenn said. "The problem is, what do I do with you while I determine where I can use you? If you're an assassin and I let you out among my people, what will you do?"

"I wasn't sent to hurt anyone," he said.

Vohn snorted. One of the guards inside the tent spat on the ground.

"You realize how ridiculous that sounds," Rhenn said. "You're a killer, Khyven. Perhaps the best I've ever seen. You're saying you weren't sent here to do what you do best?"

"I wasn't."

"Then what were you sent to do?"

"To lead Vamreth to your hidden camp," he said.

Again, that nearly imperceptible narrowing of her eyes, like she could tell when someone was speaking the truth. "You speak freely for a spy."

"This was to be my final test," he said. "My fiftieth bout.

Vamreth is desperate to find you. He discovered Vohn's interest in me. He wanted to exploit it."

"And what is your reward for this fiftieth 'bout?'"

Khyven hesitated. "A barony," he said huskily. "I was to get a knighthood for my final bout. The king said he would make me a baron if I could show him the way to your camp."

Dead silence filled the tent, and Vohn trembled with rage.

"And you love Vamreth so much that you'd be his sneak thief and assassin when you're actually a warrior?"

"Vamreth holds my leash. He has the power to make me do what he wants." Khyven shrugged and tried to look casual, but his heart began to race and the euphoria began to swirl in his belly. This was going to boil down to a fight. In the end, it *would* be his final bout, and what a legendary bout it would be—

"Leave us," Rhenn said to everyone in the tent. "Everyone but Lorelle."

"My queen!" Vohn exclaimed. Three of the other guards in the room protested, shaking their heads.

"Your Majesty—"

"You can't be alone with this villain—"

"That's exactly what he wants—"

Rhenn flashed an imperious glance at the lot of them. They quieted. Slowly, the first of the four guards left the tent. After a moment, the other three reluctantly followed.

Vohn planted himself between Khyven and Rhenn. "No, my queen."

"No?" Rhenn said, and her smile returned.

"He's here to kill you!" Vohn spluttered. "You have to protect yourself."

"Lorelle will protect me," Rhenn said. "Go, Vohn. Please."

Vohn's fists trembled, and he spun to face Khyven. "If you hurt her…" His voice was so thick with emotion that he could barely speak. "I will make your death more horrible than you can imagine." The little Shadowvar spun on his heel and stalked through the doorway, batting the flap aside.

Lorelle had not moved a muscle during the entire exchange,

but as Vohn left, she gracefully raised her blowgun and pointed it at Khyven's face.

Rhenn held up a pacifying hand. "Lorelle," she said, and shook her head.

Lorelle didn't lower the weapon.

Rhenn contemplated Khyven.

"He holds your leash?" she said.

"Well, you do now. That's the way the world works. Some hold leashes and others wear collars."

"A poetic ringer," Rhenn said. He could see the change in her posture. Tense, ready. She expected him to try something. Perhaps this was a test to see if he would.

"How did you end up in the Night Ring?" Rhenn asked.

The question seemed to come out of nowhere.

"What does that matter?"

"Because I'm holding the leash."

Khyven calmly glanced at Lorelle, who was still pointing the blowgun at him.

"Everyone knows the name Khyven the Unkillable," Rhenn said. "What I don't know is how you got into the arena in the first place. You've been there for two years. Where did you come from?"

He'd come from the old man's camp, but before that… Khyven didn't know. His earliest clear memory was the old man feeding him soup in one of his huts. Anything before that was stuck behind a misty wall at the back of his mind. The only thing he remembered before age eleven was murky. Flashes of fire and screams…. That's all he knew.

"I was thrown into the Night Ring because they caught me with weapons without permission from the king," he said.

"Ah," she said. It was illegal to own weapons and practice the art of warfare in Usara without the express permission—and oversight—of the king's knights.

"You were alone?" she asked.

Khyven hesitated. Giving her the information about Vamreth had been easy. Giving her information about the old man and Nhevaz… that was completely different.

"I was alone." He glanced up at her.

She shook her head, smiling that wry smile. "You're a bad liar, Khyven the Unkillable."

He shrugged.

Her gaze softened. "Who did he kill?" she asked.

"He… didn't."

"Tell me," she said.

"It doesn't matter," he said.

"It's the only thing that matters," she said.

Silence fell between them.

"It wasn't Vamreth," Khyven finally said emotionlessly. "It was a man named Vex."

"Vex the Victorious," she said.

"It doesn't matter because it's the way the world works. They died because they weren't strong enough to stop Vex. That's all."

"Who wasn't strong enough?" she asked.

"An old man. Two other boys I grew up with. And… and someone else."

"Who else?"

"Why do you care?"

"Tell me, Khyven," she requested softly. For the first time, it didn't sound like a command.

"Someone I looked up to," he finally managed to say, and his damned voice cracked. He cleared his throat. "But he failed. They all died. That's all."

Rhenn knelt in front of him. Her hands slipped over his and he almost fell over backward in surprise. Every muscle in his body tensed. If his mission had been to kill her, he could have done it a half dozen ways with her so close. Even Lorelle tensed.

"I'm sorry, Khyven," Rhenn said. "For what happened to you. For what Vamreth did to you. He killed my family, too. And Lorelle's."

"Just tell me what you want from me," he said roughly. Why was he getting emotional? He didn't even know these people. "I'll do it. Let's get to it."

Rhenn squeezed his hands, then let go and stood up. Khyven

couldn't meet her gaze.

"Khyven," she said. "I want you to consider that it's not an accident you're here. Maybe you *do* belong here."

Khyven said nothing. His emotions twisted up into a ball in his belly and he couldn't find any words.

He heard Rhenn and Lorelle move as they both went to the tent flap.

"A man like Vamreth can't make you a knight, Khyven," Rhenn said. "All he can do is make you an assassin."

Khyven finally glanced up. For the first time since he'd met her, Rhenn actually looked like a queen. Even her wild hair seemed like a crown instead of a tumbling mess.

She said, "A knight is made by acts of valor. A man like Vamreth, who thinks a knight can rise from an act of treachery, doesn't understand what a knight really is. He certainly cannot make one."

"You're just letting me go?" he asked.

Her wry smile returned. "Not yet. As you suspected, I need you for something. But maybe you need us for something, too. Still, you'll be as free as the rest of us inside the camp."

Lorelle frowned and glanced at Rhenn.

"And my amulet?" Khyven asked.

"Well… That we'll keep. For now. If you want to brave the noktum without it, you're free to make that choice, too," she said. "In the meantime, come see what life is like without Vamreth's boot on your neck. You might enjoy it."

She left, but Lorelle stayed behind, her brown eyes watching Khyven like she was memorizing everything about him. She seemed about to say something, then she turned and left the tent.

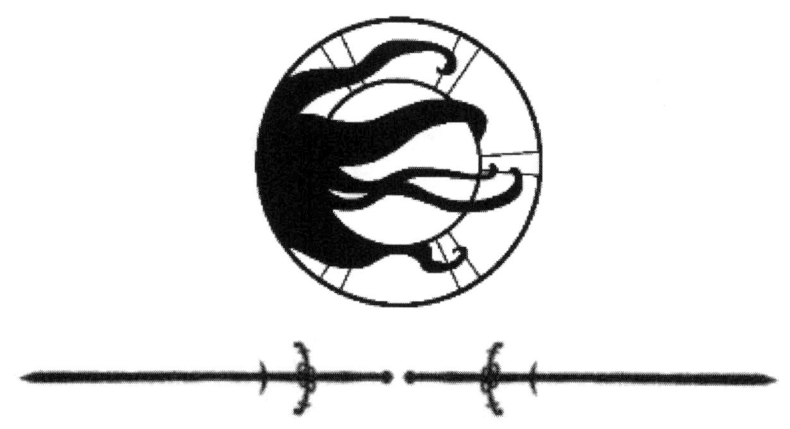

Chapter Fourteen

KHYVEN

Khyven sat for a long time thinking about Rhenn's words before she left the tent. He was in a strange new land, but it was still a cage. It was all the same. Everyone vying for control and power. In fact, of all the manipulations he'd ever experienced, this might be the worst. He didn't know how Rhenn had done it, but she'd cracked him open like an egg, made him talk about things he had no intention of talking about.

He still wasn't completely sure how she'd done it.

It was similar to the feeling he'd had with Vohn that first day they'd met. Khyven felt weaker somehow. Off balance. Plagued by doubt.

He stood up and shook it off. He remembered his truths. This was the same situation as ever. Everyone was an enemy. Those in power had forced him into a corner and taken what they wanted. With the masters of the Night Ring, manipulation had come through fear and pain. With Rhenn, it was going to come through a pretense of friendship.

Well, two could play that game.

When Khyven had first come to the Night Ring, the masters had demanded a fighter. He'd given them a fighter. If Rhenn demanded a friend, he'd give her a friend.

He could hear the people outside moving around, talking, presumably setting up for something. Khyven emerged from the tent.

At first, he watched as the men and women of Rhenn's camp went about their duties. A half dozen cooks turned spits, roasting a half dozen sheep over cooking fires. A rudimentary stage had been created out of logs and a few planks, and tables had been set up along either side, creating a wide aisle. Rhenn's people put baskets of bread, apples, and blueberries upon the tables, and Khyven began to wonder where they'd found all this food. How was Rhenn able to keep this small village going out here in the middle of nowhere? Were they stealing sheep? Or did they have a flock somewhere nearby, outside the noktum? Surely, they couldn't have a flock *inside* the noktum. The creatures would be devoured in seconds.

As Khyven wound his way through the lively camp, everyone watched him. He felt everything from surreptitious glances to outright stares. A forge stood on the far side of the camp, near the wall of the noktum. An anvil and bed for hot coals had been set up. It was the only stone structure in the entire camp. He moved toward it and saw the blacksmith inside making a sword.

The smith's hammer rang in a quick cadence, then he flipped the sword, and his hammer pounded again. As Khyven drew near, the smith raised his head. His gaze was cool, not as suspicious as most of the others within the camp, but unflinching.

Khyven felt the approach of the guards before he turned to look at them. The four who had been in the queen's tent had shadowed him to the smithy, and the unspoken message was clear: *Look if you like but come near any of the weapons and you'll find out just how limited your freedom is.*

Khyven turned, gave a winning smile to the four guards, and

walked away from the smith. The ringing of the hammer started up again.

He spent the hours before sundown exploring the camp. It was huge, and far more sophisticated than he'd thought at first glance. The organization was impeccable. There were a multitude of tents, as well as an array of sleeping pallets laid out for newcomers. There were several looms and seamstresses who seemed entirely dedicated to creating the fabric for tents. There were two other wooden structures, one with a closed door and a heavy lock. Perhaps for the storage of valuables? Weapons?

As the people of the camp became used to him wandering around and looking, the quiet gradually became filled with talking and even laughter. Khyven couldn't help but see a marked difference between this place and the city of Usara. In the Night Ring, the prevailing atmosphere was fear, even in the halls of the palace. Khyven had become so used to it that this seemingly easy-going crowd unnerved him.

Her boot is still on their necks, he thought. *They just don't see it, and that's even more insidious.*

She didn't use fear to control these people. She used happiness. She made them love her, and then they did whatever she wanted.

It was a new avenue to power. He looked forward to learning it.

Soon after the sun went down, the feasting began. Soon after the feasting, the drinking began. Khyven put lamb and roasted vegetables on a plate and walked away from the crowd to lean against a tree and eat. He watched the people, who seemed genuinely happy, and he pitied them their blindfold. He watched Rhenn move through the crowd like she was one of them, always with a cup in her hand. She clinked mugs with this person and that, and her retinue followed.

Though they didn't make themselves obvious, Khyven spotted the two guards who stayed close to the queen. They ate, even drank, but they were never more than a dozen paces from her. A long-nosed, curly-haired fellow followed her as well, and

Khyven suspected he was some kind of paramour. Moreover, he didn't look Usaran. His clothes were clean, well made, and the style was foreign to Khyven. The nobles of Usara didn't dress like that. This man was clearly a noble of some kind.

Lorelle, of course, was always close to the queen. He didn't see her blowgun, but then he hadn't seen it when she'd used it on him, either. Not until after the dart had stung him.

The ale began to flow and the denizens of Rhenn's camp got more raucous. A trio of musicians took the stage and played, and people danced on the grass in front of it. After walking down the slope into the crowd to refill his ale mug, Khyven retreated again to his tree. He enjoyed the euphoria of the alcohol and the movements of the dancers. His gaze caught on Lorelle at the edge of the dancing area. She was sitting on a table with her feet on a bench. She wore a mild smile—the first he'd seen on her—and Khyven's pulse quickened. Caught up in watching her, he forgot to keep track of the queen.

"The dancers are fun to watch, yes?" Rhenn said.

Khyven started and turned to look at her. The queen emerged from between the trees. She'd divested herself of her armor and she was wearing a peasant shirt with a sleeveless brown tunic pulled over it. Golden embroidery danced along the neck of the tunic and two silver clasps were fastened to a brown cloak that draped down around her shoulders.

He quickly glanced around, but he couldn't spot either of her guards, nor any of her retinue. She'd slipped away from her followers, including the well-dressed foreigner.

"I don't know why *you're* jumpy," she said. "This is probably the safest you've been in years."

"Everyone in your camp wants me dead," he said.

"They don't. I've told them no."

"And they always listen to you?"

She winked at him. "As far as they're concerned, you're my honored guest."

He glanced at the dancers and then at Lorelle. If she was taking a break from watching the queen's back, certainly someone else was. The area between his shoulder blades itched as he thought about who might be pointing a blowgun at him from the darkness.

"Honored," Khyven said. "To be sure."

"You are," Rhenn said. "I have a job that only you can do. But first you need to see that you're on the wrong side of this war."

"You think this is a war?"

"I know it."

"And I'm going to switch sides?" he said.

"That's what's fascinating about you, Khyven. I don't think you've actually picked a side. I'm going to convince you to do that. You're more one of us than you imagine."

"I thought I was a deadly assassin."

She chuckled. "Vohn thinks you are, but I think you're what you say: a ringer pressed into service as a spy."

"Do you always size people up this quickly?"

"I only have so much time." She held her palms up and winked. "But it wasn't difficult. Real spies can actually lie, and none of them can fight like you."

"An assassin would know how to use a blade."

She shook her head. "Certainly, an assassin knows how to handle a blade, but the toe-to-toe fighting skills you have... that's a different beast. You're a brawler and a swordsman and you don't flinch when a blade flashes past your nose. Unlikely behavior in an assassin, but perfectly normal for a ringer."

"Are you hoping I'll contradict you?" he asked.

"I think maybe you don't see something about yourself. I'm going to encourage you to look at that."

She was leading him down that path again, but he wasn't going there.

"Lorelle has pointed ears," he said, intent on breaking Rhenn's spell. "What race is she?"

Rhenn glanced at her friend, who was sipping from a cup of ale and watching the musicians play. "You've never seen a Luminent before?"

"She's a *Luminent*," he murmured. He thought of the old

man's tales about Taur-Els, Shadowvars, Giants, and Luminents. He'd never mentioned pointy ears. "I wasn't sure they were real."

"So, you've been standing up here watching *Lorelle* all this time," Rhenn said. "I thought you were watching the dancers."

"She's breathtaking," Khyven said, far more comfortable talking about women than about his past. This topic had no unseen pitfalls.

"Well, you're in luck, ringer. I know everything there is to know about Lorelle. If you've set your hat for her, I can help you."

"I'm sure you could, but why would you? What is the price?"

"Not everything has a price. I want my people to be happy."

"I see."

"You sound skeptical," Rhenn said.

"I do that when I hear a lie."

Her smile widened. "Then here's your chance to test my sincerity, Khyven the Pretty."

"Oh?"

"I'll tell you how to woo Lorelle. There's a secret. One little secret, but I've seen it work on her over and over."

"What is it?"

"I'll tell you in a moment. But did you know," Rhenn said, "that most Luminents wouldn't even look at a Human romantically? Wouldn't even consider it. We're uncouth to them. Loud and obnoxious, unable to govern our emotions. But not Lorelle. She's weak in the knees for Humans. You just can't see it. She puts on the typical Luminent facade—I'm sure you've noticed. Calm face, intent eyes. You've got to be willing to push through that. It takes some doing."

"Good to know."

"And here's the secret. You'll like it. Are you ready?"

He nodded.

"Lorelle has a weakness for poetry," Rhenn whispered. "You ply her with poetry, fill a cup for her, and she will fall into your arms."

"Really?"

"I've seen it happen. Time and time again. But you have to push past that facade."

Khyven watched Lorelle, smiling and looking at the dancers. He thought of kissing those lips, of putting his arms around that slender waist.

"Well… thank you," Khyven said.

"You're welcome."

He glanced down at Rhenn, and she held up her hands. "I can see that look in your eyes. Don't let me hold you up. We can talk about the job I have for you tomorrow. Tonight is for pleasure. Go ahead."

"Again, thank you." He bowed to the queen and crossed the glade, remembering to stop and pick up two fresh cups of ale. He was a dozen paces away from Lorelle before she noticed him.

Her contented look vanished and the facade Rhenn had mentioned leapt into place.

"The music is amazing," he said.

She looked at him, then glanced back at the copse of trees where he'd been. Rhenn was still standing there and she raised her cup to Lorelle.

A flicker of annoyance crossed her face, there and gone, then she turned her glorious brown eyes on him.

"It is amazing," she agreed.

"It's like floating sunshine, dancing about," he said.

Lorelle's lips twitched and she cleared her throat. "Yes."

"Would you like another drink?" He offered her one of the two mugs. Again, she glanced at Rhenn across the glade, who gestured with one hand, palm up, as if to say *Go ahead.*

"Thank you." Lorelle took the mug and set it on the table next to her.

"I was watching the dancers," Khyven said, "and I couldn't help but notice you."

"You couldn't," Lorelle said, and he wasn't sure if it was a question or not. The firelight played across her slender neck. She was simply exquisite.

"I've never seen a Luminent before. Are they all so beautiful?"

"Beauty is different for every person," she said. "What else did Rhenn tell you?"

"Nothing really." He raised his mug. "A toast?"

For half a second, she did nothing, then she gave a little nod, picked up the mug, and tapped it against his.

"To the moon," he said. "And to how it dances through your hair."

He thought for a moment she might smile and a thrill ran through him. He imagined it would be the most wondrous thing to see her smile.

"Mmmm poetry," she murmured in her dusky voice and took a sip from the mug.

"May I?" He indicated the table where she sat.

"Please," she said. He sat next to her, almost close enough to touch.

"Tell me," he said, "do Luminents dance?"

"They are the finest dancers on Noksonon," she said without hesitation.

He raised his eyebrows. "Really?"

"Do you know nothing of Luminents?"

"Only the beauty I see when I look at you."

She took a deep breath and stretched, as though she had inhaled the compliment and it was coursing through her body. His heart beat faster.

"And Rhenn, did she tell you about our culture?" Lorelle asked.

"Only that… well that Luminents don't often interact with Humans."

"That's what she said?"

"Yes."

"And that I am the exception."

"I didn't need Rhenn to see that you are exceptional."

"Mmmm." Lorelle purred. "I think I understand now," she said softly, leaning toward him. She touched his arm, her fingers tracing so delicately it felt like a butterfly. Her caress reached his shoulder, then her fingers slid along his neck. Lorelle gave a guilty smile and leaned into him, touching her forehead to his. "She told you my secret, did she?" she whispered, sounding a little embarrassed.

"I won't tell anyone else," he said, his heart thundering. All he could see were her pale pink lips, and all he could feel was the ache of need in his chest. He put his hands around her waist, felt the warmth of her taut body beneath the fabric. He wanted to crush her to him, but he waited. Best to let her come to him. Best to unleash her desires, let *them* guide the kiss.

"You promise?" she breathed.

"I do."

"Then I will tell you another secret," she said.

Something sharp stuck his neck, like the dart she'd shot at him earlier that day.

He jerked back and reached up. His hand came away with a spot of blood. Lorelle's sultry gaze went impassive again. He looked at her hand and noticed a thin silver sheath around her pinky finger. It was decorated with a spot of his blood.

"Rhenn likes to play pranks," Lorelle said as his world began to fall sideways.

Khyven craned his neck to look at the queen. She stood at the edge of the trees, holding her sides, doubled over with laughter.

"Good night, Khyven," Lorelle said. "Again."

Khyven's legs and arms stopped working and he crashed to the ground.

He heard the laughter of nearby people swirling all around him.

He saw Lorelle standing over him, looking down, shaking her head.

Everything went dark.

Chapter Fifteen

LORELLE

"That wasn't funny," Lorelle said as she reached the trees on the small rise. Rhenn was still laughing.

"By Senji," she giggled, having a hard time drawing enough breath. "It most certainly was."

"You have a cruel streak," Lorelle said, glancing back to where she'd left the prone ringer.

"He came here to reveal us to Vamreth," Rhenn said between breaths. "If almost getting to kiss you is his worst punishment, he's the luckiest man alive."

"I wasn't talking about him," she said.

"Oh please," Rhenn said, walking toward her tent, settled atop the rise where everyone in the camp could see it. "I sent you a gift. He's handsome and you hate him. You could have kissed him all night long and felt nothing, and then you'd have had a kiss."

"You're reckless, Rhenn."

"And then some," she agreed, opening the tent flap and heading inside. Lorelle followed, shaking her head.

"You could have at least kissed him before you stung him,"

Rhenn said. "Would that have been so awful?"

Lorelle didn't respond to that.

"Tell me you didn't enjoy teasing him," Rhenn said. "You played the role with such relish."

Despite herself, Lorelle cracked a smile. "You are the most fallible person I've ever met."

Lorelle knew that Rhenn only wanted to help, but Rhenn understood better than anyone why kissing, laughter, sorrow… why *all* of these things might be a danger to Lorelle. Any large emotion could carry her away. She wasn't Human like Rhenn.

Rhenn's prank reminded Lorelle how precarious her situation was. Every time her emotions broke free, she thought of Lumyn. She'd even considered leaving Rhenn for a few months, going home, finding a Luminent mate, and returning as soon as possible. Creating a Soulbond with another—finding a real mate—was the only thing that would remove the pressure Lorelle felt.

But she couldn't stomach the idea of leaving Rhenn vulnerable for even a single day. Rhenn's life had become increasingly more dangerous. Rhenn had the right of it: it was only a matter of time before Vamreth found them. How could Lorelle possibly have clarity of mind enough to open herself to a life-mate—to travel for weeks to her homeland and spend who-knows-how-long actually finding someone suitable—when she was constantly worrying about Rhenn?

But the pressure was building. Lorelle was already past the age when most Luminents bonded, and it wasn't like she was sitting alone on top of a mountain, meditating. She was stuck in a camp full of Humans, the most emotionally volatile race on Noksonon. Every day presented another opportunity for Lorelle to slip. To fail. To accidentally begin the bond with someone near her. How much longer could she delay?

"Come now." Rhenn put a hand on Lorelle's shoulder. "We all deserve a little fun. There's far too little to be had. A kiss… A laugh… If we can't laugh, what will become of us?"

"Do you want me to return to Lumyn?" Lorelle asked. "Is

that what you want?"

Rhenn's hesitation, despite her smile, said it all. "No, of course not."

"You do," Lorelle said.

"I want what's best for you," Rhenn said.

"And this is your way of forcing me into it?"

"Lorelle, I don't want to force you into anything, but you're suffering."

"I suppose leaving you alone to be slaughtered by assassins or Vamreth's mages… that will ease my suffering?"

"I'm not helpless."

"All it takes is one dart, Rhenn."

"I see your pain every day," Rhenn said. "How much longer can you hold it in? Maybe it isn't the worst idea for you to return to Lumyn, at least for a little while."

"A little while could be a year. It could be more. And you aren't even thinking of what happens if I should succeed. It means finding someone who matters to me more than you do. That's what a Soulbond is, Rhenn. That person would matter to me most of all. It means I might never come back here."

"I know."

"So, it is fine for you if I decide you and your kingdom are not my business anymore?"

"We all have our own lives to live." Rhenn's wry smile faded. "Our own choices to make. This doesn't have to be your war."

"How dare you say that to me." The edges of Lorelle's hair flickered, glowing with a soft silver light.

"Lorelle—"

"He killed my parents," she said in a whisper. "He killed yours…" The glow brightened, and she shut her eyes, turned her face away.

"Lorelle, I'm sorry—"

"I'm not talking about this anymore," she said. She breathed silently in and out. She envisioned a white wall in her mind, with a tall, thick wooden door and an enormous lock. She pushed her anger and despair through that doorway, slammed it shut, and locked it tight.

"I'm sorry," Rhenn said again. "I don't *want* you to leave, but you have to consider it. Everyone has their breaking point. All it is going to take is one moment, one slip, and then what?"

Images rose in Lorelle's mind of a woman back in Lumyn who the villagers had called Sad Sovere. It was one of Lorelle's oldest memories, from when she was a child, when her family still lived in the Luminent kingdom, but she had never forgotten it. Sad Sovere staggering down the street like her muscles could barely move her legs. Lorelle had rushed to help her. She had put her shoulder beneath the old woman's hand to keep her upright, and that's when Lorelle had seen the woman's milky eyes, her slack face, her hopelessness.

Lorelle had only glimpsed Sad Sovere for a stunned second before her parents had scooped her up and taken her away, but she'd never forgotten it.

"There's nothing you can do for her, my little song," her mother had said. "It's the half-life."

"What's the half-life?" Lorelle had asked.

"A failed bonding," her mother had said. "She gave her soul to another but didn't receive theirs in return."

"Will that happen to me?" Lorelle had asked.

"No, my little song," her mother had said. "You have us and we will train you. We will counsel you. When you bond, you will be ready. It will be beautiful, the most beautiful thing you can imagine. It will be like it was for your father and I."

Lorelle came back from her reverie and the chill of the memory helped her lock that door within her mind. She looked down at Rhenn.

"I'm not leaving you," she said.

Rhenn searched her eyes, then slowly nodded. "Very well," she said. "Very well."

Lorelle cleared her throat and changed the subject. "So tomorrow, the nuraghi?"

Rhenn had been planning an excursion into the noktum for more than a week. She had announced that it was time to explore the Giant castle in the noktum. Vohn, the noktum expert among them, had called it a nuraghi.

Rhenn nodded. There was a great deal of debate among Rhenn's advisors about the wisdom of poking about in the nuraghi. Lord Harpinjur said they should leave well enough alone. He'd argued that finding the amulets and the cache of totems that held back the noktum had been Senji's own blessing and that they should take it and leave it at that, not tempt Fate.

But Lorelle knew that Rhenn would never stop at that. She would never leave a possible advantage behind just because of danger. Rhenn argued that if they hadn't taken the risk to get the amulets in the first place, they wouldn't be where they are now.

No doubt Rhenn envisioned treasures beyond imagining within the nuraghi itself. Maybe something large enough to obliterate Vamreth and his frighteningly large army. Maybe she was right.

"If you and your best fighters vanish into the noktum, who is going to watch the spy?" Lorelle asked, fearing that Rhenn would say it would be Lorelle herself. That would precipitate an argument. Lorelle wasn't letting Rhenn go into the nuraghi without her.

"Oh, we're going take him."

"*Take* him?" Lorelle asked.

"You want me to leave him here?"

"I will put him to sleep. I have something that could—"

"This will be a good test."

"A test…?" Lorelle sighed. "Lotura give me patience. I feel a headache coming on. You actually *do* want to recruit him. You don't just want to hire him as your champion at the Burzagi Tor. You want him as part of your band."

"I think we can mold him," Rhenn said.

"He was sent to destroy you," Lorelle said.

"So dramatic," Rhenn chided. "He's a ringer. A ringer fights to stay alive. That's why he came here. He's a survivor, not a spy."

"You think too highly of him. He's a killer in service to Vamreth. You're not going to recruit him to your cause."

"You're right. I'm not. You are."

"I—" Lorelle cut herself off as she saw where Rhenn was going. "No."

"You can do it."

"No."

"He's in love with you." Rhenn sat down on the smooth pine bed that Pohvul the blacksmith had made for her. The man was a genius with iron, but he was also a fair hand at woodworking.

"You Humans throw that word around like you know what it means." Lorelle put her hands on her hips.

"He's been watching you since the moment he first saw you," Rhenn said.

"His brain was addled by *somnul* when he first saw me."

"True love." Rhenn grinned.

"He wants to rut. And I'm exotic to him."

"He's smitten."

"I'm sure. And he was undoubtedly smitten with dozens of other women before me. Human love is not a binding thing. It doesn't tie him to your cause any better than dangling a roasted chicken leg in his face."

"An excellent analogy," Rhenn said. "We must keep him hungry."

Lorelle rolled her eyes. Rhenn had latched on to another of her ideas and nothing was going to pry her away from it.

"Besides, you get to play the temptress again," Rhenn said, setting her cup on a stump growing through the middle of her tent. She'd placed her bed so she could use the stump as a nightstand. "Which you obviously liked."

Rhenn was baiting her, so Lorelle didn't respond to the hook. "This is ridiculously transparent," she said. "He won't fall for it."

"You underestimate the stupidity of a man in love."

"Stop using that word," Lorelle said. "You obviously don't know what it means."

Rhenn chuckled, pulling off her boots and clothes and donning the lightweight linen bed clothes she'd had made. Once she was dressed for sleep, she sighed and fell back onto the bed.

"He tried to kiss me, I poisoned him," Lorelle persisted. "He is well aware I'm not interested."

"Foreplay," Rhenn said, snuggling into the soft bed.

"What?"

"You've only ensured he'll chase you. Trust me."

"Humans are bizarre. Is this actually how you attract a mate?"

"It's fun. You'll see. Think of it as study. Further your education."

Lorelle shook her head.

"You'll see." Rhenn let out a breath and closed her eyes. "I have a feeling about him."

"And you are certain about taking him to the nuraghi?" Lorelle asked.

"Yes."

"It is a singularly bad idea. With all the other dangers, it will be impossible to keep an adequate watch on him."

"It will be a good test."

"To see if he takes the opportunity to kill you?"

"Exactly."

Lorelle sighed. "I love you, Rhenn, but you are insane."

"The best way to know a man's intentions is to provide him a clear shot at the target he craves." Rhenn winked. "A *seemingly* clear shot, at least."

"I suppose this is where I come in."

"It's like we think with one mind."

"Two people in your head would explain a lot," Lorelle said.

Rhenn chuckled. "We offer him two targets that are impossible to resist, you and me. Let's see which one he chooses."

"A good queen doesn't risk her life over and over every day." Lorelle shook her head.

Rhenn yawned. "Oh, Lorelle," she murmured. "That is exactly what a good queen does. We have far too much ground to cover in far too short a time. We can't afford to tiptoe through the woods. Not today. Not tomorrow. Not until Vamreth is dead."

"I'm going to sleep," Lorelle said.

"Tell me you'll do it," Rhenn said, cracking open one eye.

"I'm not a seductress."

"You won't have to be," Rhenn said. "He'll come to you."

"I don't think he will."

"Trust me."

Lorelle looked down at her friend and a surge of respect and love rose within her. The woman never stopped trying. She was always thinking of every possible way to achieve her goal. She had built this camp from nothing. The two of them had started as fleeing children, and now Rhenn was a legend: the Queen-in-Exile. Now, two lords had come to her side, a handful of knights, and close to a hundred and fifty people who could actually fight. Rhenn had created a rebellion and Vamreth was frightened enough to send spies to kill her.

She'd done all that by following her instincts. As frustrating as Rhenn's recklessness could sometimes be, Lorelle couldn't ignore the results.

"I will do my best," Lorelle said softly.

Rhenn smiled and closed her eyes again. "Just stay close to him. He'll take care of the rest."

"Sleep well, Your Majesty."

"Mmmm hmmm," Rhenn said, sounding like she was halfway asleep already.

Smiling, Lorelle left the tent.

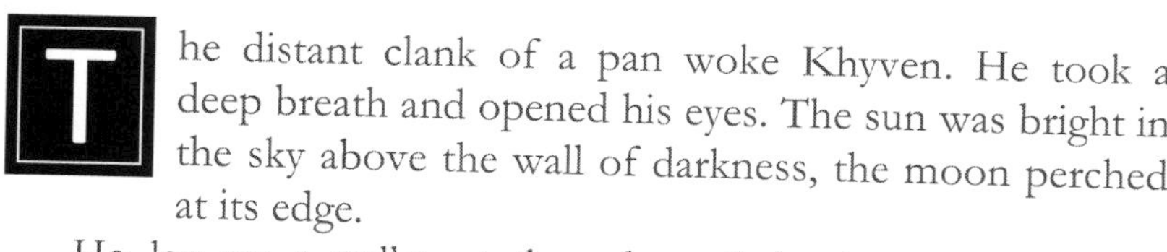

Chapter Sixteen

KHYVEN

The distant clank of a pan woke Khyven. He took a deep breath and opened his eyes. The sun was bright in the sky above the wall of darkness, the moon perched at its edge.

He lay on a pallet at the edge of the large, unsheltered sleeping area. Several dozen others lay on similar pallets, snoring away. Down the slope, the cook fires were already alive and the smell of eggs and bacon floated up the hill.

He rolled onto his side and sat up. His neck ached from Lorelle's drug even worse this time. As he tried to shrug off the aftereffects, he noticed two guards a short distance away. Both were watching him.

In the light of the new day, he had a decision to make, and the sooner the better. Was he going to try to escape this place? Or was he going to do Rhenn's bidding?

He glanced around at the wall of the noktum—

And saw Lorelle.

She was emerging from the trees where Rhenn had delivered her prank last night.

The Luminent wore a hooded tunic, the body of it trapped by a leather vest, the sleeves rolled up to mid-arm. Four thin belts encircled her slender waist holding various pouches and a sheath for her blowgun. Her woodsman's breeches stopped at mid-calf, revealing a flash of smooth, pale skin before her slipper-like shoes began at the ankle.

Her light, graceful movements seemed designed to draw his gaze. Despite the fact she had poisoned him twice, he was immediately enthralled by her; he just couldn't look away.

She stopped next to him, staring down.

"Did you sleep well?" she asked.

"Like I was drugged," he replied.

"Hmm," she said. He thought maybe she wanted to smile, but she didn't.

"The queen requested I wake you," she said.

He glanced over his shoulder at the cook fires. Several people were already lined up, piling bacon and eggs onto wooden plates.

"Are you hungry?" he asked.

She followed his gaze, hesitating, but then she nodded. "Very well." She started down the slope.

He leapt to his feet and caught up with her. Her head held high, she didn't once look at the uneven terrain, yet she never stumbled. It was like her feet already knew every bump and rock of the meadow. She practically glided along.

"So," Khyven said as they joined the line and picked up plates from a lopsided table, "you've poisoned me twice now."

She didn't respond, just put eggs on her plate and a single strip of bacon. He filled his plate and threw a handful of bacon on top, then followed her to a patch of empty grass with the many people who had already hunkered down to eat. He noticed that everyone deferred to Lorelle almost as much as they did to Rhenn.

She settled herself.

Khyven plopped down opposite her and shoveled in the hot food. It was wonderful.

"Why did Rhenn send you?" he asked after swallowing his first mouthful.

"Excuse me?"

"To get me, to bring me. She has lots of people to do things for her. Why send you?"

"I happened to be there," she said.

"Is that so?"

She didn't answer and they ate in silence for a while.

"You seem to be taking your captivity fairly well," she said.

"This is the nicest cage I've ever been in," he said around a mouthful of eggs.

"Vohn said you were living at the palace."

"I was a free man by then."

"Were you?" she asked.

He grinned while chewing. He swallowed and pointed his finger at her. "A fair point. Still, there is an… easiness about this place. Vamreth's axe could fall at any moment, yet you all act as though it won't. That's…" He shrugged. "It's interesting."

"You like it," Lorelle said.

He hesitated, then nodded. "I suppose I do."

"It's what freedom feels like."

"Oh, you don't really think you're free, do you?" Khyven asked.

"Why would you say that?"

He chuckled. "How should I count the ways?"

Lorelle set her fork at the edge of her plate, stopped eating, and watched him with flinty eyes.

He waved at the noktum. "First, you're trapped. Anyone who steps into the noktum without an amulet will be devoured. It's like standing beneath a teetering boulder. That power will crush you the moment it gets the chance. And, of course, there's Vamreth. You can't hide from him forever. Your trick with the noktum is impressive. No one would think of it out of hand, I'd wager, but there are trails that lead here. New recruits. They come from somewhere. People will miss them, ask about them. And food. I mean, where did all this food come from? Vamreth's going to find you eventually, and he has a thousand fighters. Another teetering boulder. That power will crush you the moment it can."

Lorelle had gone completely still.

"And let's not forget the most obvious one of all. Rhenn rules here, just like Vamreth rules in Usara. No one is actually free, except maybe Rhenn."

"You have no idea what you're talking about," Lorelle said in a frosty tone.

"In the end, only the powerful are free," Khyven said. "They're the only ones who are safe. It's the law of the world."

Lorelle lapsed into silence and she began eating with slow, measured movements. Her jaw worked as she chewed. She looked over the camp, kept her gaze anywhere but on Khyven.

"So, Rhenn seems to understand people," Khyven said conversationally. "It's like everyone is a book to her and she just opens them up and reads them."

Lorelle took a bite of her bacon, chewed, swallowed, then looked at him. "She is a good queen," she said evenly.

"I imagine everyone here agrees with you."

"What is your point?"

"That she knows how to manipulate people. She's the best I've ever seen." He gestured at the people getting their food and happily talking with one another. "Look at them. She's convinced them this is freedom, like she's convinced you, and they love her for it. That's a feat."

"They love her because what she is doing is right."

"You don't think she's manipulating them."

"Of course not."

He smiled, ate another spoonful of eggs. "I see. Just like it was chance that you came to wake me up."

"It was," Lorelle said, but there was a slight tightening around her eyes.

"You just happened to be in the tent when Rhenn said she needed to see me?"

"That is correct."

"And you just happened to have the time to sit down with me and have breakfast?"

Lorelle didn't say anything.

"Rhenn sent you on purpose," Khyven said. "You, specifically."

"I told you—"

"She knows I find you attractive," Khyven said, "and you are the dutiful subject."

Lorelle lifted her chin.

Khyven set his plate aside and held his hands up in a pacifying gesture. "Don't be upset. I don't mind. She's right. I love seeing you. I'm accustomed to appreciating what I like from within the confines of my cage. At least I get to look at a beautiful woman while I do it. Far better than the Night Ring. I can play the slave—Senji knows I can—I just like understanding how I'm being manipulated," he said.

Lorelle stood up. "There are no slaves here, Khyven. Rhenn is not Vamreth. These people are content because they're on the right side of this war, and her generosity of spirit is the only reason you're still alive."

"I'm still alive because your queen needs me. She sent you to secure my interest. A little invisible shackle."

Lorelle's dark eyes had gone flat. "Leave anytime you wish, ringer."

"With my amulet?" he asked.

She didn't reply.

He chuckled. "Like I said, I just like to know how I'm being manipulated."

Khyven had positioned himself so he could keep an eye Rhenn's tent, which was larger than all the rest, so he saw when the flap opened. The queen emerged and said something to a young man standing outside. He went running off and Rhenn turned her attention down the slope, fixed a gaze on Khyven and Lorelle, and headed toward them.

"Time to prove my loyalty," he said.

Rhenn stopped before them, boots thumping on the matted grass. "Feel like an adventure today, Khyven the Pretty?" she asked.

He stood up. "Is this the business you mentioned?"

"No," she said. "Call it a side adventure."

"So, it's a test?"

Rhenn paused. She flicked a glance at Lorelle, then her wry smile widened. "Something like that."

Khyven conspicuously turned and regarded Lorelle. "Don't worry," he said. "I'm not going anywhere."

He was gratified to see the barest blush on Lorelle's cheeks. He couldn't tell if it was from anger or embarrassment, then decided it didn't really matter.

This camp was a new arena, but it had the same basic principles. Stay on your toes. Look for manipulations. Navigate safely through them. Survive.

Rhenn extended her fist, then opened it. Khyven's amulet dropped out and dangled from her fingers. "We're going into the noktum."

A thrill of fear went through him as he thought of the pack of Kyolars and those fanged, flying otters that had paced him and Vohn all the way from the Night Ring.

Rhenn's eyes twinkled. "Don't get separated from the group," she said. "It's dangerous in there."

"Danger is where I live," he said.

"So it seems," Rhenn said.

The young man Rhenn had spoken to outside her tent returned with half a dozen other people: four of Rhenn's knights, Vohn, and a burly giant of a man who was nearly as tall as Khyven and twice as wide, all of it muscle. The big man wore a dun-colored tunic chopped off at the shoulders, a thick, black belt, and brown trousers. He also had a longsword strapped to his back.

They all wore Amulets of Noksonon.

Rhenn started up the slope without a word, heading directly toward the noktum. When she reached the twenty-foot-tall wall of night, she turned, her rakish silhouette framed by the darkness.

"Everyone knows what we're doing except this one." Rhenn gestured at Khyven. "Khyven, we're looking for these." She lifted her amulet from her chest. "We're also looking for those." She let the amulet fall and pointed at the posts designating the shape of the camp, each topped with large-headed, onyx ravens. "There are undoubtedly innumerable other artifacts in there that do things we can only guess at. Anything you find that looks useful, run it by Vohn or me before you take it."

Khyven glanced at Vohn. The Shadowvar scowled at him.

"If he says don't touch it, don't touch it," Rhenn finished. She turned her attention to the group. "We'll head straight for the nuraghi. Don't waste time getting distracted. I'm giving us one hour. The amulets will last twice that if we stay close together, so let's stay close together. Does everybody understand?"

Everyone grunted assent.

"The amulets last longer if there's more of them?" Khyven murmured to Vohn. Vohn glared up at him, then looked back at Rhenn without saying anything.

"Let's go," Rhenn said and she walked into the wall of black, vanishing from view. Lorelle followed, and then the rest plunged into the wall, all except Vohn, who stood with his hands on his hips watching Khyven.

Taking a deep breath, Khyven followed. He expected some kind of tingle as he passed through the barrier, maybe that sensation of cold again, but this time there was no sensation whatsoever. He simply went from a place of light to utter darkness.

Chapter Seventeen

KHYVEN

He experienced that same feeling of being clipped loose from life, like a feather floating between the stars. He quickly reached up and ran a finger around the edge of the amulet as he'd seen Vohn do.

The landscape resolved into gray ground with patches of charcoal gray grass and even darker gray forest ahead on their left.

Rhenn was moving toward the castle in the distance and her band followed her. With Vohn behind him, Khyven fell in line. They hiked for at least half an hour and the castle loomed larger and larger. Khyven was stunned at how huge the castle really was. A dozen towers spiraled up from the sprawling hulk of the edifice, barely half of them still intact. The rest had crumbled, their half-shorn jagged tips reaching feebly into the air.

The walls of the main structure looked like they'd been made from black granite, but everything in this place was different shades of dark. Khyven wondered if it would be gray granite—or even marble—if seen in daylight.

Everyone stayed close together. Since they'd arrived only a

few Kyolars had paced them, and those from a distance. The fanged flying otters zipped across the sky, but much higher than they'd done with Khyven and Vohn alone. The necklaces didn't exude sunlight, but apparently the effect was the same to the creatures.

They finally approached the stone wall surrounding the castle. The path they'd been following—just a dirt aisle bordered by fist-sized stones—opened onto a real road with tight-fit cobblestones. As Khyven walked the road, he studied their amazing configuration. It was as though the asymmetrical stones had been hewn to fit together, except no two were the same. What stone mason would spend that much time making each individual stone the exact, unique fit for the other random stones around it?

A chill went up his spine and he began to suspect that no mortal stonecutter had hewn them and no mortal mason had placed them. This road had been made by magic.

They followed the eerie, perfect path up to the crumbled wall. The huge, twisted gates had been ripped away long ago and tossed aside like toys, one set outside the ravaged wall and one on the inside. Crumbled stones lay in a pile, blocking the entrance to the courtyard, but the cobblestone road continued after, leading toward the distant archway at the front of the castle.

Rhenn stopped before the rubble, turned, and faced them. She beckoned them closer.

"Now," she said when they had all gathered nearer. "The necklaces protect us in the noktum at large, that much we know. But we've never been into the nuraghi before. For all we know, the effectiveness of the necklaces ends at the wall. If that happens, get back across that line." She pointed at the apex of the rubble.

A rumble of assent went through the group.

"We are going to stay in sight of each other," Rhenn said. "If you find a magical artifact, let Vohn know. Do not leave your group, and don't pick it up unless it's a necklace or a raven totem. Anything else, we talk to Vohn. Any dead bodies in there are likely to have a necklace. You see a skeleton, search it."

"How do we know if something is magical?" Khyven asked.

"If it's still intact, it's probably magical. No one has ever explored this place. The Giants abandoned it almost two thousand years ago. The only things that would survive that long would be stone, steel, bones, and anything magical." She paused, looked at each of them. "Keep eyes on each other, okay? No wandering off."

"Yes, Your Majesty," several of the knights said. Vohn nodded. Lorelle said nothing.

"Lorelle and Gohver, you come with me," Rhenn said. "And you too, Khyven the Pretty. I don't want you getting spooked on your first trip." She winked. "Vohn, you take the rest. There is a lot of space in this castle. We can't see it all today, and if we do this wrong we won't be seeing anything ever again. Small bites for now. If by some chance you get separated, come back to this archway. Wait ten minutes for the rest of us. After that, you bolt for camp. Understand?"

Everyone nodded.

Rhenn stepped deftly up and over the rubble. Lorelle followed, then the big, thick man named Gohver looked at Khyven. He gave a grin that was missing teeth and pointed with his chin that Khyven should follow Lorelle.

Khyven climbed up one side and danced down the opposite slope before continuing on. Gohver tromped up and down right behind him, glancing this way and that. Khyven noticed that as the second group came up and over the rubble the Kyolars and the flying otters moved closer, bunching against the edge of the gates, but they didn't enter the courtyard.

That gave Khyven a chill. If the fanged otters and the Kyolars didn't want to come here then what was in this place?

"Quickly now," Rhenn said calmly. "Stay sharp. Stay close. Whatever is in here, we face it together."

They walked up the wide path. Crossing the courtyard seemed to take forever. The space between the gates and the castle had to be three times the size of the courtyard of the

Usaran palace.

"What is this place?" Khyven murmured.

"Nuraghi," Gohver said.

That was the word Rhenn had used. He felt he'd heard that word before, but he couldn't remember where. Had the old man told him about it?

"What's a nuraghi?" he asked.

"Castle," Gohver murmured and Khyven shot him a frown.

Gohver showed his gap-toothed grin again. It was an evil kind of a smile, Khyven decided, something he imagined a puppy would see right before Gohver drowned it. "An *old* castle," Gohver said.

They continued down the path at a swift walk.

Huge sculptures rose through the shin-high black grass and Khyven again wondered what it would look like in the sunlight. He still wasn't sure how he could see any of this in the first place.

He studied the sculptures. Most had crumbled, littering misshapen stones across the courtyard, but some were intact. The closest loomed over them as they neared. One depicted an eighteen-foot-tall man—or what Khyven assumed was a man—on a pedestal. The figure looked forward, intense, as though he could light the horizon on fire with his gaze. The more Khyven stared at the sculpture, the more the face seemed to change. The brows furrowed, creating lines of rage. The mouth turned down in a sneer, showing teeth. The eyes elongated—

Khyven broke his gaze away, shook his head, and looked again. The statue had returned to its previous intense gaze, frozen in time.

His heart hammered and he swallowed. He hurried past the thing and didn't look at it again.

"Who built this place?" he murmured over his shoulder at Gohver.

"Giants," the thick man said. "Don't you know about the noktums?"

"Giants? Giants weren't actually real."

Gohver showed his horrible smile again, but he didn't say anything.

Rhenn arrived at the base of the stairs. Each step was as tall as a bench and twice as deep. From a distance it had looked like an elegant, sweeping stairway. Up close it looked like another massive sculpture. Surely no one was meant to actually walk up this.

"Giants, huh?" Khyven murmured to Gohver.

"Made during the war," Gohver said.

"What war?" Khyven asked.

"Some ancient war. Heard Vohn talk about it sometimes. Giants against Giants."

"What?"

Gohver chuckled.

"Enough," Rhenn said, stopping at the base of the enormous steps. "You want a history lesson, Khyven, ask afterward. Right now, we focus. We pay attention. Now, we all know it's a bad idea to attack creatures in the noktum. Bohlen taught us that, the poor bastard. The moment you spill blood here, every creature within a mile is going to come out of the woodwork. Spilling blood is like lighting a torch. And I'm going to assume that, as bad as it is outside the walls of the nuraghi, it's twice as bad inside. So, no attacking anything unless it's life or death. Understand?"

Everyone nodded.

"We're going to spend half an hour here. That's all. Half an hour. Vohn will be our timekeeper. Then, whatever we have that's what we have and we're done and we head back to camp as quickly as we can. When I give the signal, you drop what you're doing and move. Does everybody understand that?"

Nods all around.

Rhenn turned and started up the stairway, one huge step at a time. They followed.

"What's wrong with lighting a torch?" Khyven whispered to Gohver.

"Nokkies hate light. Bring real light into this place and even the necklaces won't protect you. The nokkies won't care about their own hides anymore. They'll go crazy, swarm ya, even though the necklaces burn 'em."

They concentrated on climbing. There were over a hundred steps and Khyven's thighs were burning by the time they reached the top. A wide, circular landing led to twenty-foot-tall steel-banded doors in an unfathomably tall wall. Khyven stared upward and the dark walls seemed to go up forever. It made him dizzy. He turned his focus to the doors.

The wood had decayed and the doors sagged in their thick, iron bands. There was a space in the right door that was almost large enough for a person to walk through. Rhenn inspected the gap, but Khyven noticed she didn't touch the doors.

"We go through here." She dropped her voice to a whisper. Khyven took the cue and stopped asking Gohver questions. As lithe as a flying otter, Lorelle slithered through the hole before Rhenn could. With a disapproving shake of her head, Rhenn followed, crouching low and stepping through the hole, passing without touching.

Gohver nodded at Khyven, and he went next. He wasn't as small or graceful as Rhenn or Lorelle and his shoulder brushed the top of the wood. His sword's sheath clanked against the bottom. He winced as he came into the great room beyond. Both Lorelle and Rhenn looked back at the noise with disapproving frowns.

Gohver didn't enter any quieter.

Khyven turned his attention to the great room. Soaring, vaulted ceilings went so far up they vanished into shadow. Perfectly fitted black stones created three arches—one on the wall before them, one to the left and one to the right—and each was taller than the highest point of the Usaran palace

The walls between the arches bore alcoves with sculptures, all still intact, and flat spaces where once had been paintings and tapestries, though all that remained of the tapestries were steel rods suspended on the wall. Tilted, rotting frames showing the bare stone walls behind were all that remained of the paintings. Only wispy threads around the edges showed that canvas had ever been attached to them. There were at least half a dozen lopsided chairs in various stages of decay, as well as two large divans whose coverings and legs had rotted away long ago, looking more like squarish piles of wood than anything else.

And there were five skeletons.

One, its head tilted forward, chin to bony chest, was almost folded in half within the remains of a chair. A second lay amidst the rubble of one of the divans.

The other three lay on the floor, two face-down and one face-up grinning at the lofty ceiling. Each of the skeletons, were they to stand up, would be at least ten feet tall.

Chills went through Khyven. He felt like a mouse invading the house of a long dead lion. Everything here was on a larger scale. The chairs, the archways, the stairs. Even the paintings and sculptures. Gohver, Rhenn, Vohn… were telling the truth. This place had been built by Giants. Those skeletons belonged to Giants. But even as he stared at them, he could barely believe it.

Rhenn pointed at the corpses. "Vohn," she whispered. Vohn's group fanned out and searched them. Each came up with a necklace, and Rhenn smiled.

"That's more than we found in weeks of searching the outskirts," she said. "This trip is already worth it. Anyone see any totems?"

Vohn shook his head.

"Maybe that was a one-time thing," she said. Vohn nodded.

Rhenn's group began searching the walls, behind the sculptures, along the floor, amongst the debris, and finally all around—and inside—the enormous fireplace, which was big enough to fit a pair of horses on roasting spits.

Khyven leapt to the task, but he didn't put his whole heart into finding anything. He planned to rise within Rhenn's court just as he'd risen within Vamreth's and finding a few trinkets wasn't going to win him anything. He had to play to his strengths. If he could save the queen from some nightmare beast, that would do it. So, while he went through the same motions as the rest, he stayed close to the queen and kept his eye out for any beasts that might creep in through the archways or fly down from above.

He noticed that Rhenn, while she did some searching, mainly kept her eyes on the rest of the group, making sure no one left the main room. When they'd finished searching, she motioned everyone together in the center.

"Anything?" she asked.

Everyone shook their heads except for Vohn, who held up an odd pentagonal ring. It was made of metal and encrusted with jewels. Khyven assumed it was gold, but he couldn't see colors in this place.

"I don't know," Vohn said. "If it is magical, I don't know what it does."

"Keep it," she said. "We'll see if we can figure it out."

He put it into one of his pouches.

"We're moving that way." She indicated the giant arch to the right, which opened onto a long hallway. From here, Khyven could see more sculptures, more frames with missing or ripped canvas, and a twelve-foot-tall doorway along the left-hand wall. The right-hand wall held arched windows.

The group quietly followed Rhenn. The unraveled tatters of a long rug ran the entire length of hallway, which must have been as long as two entire Night Rings put end-to-end. At the far end was another archway.

"Senji's Boots…" Khyven murmured.

"We search the hall, nothing more," Rhenn commanded, and they set to it.

Khyven continued his pretense, all the while keeping an eye on Rhenn and looking for creatures. It surprised him that they'd been in here for at least a quarter of an hour and nothing had attacked them. Nothing had even approached them. It made the hairs on the back of his neck stand up.

He glanced back at the archway through which they'd entered. He could barely see the edge of the giant fireplace. So many things here didn't feel right, but a singular question occurred to him. Why would these Giants bother crafting a fireplace if everything in this benighted land hated fire?

He turned to ask Gohver, but the big man wasn't with him

anymore. Khyven's gaze flicked about the party. He located Rhenn and Lorelle, Vohn and the other knights.

Wait... where was Gohver?

Khyven jogged back toward the archway and spotted the big man just inside the first room regarding a giant black sword on the wall. Relief flooded through Khyven. He glanced at the rest of the group, which was about halfway up the hall. Rhenn was relatively safe, surrounded by her band and preoccupied with something Vohn had discovered in the fist of one of the sculptures. Khyven went into the room.

"Gohver," Khyven whispered. "Stay where we can see you, huh?"

Gohver didn't say anything. He seemed mesmerized by the sword.

"Gohver," Khyven whispered.

"You see this?" Gohver asked without turning.

"A big damned sword," Khyven said. The thing was made of some dark metal and it had to be at least six feet long. Larger than a two-handed sword, meant for a Giant. Khyven wasn't even sure he could lift it, let alone wield it. The blade was pointed at the vaulted ceiling and its hilt was just within Gohver's reach.

"Leave it," Khyven said. "Let's go tell Vohn and we'll come back."

"It's a beauty."

Khyven came closer. The blade seemed to lengthen before his eyes, the point stretching toward the ceiling. The edges became serrated, then straight, then serrated...

He shook his head, and it was just a sword again. He felt the same repulsion he'd felt when the statue outside the castle had seemed to come alive.

"Leave it," Khyven warned, but Gohver was already reaching out to grasp the hilt. Khyven winced, but nothing happened to the big man. He lifted it from its hook and, astoundingly, held it up with one hand.

Khyven stared in stupefaction.

Gohver turned, a goofy smile on his face, exposing his

missing teeth. "By Senji's Spear, Khyven," he said. "It's as light as a stick. I could hold one in each hand."

It didn't seem real. The sword was taller than Gohver. It should have weighed at least ten pounds, but he waved it about like a dagger.

"See? Magic," Gohver said.

"I wouldn't believe it if I wasn't looking at it," Khyven murmured.

Gohver winked at him. "Still want me to leave it? I think this is the kind o' magic the queen is looking for."

Khyven's response stuck in his throat. The sword still made him uneasy. "Best bring it to her, then—"

A shadow detached itself from the ocean of dark above.

"Gohver!" Khyven drew his sword as the thing dropped toward Gohver. Gohver whipped up his new blade. At the last second, the creature—a giant bat with talons—changed targets. It shrieked as it hit Khyven.

Curled needles sank into Khyven's sword arm and side before he could react. His sword clanged to the floor and he cried out. Gohver, who had crouched into a defensive position, leapt forward, swinging that enormous sword.

The bat-thing lifted Khyven like he weighed nothing, avoiding the black blade and shooting upward.

"Khyven!" Gohver called out.

The astonished Gohver became smaller and smaller as the creature hauled Khyven into the air. He could hear Gohver shouting, heard Rhenn shouting back. Booted feet pounded from the hallway into the room as the entire party burst through the doorway, but they were far too late. Khyven saw them only for a moment before the giant bat swept him away into some opening high in the wall.

The room vanished from view.

Darkness swirled and Khyven struggled, but no matter which way he moved, the claws sank deeper. He gasped.

The bat shot through a short tunnel into a circular room. There, it threw Khyven to the ground with a shriek.

He tumbled to a stop and gritted his teeth against the

puncture wounds in his arm and side. He'd dropped his sword when the bat-thing had snatched him up, but he still had the wooden sword in his belt. He'd kept it with him as a joke when they'd headed into the noktum, but now it was the best weapon he had.

He pulled the practice sword and ignored the pain in his arm. The bat-thing opened its mouth, which was more a hole in the center of its narrow face. Five fangs—looking more like pointy, curled fingers—lined the maw. It hissed, but the bat also limped, as though grabbing Khyven had burned it.

The amulet, he thought. *The amulet hurt this thing, but it wasn't enough to keep it away.*

He wondered if the amulet was failing. They'd been in the noktum for over an hour, and now he was separated from the group.

He looked around the room for an escape, but there were no windows and only two ways in: the hole through which they'd flown and an elegant, spiral staircase that went upward into darkness.

If Khyven went back through the tunnel, he'd drop four stories to the flagstones, and the stairs… well, the stairs went up. They'd lead higher and deeper into the castle. He could only guess at how many beasts remained undiscovered in this place. Running deeper into the castle seemed like suicide.

But there was nowhere else to go. He held the practice sword before himself as he circled toward the stairs, but the giant bat-thing didn't attack him. It crouched in the corner, wings folded, and watched him.

"What's it going to be?" Khyven growled. The creature shrieked, sidled toward the tunnel, and dove into it.

Khyven stood there, confused. For a moment, he didn't know what to think.

Cautiously, he crossed the room and peered into the tube, but he couldn't see anything except a circle of grayish light at the far end.

"Well," he murmured to himself. "I guess I'm not your

dinner today."

"No," a chilling voice said from behind him. "You're mine."

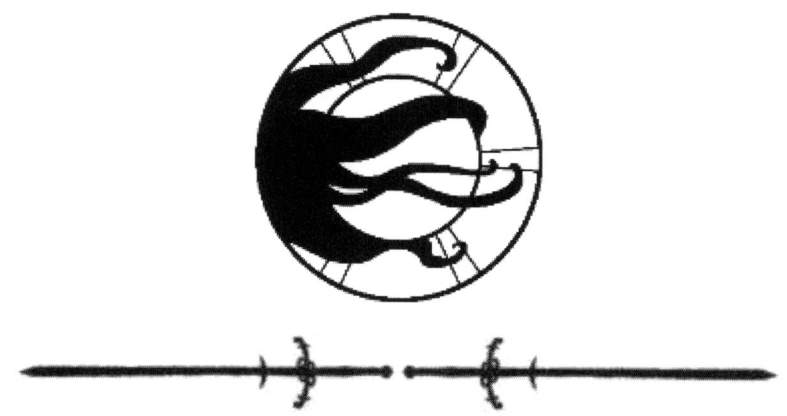

Chapter Eighteen

KHYVEN

Khyven spun and almost fell backward into the short tunnel.

Two taloned bird feet descended from the darkness of the stairway. Thin legs came into view, tall and scaled, bent backward at the knee. The blanket of night fell away from the creature and Khyven's breath caught in his throat.

It was an enormous raven, over twelve feet tall. Its head was mostly beak, a wicked-looking thing that ended in a point that a spear would envy. Large, dark eyes watched Khyven from behind its beak, its black wings were folded back against its sleek body.

"Senji Boots…" Khyven said. He wanted to back away, but he had nowhere to go. The thing seemed to fill the room.

The giant bird, quite impossibly, spoke. That long beak moved, sawing up and down, and perfectly intelligible words came out. "A god? No. I am the keeper of this nuraghi."

Khyven gaped. He pressed his back to the wall.

"I don't usually concern myself with trespassers personally," the giant bird said. "But I've been so… lonely lately." It drew a deep breath and exhaled. "And hungry. When you stole the sword, I simply couldn't resist."

Khyven flicked a glance at the stairway behind the bird.

"A trade," the bird continued. "Your life for the sword. Your friend can keep the blade for the rest of his short life and I shall sate myself upon the rest of yours. I haven't tasted live Human in a long time. Ezwyne does his best, but so few brave the noktum these days."

"Stop," Khyven warned, holding his wooden sword forward. He yanked his dagger from his belt and his heart thundered. He waited for the euphoria to flow through him, but it was slower, less eager. It was like the first times Khyven had used it in the Night Ring after the old man and Nhevaz had been killed.

"Please," the bird said, "put the weapons down. Can we not have a pleasant conversation before I feast? Can you not simply resign yourself to your fate? Look at me. I have been here for centuries, destined to stay here until my master returns. A slow, torturous cataloging of identical days. Do you see me complaining?" The bird shook his head. "No. Struggling against your fate does nothing, Human, and attacking me with your little sword will do even less..." It trailed off and cocked its bird head, perplexed. "That is a wooden sword."

Khyven glanced at his sword, then up at the bird. "Yes."

The longer he kept the bird talking, the less it would be eating.

"Dendryn met a Human who uses a wooden sword," the bird said.

"Dendryn?"

"One of my Kyolars. The Humans lured her into your slaughter box through the Night Door," the bird said. "I do tell my Kyolars to stay away, but every time I remove the helm, they just do what they want to, and let's face it, they are what they are." The bird cocked its head.

"You're talking about the Night Ring," Khyven said.

"Yes. Dendryn fought a Human there who used wooden swords. He spared her when he could have killed her. That's you, isn't it? I thought you looked familiar. You're Khyven the

Unkillable."

"Yes, that's me!"

"Ah," the bird said. "That is what I thought. Did you really make the arrogant proclamation that we of the noktum should fear you?"

"You were watching?" he asked.

"Not I personally. Ezwyne saw you." It ruffled its wing out from its side then settled again. "I was wearing the helm at the time, so I could see through Ezwyne's eyes. Bold words, Khyven the Unkillable." The bird shook its large head, the pointed beak waving back and forth like a blade.

Khyven watched the spear-like beak cautiously and kept his sword up.

"But you didn't kill Dendryn," the bird said. "That was new. No Kyolar has ever ventured into the Human slaughter box and emerged again. Why spare her? Was it to make your speech?"

"I… I don't know why," Khyven said.

"Well, it was honorably done, and the honorable deserve honor, so I will tell you my name before I eat you. Khyven the Unkillable, I am Rauvelos the Night Shadow." The bird inclined its neck in a kind of bow. "Well met. I think we should be friends, for as long as that lasts."

"But I… spared the Kyolar," Khyven said.

"Well, I must still eat you," Rauvelos said. "Surely you must see that."

"Not really, no." He edged toward the hole, contemplating rushing into the tunnel and taking his chances with the fall. Maybe he could try to climb down…

"Come now, serve your fellow Humans," Rauvelos said. "Your little band absconds with Daelakos's sword even now. I could use the helm to stop them. I could bring all the creatures of the noktum down upon them. But have I? No. I allow them to escape. A sword of Mavric iron is worth a dozen Humans, yet I shall let it go for one."

Khyven edged backward. He let the euphoria build within him and the blue wind swirled about the bird. Khyven looked for weaknesses, the little blue funnels that would—

"Where did you learn to do that?" the bird asked abruptly. He cocked his head left and right, as though trying to see Khyven better, and took a step away.

"You can see the wind?" Khyven asked. The bird was the first to ever mention the wind, except the old man and Nhevaz.

"I am the steward of this castle, Human. I can feel magic when it is used upon me," Rauvelos said. "Where did you learn…" It trailed off, staring at Khyven's chest. "Your amulet…"

Khyven flicked a glance down at the softly glowing amulet, then back up. "Yes?"

"Lords of the Dark—You didn't steal it, did you? Not like the others." The bird drew itself up to its considerable height.

"N-No," Khyven said. "It was given to me—"

"By whom?" the bird interrupted impatiently.

"My brother."

"Brother?" the bird said. "I hardly think so. Who was he? What was his name?"

"Nhevaz—"

The bird jerked, then stabbed his beak straight at Khyven.

He blocked with his sword, but the bird twitched its head, batting aside the wooden blade so fiercely Khyven almost dropped it. "Show me the back of the amulet!" Rauvelos demanded.

Khyven fumbled with the amulet and turned it over. He'd looked at the simple, graven symbol on the backside so many times he barely thought of it anymore. He'd always thought it was an artisan mark, perhaps the symbol of Nhevaz's family.

The bird backed up so quickly and so far it ascended the first step of the stairway. "Nhevalos…" he hissed.

"Nhevalos?" Khyven said.

"That is the mark of Nhevalos," Rauvelos said.

"Are you talking about Nhevaz?"

The bird went completely still, watching Khyven with those huge, glistening eyes. The silence stretched for so long that the bird might have become a statue.

"Are you talking about—?"

"Khyven the Unkillable," Rauvelos interrupted again. He bowed his great head. "Please accept my apologies."

Khyven was dumbstruck. "Uh, I… All right," he finally managed to say.

The bird cocked his head, regarding Khyven as though he was a puzzle. Finally, Rauvelos said, "You need not fear me any longer, Khyven the Unkillable. I will not hurt you."

"Why? Who is Nhevalos?" Khyven demanded. "Is that Nhevaz?"

In answer, the bird launched itself at Khyven. He whipped his sword up, but the thing batted it aside, grabbed Khyven with enormous talons and spiraled into the hole like a spinning arrow. Khyven gasped, but they shot through the tunnel and into the room before he could even take a breath.

"Be at peace, brother of… Nhevaz," Rauvelos said. Khyven suddenly realized that, unlike the bat-creature, Rauvelos had not pierced Khyven with its claws. The giant bird soared around in a wide circle, descending further and further down. Finally, it deposited Khyven on the floor and deftly alighted a few steps away.

"Please answer my question," Khyven said.

Rauvelos regarded him. "You are free to walk this noktum, Khyven the Unkillable. Wear your amulet and my creatures will recognize you."

"Please," Khyven said. "Tell me what you know. How is Nhevaz connected to this… Nhevalos." Khyven waved his sword at the darkened room. "To this place?"

"What did"—the bird paused every time he said Nhevaz's name, as though he was reluctant to speak it—"Nhevaz tell you about the amulet?"

"He said it made us brothers."

"Did he say anything else?"

"No."

The bird nodded his head. "Very well."

"What does it mean?"

"If he did not say, then I may not."

"No, please—"

"Go to your friends, Khyven the Unkillable," Rauvelos said.

"They're not my friends."

"Aren't they?"

"They're just—Tell me about my brother!"

The giant bird chuckled, its sword-like beak parting.

For an instant, Khyven could see Rauvelos's straight black tongue. The bird unfurled his wings and launched into the air. Seconds later he vanished into the darkness overhead while Khyven stood alone in the eerie room. He looked for a way to get back up to the hole, to that tunnel, but there were no ladders, no stairway. Nothing. If there was another way to reach the room, it wasn't here.

For a moment, he considered searching the castle for Rauvelos.

No.

Against all odds, Khyven stood there, alive. That was enough. He wanted to be away from this place, out of this noktum.

Khyven turned and ran from the room.

Chapter Nineteen

KHYVEN

He exited the castle, ran across the vast courtyard to the crumbled gates, but he found no one waiting. Rhenn and her group had done exactly what she'd promised. They'd returned to the camp as quickly as possible. Khyven wasn't part of her band. He was just a spy who had now served a good purpose. He was expendable.

The Kyolars and the flying otters that had tracked them all to the nuraghi lingered nearby, but they stayed at a distance as though they recognized him.

Wear your amulet and my creatures will recognize you…

Khyven suddenly wondered if he should return to the Queen-in-Exile's camp at all. He had his amulet. He could travel the noktum at will. Why not go back to the Night Ring, fulfill his promise to Vamreth, show the king where the traitors lay?

An image came to his mind, of King Vamreth and his Knights of the Sun, the Dark, and the Steel pouring into the camp, slashing and killing. He imagined swords cutting Rhenn down as she fought like a wildcat.

He imagined swords piercing Lorelle's lithe body, her

blowgun clenched in a dying fist…

Khyven stood there for a long time, so long that he began to feel the darkness like a weight.

He took the path back to Rhenn's camp.

In minutes he saw the end of the makeshift path and the shimmer of the noktum's barrier—the entrance to the camp.

When he was only a hundred feet away, Rhenn and Lorelle emerged. Rhenn had Khyven's sword—the one he'd dropped when the bat grabbed him—thrust through her belt. She was shaking her head, and Lorelle looked angry, like they'd been arguing.

"… irresponsible!" Lorelle said. "Your amulet barely has half its time left. Without the large group, you have ten minutes, maybe."

"I'd say twenty," Rhenn said.

"Rhenn—"

"I'm not just going to just leave him there, Lorelle. We have to try."

"He is dead!" Lorelle exclaimed.

"You don't know that."

"Rhenn…" Lorelle began, exasperated. "People snatched by the noktum don't survive. That has *never* happened. You can't help him. You'll throw your life away in a futile attempt to try, and who does that serve?"

"I brought him into the noktum."

"We all knew the risks. That was our choice—"

"He didn't choose."

Lorelle clenched her fists in frustration. The edges of her hair began to shimmer, bringing color into the noktum for the first time. A buttery yellow light filled the gray air. "He was a spy for Vamreth! Who cares if—"

Both of them stopped talking at the same time.

Their heads jerked to the side as they spotted Khyven. He imagined he must have seemed like a ghost materializing out of the darkness. Rhenn's mouth hung open and Lorelle's large brown eyes were as wide as he'd ever seen them.

Lorelle stepped in front of Rhenn. Her blowgun came up.

"It's a changeling," she whispered.

Khyven held up his hands. "I'm no changeling. I'm just me…"

Rhenn put a gentle hand on the tip of Lorelle's blowgun, lowering it.

"What happened?" Rhenn asked.

"A lot. I… was snatched by a bat," he said. "But the amulet burned it. I… fought it." He showed them his puncture marks. "It left."

"Gohver said it took you up into the darkness. How did you get down?"

"It dropped me in a room. I beat it back with this…" He patted the wooden sword at his side. "I escaped into the castle, ran down and around. It's all a bit of a blur, actually," he said. He didn't mention Rauvelos. "Somehow, I managed to get back to that foyer and then through the front doors."

"They didn't chase you?" Lorelle asked.

He shrugged. "I guess once that bat-thing had been burned by my amulet it decided to leave me alone."

Rhenn's face broke into a little smile. "You beat that thing back with a wooden sword?"

"It's turning out to be handier than I would have guessed," he said.

"You may be the luckiest man I've ever seen," Rhenn said.

"I won't disagree with that." Khyven glanced over his shoulder in the direction of the Kyolars and bizarre, fanged otters. They'd stayed at a respectful distance up to now, but they were creeping closer, drawn by Rhenn and Lorelle. "You sure you want to stay out here talking about it?"

Rhenn clapped a hand on Khyven's arm. "You really are Khyven the Unkillable. To the camp then."

"Rhenn!" Lorelle objected.

Rhenn sighed. "A moment ago, you didn't want to go after him because he was dead. Now he's alive and you want to leave him in the noktum to die."

"He could be a changeling," Lorelle persisted.

"Have you ever seen a changeling?" Rhenn said.

"There are many—"

"Stories. I know. Have you ever seen a changeling? Seen it come out of the noktum?"

"There are many things about the noktum we don't know," Lorelle said.

"Have you ever seen a changeling?" Rhenn repeated flatly.

"No," Lorelle admitted.

"Then maybe we don't throw a life away because of a spooky children's story." Rhenn turned back to Khyven and pointed at his wounds. "We should tend those."

Khyven looked down at the blood spots on his sword arm and his side where the bat-thing had punctured him. "They're not as bad as they look."

Rhenn smiled. "Be that as it may, Lorelle's going to take a look at them. We've had a few people poisoned in the noktum and she's spent some time concocting antidotes. Some of them might even work."

Lorelle's hair had stopped glinting and she narrowed her eyes. She turned and went back through the wall of darkness, vanishing from sight.

Rhenn chuckled. "Don't mind her," she said. "She gets upset whenever I'm right."

"She thought I was dead."

"Everybody did."

"Not you," he said.

"It's my job to doubt the worst." She winked.

"You were actually going to come look for me in the nuraghi?" Khyven asked.

"Of course not." She scoffed. "That would be ridiculous. I was just trying to annoy Lorelle."

He watched her face. She returned his gaze with an enigmatic smile. "Come. Let's get you a drink...."

They went through the edge of the noktum and emerged into the sunlight of Rhenn's camp and her two knights fell in behind them. As they approached the camp, word of their arrival spread ahead of them. Vohn was the first to appear, looking at Khyven at least as suspiciously as Lorelle had.

"Vohn, would you mind grabbing a couple of ales for this ringer and me?" Rhenn asked.

"It's not even noon," Vohn said.

"Two ales, if you please, sir," Rhenn said.

"What happened?" Vohn pressed.

"That's what we're going to determine, but we'll need some ale." She turned and guided Khyven away from the growing crowd behind Vohn and toward her tent. With a frustrated frown, the little Shadowvar turned and headed downhill.

Rhenn led the way to the tent, pulled aside the flap, and ushered him inside. Her two guards took up positions inside. They both watched Khyven. He couldn't remember either of them talking, not even in the noktum.

"Have a seat," Rhenn said, indicating her rudimentary throne. There were four other chairs and a table at an angle off to the side, all presumably for Rhenn to hold her limited court, but she had clearly gestured toward the throne.

So, he went and sat down in it. He thought of Vamreth in his gilded throne above the Night Ring, or the tall, mahogany chair in the room behind the golden doors. The seats of power.

Even here, in this camp, a throne was power. The person who sat here commanded everyone outside the tent. Khyven tasted that power in his imagination, that ability to move others, as opposed to being the one being moved. The person sitting in this chair had no worries.

"Feels odd, doesn't it?" Rhenn asked, flopping into one of the other chairs and putting her feet up on the table. Her boots clomped, *thunk thunk*, on the wood.

Vohn ducked between the flap and the tent wall. The guards didn't even look at him.

He set two full, foamy mugs on the table. He looked annoyed, but he left without a word.

"Is he always angry?" Khyven asked.

"Everything is serious business to Vohn," Rhenn said. "He

cares deeply about everyone in this camp and he likes things in tidy little stacks and boxes. You don't fit on a stack or in a box. And he's mad at himself."

"Mad at himself?"

"He vouched for you, brought you here, then you turned out to be a spy. He probably hoped you'd die in the noktum."

"Oh."

"No." She chuckled and drank from her mug. "He didn't hope that. I'm joking. He looks demonic and talks tough, but Vohn has a soft heart. He's also one of the finest minds in Usara, but he's not a fighter. I'm not even sure he believes in bloodshed. He's probably been wrestling with the very notion of you, the danger he brought to my camp, and it's more frustrating for him since I decided to take you in."

"Why *did* you do that?" Khyven asked.

"I don't waste resources," she said.

"Right. My job."

"Exactly."

"You're an odd ruler," he said.

She laughed. "I'll take that as a compliment, considering the other ruler you know." She bowed at the waist, an interesting feat while she was sitting down.

"Orig, Chellit," she said to her guards. "Do me a favor, would you? Head down the hill and bring one of those kegs up here." She held up her mug. "This is good for a start, but we're going to need more. Grab one of the small ones."

The guard on the left, the stocky one, shook his head with his brows furrowed. He grunted and pointed at Khyven.

"No, he's not going to kill me," she said. "I'll be fine."

The knight looked disappointed and he didn't move.

"I tell you what, if he kills me, cut his arms off and throw him in the noktum without his amulet," she said. "Will that suffice?"

The knight still looked reluctant, then let out a breath and left the tent. The other knight followed.

"They don't talk?" Khyven said.

"Vamreth cut their tongues out," she said. "That's what you get for being loyal to Vamreth. They were henchmen. Not knights—not even butcher knights—but fighters. During one of their assignments for him they apparently saw something they shouldn't have. So Vamreth gave them a flowery speech about loyalty and sacrifice, then cut their tongues out so they could never tell anyone what they saw." She sipped her ale. "Magnanimous bastard, isn't he?"

"Couldn't they just write down what they'd seen?"

"*That's* your question?" she asked.

He shrugged.

"You don't stand on sentiment, do you?" she asked.

"Sentiment never saved my life," he said.

She watched him with narrowed eyes. "Ironic," she said. "It's saved mine time and again."

"Maybe it's different in the Night Ring," he said.

"Maybe it is," she said, then, a moment later, "Neither of them can write."

"The knights?"

"Yes."

Khyven glanced at the tent flap, then back at Rhenn. "If they can't write and they came here with their tongues cut out how do you know Vamreth gave them a flowery speech?"

She chuckled. "You don't miss much, do you?"

"So how do you know?"

"Vamreth isn't the only one with spies," she said.

So, Rhenn had one of her loyalists in Vamreth's court. She had a spy next to the king. He thought of all those close to the king and wondered who it might be. One of Vamreth's knights? Maybe even one of his elites? Someone who had sympathy for Rhenn's cause.

"You're full of surprises, aren't you?" Khyven said.

"Says the man who just escaped from certain death."

"Actually, escaping certain death is what a ringer does."

She chuckled. "Let us drink, Khyven the Unkillable, and you can tell me your story again."

He nodded and took a swig of ale. It was actually cool and it went down smoothly.

Lorelle gracefully sidestepped through the tent flap balancing a porcelain basin full of steaming water, several white rags draped over her arm, and a weathered leather bag in her hand. She stopped short when she saw Khyven sitting on Rhenn's throne. If her glare could have killed him, Khyven would have died on the spot. Lorelle shifted the glare to Rhenn, who raised her glass in salute.

"Get out of that chair," Lorelle said.

"She told me to sit here," he said.

"Get out of the chair or I'll leave that wound to fester and eat your irreverent heart." Lorelle set the bag on the table, pulled one chair on either side of the corner, and waited.

Khyven got up and sat where Lorelle wanted him to sit. "I think you like for her to hate me," he said to Rhenn. "You knew she wouldn't want me sitting there."

"I offered. You accepted," Rhenn said. "Every choice a person makes defines them."

"Is everything a test with you?" Khyven asked.

Rhenn just smiled.

"Strip off your tunic," Lorelle said.

Khyven did, gingerly avoiding his injuries, and laid it on the table.

Lorelle, her face again expressionless, cleaned his arm and his side with a white cloth and warm water from the basin. She treated both wounds with a salve that looked like green mud. Her hands were gentle. Everywhere she touched him, he felt a thrill.

The two mute knights returned with the keg and put it on the table next to Rhenn. She finished her mug and slammed it down. "Perfect timing, milords," she said. They took up their positions on either side of the flap, but she waved them away.

"You two may go have some lunch, if Basant is serving," she said. "If not, have an ale yourselves."

The knights hesitated.

"I have Lorelle. She'll protect me from the ravening ringer,"

Rhenn said.

Lorelle rolled her eyes, but she didn't say anything. Instead, she concentrated on the bandage she was wrapping around Khyven's middle.

After a moment's hesitation, the knights left the tent.

"So, there was a giant bat…" she prompted, filling her cup from the keg.

Khyven related the version of the tale he'd already told her. The bat grabbed him. He fought the bat for an untold number of minutes until it dropped him. He got up, shook himself off, and ran to catch up.

Rhenn asked some questions and he answered them. They both drank from their cups. Khyven, admittedly, wasn't much of a liar, but Rhenn seemed to buy the story.

Of course, Khyven thought as they downed mug after mug of ale, who wouldn't buy that tale? Or rather, who *would* buy the *actual* tale. A giant, malevolent raven decides to let Khyven go because of the inscription on the back of his amulet? Better to go with the bat story.

Once he finished, Rhenn told stories of her own, of the recent escapades of her band of rebels. Every time she refilled her mug, she offered the same to Khyven and he found himself struggling to keep up. She was barely more than half his weight, but the woman drank like a veteran seaman. She seemed to think she could outdrink him, so he picked up the gauntlet.

Little warning flags popped up in his mind. He really shouldn't be getting drunk with this woman, but he told himself he was succeeding in gaining Rhenn's trust. After all, she seemed far more interested in the next beer—in their drinking competition—than in anything else. And by Senji's Blond Braid, the woman could drink!

Lorelle also had a mug, but she barely sipped from it.

By the time he finished talking, Khyven was happily drunk. One of Rhenn's knights entered the tent and informed them that Basant and the cooks had finished preparing lunch.

"That's exactly what's needed," Rhenn stated, standing up.

He stood with her and found his legs were wobbly.

"Come, my friend." She put her arm around Khyven's waist to steady him. "Let's get some food down you." She guided him to the tent flap.

They descended the slope to the eating tables near the makeshift stage and the cook fires. When they arrived they drew a crowd. A few of the knights from the expedition clapped Khyven on the back. Soon, Gohver arrived, came over and shook Khyven's hand.

"Saved my life, this one," Gohver said. "That nokkie would have got me if this ringer hadn't drawn his sword and stepped into its path." His hand was warm—almost hot—as he gave Khyven a vigorous handshake.

Khyven didn't remember the attack that way at all. He hadn't been moving to save Gohver, but to protect himself. Gohver thought Khyven had saved his life. If Rhenn believed it, too, that could only serve him.

Khyven said to Rhenn, "Gohver pulls this artifact off the wall just before the bat arrived. A Giant's sword. It's as tall as he is, I swear."

"I saw it," Rhenn said. "Gohver's been playing with it since returning to camp. I'm surprised he left it in his tent to come say hello." She chucked him on the shoulder.

"In my hands, that sword could cut through a dozen o' the false king's men," Ghover said. "Best piece of magic we've pulled out of the noktum." He clapped Khyven on the back once more. "Eat up, ringer. You deserve it." Gohver headed back up the hill toward his tent, obviously bent on practicing more with his frightening sword.

Before long, the band began playing again and the day turned into a party just like the previous night. Rhenn's paramour showed up and she introduced him to Khyven. It turned out the handsome foreigner who had been following Rhenn around yesterday was Alfric, prince of Triada.

Prince Alfric seemed stiff and diffident as he shook Khyven's hand. It took Khyven all of two seconds to spot that the prince was jealous. Rhenn kept putting her arm around

Khyven as they talked and drank and laughed. Every time she did, Alfric stood a little straighter, but just when he looked like he was going to spin on his heel and stalk away, Rhenn reached up and grabbed hold of his tunic. He frowned and opened his mouth to protest and she pulled him into a long, sensuous kiss.

He blinked when she let him go and she patted the seat next to herself. The mollified prince sat. Without wasting a second, she turned to Khyven, kept talking, and motioned for someone to bring Prince Alfric a beer. He began drinking with them.

Every new thing Khyven discovered about Rhenn made him look at her in a different light. When he'd first arrived she'd been a tavern brawler. Later, a queen full of majesty and gravity. In the noktum, a leader, terse and efficient. Now she vacillated between all of these personalities, seemingly at random.

The day spun on. Khyven and the rest of the camp ate a succulent goat stew, full of chunks of sweet carrots and potatoes and served with a rough soft brown bread that was perfect for sopping up every last bit of stew in the wooden bowl.

After the meal, Rhenn pulled both Alfric and Khyven to the busy dancing ground in front of the stage. Khyven danced with partner after partner, including Rhenn for a short time. He even danced with one of the mute knights, both of them drunk and laughing.

But he did not dance with Lorelle. She did not join the throng, instead she sat watching, as she had done the night before. Khyven spun through partner after partner and kept telling himself he was going to visit Lorelle, challenge her to prove that Luminents were the best dancers on Noksonon.

Before he knew it, the sun was setting, spreading orange and yellow wings over the top of the noktum wall. He felt dizzy and wholly happy. He couldn't remember the last time he'd felt this way.

He stumbled away from the dance floor, made it all the way to the edge of the trees and collapsed against one of them.

He leaned his back against the trunk and watched the chaotic mélange of humanity. The dancers. The watchers. The people cheering and drinking and feasting. The cooks and servants clearing tables.

These people were so different than those in Usara, from the ringers in the cages to Vamreth's court. In Usara, it seemed everything was held in place by the mandate of the king, and woe be to those who stepped outside those designated lines.

Here, there were no lines. Rhenn's knights didn't wear plate mail. Many didn't even seem like knights. They were just part of the throng. There seemed to be no hierarchy to this camp, just as there seemed to be no order to Rhenn herself. She danced with whomever, and her subjects loved it. She kissed princes to whom she wasn't betrothed. She dove into the noktum when it suited her, began drinking in the morning and commanded an informal feast when it suited her.

He tried to imagine Vamreth dancing with his people in the great banquet hall at the palace. He couldn't even picture it.

For the first time, Khyven imagined himself as one of Rhenn's people. What would that be like?

He shook his head. It was a dangerous thought. Like ringers trusting nobles in Usara. Like the Night Ring masters and their insidious games of the mind. Rhenn had a job for him. She'd be as nice as required until he fulfilled that need. This was just her method of manipulation.

But since Khyven was here, he figured he could still appreciate the view.

His gaze settled on Lorelle, still sitting on a table at the edge of the dancers, watching them move and twist, grasp and release, whoop and laugh. Her faint smile, her golden hair, the delicate point of her ears cleaving through, the elegant slope of her neck… The woman lit a fire inside him and he couldn't look away—

He felt—more than heard—someone behind him, and he turned. Rhenn appeared from between the trees, as silent as the air itself.

"You like to sneak up on people," he said.

"Appreciating the dancers again?" Her eyes twinkled like she knew exactly what he'd been appreciating. She sat down next to him.

"I find her exquisite," he replied. Lorelle had turned and she was watching Rhenn and Khyven coolly across the distance. Lorelle always seemed to know where her queen was.

"She *is* exquisite," Rhenn said.

"And you keep setting me up to look like a fool in front of her," he said.

"You make your own choices, Khyven the Unkillable." Rhenn chuckled.

"So you're *not* trying to sabotage me."

Rhenn, who was in the middle of a long pull from her mug, tipped it back down with a little cough. "The opposite, my friend." She said around a mouthful of ale, then swallowed. "I've been helping you at every turn."

"Prove it."

"Ah, a dare," Rhenn said, wiping the back of her hand across her mouth.

"Tell me how to court her," he said.

"You mean bed her."

Khyven didn't answer, and Rhenn chuckled again.

"You know her better than anyone," Khyven said. "What can I do?"

"It's a tall order. A greater woman doesn't exist in all the kingdoms," Rhenn said.

"You tell me how and I'll do this thing for you, the thing you want me to do."

"Without even knowing what it is?" she asked.

"Yes."

"You're a brave man, Khyven. I like that. I really do."

"So, give me a real chance," he said.

"What makes you think you deserve a real chance with Lorelle?" she asked.

"Because I do."

"You *did* save Gohver's life today." She watched him with sly eyes. There was no way Rhenn could have seen what happened in that room, but her gaze seemed to say she knew Khyven hadn't defended Gohver today, only himself. He held her gaze and tried not to give the truth away.

"Very well," Rhenn finally said. "I'll give you advice."

"Thank you."

"My advice is this: don't pursue her. It isn't going to happen," she said.

"That's no advice."

"You will only set yourself up for failure." She raised her mug. "Your attempts would afford me more opportunities to laugh, but I must bid you to stop." She watched him and sipped.

"Why is it never going to happen?" he finally asked.

"There are many reasons," she said.

"I don't see why—"

"Have you ever kissed someone?" she asked.

"What?"

"Kissed someone," she repeated. "Anyone."

"Of course I have."

"She hasn't," Rhenn said.

He opened his mouth to retort, but nothing came out. He glanced at Lorelle, then back at Rhenn.

"That can't be true," he said.

"She hasn't flirted," Rhenn said. "Hasn't had a fling, and she won't until she chooses a mate. It's the difference between Luminents and Humans. She can't afford to do what we do."

"What do we do?"

She nodded at the dancing throng. "That, down there, the abandon. The casual way we throw our emotions about. You could go down there and flirt with whomever you wanted. Any of us could, and they could flirt back. You could dance with them, kiss them, bed them. Lorelle cannot."

"Is chastity a Luminent custom?" he asked. He'd heard the Sandrunners were fanatical about chaste brides. Women who lost their virginity before marriage were relegated to a lower caste in Sandrunner society, rag women or prostitutes.

Rhenn took a long gulp, wiped her mouth with her sleeve and shook her head. "Not a chastity thing. A physical thing. A… magical thing."

"Magic?"

"Luminents are magical beings, created by the Giants long

ago."

"The Giants created an entire race...." Khyven said in a dull tone. He didn't believe that for a second.

"Many of them."

"You don't believe that," Khyven said. "The gods created the races."

Rhenn laughed. "You're a strange man, Khyven. You just spent the morning in the noktum. You saw those skeletons. Who did you think were the masters of that nuraghi?"

"Maybe Giants did exist, and maybe they lived in that castle, but they didn't create people. Only Grina and Lotura and Senji—only the gods can do that."

"Mmmm," she said, taking another sip.

"What magic does she do?" Khyven asked, wanting to direct the conversation away from tall tales about godlike Giants and back to the point at hand.

"She doesn't *do* magic. She *is* magic," Rhenn said. "Did you know she weighs less than I do?"

"You're drunk," Khyven said, realizing this was another one of her pranks. Lorelle was nearly Khyven's height. Rhenn was a foot shorter. "That's not possible."

"I *am* drunk," Rhenn said. "And it *is* possible. She weighs less than a hundred pounds. Yet she's still as strong as you or me." Rhenn hiccuped. "Well, me anyway. That's a Luminent."

He thought about how Lorelle always seemed like she was floating. Her movements so graceful and controlled.

"Best dancers on Noksonon..." he murmured.

"What?" Rhenn asked.

"She said Luminents are the best dancers on Noksonon."

"Oh, they are." Rhenn nodded. "It's breathtaking to watch them. Their leaps... Well, let me just say that when you watch a Luminent dance, you fully understand the difference between them and us."

"That's why Lorelle always looks like she's half-floating."

"She could jump straight into this tree and grab that sixth branch. Right there." Rhenn squinted and pointed a finger at the limb. "And she could clamber the rest of the way like a squirrel."

He leaned to the left and squinted up at the branch. It had to be twelve feet above him.

"She also has a natural immunity to the noktum," Rhenn said. "She's gone in without an amulet and the nokkies didn't kill her. Part of why the Giants created them, I would wager."

"I thought I saw her hair… When you two were arguing as I returned, I thought I saw it… glow. I told myself I was imagining things."

"No that's real. When she gets upset, that sometimes happens."

"So, you're saying this Luminent celibacy is magical like her hair?"

"I'm getting there." Rhenn took another drink, looked at him sideways. "Are you this impatient in your Night Ring fights, ringer?"

"Usually."

She chuckled. "Some of her magical abilities help her and some hurt her. As I mentioned, Humans can dally with who they like. Kiss and change their minds. Philander about. They can be—well, as chaotic and twisted up as we are. Luminents cannot. They can't be chaotic. After a Luminent comes of age, after their bodies mature, their emotions reach out to others, much like the tendrils of the noktum. Luminents have a powerful physical need to bond with another. If she isn't careful, if Lorelle's emotions get too powerful, they could overwhelm her, and she would reach out to someone—a Human, even—she could bond by accident."

"What's so bad about that?"

"This isn't some starry-eyed infatuation, Khyven, a fling for fun. A Luminent's emotional outreach is permanent. When one Luminent bonds with another, she gives away half of her soul. The core of her reaches out and weaves into another person, binding them together forever. Half of her soul; half of herself."

Khyven glanced back at Lorelle, who was still watching them.

Rhenn took another swig. "Which is, I gather, exquisitely

pleasurable… if she gives herself to someone who gives half of their soul back to her. I hear a successful Luminent bonding is so joyous it's beyond Human comprehension."

"That doesn't sound bad," Khyven said.

"Not bad at all. But the problem is this: if she bonds with someone who does not—or cannot—bond with her in return, she *loses* half her soul. It goes with them or floats up into the sky or something. She loses it. It's gone, and the best parts of her go with it. Most Luminents of a failed bonding commit suicide. They simply cannot bear living with only half a soul. Those who don't commit suicide don't live for long. They slowly become weak, prone to sickness. Most die within a year after a failed bonding."

Khyven didn't say anything. He glanced at Lorelle.

"A Luminent cannot bond with a Human," Rhenn said.

"But you said she could—"

"The bonding *can* happen, but it would destroy the Luminent. Most likely, anyway. A Luminent can bond with the Human, but it's highly unlikely the Human could bond back. Humans cannot reach the level of commitment required. If your positions were reversed, would you give half your soul away?"

"Well, I…"

Rhenn chuckled. "Honestly, Khyven, how could you commit to Lorelle when there are so many other beautiful women out there? Imagine this, if she did bond with you, she could feel every infidelity in your heart. There are no secrets between the Soul-bonded. I know my own kind when I see one, Khyven, and you're a philanderer. You see something you want and you go after it. I imagine that, once you have it, you grow bored and look for your next target."

He glared at her, but he wondered if she was right.

She held up her hands in a pacifying gesture. "Easy. As I said, I am no better. I couldn't muster that kind of commitment. Let's face it, we're Human. We want what we want." She shrugged. "I told her when you first arrived that you were smitten. You know what she said to me? I believe her exact words were 'He wants to rut with me because I'm exotic.' Be honest, tell me she's wrong."

Khyven looked at the grass. "She's wrong," he said.

"You're a bad liar."

"Maybe *you're* wrong."

"Maybe I am. Are you willing to bet her life on it?" she asked. "I think the answer to that question answers all the questions."

He fell silent.

"You asked for my advice, Khyven, and my best advice is don't pursue her. At best, it will frustrate you. At worst, you could kill her. If you somehow managed to win her affections, she would ultimately pay the price."

Khyven ripped a bit of grass from the ground, tossed it. He ripped another bit, tossed it.

"I can see you're not going to listen to me," Rhenn said. "Since I'm being honest and all, I'll say one last thing: it's going to be fun watching you try. You're handsome and charming, but those are thin arrows against a castle wall. She's not going to let you in. So, when you fail, remember I told you so. Remember *why* I'm laughing at you."

"I like it when people underestimate me," Khyven said, ripping up another tuft of grass and tossing it.

"You like to conquer things. Go forth. Conquer." Rhenn picked up her mug, looked at its empty bottom, then set it back down with a sigh. "It will be fun. For me, anyway."

Khyven went silent.

"Well..." Rhenn slapped her thighs and stood up. "A fine talk, this, but we have a long journey tomorrow. Best get some rest."

"Journey?"

"It's time for you to serve your purpose."

"Which is?"

"I thought it didn't matter. I thought you were in for all, Khyven the Brave. Khyven the Impetuous. Khyven the Lovesick."

Rhenn left him sitting there and he turned his gaze back to

Lorelle. Once Rhenn stood up, though, the Luminent turned her attention back to the dancers.

Khyven watched her for a long time before wandering away to find a good place to pass out.

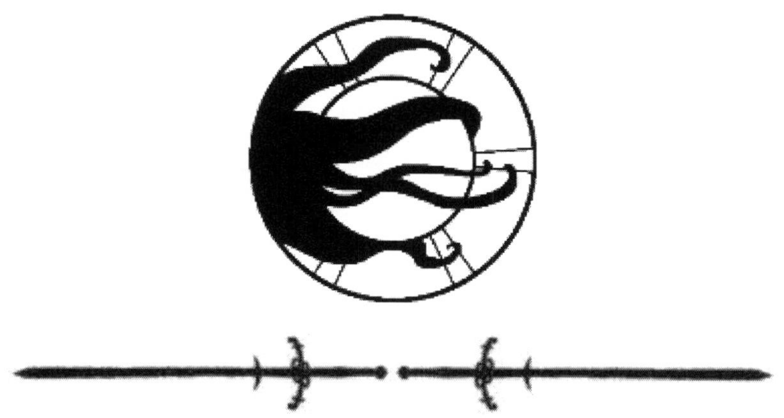

CHAPTER TWENTY

KHYVEN

A scream pierced the morning.

Khyven sat bolt upright on his pallet so fast he fell sideways. He hit the ground and felt like someone had struck him in the head with a hammer.

"Ugh," he muttered. The hammer hit again, and then again, and then again.

A second scream pealed through the air and Khyven blinked his gummy eyes. *Senji's Boots, what's happening?*

Everyone around him had also awoken. They were scrambling toward the sound of the noise.

Instinctively, Khyven reached for his sword, then realized he didn't have one. They'd taken it from him when he'd returned from the noktum.

Voices filled the air. People near Khyven murmured, and louder voices came from the direction of the scream.

Basant the cook waddled up the hill past Khyven, a cleaver gripped in his thick hand.

"What's happening?" Khyven muttered, standing up.

"Don't know," Basant said. "Nokkie come through, maybe?"

Despite his pounding headache and the nearly overwhelming urge to vomit, Khyven held down his bile and kept pace with the cook.

"That ever happened before?" Khyven asked, and his pounding head told him in no uncertain terms that he needed to stop speaking.

"Not since I been here," Basant said.

In the thin, yellow morning light that poured over the rim of the noktum, the entire camp was clustered around something.

Another few steps and Khyven almost vomited. His stomach sloshed about like a ship in a storm, and that damned hammer kept tapping, lightly asking him if he could just lay down and die quietly.

He wrenched his faculties together for the moment and assessed what was happening. There was no anticipation in the faces of the crowd, only revulsion. There was no movement among the people, only a stunned quiet. Whatever the crowd was looking at, it wasn't a fight.

This was something else.

"Make way!" someone shouted, and Khyven turned. One of Rhenn's knights motioned with his hands that everyone should back away. Behind the two knights, Rhenn strode forward, already dressed in traveling leathers with a red cape fluttering behind her. She didn't look any worse for wear for having drunk Khyven under the table last night. Lorelle followed close behind like a flowing wind, her blowgun already in hand. The crowd cleared away and revealed what they were gawking at.

It was Gohver. Or what was left of him.

He lay on his belly, one leg cocked up under him, one stretched out, one arm bent under him, one reaching forward, gripping that monstrous sword he'd taken from the noktum.

He'd obviously been trying to crawl somewhere. The fist around his prized sword was grossly deformed, like a sheep's bladder that had been stuffed full of rice. The grisly, bubbled flesh continued up his arm, culminating in a giant tumor of flesh on his shoulder. The growth pressed into his head where it had fallen against the grass.

His face was covered with the same sickly bubbles. The left side of his body had fared better, but it still showed similar signs.

Rhenn stood before the body with a furrowed brow. She hesitated only a moment. "Who found him?"

"Me, Your Majesty," an old woman came forward, wringing her hands. Her eyes were wide, chin high. It looked like she might scream again. "It's a sign from the gods. We's not meant to live inside these walls. We's not meant—"

"Enough," Rhenn said. Basant guided the old woman gently away. "Where is Vohn?"

No one answered.

Rhenn raised her voice. "Someone find Vohn—"

"I'm here, You're Majesty," Vohn called, running toward them from the other side of the group, a pair of spectacles perched on his flat nose. The crowd parted. It was obvious Vohn had just come from the cluster of small tents where Rhenn's high level advisors and knights slept.

"What is this?" Rhenn said.

Out of breath, Vohn held up a book. "That's…" he huffed, "that's what I went to find out."

"Did something attack—"

"Rrrgghfllth!" Gohver said, pushing himself over onto his back.

Curses, gasps, and shouts went up in the crowd as they leapt away.

The big man's eyes were swollen shut. Red strips of flesh sloughed away from his face. His lips were so swollen and peeled that he couldn't form words, though he tried. "Thhhfl… sssrrrrkk."

"Lorelle, get your kit," Rhenn commanded.

Lorelle spun and darted into the trees like a deer, a blur in the morning light. Despite everything Rhenn had told Khyven about Luminents, he was astonished at how fast she moved.

Rhenn strode toward Gohver, but Khyven leapt forward and caught her shoulder. Both of her knights shouted, drew their swords, and pointed them at Khyven.

"Don't," Khyven said, shaking his head at Rhenn. "Don't

touch him."

Rhenn frowned at Khyven, but after a moment, she nodded. She held up a pacifying hand to her knights and they lowered their swords.

"Talk to me, Vohn," Rhenn said.

The little Shadowvar's horns glowed in the morning light as he thumbed through the huge tome in his hand. He nodded, adjusted his spectacles, but didn't answer the queen.

"Vohn…" Rhenn warned.

"The sword," he said. "It has to be something about the sword."

"What about the sword?" she asked.

"It's magic. I just figured—"

"Mavric iron," Khyven said suddenly. "Look for Mavric iron."

Rhenn looked at him sharply. "What is Mavric iron?"

"Something… I heard of," Khyven said, remembering Rauvelos's words.

A sword of Mavric iron is worth a dozen Humans, yet I shall let it go for one….

Vohn grunted, his finger on something in the book as his eyes flicked back and forth, reading. A deathly quiet fell over the camp.

"Skkkgvvvsss," Gohver muttered. It seemed like his entire body was turning to mush. Khyven *really* wanted to vomit.

Then another thing the giant raven had said came to his mind.

Your friend can keep the blade for the rest of his short life….

At the time, Khyven had been so concerned with his own life that he hadn't understood the implication, that Gohver didn't have long to live because he'd taken the sword. But now, as he stared at the wreck of Gohver's body, that's exactly what it sounded like.

Lorelle arrived, carrying her satchel. She immediately moved toward Gohver, but Rhenn blocked her with a hand, shook her head.

"Wait," Rhenn said.

"He's dying."

"Yes, and we don't know why. You touch him, it might be you next. This is Giant magic. Give Vohn a moment."

"I have it," Vohn said, glancing at Khyven with a disbelieving expression. "Khyven is… Well, I think he's right. It's Mavric iron."

"What is Mavric iron?" Rhenn asked evenly.

"It's… well, there isn't much about it in here," Vohn said. "But it's…"

"Vohn!" Rhenn prompted, clearly annoyed.

"It's deadly to Humans. That's… That's what it seems based on the text. Mavric iron can only be wielded by Giants. If a Human wields it… If they wield it, they don't for long. Hours, maybe, and then… this."

"Is it contagious?"

"I…" Vohn looked at text, then back at Rhenn. "It just says that if a Human touches the metal, the magical properties in the metal will… It will take a Human body apart. It says something in a very old language. I think it means melt. I could be wrong."

"What does it say about healing someone who touches it?" Lorelle asked.

"Wait," Rhenn told Lorelle.

"Rhenn," the Luminent said impatiently.

Rhenn shook her head.

"At least let me try," Lorelle said.

"Not while he's holding that sword."

The crowd gave even more room to the deformed Gohver as they understood that proximity to the sword was the danger.

Rhenn started forward, but Khyven touched her shoulder and said, "I'll do it."

"This isn't a sword fight," Rhenn said.

"I beg to differ." Khyven winked and started forward.

Rhenn whipped the red cape from her shoulders, wadded it up and flung it to him. He snatched it out of the air.

"Don't touch it, Khyven the Brave. Wrap it," she said.

He nodded and approached Gohver carefully.

Gohver made a guttural noise that vibrated his ruined lips. Khyven winced, knelt next to the sword, and threw the cape over the blade. Taking a deep breath, he bunched the cloth and pulled the sword from Gohver's swollen fist. Loose flesh and muscle tore free as the hilt came away. Khyven fought back the bile that rose in his throat.

Finally, he hefted the swaddled sword. The damned thing weighed as much as a willow switch and was warm to the touch.

Senji's Spear! What is this thing? "Out of my way," Khyven said to the crowd. They leapt out of his path as he strode toward the wall of the noktum. He broke into a run and when he reached it, he locked his stance and hurled the sword and cape into the darkness with all of his might. It vanished the moment it hit the edge of the noktum.

Breathing hard, Khyven stared down at his hands. They were warm, and a trickle of fear ran up his back. But the warmth faded as he walked back to where Gohver lay. Lorelle already had her kit open and a vial in hand.

"Drink this," she said softly to the dying man.

"Ffffkkklllttt," Gohver managed. Lorelle parted his swollen lips and poured the liquid in. Gohver coughed, and the distended parts of his body moved, shivering in sickening ways.

"We need to get him to a tent," Lorelle said. "I need privacy. And good light."

"Take him to mine," Rhenn said.

"No," Lorelle said firmly. "We'll go to Gohver's tent. He has a table. We put him on the table, and I can work on him properly."

No one moved to pick up Gohver.

"I'll help carry him," Khyven said, stepping forward.

"Should have kept that cloak," Vohn muttered as he joined Khyven.

Rhenn started toward him, but her two knights leapt in front of her and took up one side of Gohver's body while Khyven and Vohn took the other. Together, they brought Gohver to his tent. Khyven cleared the clutter of plates and cups on the table with a quick sweep of his arm, and they set him on it.

Lorelle followed, set her satchel on the table. "Thank you, gentlemen," she said. "Now please leave."

Everyone looked to Rhenn, and she nodded.

"You too, Your Majesty," Lorelle said.

"I'm staying with you," Rhenn said.

Lorelle shook her head. "You aren't. We barely have any information on Mavric iron. As far as we know, it actually is contagious."

"Then you cannot stay here either," Rhenn said.

Lorelle locked gazes with the queen. "We must take risks sometimes."

Rhenn cocked her head and frowned.

"Whatever did this to him is now inside his body. If one of us is to join Gohver in his fate, let it be only one. Go, Your Majesty."

Rhenn clenched her jaw.

"I will tell you if I can stop what's happening," Lorelle said.

Rhenn opened her mouth, shut it. She turned and gestured for everyone to follow her out of the tent.

The crowd had migrated to outside the tent, so Rhenn ordered everyone to return to their tasks. Then she, her two knights, Vohn, and Khyven waited while the sun climbed slowly into the sky.

Khyven couldn't remember ever feeling this awful. His head pounded, his stomach was sick, and he was aghast at what had become of Gohver. The man's great prize had been his undoing, and what a grisly end. Khyven couldn't imagine a more horrible fate.

The sky lightened, and finally the sun topped the edge of the noktum, bringing full daylight to the somber camp. Lorelle emerged from the tent, and her hair shimmered with a light of its own.

"He is dead," she said softly. "I tried… many things. Nothing worked."

Her hands were covered in pus and gore. Tears stood in her

eyes, but her voice was steady.

"A basin with water," Rhenn ordered. One of the knights ran down the slope and shouted orders below. A dozen people rushed to obey.

Rhenn approached Lorelle, but she shook her head. "Please wait, Your Majesty. Let me get clean."

Rhenn paused, then nodded. "It's going to be all right," she said quietly.

Lorelle didn't respond. She just swallowed, holding her hands in front of herself, and fixed her eyes on the horizon.

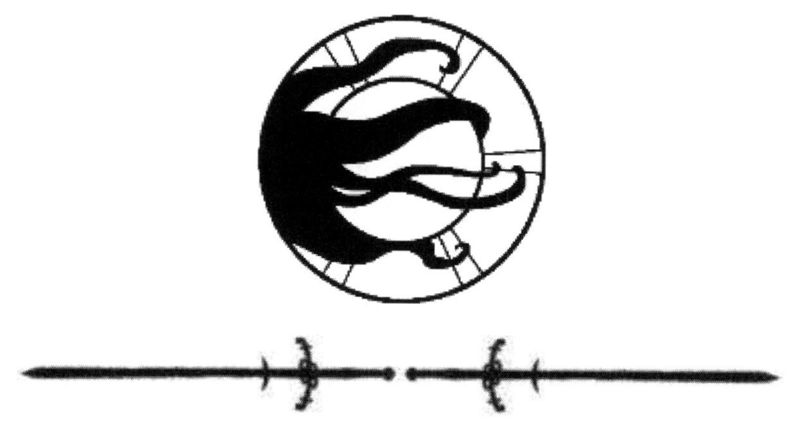

Chapter Twenty-One

KHYVEN

With heavy hearts, they buried Gohver that afternoon at the farthest edge of the camp. There were a dozen other graves there, most marked with wooden markers, some with crude headstones.

Everyone attended, and for the rest of the afternoon and night the camp was quiet. Khyven spent the time alone, and when it was time to sleep, he went to bed without speaking to anyone.

The next morning, the camp awoke as though it was just another day. Rhenn emerged from her tent, this time with a blue cape draped around her shoulders, and began organizing a group of people for the journey they would have taken the day before, if not for Gohver. The chosen few hustled about the camp, saddling horses and loading supplies.

When the dozen men and women Rhenn had chosen were ready, they exited the hidden camp by using four of the raven totems. Fixed atop staves, Rhenn's knights approached the wall of the noktum, staff-point first, and the noktum rippled and bent away from the totems.

As it turned out, the noktum on one side of the camp was

only a dozen feet thick. Of course, it was impossible to tell that until the knights marched into it, staves held high. The noktum bent away from their advance and soon opened into the rest of the normal, daylight-drenched land.

The knights held their positions as Rhenn and two-dozen of her closest advisors and fighters rode out with her. It looked like those who entered and left the noktum camp this way did so at a different point along the wall each time. A half dozen people followed them out and immediately began hiding their passage by roughing up the dirt and wiping away all tracks. Once on the other side, the knights backed into the camp and the wall slithered forward. Once the totems were back inside, the noktum reasserted itself until it reformed, tentacles reaching out lazily, and there was nothing to show a camp existed behind it.

A vanguard preceded the queen; scouts had been sent out a half hour earlier to ensure none of Vamreth's hunters were close by. Lorelle and Vohn rode on either side of Rhenn and four guards encircled the trio.

They rode for fifteen minutes before they came to a small road—barely more than a goat path—and clopped onto it. The road ran roughly north-south, and Rhenn turned her band south.

"Spare the horses for now," Rhenn commanded. "We can walk. If we need to run, I want them rested."

"Yes, Your Majesty," Lord Harpinjur said. He was a ruddy-faced man with white hair, a bulbous nose, and a long, thick mustache. The Baron of Harpinjur was well into his fifties, but he was still a fit, muscled man. Khyven had heard stories of Harpinjur's prowess with a blade even before he'd come to Rhenn's camp, and the baron seemed to be one of Rhenn's top advisors. Khyven had seen him approach her a couple of times inside the noktum, but now that they were outside, he stayed close to her, almost as though he'd appointed himself her personal bodyguard.

Khyven rode near the back of the group while trying to master his mount, and it wasn't going well. The horse kept wanting to crop the tasty-looking grass, and Khyven had to fight to keep the beast going forward while making sure he didn't fall out of the saddle.

Khyven's equestrian education was rudimentary at best. The old man had given him a few lessons. He knew how a bridle worked. Pull the reins left and the horse was supposed to go left. Pull them right, and they were supposed to go right. But there seemed to be more to it than that. It wasn't like wielding a sword, where if one understood one's own balance and the balance of the sword, the two merged together in a dance that gave Khyven full control.

The horse had a mind of its own, and making it do things was more like making demands of a reluctant child. Sometimes the horse did what Khyven wanted and sometimes it didn't. At an easy walk, like right now, he could make the horse go in the right direction, but if a cadre of Vamreth's knights were to burst out of the woods, Khyven would have to leap to the ground in order to fight. Sword fighting from horseback would be a disaster.

"Got the gist of it yet, Khyven the Unkillable?" Rhenn asked.

He glanced up and saw her twisted halfway around in her saddle, easily managing the reins though she wasn't even looking where she was going.

"I don't think he likes me," Khyven said, yanking the reins again to keep the horse from going off the path.

"That's a mare," Rhenn said.

"A what?"

"It's not a 'he.'"

Khyven frowned. "I don't think *she* likes me," he said.

"Maybe she's met you before." Rhenn chuckled.

"Funny," he said, pulling hard upward to keep the horse from cropping at a thatch of grass.

"I find it interesting how you can be so good at some things and so bad at others." Rhenn beckoned with two fingers. "Come up here, we have to talk."

He kicked his heels into the flanks of the horse and it jerked forward reluctantly. Once he pulled up alongside Rhenn on the right-hand side, the horse kept pace with her, thankfully. Lorelle, riding on Rhenn's left, merely glanced at Khyven before turning her gaze back to the road.

"How did you know about the Mavric iron?" Rhenn asked.

Khyven had known this moment would come. There was no earthly reason for him to have known something that Vohn, with all his books and education, didn't know. He'd prepared his lie. He didn't want to tell Rhenn about his past, his time with the old man, his adopted brothers, and Nhevaz, but after thinking it through, he'd come to the conclusion that he'd rather talk about that than the giant raven.

"My… mentor mentioned it to me," he said reluctantly.

Rhenn's eyes narrowed. "The old man. The one Vex the Victorious killed."

"Yes, the old man."

"But you didn't think to tell Gohver to leave the sword?" Rhenn asked.

"I did tell him to leave it. He ignored me. Then I got grabbed by a big bat."

"But you didn't warn him when you returned to the camp."

"I didn't know it would do that."

"Then why did you tell Vohn to look for that in his book?"

"Because the old man said Mavric iron was a Giant's metal," Khyven lied. "We were in a Giant's castle. It made sense."

"But the danger—"

"Look, the old man talked about Taur-Els and Luminents and Shadowvar, too. I didn't believe in them until I tumbled into this group. Did I think maybe Gohver's sword was Mavric iron when he grabbed it? Yes. Did I have any idea what it would do to him? No."

Rhenn watched him, as though she sensed something was off about his tale, but she also seemed to sense he was telling the truth, too.

They rode in silence. Finally, as though they hadn't talked about Gohver at all, Rhenn spoke in a cheery tone.

"So, what do you know about the Sandrunners?"

"Sandrunners?" He hesitated at the abrupt change in conversation. "Same as everyone, I suppose. They live in the desert somewhere south, past the sea. Savage primitives. They ride pamants instead of horses. They, uh, they can hide in the sand really well, I heard...." He shrugged.

She chuckled. "First, they're not primitive. They're just specialized."

"They live in tents."

"*We* live in tents," Rhenn said.

Khyven spread his hands as if to say "See?"

"You're funny," Rhenn said. "They're nomads. They move with the sandstorms. You can't build a castle in the desert. Sandstorms would wipe them out."

"Which is why you shouldn't choose to live in the desert, seems to me."

"Open your mind, Khyven. If you go in there thinking they're primitive, you're going to underestimate them. And they'll kill you for it."

"This is the job you were talking about."

"I want you to fight their Champion of the Sun."

Supposedly, every kingdom on Noksonon had their singular champion. Most were called the Champion of Night because, according to Usaran theology, back in the beginnings of Human civilization, the gods had declared that each kingdom must have a champion to stand against the darkness.

In the holy books of Senji, there was talk of the Day of Eternal Night, a cataclysm where the forces of good and evil would clash in an epic battle, or something like that. Whatever, the priests of Senji said that the fate of humankind would be decided at that time and every kingdom's Champion of Night would rise, join forces, and defeat the evil that would seek to destroy humanity.

So, every kingdom was supposed to have a Champion of Night, and that one person was supposed to be the greatest fighter in the kingdom.

Except most kingdoms, like Usara, saw the Champion of

Night as an irrelevant, religious throwback, a ceremonial title. In Usara, the Champion of Night was Sir Ohvan Verigund, first among the Knights of the Dark. The holy texts said the Champion of Night was supposed to be the best fighter in the realm, but while Sir Ohvan was a respectable fighter, there were at least a half dozen others who were better. The Knights of the Sun, for starters. And, of course, there was Vex the Victorious. Only the devout saw Sir Ohvan as anything more than a half-decent swordsman.

Other kingdoms took the old edict of the gods seriously, like Triada. The Triadan Champion of Night, Sir Staaven Ector, was not only hailed as the finest blade in the land, but in all the northern kingdoms. Khyven had often wondered what a fight between Vex and Sir Staaven would look like.

The Sandrunners, though they weren't exactly a kingdom, also had a champion, but they called him the Champion of the Sun. The Sandrunners, as far as Khyven knew, didn't have castes of knights like the other kingdoms. Their fighters were called Lantzas and their Champion of the Sun was a Lantza named Txomin.

In the Night Ring, great fighters were often a topic of conversation among the old hands and Txomin was a name Khyven had heard before. He was reputed to be a fearsome fighter, but Khyven didn't know much beyond that.

"You want me to fight Txomin?" he asked.

"The Sandrunner culture has many flaws, but—"

"Like the fact that their women are slaves?" Lorelle said without looking at them.

Rhenn gave Lorelle a brief frown. "Their women aren't slaves."

"Except they are," Lorelle insisted.

"They have a male dominant society," Rhenn said to Khyven. "But—"

"And Rhenn wants to throw herself at their mercy."

"But," Rhenn emphasized, "their rigid rules may work in our favor this time. They are driven by tradition, duty, and religion. If we play precisely by their laws and religious doctrine, we may

be able to get what we need."

"Which is?" Khyven asked.

"An army," Rhenn said.

"They have an army?"

"I need three hundred of their Lantzas to fight for me," she said. "Three hundred would be enough for my plan."

"Three hundred… Why would they give you even *one* Lantza, let alone three hundred?" Khyven glanced incredulously at Lorelle. The Luminent didn't make eye contact, but her frown indicated she agreed with Khyven.

"No," Rhenn said. "They would never give a *woman* three hundred Lantzas."

"They wouldn't give *anyone* three hundred Lantzas. What ruler would give away his fighters?"

"He wouldn't. That's why you're going to become their Burzagi."

"Their what?"

"Their leader. Their Zagi of Zagis."

"*I'm* going to do that?" he said. "Become the king of the Sandrunners."

"You're going to do that."

"How am I going to do that?"

"Well, I'm glad you asked that, Khyven the Unkillable," Rhenn said. "You're going to challenge for leadership at the Burzagi Tor."

"The what?"

"They're not going to let you," Lorelle interjected.

"They *are* going to let me," Rhenn said. "Or they'll let him, rather."

Lorelle shook her head.

"The Sandrunner scriptures are clear," Rhenn said. "Any man can challenge for leadership at the Burzagi Tor, once every year on the day of Highsun, if they're willing to pay the price for failure."

"Death," Khyven said.

"Yes. But if the challenger defeats the Champion of the Sun, he becomes the Burzagi or chooses the Burzagi to sit on the Sandrunner throne."

"You want me to risk my life for a scheme that your sister-in-arms over there doesn't think will work?" Khyven asked.

"Do this for Usara and our slate is clean," Rhenn said.

"For Usara?" he said. Despite what Rhenn might like to believe, she was not Queen of Usara.

Rhenn held his gaze, seemingly daring him to say it.

"No," Khyven said.

"You won't do it?" Rhenn replied. Lorelle and several others, including Lord Harpinjur, turned to look at Khyven. Lord Harpinjur's hand shifted from his reins to the pommel of his sword. If Khyven had ever doubted he was a prisoner here, it was suddenly glaringly obvious.

"Not for nothing, anyway," Khyven amended.

Rhenn's wry smile curved her lips. "And what is it you want?"

"Make me a knight," he said.

Lord Harpinjur scoffed. Even Lorelle raised her eyebrows a little.

"You wish to be a knight?" Rhenn said.

"For my fiftieth bout in the Night Ring, I was to be made a knight. Vamreth told me to spy on you and reveal your camp's location, but instead you caught me. Now you want me to go into possibly my toughest bout yet. Interestingly—if we don't count our little scuffle, Your Majesty—this would be my fiftieth bout. Seems to me the reward should be the same."

"You are no knight, ringer," Lord Harpinjur said in his gravelly voice.

"Not yet," Khyven said.

"You," Lord Harpinjur said, "don't have the heart of a knight. A true knight serves his queen. He does not barter for—"

"It's a deal," Rhenn interrupted the baron. "You want to be a knight? I will make you a knight."

"A Knight of the Sun," he said.

"Unthinkable!" Lord Harpinjur spluttered.

"I will make you a Knight of the Steel," Rhenn said. "You may earn your merits within that order and, if appropriate, advance to the next."

"I think winning your kingdom back for you earns quite a few merits."

"You insolent cur!" Lord Harpinjur spluttered. Riders at the front of the column turned in their saddles. "You're a blackguard and a swindler. This is your queen—"

"King Vamreth would say otherwise," Khyven said.

Lord Harpinjur's sword leapt out its sheath and Khyven pulled his horse to a stop just out of Harpinjur's range. He put a hand on the pommel of his sword but didn't draw. He didn't need the blue wind to size up Harpinjur. The fight would be over as soon as it began. The old man had been a great swordsman once, but Khyven could carve him up. Once Khyven drew, that's exactly what he would do.

Rhenn seemed to sense it, too, and her voice cracked like a whip.

"Enough!" she said. "Calm down."

"Your Majesty...." Lord Harpinjur glared at Khyven and spoke to Rhenn through his teeth, though he somehow managed to make it sound respectful. "Allow me to stand in for you. Bind this treasonous spy with rope and drag him behind his horse until he learns his place. I will rout the Sandrunner's champion for you and win what needs winning. You have no need of this cur."

"I cannot allow that, Lord Harpinjur," Rhenn said. "You are far too valuable to risk in this gambit. Not only do I need you to help bring the other nobles of Vamreth's court to me, but should Khyven fail, I will need you to spearhead our escape. He is my choice for this endeavor."

Lord Harpinjur sneered. That almost prompted Khyven to draw his blade, but then Harpinjur sheathed his sword with a clang.

"A wise move, my lord," Khyven said in a dark voice. "Draw on me again and—"

"Khyven!" Rhenn cut him off.

Lord Harpinjur bristled. The lord's hand twitched, ready to move toward his sword again. By this time, the entire troupe surrounded them.

Impatient, Rhenn signaled everyone to continue and she ordered Harpinjur to lead the way. Reluctantly, he did so. Once Khyven and Rhenn were riding together in the center of the procession again, relatively alone, she turned her gaze back to him.

"You shouldn't provoke him," Rhenn said.

"Me?" Khyven said, showing his teeth. He'd mostly regained his temper by then. The pompous Lord Harpinjur reminded Khyven of the old man, except Khyven didn't have any reason to listen to Harpinjur. He'd learned his lessons. He'd come through the fire, and he didn't need some old windbag telling him what kind of person he was.

"Yes, Your Majesty," he said flippantly.

"You realize if you fought him, you'd die," she said. "You're good, but you're surrounded by men and women who would kill for Lord Harpinjur."

"Or die for him," he said.

She chuckled. "Very well, Khyven. I will offer you this: If you succeed, I will make you a Knight of the Dark. You've proven already that you can swing a sword as well as any Knight of the Steel, and if you defeat the Sandrunner champion you'll have done a great service to the crown. But understand this: there's more to being a knight than feats of arms. A true knight has his queen's complete trust. When you earn that—and only then—you will have what you seek."

Khyven already knew what his answer was, but he let the silence stretch. Let her wait upon him. Let her understand what it felt like to have a need withheld.

"I accept," Khyven said.

"Good," Rhenn said. Her eyes twinkled, and that wry smile of hers played at the corners of her lips.

Khyven couldn't help smiling in return. He found it hard not to like Rhenn, despite her manipulations.

Rhenn turned her focus forward, and Khyven's gaze slipped

past her to Lorelle. He found she was watching him.

His heart beat faster. He wanted to say something, to try to tease out what Lorelle might be thinking, but he couldn't with Rhenn between them.

Lorelle looked forward again, and it was as though the moment had never happened.

Chapter Twenty-Two

KHYVEN

"We have to be careful," Rhenn said as they approached the Burzagi Tor. She adjusted the headband and the side veils attached to them that kept blowing in her face.

"Yes," Khyven said.

Flat desert stretched as far as the eye could see in every direction except before them. They'd been riding over sand on the back of pamants for three days. Earlier that day, the golden spike of the Burzagi Tor began to resolve against the horizon and the thing had just gotten larger and larger as they approached.

"So careful," Rhenn reiterated. "You have to remember everything we told you."

"I remember," Khyven said.

"You make even one mistake and it frees them from the customs."

"I remember that, too," he said.

"Because if you—"

"He has it," Lorelle interjected.

"He forgot the sequence of bows," Rhenn reminded them.

"That was two days ago," Lorelle said.

Rhenn didn't respond to that. They'd been drilling the nuances of Sandrunner ceremony, not to mention terminology, since they had begun this two-week journey. Khyven had learned the names of the Sandrunner Zagis and Burzagis, most of their prominent Lantzas, and some of their Jakintzus, which were the Sandrunner all-female caste of mages.

"It will be fine, Rhenn," Lorelle assured her.

The last week had been difficult. It had reminded Khyven of his grueling education under the stern eye of the old man. The Night Ring seemed simple by comparison. Of course, Khyven's life in the Night Ring had never been safe, but he had become better at it. Every bout he survived taught him how to better survive the next. This last year, the routine of the Night Ring had become normal, if never safe. He knew what he was doing every time he stepped into the arena.

With the old man—and with Rhenn's, Lorelle's, and Vohn's tutelage—every day had brought a new, unexpected trial. Every day had stretched the abilities of his mind rather than his body. They all had something to show him, and it started as soon as the sun came up and only finished after the sun had long gone to bed.

In the beginning, Lorelle had fought against the very idea of going to Burzagi Tor. Rhenn was the one full of confidence.

But sometime during the two-week journey, their roles had switched. Rhenn had gone from jaunty to serious to downright twitchy. Conversely, Lorelle had gone from skeptical to reassuring. At first, Khyven had assumed Lorelle was just trying to make her friend feel better, but the Luminent's confidence in the plan—and her compliments of Khyven—had grown so convincing that even Khyven had begun to believe her.

He liked that a lot.

They'd traveled south to the Hundred Mile Sea, then taken a ship across the waves to the Eternal Desert. At the edge of the desert, they had outfitted everyone in the group with Sandrunner attire, from sand cloaks to viper boots to Sandrunner headdresses for the women. All women were required to wear a headband with veils that covered the ears. Apparently Sandrunners considered a woman's exposed ears scandalous, a lascivious enticement.

Rhenn hated it. She'd been struggling with the thing for days. The headband fought her like it had a life of its own, refusing to stay in place around her unruly hair. Whenever the wind blew, the veils flew into her face. She growled a bit louder each time it happened.

The Burzagi Tor was a natural sandstone monolith in the midst of an oasis. Palm trees and vibrant green surrounded the jutting spire of gold.

"This isn't without precedent," Rhenn said. "In 1342, King Joran sent a champion to take control of the Sandrunner tribes. He ruled them for fifty years before he died."

"You told me that," Khyven said.

"I'm just saying—"

"He has it, Rhenn," Lorelle said softly, laying a hand on her friend as the pamants carried them ever closer to the Tor. She turned to look at Khyven and he thought he actually saw compassion in her eyes. "How do you feel, Khyven?"

He chuckled. "Are you worried for me?"

The compassionate look faded. "If you lose, they will kill you. Either way, I shall be happy."

He chuckled again.

No one spoke as the hot breeze blew across them and they swayed to the odd gait of the pamants. Khyven didn't like pamants any more than he liked horses, but he was getting better at riding. At least he no longer felt like he was going to fall off every other moment.

"You do not seem afraid," Lorelle said after a moment, her voice serious.

"This is what I do," he said.

She got that contemplative look she'd had when they'd first left Rhenn's camp. "I think he's ready, Rhenn."

Rhenn took a deep breath. "Of course he's ready," she said, but worry still creased her brow.

A gathering place had been created around the Burzagi Tor.

The wide, hard-packed road led right into the lush vegetation surrounding the Tor, and it was busy. Other Sandrunners pulled carts and rode pamants next to them, but because they were dressed like Sandrunners, no one paid them any attention.

Lord Harpinjur and two of Rhenn's knights led the way. Khyven came next, which was the traditional position of the Zagi of a tribe, with Rhenn, Lorelle, Vohn, and one of Rhenn's female knights riding together in the center, dressed in the billowing garb of Sandrunner women, while the rest of the retinue followed behind.

The thick jungle gave way to an immense, wide-open space. Water flowed around the Tor like a moat, and tents had been pitched everywhere except for a hundred-foot circle of gray stones placed around the towering spire of the Tor. Khyven had no idea where those Usaran-like stones could have come from. There wasn't a mountain for a hundred miles in any direction.

Sweat dribbled down his back and his ribs as he surveyed the scene. There were clearly five different camps; the clustered tents were of distinctly different colors. In one camp, the tents were red. In another, blue. A third was dark brown. A fourth, gray. The fifth was gold and appeared to be the largest group.

None of the colored tents mixed. There was at least a twenty-foot gap between each camp.

In the center of it all, of course, sat that stone ring and the Burzagi Tor. The thing was easily a hundred feet in diameter at its base and it towered toward the sky, taller even than the mighty spires of the nuraghi. It seemed impossible that it stayed up, and Khyven wondered if some eldritch force kept it upright.

Bright sunlight lit up the Tor like a spike of gold. The colored tents surrounding the ring were like servants bowing in supplication.

"Wow," Khyven said at the immensity of the place.

"Put away your amazement," Lord Harpinjur said. "You are supposed to be our Zagi."

Though Rhenn and Vohn had begun to treat Khyven as a friend over the past two weeks—even Lorelle had softened somewhat—Lord Harpinjur still looked at Khyven like a mangy cur.

The wide road led to a stone archway before the encampment. Three Jakintzus, the female holy women, stood before the arch in long, gold robes. As each group approached, they spread across the road into the camp and waited. The leader of each group dismounted from his pamant, walked forward, and performed obeisance to the Sandrunner gods, Grina and Lotura—a series of bows that ended in a descent to the knees and a pressing of the forehead against clasped hands.

When it was their turn, Khyven did as he'd been trained, hopping off his pamant, walking up to the Jakintzus, performing the hand motions that flowed into a bow that became kneeling and finally ending in a full obeisance.

All three Jakintzus touched him on the shoulders. He rose to his feet and the group passed into the environs of the Burzagi Tor.

They were going to set up their tents conspicuously away from every other group. They had taught Khyven that trying to assume a part of another tribe's camp would be a grave affront that would trigger an entire set of challenges and problems. They had purchased black tents—something no true Sandrunner would use on the baked Eternal Desert—to show immediately that they were outsiders.

They found a small spot away from the rest of the tribes, and as soon as they began erecting their tents, an audible buzz went through the entire camp. All the denizens of the Burzagi Tor seemed to notice them at once.

"Well, we're committed now," Khyven said.

"I'll find out what phase we are in," Lord Harpinjur said.

They had educated Khyven on how challenges were met. The fight for leadership at the Burzagi Tor lasted for five intense days. Contenders fought each other until only one remained. The final battle between the current Champion of the Sun and the top contender always occurred on the last day.

All of the Sandrunners gathered in this place, and all of the contenders put their names on the Jakintzu's list. The list could grow or shrink as anyone who wished could add—or subtract—their name from the list. This could go on for a long time. Some

Tor gatherings had lasted an entire month as the list grew and shrank. But the moment one of the contenders challenged another contender, the waiting was done, that's when the official five days began. From that point forward, while names could still be added to the list, none could be removed. If one's name was already on the list, that person had to fight to the death.

They finished setting up the camp, and Lord Harpinjur returned just as the last tent was being erected.

"Have the official five days started yet?" Rhenn asked.

When Lord Harpinjur answered, he didn't look at Rhenn, but instead faced Khyven, as they had practiced. If Lord Harpinjur showed any deference to Rhenn, that would be seen as disrespect to the Burzagi and the Sandrunner culture. It was one of the unspoken rules that, if broken, would put them outside Sandrunner law, therefore unable to avail themselves of Sandrunner law.

"We are in the fifth day," Lord Harpinjur said.

"The fifth!" Rhenn exclaimed.

They had almost missed it. That would have been disastrous. It would have made the entire trip for nothing.

Lord Harpinjur frowned at Rhenn's outburst and she quieted herself, bowed her head, and looked contrite. Her next words came out as a harsh whisper.

"The final fight is tonight?" she asked.

"That is correct," Lord Harpinjur said, still facing Khyven. "As the sun sets behind the Tor."

"We have to get him on the list. Did you sign him onto the list?"

"Not yet," Lord Harpinjur said. "The moment we put his name on the list, the top contender, a Lantza named Ferbasi, will challenge. He will want as much time to rest before his bout with Txomin, so he won't wait."

"So, the moment we sign up, he attacks?" Khyven asked.

"Yes, and once the challenge is made, you will be immediately escorted to the Sun Ring with the weapons you have," Lord Harpinjur said.

Khyven had learned the ring surrounding the Burzaghi Tor

was called the Sun Ring, a conspicuous counterpoint to the Night Ring in Usara. Khyven had spent a great deal of time wondering if there was actually some historical connection between the two places. They seemed to serve a similar purpose.

"I had hoped to give Khyven a night to rest," Rhenn said.

"That isn't going to happen," Lord Harpinjur said. "Frankly, the sooner he gets over there and signs up, the better. Ferbasi isn't wrong about wanting time between the bouts. It's already midday, so we only have six hours between the fights, at best. Khyven needs that time as badly as Ferbasi, assuming he wins."

"Assuming that," Khyven said drily. He wasn't sure if Lord Harpinjur actually wanted Khyven to win. "Let's go."

There was no point in pretending to be a Sandrunner anymore, so he took off the silly, billowing robe he'd been wearing. He also divested himself of any accoutrements he didn't need and left only his sword, his waist dagger, his boot dagger, and the wooden practice sword.

"Leave that thing," Lord Harpinjur said, nodding at the practice sword.

"I'll keep it," Khyven said. "Ever since I chose to use it, the most unlikely things have happened to me. I think it brings luck."

"It brings extra weight," Lord Harpinjur said, but he didn't say anything more.

"Where is the list?" Khyven asked.

Rhenn touched Khyven's elbow, and he paused.

She caught his glance and murmured, "Fortune."

"Fight well," Lorelle added. Vohn watched Khyven before nodding and turning away.

Khyven winked. "Be back in a moment."

Lorelle rolled her eyes and Rhenn grinned.

Lord Harpinjur led Khyven through the gathering throng of Sandrunners. Everyone wanted to see the newcomers. The crowd clustered close but didn't obstruct. In fact, they instinctively cleared a path all the way to the edge of the Sun Ring.

Lord Harpinjur stopped at a waist-high stone pillar with a

flat top. Behind it stood a stooped woman with ice blue eyes and white hair, another Jakintzu. Her gaze barely touched on Lord Harpinjur before settling on Khyven.

"Foreigners," she said.

"I have come to contend for leadership," Khyven said.

"Sign the scroll," another voice said.

Khyven turned and a big Sandrunner approached, as tall as Khyven was. The man wore a studded leather "X" over his well-defined chest, a studded leather headband around his forehead, the billowing pantaloons that most Sandrunner men wore, and no shoes. His black ponytail almost reached his waist and a longsword hung across his back, slanted so he could draw what looked like a hand-and-a-half sword over his left shoulder.

Khyven sized him up in a second. The man was probably about the same strength as Khyven, perhaps a little stronger, and it looked like he had about the same reach.

"You must be Ferbasi," Khyven said.

"I am Ferbasi the Slow, champion of the Ilunsenti," he said in a deep voice.

"The slow?"

The big man grinned, showing a gap between his long front teeth.

"Why do they call you Ferbasi the Slow?" Khyven asked.

"Sign your name, foreigner, and I will show you," Ferbasi said. "The sun will soon set and it will be the time for the Ilunsenti to rule."

Khyven looked at the Jakintzu woman. She slowly shook her head, as though warning him not to sign his name on the scroll.

"Very well," he said. He took the quill and signed "Khyven" and then, after a moment's hesitation, added "the Unkillable" next to it. No sooner had he set the quill down than Ferbasi the Slow touched Khyven's shoulder, so viper-quick that Khyven didn't have a chance to dodge.

"I challenge this foreigner," the Sandrunner said.

So, his name is ironic, Khyven thought. *Ferbasi the Slow is Ferbasi the Blindingly Fast.*

The Jakintzu raised her voice like a god speaking from the

clouds. Khyven was stunned at how well it carried, striking out across the gathered crowd like a shrieking whistle.

"Ferbasi the Slow challenges Khyven the Unkillable," she said. "The duel will take place immediately."

Ferbasi was already walking toward the Sun Ring, and Khyven followed.

"It is good of you to do this," Ferbasi said over his shoulder. "I was only able to fight one coward before today. My clan says it is bad for me to fight twice in one day, but I say no."

"Oh?" Khyven said conversationally.

"No," Ferbasi replied. "I say Txomin has defended his Zagi for too long."

Usually, the Lantza who won the challenge at the Tor became the Burzagi himself, but the Burzagi of the currently ruling clan, the Hareazko Clan, was not Txomin. Txomin was his champion only, which was allowed under the Sandrunner rules. Txomin had defended his Burzagi's throne for five years.

Shoulder to shoulder, Khyven and Ferbasi continued toward the Sun Ring.

"Five years is too long for a coward to rule the people of the wind, to rule those who value real strength," Ferbasi said loudly enough for all to hear. "And I say that two fights before I face Txomin is one more fight where he can see that I have come for him. He can see that he should be afraid."

"I see."

They entered the ring and the Jakintzu, who trailed behind them, closed a knee-high gate. She stepped onto the edge of the knee-high stone wall and raised her hands, announcing once again the battle that was about to take place.

"You are a foreigner," Ferbasi said. "You were unwise to come here, but I like you."

"Do you?" Khyven said.

"I will do you the favor of killing you quickly," he said. "I do not do this for everyone."

"Ah," Khyven said. "Ferbasi the Slow."

"Defeat quickly, kill slowly," Ferbasi said.

"Clever."

"It strikes the fear," he said.

"I see." Khyven slowly and deliberately drew the practice sword from his belt rather than his real blade.

Ferbasi raised his eyebrow.

Khyven smiled.

"Begin!" the Jakintzu shouted.

Ferbasi struck immediately. Like a lizard's tongue, his hand-and-a-half sword flicked out. If the Sandrunner hadn't given Khyven a glimpse of how fast he was just before the bout, Khyven might have been taken by surprise.

But the Sandrunner had tipped his hand, and Khyven had fought fighters who were faster than Ferbasi before. Speed could be beaten if a ringer stayed vigilant, flexible, and constantly in motion.

Khyven lunged forward at the strike, swaying to the side at the same time.

Ferbasi's blade missed him by an inch, whipping past Khyven's head. Ferbasi tried to drag the edge along Khyven's neck as he recovered from his lunge, but Khyven's wooden sword was already there, so the blade sliced harmlessly into wood.

Khyven pushed Ferbasi's blade away and backed up, still smiling. Ferbasi seemed surprised that Khyven wasn't dead. He'd obviously been confident that his first strike was going to be the only strike. His brows furrowed, and he looked again at Khyven's choice of weapons.

"You will throw your life away using that wooden sword," Ferbasi said.

"No," Khyven said. "When I defeat you. It will strike the fear."

Ferbasi's cocksure attitude became a frown. His eyes narrowed and he swung his steel blade back and forth so quickly it became a blur. He made a figure eight with it, slicing the air on either side of himself as he sidestepped, graceful as a cat, looking for his opening.

It was a magnificent show of control and grace, a distraction

Ferbasi had probably used before to capture an opponent's attention before a deadly strike.

Khyven's pulse began to race and the blue wind appeared. It flickered around Ferbasi, the barest hint of sky blue slowly deepening into a dark blue.

Two blue funnels appeared in Khyven's vision, one on the left side of Ferbasi's neck, and the other high on his belly. The blue lanced out at Khyven and he danced with it. The flat of the Sandrunner's blade clacked against Khyven's wooden sword as he parried, the steel coming so close to Khyven's neck that he felt it. He spun and gave a short push, sending the strike wide. He whipped his sword around in a tight circle and thrust for the funnel just below Ferbasi's ribs.

The tip of the wooden sword hit Ferbasi's bare flesh so hard it broke skin and nearly bent the Sandrunner in half. The air whooshed from his lungs and he stumbled backward.

Five funnels appeared around the Sandrunner like an explosion of flowers. Khyven struck the one at Ferbasi's left temple with all his strength. The *thunk* sounded throughout the Sun Ring. Khyven whipped his sword around and whacked at Ferbasi's right temple.

Ferbasi's head snapped left then right and he dropped like a stone.

He sprawled across the ground, limbs as limp as rags. His sword spun away, sliding to a rest against the golden spire of the Burzagi Tor. The man was unconscious, but Khyven leaned over him anyway, looking for movement. The Sandrunner's eyelids drooped, his eyes half-rolled up into his head.

The spectators went dead silent. There was no cheering, just an entire kingdom of slack-jawed nomads.

"Oh," Khyven said loudly. "Ferbasi the *Slow*... Now I understand."

He turned away from the defeated Sandrunner and made a point of not looking at anyone except the Jakintzu, who seemed as shocked as everyone else. Cultural protocol dictated that he make obeisance to her again before he did anything else, so he did. The hand motions. The bow. The kneeling. The head-to-clasped-hands gesture.

He stood and walked back to the entrance of the Sun Ring.

Lord Harpinjur was waiting for him and the baron looked thunderstruck. Neither of them spoke as Khyven preceded him—as the victorious leader of a Sandrunner Clan would—and they walked back to their black tents without a word.

He went straight into the largest tent, Harpinjur at his heels. Seconds later, Rhenn, Lorelle, and Vohn piled inside. Vohn's eyes were wide. Lorelle was actually smiling.

"By Senji's sword," Rhenn breathed. "That was…" She couldn't seem to find the word.

"Impressive," Lord Harpinjur supplied, but he looked troubled, like he'd expected Khyven to fail and wasn't sure what to think now.

"Impressive?" Rhenn said. "That was amazing! It was like you knew where he was going to strike before he did. Khyven, I—I don't know what to say." She shook her head in wonder. "Were you going easy on me when we fought?"

"I liked you better than I liked Ferbasi," he said.

"You need rest," Lorelle said.

"Or a drink," Khyven said.

Lorelle frowned.

"Or perhaps a kiss?" Khyven said. "For the hero of the hour?"

Harpinjur growled. Rhenn coughed, put her hand over her face, and tried to suppress her grin.

Lorelle's eyes went flinty. She turned and left the tent.

"I guess not." Khyven looked at Rhenn.

"You are a man who likes to live dangerously," Rhenn said.

"Well, I might die in a few hours. Do you think she'd kiss me if she knew?"

"Rest now," Rhenn said. "In all seriousness, Lorelle is right."

"Very well," Khyven said. Someone had laid down a bedroll in the big tent, but it was the only one. They only had five tents and sixteen people.

Lord Harpinjur slapped the flap aside as he left. Rhenn gave a mock bow. "You are the Zagi," she said, and backed out still bowing until she was gone and only Vohn remained.

He studied Khyven, much like he'd done the first time they'd met. His dark eyes glistened in his dark face. Khyven returned the gaze. He considered making a wry comment, but he held his tongue.

"Why are you doing this?" Vohn asked.

"For a kiss," Khyven answered. "Didn't you hear?"

"No." Vohn shook his head, and he seemed bothered. "You've upheld the pretense. Traveled across the desert. Why are you doing this?"

Khyven cocked his head. "I was—Well, Rhenn asked me."

"Is it just for power?" Vohn asked. "A knighthood? Is that what you really want? Why are you here?"

"The queen isn't keen on letting me go, in case you hadn't noticed. She's had me hemmed in from the day I arrived."

"Based on what I just saw you could have fought your way to freedom at any number of moments. Libur's Sparks, you could have left that day in the noktum, but you came back to the camp instead. Now you're risking your life for the queen when you could have returned to Vamreth and exposed her camp."

"Every man dies," Khyven said, echoing the Shadowvar's words from their first meeting. "Maybe I'm trying to save my soul."

Vohn's brow furrowed. "Every time I judge you, I turn out to be wrong." He went to the tent flap but stopped as he opened it and looked over his shoulder. "I want to believe in you, Khyven the Unkillable. I suppose by tomorrow, I'll know whether or not I was a fool."

He seemed about to say something more, but then left.

Khyven stood there, staring at the tent flap. The giddy lightness of his victory suddenly felt like a weight. It pulled down at the center of his gut. In the Night Ring, it had always been simple. Kill or be killed. Suddenly, none of what he was doing seemed simple.

Now, for the first time, he held someone else's dreams in his hands, not just his own, and Khyven wasn't sure he liked it.

He wasn't sure he liked it at all.

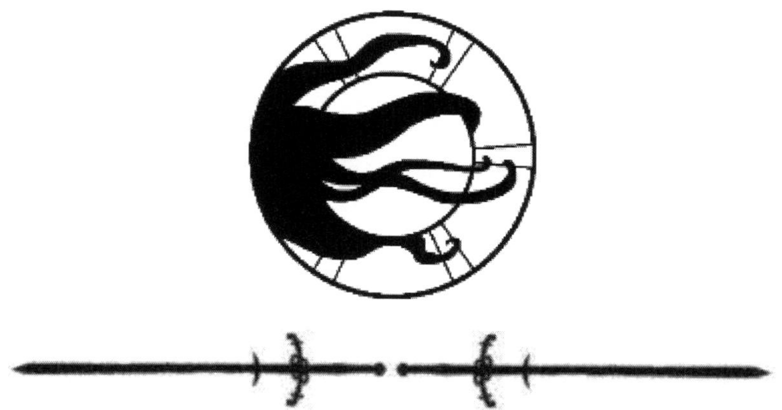

Chapter Twenty-Three

KHYVEN

hyven actually did lay down, and though his mind was filled with Vohn's question and the possible answers… he drifted into sleep.

He woke with a start, with Lorelle standing over him. He hadn't heard her come in. Khyven had trained himself for two years to wake from sleep if someone approached him.

He blinked and sat up.

"It's time," she said.

"Very well." He shook his head. Sweat plastered his hair to his head and was beaded all over his body. The tent had been a hot box. It was a wonder he'd been able to sleep at all.

"May I give you a gift?" she asked.

Khyven grinned. "Is this where I get my kiss?"

She frowned. "Stand up."

He stood up. "Are you going to poison me again?"

"The opposite, in fact."

"The opposite?"

"Sandrunners use poison," she said. "Quite often, in fact."

They hadn't taught him about that on their journey here, and

Khyven wondered if they'd kept it from him on purpose. "Poison isn't allowed in the Night Ring."

"Well, it is allowed in the Sun Ring," she said. "It comes from living with snakes, I suspect."

"And you're going to give me the antidote?"

"*An* antidote," she said. "There are a dozen venomous snakes in the Eternal Desert and even more poisons derived from them. I cannot possibly know what Txomin might use, if anything, but I have put together a cocktail of the most likely."

"Is this where you stick me with another dart?"

A small smile flickered across her lips and she held forth a vial. "Just drink it."

He popped the cork and downed the liquid. It tasted like blood and metal.

He made a face. "That's awful."

"Just for you," she said and turned to leave.

"Lorelle."

She stopped and turned her glorious, depthless brown gaze upon him. His mind raced, looking for the perfect thing to say to her, but nothing came. Instead he just said, "Thank you."

"You are welcome." She hesitated, then left.

He emerged to a small crowd outside the tent. Not only were Rhenn, Lord Harpinjur, Vohn and the rest of Rhenn's retinue standing in a semi-circle, but a crowd of Sandrunners were clustered behind them. Apparently, everyone wanted to see the strange, foreign Zagi who had bested Ferbasi with a wooden sword.

Khyven cleared his throat. He was used to crowds staring at him, but somehow this was different, and he suspected it had something to do with the weight Vohn had put upon him. Khyven's life wasn't the only thing hanging on this fight. All of Rhenn's hopes—and the hopes of everyone who followed her—were as well.

He shook his head. He needed to cast off that feeling. He needed to focus.

"You look sweaty," Rhenn said.

"Nice choice on the black tents."

"Are you rested?" she asked.

"I'm ready."

"Good. Because Txomin is already in the ring, strolling around like he's gardening in the shadow of the Tor."

"Fear tactics," Khyven said.

"I know that. I just wanted to make sure you did," she said.

"Should you be talking to me like you're giving me orders?" He tipped his chin to the surrounding Sandrunners.

"My apologies, Zagi," she said deferentially. "Am I bothering you?"

"You've been bothering me ever since I arrived at your camp."

She chuckled and her wry smile faded to a soul-searching gaze. "Are you ready?"

"I'm ready. Let's get about it."

Rhenn bowed, as was Sandrunner protocol, and Khyven passed her. The entire throng parted for him, again creating an aisle straight to the Sun Ring.

Within, a single man paced the edge of the stones, just as Rhenn had described. Unlike Ferbasi, this man was notably smaller than Khyven, not even six feet tall, and slighter of build. Ferbasi, despite his size, had been a speed fighter, and Khyven could only guess how fast Txomin must be. The Sandrunner Champion of the Sun looked like he was seeking the perfect stone on the floor of the ring, strolling lazily with calm contemplation.

Lord Harpinjur approached Khyven, though the baron respectfully stayed back a pace.

"Take that silly wooden sword off, Khyven," he said.

"I was thinking about using it."

"No," Lord Harpinjur said.

"No?"

"Are you the best swordsman in Usara?"

A vision of Vex the Victorious stabbing Nhevaz in the back flashed through Khyven's mind. "I don't know."

"Well, Txomin is the best swordsman among the

Sandrunners. You got lucky with Ferbasi. Don't press it."

"Lucky?"

"Yes, damn it."

"Imagine how sweet the victory will be if the Sandrunner champion faces me with steel and I best him with a practice sword," Khyven said.

"You got their attention with Ferbasi. Leave it at that. If you pull a practice sword on their champion it will be seen as an insult. If you defeat him with it, that will be a mortal insult. They might not be able to bear it. It is possible they will throw their traditions and rules to the wind, swarm us, and kill us. This isn't the time to flaunt your skill. This is politics. You aren't just playing to a crowd in the Night Ring anymore. You're striking at the heart of an entire people. Show respect."

Khyven stopped just before the old Jakintzu, who once again stood at her stone podium, and he turned to face Lord Harpinjur. The entire crowd stopped around them.

"Thank you for your counsel, Wise Lord Harpinjur," Khyven said. "But how about we do this? You stay with the queen and do… whatever it is you do. I'll leave that job to you. You leave the fighting of the battles, the gaining of the Sandrunner throne, and the swordsmanship to me. Do we have a deal?"

Lord Harpinjur's face turned purple. His bushy white mustache quivered and Khyven saw a flash of the baron's teeth. For a moment, Khyven thought Harpinjur was going to spit vituperations, maybe even draw a dagger and attack, but the old knight turned abruptly and stalked away.

Khyven faced the Jakintzu and made obeisance, ending up on his knees. She nodded sagely and motioned to the entrance of the Sun Ring.

Txomin paused, looking up as though sensing Khyven's entrance. The champion was at the far side of the ring and he turned. He was a hundred feet away, but it seemed Khyven could see his eyes like they were standing a foot apart. Txomin had jet black hair, straight as an arrow and tied into a ponytail that went to his waist. His face was narrow, like an inverted triangle, and his eyes were little black diamonds.

Txomin bowed gracefully, straightened, and slowly drew his sword from the sheath across his back. The bright steel glimmered in the sun and Khyven estimated it was about the same length as Khyven's own steel blade, perhaps slightly shorter, but he had no doubt Txomin had the skill to ensure that blade went wherever he commanded it go.

They began walking toward each other and the center of the ring. The crowd went silent.

Khyven's heart raced and the blue wind appeared. It flickered at Txomin's feet, dancing like swirling dust. When he and Txomin were ten feet away, Khyven reached to his hip…

And drew the practice sword.

A murmur went through the crowd. Txomin smiled, coming closer. He was eight feet away now, close enough to strike. The blue wind swirled and lanced out at Khyven. He moved to the right—

—at the last second, the blue wind curved into his path, spearing toward his chest. With a cry, Khyven twisted, but instead of going into his chest, the wind blew through his left arm.

Txomin's blade came right behind it, slicing through Khyven's tunic and into his flesh. He gasped and stumbled away. Spears of blue wind sprouted from Txomin, surrounding Khyven, coming at him from every direction.

He had never seen anything like this before. The blue wind had always proceeded his opponent's strike. Sometimes there were two if Khyven's foe attempted a double strike, but he'd never seen more than two, and certainly never half a dozen blue spears launching at him.

He threw up his sword against the darkest blue and Txomin's bit into the wood a split second later, cracking the sword in half. Desperate, Khyven slugged Txomin in the face. The strike actually connected, though Txomin was already flinching away—

—like he knew it was coming.

The realization hit Khyven like a mallet. Txomin could see

the blue wind. He could see it just like Khyven.

Khyven took the brief moment while Txomin recoiled from the punch to leap back. He dropped the broken practice sword and drew steel. The blade rang against the scabbard as Khyven stared at Txomin in disbelief.

Txomin backed up and stalked Khyven in a lazy circle, seemingly happy to wait after his lightning-quick assault.

At Khyven's expression, Txomin smiled, his lips making a V on his angular face. "Did you think you were the only one, Khyven the Unkillable?"

"You can see the wind!" Khyven exclaimed.

"Wind? Is that how you see it?"

"A blue wind."

Txomin chuckled. "You don't even know what you're doing, do you? You barely comprehend it."

Memories of the old man and Nhevaz flashed through Khyven's mind. Their impatience, the constant lessons, and the relief when Khyven had finally seen the blue wind. A dozen questions filled Khyven's mind…

… and he was suddenly sure that was exactly what Txomin wanted, to take Khyven's mind off the fight. To make him doubt. To make him ponder things that didn't matter right now. He forced himself to focus.

If he can see the blue wind, then he can predict my moves just as I can predict his, he thought.

There would be no advantage for Khyven in this fight, just skill against skill.

Khyven had come to rely on the advantage of the blue wind. How could he…?

No!

He shook the doubts from his head and took hold of his shaken confidence. He had to be ready for Txomin's next assault. Khyven would just have to fight with the honest skill he'd earned over the last two years.

Txomin continued his lazy, distant circling as though he was waiting for something.

Waiting for something…

Khyven looked down at the blood on his sleeve. The cut on his arm wasn't deep, but it was deep enough for poison. He felt it then, a tingling in his limbs, and an illness, like something rotten was coiling inside his belly.

Khyven looked up from his wound to Txomin and the champion's smile confirmed Khyven's guess. Lorelle had been right. The only question was whether her antidote would keep him alive.

He had to end this fight now. He couldn't simply wait to see if Txomin had already won. If Lorelle's antidote didn't work, Khyven only had moments.

He started for Txomin and the champion slashed his sword back and forth, displaying his dexterity. Khyven concentrated on the blue wind, trying to see the funnels that would show him Txomin's vulnerabilities.

The funnels flickered at the man's wrist, then his shoulder, then his neck, but every time one appeared, it almost immediately faded. None stayed long enough for Khyven to even think of striking it.

Khyven's left eye suddenly went blurry. He blinked and it returned to normal. The poison!

With a roar, Khyven attacked. Txomin parried. A barrage of blue, swirling tentacles launched at Khyven, but he didn't watch them. He watched Txomin's eyes, the angle of his arm, the bend of his wrist, the balance of his feet.

Txomin's blade clanged off Khyven's, and he struck at a blue funnel that flickered at the champion's neck. Txomin's blade leapt up. Steel rang, turning Khyven's strike aside.

Khyven's eyesight flickered in his left eye again, then winked out. His depth perception vanished, and he could only see out of his right eye. He turned his head so that he could keep Txomin in full view.

Txomin saw the gesture, and his V-shaped grin reappeared. "We'll soon see just how unkillable you are," the Champion of the Sun said.

Khyven's right eye blurred, and he blinked it furiously. His sight came back.

His heart hammered. Despair crept over his scalp like oozing oil. A flash of memory of the old man came to him, the time he'd made Khyven fight with a blindfold.

"I can't see!" Khyven had complained.

"Someday, you may need to fight in the dark, Khyven, against someone who can see just fine. What will you do then? Will you complain to them that it isn't fair? No. You must use what you have and you must win regardless. You must trust yourself. Trust what you know."

The old man had beaten Khyven day after day with a wooden sword, coming at him while he was blindfolded. Khyven had never had so many bruises as during those final weeks before the old man's death.

It was just after the old man had abandoned the blindfold that Khyven had discovered the blue wind for the first time. The old man's attitude had changed that day, as though he'd been waiting for that exact revelation, as though that had been the entire point of his years of relentless training.

Khyven's right eye blurred again and then went completely dark. His eyesight was gone.

Instinctively, he backed up, sword in front of him. In his panic, he wanted to run, to flee the Sun Ring, to get away. He fought to control himself. He knew the moment he turned, Txomin would skewer him from behind. Even if, by some miracle, he could make it to the edge of the Sun Ring before Txomin reached him, the crowd would simply push him back. There was no help there.

Khyven's other senses sharpened. He felt the sand shift under his feet as he slowly shuffled backward. He felt the sweat on his neck, a droplet trickling down his spine. His fingers trembled where they gripped his sword. He heard the soft murmurs from the crowd as though they were whispering in his ear.

He was going to die.

This wasn't the old man training him. This was a superior foe with all the advantages stalking him.

"You must use what you have..."

What did he have? Txomin had the blue wind as well, and he had the power of sight while Khyven did not.

Khyven thought of his last fight against Nhevaz. The sole advantage he could find was Nhevaz's overconfidence. His certainty.

Txomin had that same certainty. Somehow, he knew about the blue wind, and he knew what his poison would do to Khyven. Txomin knew exactly what he was facing and he would have certainty about the outcome.

I have to give him exactly what he expects, Khyven thought. *My only advantage is knowing what he is likely to do.*

It was a gamble. If Khyven was wrong—if Txomin wasn't the arrogant sort—Khyven would die.

"You must use what you have…"

Khyven made his choice and then threw himself into the role. He didn't know how close Txomin was, but he had to lure him closer.

Khyven backed up, hunched, one hand up as though it could possibly ward off a sword. His other hand gripped his own blade. He tentatively swung it back and forth like the antennae of a bug. He intentionally stumbled uncertainly.

His heart hammered.

And then he saw the blue wind. Khyven was encased in pure darkness, but within his own mind he saw the blue wind swirl in the blackness. It swirled as though it was flowing around the form of a man, just as it did when Khyven could see, except the man was not there, just blackness.

The swirling blue approached him from the left.

Khyven let out a shaky breath and he let the blue wind be his eyes. The swirling figure crept closer. Slashes of blue flowed on its left and then its right. Khyven heard an appreciative murmur from the hundreds looking on. Txomin was playing to the crowd.

He must be swinging his sword about, putting on a show.

Khyven continued to back up, making sure he looked hesitant and scared, which wasn't difficult. He felt the poison working further, deeper into his body. His arms felt heavier and some of his stumbles were no longer staged.

What if he just waits it out? Khyven thought. *What if he—?*

The blue wind came for Khyven. Without being able to see the actual person standing in the center, it formed into a headless, tentacled monster, three swirls of blue reaching for Khyven.

Khyven focused on the wind, the shape, the intensity of it, and one of the tentacles darkened to a deeper blue.

Khyven pushed deeper, seeing… seeing…

A vague funnel swirled behind the tentacles, barely visible. A target. Not a great one. But the only one.

Txomin struck. The dark blue swirl lanced at Khyven, and Khyven lunged at it, pushing his sluggish body to twist at the last second. The other tentacles vanished as Txomin committed to the single strike…

… and missed.

Khyven felt the blade whisper past his side, almost touching, and the funnel became dark blue. Khyven thrust at it with all his strength.

His arm jolted as steel punched through flesh and bone. Txomin screamed. The blue wind flickered in Khyven's mind, recoiling. The blue tentacles drew back into a twitching mass.

Txomin gurgled and Khyven felt the man's body slide off his blade. He heard a ragged thud and the blue wind vanished altogether. Cries of anguish went up from one side of the crowd outside the ring.

Breathing hard, Khyven stood in absolute darkness. His arms felt so heavy he could barely hold them up. He wasn't done. He had to do what he came to do.

He turned toward the anguished cries, deducing they had most likely come from the Hareazko Clan, and therefore he should be facing the Burzagi of the Sandrunners.

"The Champion of the Sun is slain," he said, as Rhenn had trained him to say. "By the pact of Batasyn, I claim the right of Burzagi, to rule the Sandrunners for one year." He began turning, as though he could actually see the assemblage, and he projected his voice, recalling everything Rhenn had drilled into him over their journey. "My first command is this: Each clan will make ready fifty Lantzas. When your Lantzas are assembled, you will send them north to gather on the plains of Saffaht to await my further orders. Once there, you will know my will by the words of the one who carries this." He pulled the Amulet of Noksonon over his head and held it high. "The one who carries this will speak with my voice, and you will follow his—or her—directives."

A grumbling murmur went through the crowd.

Khyven held the amulet high and turned in a slow circle. It was like lifting a log to keep his arm up, and when it began to shake he quickly put the amulet over his head again.

"You have one month!" he said in his loudest, most commanding voice.

His leg twitched and he stumbled, then regained his balance. He suddenly realized that if he didn't leave the Sun Ring quickly, he might collapse here. That would not send a good message.

But without sight, he didn't know which way the exit was. He picked a direction and began walking, but his legs were failing. He'd have to—

"Your will be done, Burzagi Khyven," a deep, older voice shouted from behind him, louder than the others, and Khyven recognized Lord Harpinjur.

Gratefully, he turned toward the sound and walked that direction.

"Hail the new Burzagi!" Lord Harpinjur shouted again, off to Khyven's left. He realized he'd overshot and he corrected his course.

A few cheers went up at Harpinjur's statement and there was a low murmur of approval from other areas, but mostly the crowd remained silent.

Khyven kept walking and suddenly felt hands on his arms.

"Khyven," Rhenn whispered. "Khyven…"

The hands guided him forward, and he heard murmurs all around him.

"He's been poisoned," Lorelle said. "We have to get him to

the tent quickly. Can you walk faster, Khyven?"

"I can't see," he whispered. "I—I'm blind."

"You can't see?" Rhenn said. "Lor, what kind of poison does that?"

Lorelle cursed quietly under her breath.

"Quickly now," she said tersely.

They pushed Khyven faster. He rested his arms in their grips and moved his legs perfunctorily as they practically carried him. His legs felt like sacks of sand. He couldn't feel his feet.

"Khyven, you stay awake," Lorelle commanded softly. "Do you understand me? You have to stay awake."

He forced a smile. "I'll stay awake for a kiss," he said, his words slurring.

The grip on his arms tightened, and he realized he had stopped walking altogether.

"Khyven!" Lorelle said urgently.

He wished he could see her beautiful face, her big brown eyes, their edges crinkled in concern. He wished he knew which hands were hers, grasping his arms.

He wished…

Khyven was swirled away on a wash of black water, circling down and down.

And he knew no more.

Chapter Twenty-Four

KHYVEN

The next thing Khyven felt was a rocking, swaying sensation. His first thought was that he was in the tent at the Burzagi Tor and the poison was still coursing through his veins. But he felt cool, and the inside of the black tent in the Eternal Desert had been like standing inside a fireplace.

He blinked, and to his great delight his eyes didn't open to darkness. He saw blurred colors and blurred shadows. The tent had a window of some kind. There was a blurry square of light low and to his left.

He turned his head to the right, but he saw only darkness in that direction. He felt beneath him; a soft mattress, a wooden bed frame. He reached out and touched a wooden wall to his left. The bed was attached to the wall.

So, not a tent, a room.

He heard the scrape of wood against wood, like a chair scooting across the floor, and he turned toward the noise.

He heard a satisfied snuff of breath, but Khyven couldn't make anything out, just gray darkness. Then part of the darkness moved into the square of sunlight and two white horns flashed.

"Vohn!" Khyven said.

"Welcome back, Khyven," Vohn said. "You can see?"

"I—No. Not really. Just… light and some color. Everything is blurry."

Vohn chuckled. "Well then, I've been told to tell you that is a good sign. If you can see anything at all, that means Lorelle wasn't too late."

"Too late?"

"The poison Txomin used on you is progressive, according to her. Once it passes a certain point, there's nothing can be done. At best, the victim is debilitated for life, but if you recover even a bit of your eyesight, you'll recover it all eventually, as well as the rest of your faculties."

Khyven breathed a sigh of relief.

The white horns moved again, coming closer, and Khyven felt a small hand on his shoulder. "Impressive, ringer. I am not a lover of brutal combat, but even I thought what you did was something special. You won our queen what she needed."

The swaying of the ground continued.

"Where are we?" Khyven asked.

"On a ship on the Hundred Mile Sea."

"We're at sea? Already?"

"You've been unconscious for four days."

"Four days!" Khyven cut himself off.

"It was a very near thing, but Lorelle knows her craft. Maybe a handful of people in Usara know poison like she does. You're lucky." He shook his head, white horns bobbing this way and that. "But then, I think you probably know that."

"Where is she?"

"Well, I should probably tell her you are awake. They told me to alert them the moment you woke. Lorelle will be upset if I don't."

"Lorelle?"

"When it comes to reports about her patients, she's unforgiving. If I don't tell her that you've awakened, I'll get frosty stares for a week," Vohn said.

"Oh."

Vohn chuckled. "Hold tight. I'll go get them." His shadowy body moved through the light again and vanished, swallowed by the darkness. Khyven heard the door open and shut. He laid back and tried to make his eyes work correctly. The ship swayed and her timbers creaked. A lantern on an overhead hook squeaked.

Khyven had just decided it was time to sit up when he heard the thump of boots in the hall and the door opened.

"Khyven!" Rhenn's voice burst into the room. He heard her footfalls approach, but he didn't see her silhouette until she crossed the square of light. He squinted, trying to bring her into focus. He thought maybe his vision had improved a little. He could see her tumbling mass of brown hair, tied back in a messy ponytail. He could see the dark hollows where her eyes should be, a blur of flesh where her nose and cheeks would be, and a shadowy body beneath.

She sat down unceremoniously on the edge of the bed.

"You're the talk of the ship," she said.

"Am I?"

"The story of Khyven the Unkillable and the Sun Ring gets larger with every telling. You're a legend. That should please you."

He squinted, but he couldn't make Rhenn anything more than a brown-haired blur. He chuckled. "I wish I could see you better."

A hand alighted on Khyven's forehead like the flap of a butterfly's wing. He started.

"He still has a fever," Lorelle's husky voice said from above him. Khyven craned his neck, but while he felt her hand and could see her forearm, the rest of her vanished into the shadows behind him. He hadn't heard her footfalls, hadn't seen her cross the room.

"The poison is leaving his body," she said, "but he needs rest."

"I'm fine," Khyven said, trying to push himself upright. His arms felt like limp strips of leather and they shook. He couldn't get upright and thumped back against the soft bed. "I'll be all right in a second."

"I wasn't asking," Lorelle said. Something stung Khyven's neck.

"Hey!"

Rhenn chuckled. "You should be happy," she said. "That's three stabs now. She might be flirting with you."

"Damn it, Rhenn," Lorelle said.

Rhenn laughed. "Sleep, Khyven." Her voice warbled, and what little he could see of her began to blur even more as his eyes slid shut, but he felt her warm, rough hand when she clasped his wrist. "You did your job. You did it amazingly well. You've done me a great service and I won't forget it. You've earned your prize."

"Knight…" Khyven murmured, and his body felt as heavy as a stone, sinking into the soft mattress.

"A Knight of the Dark," Rhenn's voice swirled around him.

The next time Khyven opened his eyes, he could actually see. The morning after that, he was able to stand and dress himself. He made it onto the deck of the ship before Lorelle descended on him like the giant bat in the nuraghi. She made him go back down to his cabin, and then she gave Vohn—who was supposed to be watching Khyven—a scathing tongue-lashing.

But by the third day, Khyven felt more like himself and, no matter Lorelle's protests, he stood on the deck as the ship reached the northern shore of the Hundred Mile Sea.

They all disembarked and recovered the horses they had stabled in the town of Dhanere. It took them another six days to return to Rhenn's camp, avoiding the main roads to ensure they didn't run afoul of Vamreth's patrols.

By the time they rode through the thin veil of noktum separating Rhenn's camp from the rest of the lands, Khyven—under Lorelle's impassive ministrations—had fully recovered from the poison.

Rhenn had caught him up on everything that had happened while he was unconscious.

The Sandrunner symbols of power were a golden key and a golden headdress, and every new Burzagi kept them until the power changed from one clan to another. The Hareazko Burzagi had been reluctant to give them up, not only to a foreigner but to a man who had vanished—due to the poison—the moment he had won. Traditionally, the incoming Burzagi went through a ceremony in front of all the Sandrunner clans. Khyven had been unconscious, so Lord Harpinjur had held aloft his Amulet of Noksonon and stood in Khyven's stead. The Hareazko Clan had objected, but under the narrow-eyed scrutiny of the other four clans—none of which wanted the Hareazkos in power anymore—the transfer was made.

The moment Rhenn and her band returned, cries of celebration went up from those in the camp, followed quickly by whoops of victory as the tale of their success circulated.

In less than an hour, the cooking fires had been stoked and the ale kegs tapped. The celebration promptly began. Before Khyven knew it, he'd been handed a half dozen cups of ale, one after the other, everyone clapping him on the back and congratulating him.

Rhenn jumped atop a large table, scattering spoons and bowls of stew. Those sitting at the table laughed and scuttled back with what food and ale they could save.

"Khyven!" Rhenn shouted over the din of music, talking, and dancing. The music fell silent, the conversations hushed, and the dancers slowed to a stop.

"Khyven the Unkillable!" Rhenn called again, pointing at him. He approached the table. The Queen-in-Exile drew her sword and beckoned him.

Cautiously, he approached.

"Mount the table," she said, "and kneel, Champion of the Night Ring. Vanquisher of Txomin the Poisoner. Burzagi of the Sandrunner people!"

A resounding cheer went up and Rhenn grinned. She kicked a cup of ale from the table and pointed before her. "Mount the table and kneel," she repeated.

Khyven stepped onto the bench and then the table. He knelt and looked up at her.

"Your head, ringer," she said. "Bow your head."

"You're sure you won't lop it off on accident?" he asked.

She waved the sword drunkenly and chuckled. "I make no such promises. Bow your head!"

Laughing, he did so, and the flat of her sword lightly touched one shoulder then the other.

"Khyven the Unkillable," she said, and her jaunty tone became her solemn queen's voice. "I dub thee Sir Khyven, Knight of the Dark and Protector of Usara."

She tapped him on the shoulder one last time with her blade, then sheathed it.

"Rise, Sir Khyven," Rhenn said. "You have proven yourself worthy. A true asset to the crown."

Half a hundred "Huzzah's!" rose into the air. Khyven looked up and Rhenn smiled down at him. She seemed genuinely happy.

She leaned down, took his hands in hers, and pulled him to his feet.

"Thank you," she said, squeezed his fingers, and then she let them go. "Thank you," she whispered again, and hugged him.

He hesitated, then hugged her back.

She released him. "Now go. You have an adoring public to greet, dances to dance, and ale to drink. Celebrate, Khyven. Days like this do not come often. Enjoy it while you may."

He stepped down from the table, just tipsy enough that he landed off balance and stumbled. He'd attained what he'd wanted here. With his skill—and almost his life—he'd bought what was promised. He should be ecstatic, but the ring of his knighthood felt… less than he'd expected. He had expected some kind of change within himself, but he felt exactly the same.

The minstrels started up a lively tune and the crowd danced. He looked about for Lorelle, but he couldn't locate her.

He grabbed another full cup of ale from one of the many eager hands waiting to pass one to him, and he danced with whichever comely lass chose to take his hand. He danced and spun and drank until the sun went down.

As the moon rose, he staggered breathlessly away from the group, climbed the slope, and sat at his familiar tree. He looked over the gathered, happy people.

Rhenn's kingdom. Those people believed in her, believed in the fiction she had spun for them. That she was the Queen-in-Exile, destined to retake the throne.

Vamreth promised a fiction, too. That he cared about his underlings. But Vamreth actually *had* power. He had the palace, the city of Usara, the loyalty of the nobles and their scores of knights, not just a ragtag group hiding behind a thin veil of noktum.

Rhenn had Lord Harpinjur, Lorelle, the barest knowledge of the noktum, and a handful of jumped-up brawlers. At some point—probably soon—these two "kingdoms" would meet. Swords would clash. Blood would run, and that would be the end of this little party for all time.

When Khyven thought of Vamreth, he looked at those happy, ignorant dancers and saw only fools. He saw fools because he, too, had once been just like them, dancing along, thinking he lived amidst strength and certainty. The old man and Nhevaz had made him feel that way, like Rhenn made those people feel.

But Vamreth's knights had shown Khyven just how ignorant he'd been. They'd ended Khyven's foolishness with a dozen thrusts of the sword.

Power... Khyven thought. *It is the only thing that matters, the only thing in the world that ensures safety.*

Of course, Rhenn had hoped to manipulate Khyven into joining her band by enticing him to like her, her group, and to believe in her fiction.

And he *did* like her, but charisma couldn't stop a sword. It wouldn't save her from a man like Vamreth.

"So," Lorelle said from behind him.

Khyven started, then spotted her as she emerged from between the trees, silent as a moth.

"Senji's Sneaking Feet," he said. "Do you and Rhenn creep up on everyone like this?"

"Just you," she said, and gave the hint of a smile. Tonight, the beautiful Luminent wore a long, red summer dress, tight at the bosom, gathered at the waist, and flowing in folds down to her ankles. He'd never seen her wear a dress before.

She sat down next to him, put her bare feet precisely side-by-side, and laced her fingers around her bent knees.

"Tell me," she asked, "has the party lost its luster so soon?"

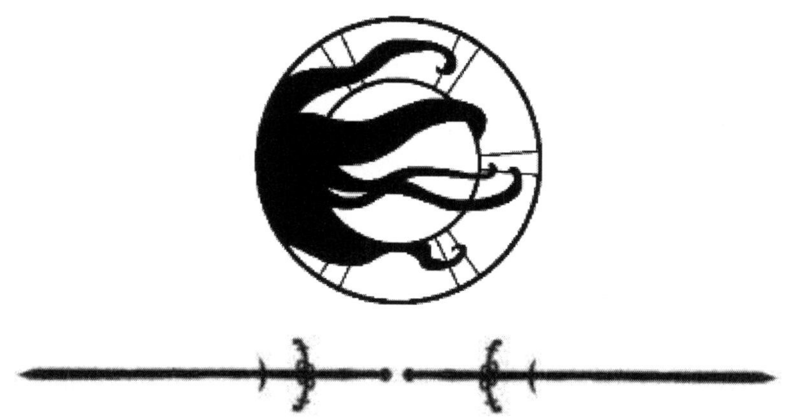

Chapter Twenty-Five

KHYVEN

Khyven tried not to stare. Every time he looked at her, she took his breath away. That dress…

He jerked his gaze back to the people.

"Are you one of those who becomes pensive when taken by drink?" Lorelle asked.

"I'm a ringer. We don't know what pensive means."

She smiled. "You are not a ringer anymore. You are a Knight of the Dark."

He almost said "Am I?" but he stopped himself. Instead, he nodded. The world wobbled a little. He cleared his throat. "You're wearing a dress."

She glanced down at her draped legs. Her eyes flew wide in mock surprise, and she gasped. "Lotura's Shadow, what has happened?"

He frowned.

Her exaggerated surprise softened and she cocked her head. "Is it so hard to believe I would wear the garment of a lady?"

"I've just never seen you wear a dress before," he said. "I thought you didn't like them."

"They are inconvenient for war, but tonight is a celebration," she said.

"There have been two other celebrations since I've been here."

"Ah, but there was a wolf in the house. One must keep one's wits about oneself when a wolf is near."

He couldn't tell if she was teasing him. "I see. And you are safe from me now, at long last?"

"I suppose only you can answer that," she said. "But I believe you've changed, Khyven. You were willing to sacrifice yourself for us—you almost did, in fact, and so, a dress. In celebration. Do you like it?"

"Very much," he said huskily.

"I even left my blowgun in my tent," she said.

"I noticed," he said, and he laughed. They both fell quiet. Lorelle turned to watch the dancers. Khyven kept watching her.

"You stare at them with such longing," he said.

She glanced at him, then glanced at her toes and let out a little breath. "Yes." And she almost sounded like he'd caught her doing something she shouldn't have.

"You get a little smile when you watch them," he said.

"I danced as a child."

"But no longer?"

She hesitated, then shook her head. "No."

"Why?"

"Because it isn't wise."

"Why?"

"I am… passionate about dancing. I could lose control."

"Of your emotions?"

Her smile receded into the impassive expression she usually wore. It felt like she'd closed an invisible door between them. She looked directly at him and the easiness had gone from her manner. "I came to say thank you, Khyven," she said solemnly. "For everything you have done for Rhenn and for her followers. The Burzagi Tor was a fool's errand. Impossible. At least I thought so, and I couldn't convince Rhenn to leave it alone. Yet somehow, you *made* it possible. I didn't believe it could be done until you did it. Watching you, your skill, your… sheer determination. Txomin sliced you, poisoned you, and you…" She looked at her bare toes again. "You prevailed. You gave Rhenn the chance she needed."

"I did what I promised."

"Yes," she said softly. "You did. And I…." She trailed off.

"You what?"

"It took me some time, but I believe I understand now."

He found himself leaning toward her. "What do you understand?" She was so close. She was wearing that red dress, and that soft tone to her voice…. Was she going to kiss him?

"Khyven," she said. "I discovered what kind of poison Txomin used on you. I know you were blind before you ever left the ring. You were blind when you stabbed him through the heart." She looked at him with her deep brown eyes. "You couldn't possibly have seen his attack coming."

"Oh…" he said, feeling disappointed. "Well, I was trained to fight in the dark."

"What you did requires more than training to fight in the dark. It requires magic," she said.

"Magic?" he said. Any hope that she might kiss him popped like a bubble.

She searched his gaze. "If you wish me to keep your secret, I won't tell. Well… I shall have to tell Rhenn, of course, but no one else need know."

"Lorelle, I'm not a mage—"

She touched his chin with her slender fingers, and his heart beat faster. "You are safe here Khyven," she whispered. "Whatever Vamreth did to you, it's over now. You're one of us, and we take care of our own."

"He didn't—" Khyven said. "I just don't know what you're talking about. I'm not a mage."

"Very well," she said, but he got the impression she thought his response was a desire to keep his secret. She let her hand slip away from his face, and he ached at its absence.

The blue wind *wasn't* magic. It was just a… state of mind, a fighting technique the old man had taught him. Part of him wanted to convince her, but part of him wanted to drop this conversation. He didn't want to talk about fighting. Not right now. He wanted….

He decided to steer it away from himself and toward Lorelle. "Tell me about Vamreth," he said.

Her eyebrows raised.

"You said I'm one of you," he pressed. "Because of what Vamreth has done to me. Why phrase it that way? What did he do to you? To Rhenn?"

"Everyone knows the story," she said.

"I don't."

"You couldn't have been younger than ten when Vamreth attacked the palace," she said.

"It's treason to talk about it," Khyven said. "I've never heard the story, certainly not from your side."

"But surely you remember."

"I don't remember anything from before I was eleven."

She cocked her head. "You don't?"

"I remember flames and screaming. I sometimes have nightmares, but there are no faces, none I recognize. I suspect something happened to my family. Something violent, but that is just a guess. It's possible I simply dream of flames and fire."

"Khyven, I'm sorry," she said.

He shrugged. "I don't remember it."

"But… your parents."

"I don't remember them, either."

She pressed her lips together and fell silent. "There are herbs…" she said finally.

"Herbs?"

"That restore memory. If you like, I might… Well, there could be a combination that would help you remember."

"My parents?"

"Possibly."

Hope rose within him like a bubble through sludge. He tried to shove it down. He didn't want to know about his parents.

Whatever had happened to them had happened because they didn't have the power to stop it. Digging up the past could only make Khyven weaker.

"Thank you," he said, smiling, "but it's best to let the past lie."

Her smooth brow wrinkled.

"And you didn't answer my question," he said. She'd deftly turned the conversation back to talking about him.

"About Rhenn and I?" she said.

"Yes."

"We were…" she began but trailed off. "It's… pretty much what you would think."

"I don't think anything. So far as I know, Vamreth was always king."

Her expression hardened. "He is *not* the rightful king. He assaulted the palace, took Rhenn's father and mother by surprise, and he killed them. He swept through the palace, slaughtered everyone loyal to the Laochodons. The blood—" She stopped, and the muscles in her jaw stood out. "If Rhenn and I hadn't already been planning to break our curfew that night, to sneak into a forbidden part of the palace, he'd have killed us, too."

"How did you escape?"

"There is a door to the noktum in the depths of the palace. We wanted to see it. That's why we were awake, dressed, prepared. That's why he didn't find us asleep in our beds. When he chased us, we went to that place, down a winding stair. When he cornered us in that room, we fled through the noktum."

"Without an amulet?"

She blinked as if to ward off tears though he didn't see any. She nodded. Breathing deeply, she put her palms flat on the grass. The tips of her hair glimmered in the dark.

"I'm sorry, Lorelle," he said. "You don't need to tell me."

She glanced at him gratefully. "It always gets to me. That and dancing." She chuckled. "For different reasons."

"I don't remember what happened to my parents," he said, "but I lost my brothers. I do remember that."

"Your brothers?"

"Adopted brothers. There was an old man who found me after… my parents, I suppose. It was me, a young man named Nhevaz, and two others my age. The old man took us all in, trained us in the use of weapons."

"Vamreth made training in swordsmanship treason for anyone not under his thumb. Where did you do this?"

"Not far from here. Close to the noktum, actually. In little wooden huts." He shrugged. "Vamreth found out about it. His knights killed the old man, killed my brothers."

"But not you?"

"I was hunting. I came late to the fight. I guess they thought they could simply take me without killing me." He shrugged. "And they were right. That's exactly what they did. They threw me into the Night Ring."

"Ah."

He nodded. "That's where I put to use everything the old man had taught me. I don't think that's where he planned for me to use it, but…."

"Was he like a father to you?" she asked.

"The old man?" He gave a rueful chuckle. "No. Or, not like the fathers I've heard of. He was demanding, inscrutable, unbending, even cruel. I suffered two broken bones under his training. I was knocked out more times than I could count."

"Oh, Khyven…. How old?"

"Eleven. All the way up to eighteen. He didn't spare me at any point."

"I'm sorry."

"But his teachings kept me alive in the Night Ring. It's what kept me alive against Txomin. In fact, I…" He trailed off and bowed his head.

"You what?"

He gave a rueful smile, knowing what it must sound like. "When I'm scared, with my back to the wall, about to die, I hear his voice in my head. His advice always sees me through. I… hate him, really. But I cling to his teachings at my most desperate moments."

"*You* get scared?"

He chuckled. "Hard to believe, I know."

"Is that what you seek, Khyven? To never be scared again?"

"I didn't say I get scared *often.*" He winked at her, once again wanting to turn the conversation away from him, but she kept her glorious, warm gaze on him expectantly.

He didn't say anything.

"The way you fight," she said. "It is unlike anyone else I've ever seen. You do not seem afraid at all. Even Rhenn, as carefree as she appears, gets a look of concentration on her face when she fights. But you… you drift away somewhere. You become that sword you're holding. I don't know how else describe it."

"Well… thank you," he said.

"You are welcome."

She hugged her knees, pushed her chin out, and closed her eyes like she was feeling a breeze. "You know what I dream about sometimes?" she asked quietly.

"Tell me."

"I dream of a large house before a green field. Trees swaying in a gentle breeze. Only my friends are there, all gathered in this one big house. Cooking for each other. Laughing with each other. Talking. Taking care of one another, and there are no swords or axes. No wars to win. No tyrants to fight. Just…" She trailed off. "Just living."

Her dream flowed through him like a warm wind, but such a thing wasn't possible, and he suspected she knew it as well as he did. There was no safety off in some gentle field somewhere. Even the old man, with all his wisdom and his hidden camp, had been found. He had fallen before Vamreth's knights.

No, the only safe place was at the top.

But he loved the look on her face as she spoke.

She opened her eyes and tilted her head against her knees to look at him. Her lips curved in the barest smile. "I think I should like to have met him."

"Who?"

"Your old man. Is that all you ever called him? Old man?"

He nodded.

"He didn't give you a name to use?"

"No."

"That seems odd."

"It wasn't the only odd thing about him."

"I should like to have met him. It would tell me a lot about you, I think."

He chuckled. "You wouldn't have liked meeting him. I'm sure of that," Khyven said. "He wasn't…"

"Wasn't what?"

He faced her, and his desire for her raced through his veins like fire. "He didn't appreciate beauty."

"Ah." Her brown eyes seemed so large.

"Lorelle…" he said, and he touched her cheek. Her skin was smooth. A thrill ran through him. He leaned toward her, brought his lips to hers—

Her fingers closed on his chin, stopped him. "Khyven, no." She pulled away, and a blush spread across her pale cheeks. The tips of her hair glinted in the darkness.

"Why?"

"You know why," she said.

"Do I?"

"Rhenn told you."

"She said Luminents and Humans rarely bond. She didn't say it was impossible."

"And that is what draws you."

"*You* draw me."

"Khyven, what you did at the Burzagi Tor was miraculous and I am grateful to you. I am intrigued by your story, by what you can do, and what it could mean for Rhenn. I would be your friend, if you allow me, but I cannot be more than that."

"The glow of your hair tells me different."

She raised an eyebrow, released his chin, and leaned back. "Do you even know what that glow is, what it means?"

"It's because of strong emotion—"

"It is called the Lueur, and even if you understood what it means, even if you *could* read it as you think you can, even if you and I were…." She shook her head. "It would not matter."

"Why not?"

"Because you are not a Luminent. You cannot give half your soul to me. Even if you could, you would still be a man of shifting loyalties, with eyes for beauty, as you say, tempted by whatever draws you."

"You speak like those are bad things."

"No, they are Human things. Your passions rule you. The needs of your heart change moment to moment, and one cannot build something permanent upon shifting sands."

"You're making assumptions."

She held his gaze and a small smile came to her lips. She touched his chin, kindly this time. "Come now, Khyven, be honest with me," she said. "In combat, you see clearer than anyone I've ever known, but here?" She tapped his chest over his heart.

"You've judged me that quickly, have you?"

"I do not think less of you. Look at Rhenn. She is a woman of many—and strong—appetites, and I adore her. But a Luminent Soulbond is—it isn't for Humans. Would you gamble your life in a fight by tying both hands behind your back? That is the kind of gamble a Luminent would take by attempting a Soulbond with even the most steady of Humans, and you are not the most steady of Humans."

"Maybe I could be," he said.

"*Maybe*," she said. "Such a key and telling word. Khyven, a Luminent Soulbond isn't a maybe, it is absolute. It would fill you with so much life, so much vitality, that in all likelihood it would spur your passions to an even more problematic height. You'd feel the need to rush around twice as fast, seek twice as many partners to kiss, fight twice as many fights." She shook her head. "No. I am not here to find a Human mate. I am here to guard my friend."

"Show me what to do, and I will do it."

"You cannot."

"They said I could not win fifty bouts in the Night Ring. They said I could not best Txomin."

"This is not a fight," she said. "And I…"

Whatever her next words might have been, she left them unspoken. For a fleeting moment, he thought he saw doubt on her face. She waved her hand at the dancers, their bodies moving in the firelight. "You are our hero tonight. If you are looking for companionship, you could have your pick of many."

"I don't want them."

"This"—she indicated her body with wave of her hand—"is a conquest for you." She gestured at the dancers again. "Take the prize you have earned, Knight of the Dark, and be satisfied. Go. Explore your Human feelings with a Human. Remember that I would be honored to be your friend, if you would allow it." She stood, and he grabbed her hand.

"What if I said I would forsake all others?" he said.

"What if saying it made it true?"

"I kept my promise to Rhenn. I will keep my promise to you."

She yanked her hand back. Her eyes flashed, and when she spoke, her voice was unbending. "I will be as clear with you as I can, Khyven: I would never attempt a Soulbond with you. You and I will never be lovers. Accept that and perhaps we can be friends." She moved into the darkness between the trees, her red dress swishing around her ankles.

He sat in the dark, his fists clenched. Finally, he stood up and stalked into the trees, the opposite direction Lorelle had gone. He walked until he found himself at the edge of the noktum at almost the exact spot he'd emerged the first time. He glanced about, but there were no knights assigned to guard him tonight.

He reached up, circled the edge of his amulet with one finger, and entered the noktum.

It took only moments before the Kyolars and the flying otters converged on him. They came close enough to sniff him, then they went away like they recognized his scent.

He almost wanted them to attack. His heart was twisted at Lorelle's unequivocal rejection. Combat would, at least, be a distraction from that, but apparently Rauvelos had been true to his word.

He walked east, found the edge of the noktum and pushed through into the darkened forest beyond Rhenn's camp. Even the tentacles—which lazily quested for living flesh at every part of the noktum except within Rhenn's camp—didn't try to reach for him.

Khyven couldn't stop picturing Lorelle in his mind's eye. Her graceful way of moving. The lightness of her. The thin, asymmetrical braids in her blond hair. Her deep brown eyes looking into his soul, and that flicker of light at the tips of her hair…

Still drunk, Khyven staggered through the forest. He didn't know where he was going until he reached edge of the forest and gazed upon the walls of Usara.

He stood there for a spellbound moment. It seemed there was a wall between Rhenn's camp and his old world, and he stood atop it. He'd been on the cusp of greatness within Vamreth's court, and he'd been welcomed by Rhenn's camp of dancers and drinkers.

"You're one of us now…"

"You and I will never be lovers."

He broke from the trees and walked toward the gates. The guards standing atop the wall saw him immediately and shouted down to their fellows, who turned.

Spears came to the ready.

Khyven marched up to the portcullis.

One of the guards behind the grate recognized him. "By Senji, that's Khyven the Unkillable!"

The second guard's eyes flew wide. Both stepped away like Khyven was a ghost. Their hands shook on the hafts of their spears.

"You died," the left-hand guard said.

"Tell King Vamreth that I have returned," Khyven said. "And I have what he wants."

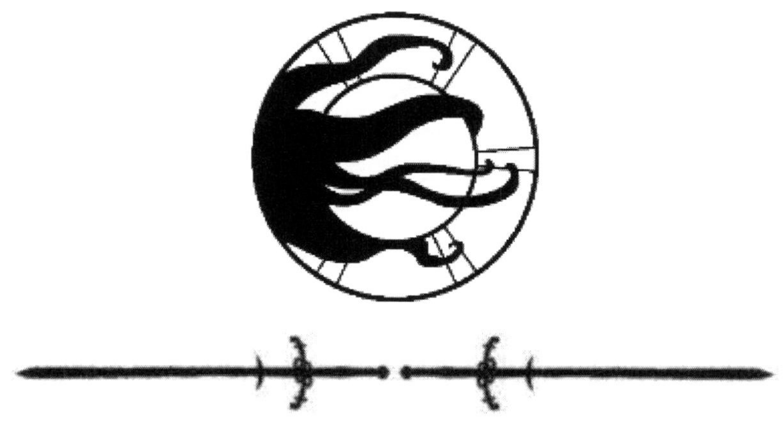

Chapter Twenty-six

KHYVEN

One guard ran as fast as his legs would carry him, vanishing into the darkness, headed for the palace. A second escorted Khyven while the other two remained at their posts. He felt the comfort of familiar sights. The cobblestone streets, the close shops and houses, the hulking silhouette of the Night Ring in the distance.

He thought of Rhenn, of Lorelle, and Vohn and a coldness descended on him, seeming to close in on him like a cloak made of snow.

They are not my responsibility, he thought. *Rhenn's camp was a fiction, a lure to yoke my swordsmanship to her cause, just as Vamreth wishes to yoke my swordsmanship to his cause. That's all. The drinking and dancing. Lorelle. All a lure. It was simply a different way to build power. Rhenn and Lorelle are not my family. In the end, Vamreth has more to offer.*

The guard took him through the palace guard post, across the courtyard, up the steps, into the grand foyer—silent at this time of night—and to the right, straight to his old room.

Everything was the same, as though Vamreth never doubted

Khyven would return. It should have comforted him, but it didn't.

The guard hesitated, then bowed to Khyven before he closed the door. Khyven stood alone in the eerie room, as though he'd never left here in the first place, as though he hadn't been away for weeks, as though Rhenn's camp had never existed.

This is what I wanted, he thought. *Tomorrow, I'll be a baron.*

He went to the credenza, the last place he'd touched before he'd gone to his final bout in the Night Ring. He took off his sword and placed it there, then went to the window where Shalure had framed herself.

Shalure… He would see her again. She would be his at last. He thought back on how her kiss had enflamed him….

And Lorelle's image floated before him.

He shook his head and clenched his teeth, forced himself to conjure Shalure's face. Her full lips. Her tantalizing, scheming smile. Her sultry eyes that promised everything he desired… once he was a knight.

A knock sounded at the door, and Khyven turned. It had to be the elites.

He went to the door and opened it, but instead of the king's Knights of the Sun, three men dressed as servants and three women dressed as dancers stood outside his door. They bore a cart with expensive clothes, many jugs of water, plates of steaming food, and a small keg of ale.

One of the pretty young dancers curtseyed.

"We've come with your bath, milord," she said.

"It's past midnight."

"Of course, milord," she said. "His majesty commands that you take your ease, have your fill of drink, food, sleep"—she looked at him through her lashes—"and whatever else milord wishes."

For a moment, he didn't know what to say. Instead, he stood aside and they brought the cart into the room. Half of them efficiently filled the bath while the other half set out a banquet of delights on the table by the window.

The three men left, leaving the three scantily clad women

behind.

"Feast, milord," the one who had first spoken said again. "Or would you like us to feed you?"

"I can feed myself," he said. "Thank you."

"And your bath, milord? Would you allow us to assist you there?"

His reward. A tantalizing benefit as one of the powerful, for assisting Vamreth. For rising through the ranks of status in this court. For being what Khyven had told himself for years that he wanted to be.

He hesitated, then nodded to the dancer. She moved forward gracefully and began to unlace his tunic, her slender fingers working at the knots.

He clasped them, stopping her. "Wait."

"Milord?"

"Just wait. I… I can manage the bath on my own."

She looked confused, looked at the bath, and back to him. "And… after, milord?"

"The food and bath are enough. Thank you."

She hesitated, looked over her shoulder at the other two women, who looked equally baffled.

"Milord, if we have done something to displease you, I assure you that we—"

"You've done nothing wrong. I am tired and hungry only. I will bathe myself."

A wrinkle appeared on the girl's forehead between her brows. "But… milord—"

"Thank you. That will be all," he said.

She bowed her head and bobbed a quick curtsey. "As you wish, milord." The three of them backed toward the door in unison, opened it, and left.

Khyven stood for a long moment, watching the door, wondering at his own actions. He heard Lorelle's voice in his head.

"You are man of shifting loyalties, tempted by whatever draws you."

He tried to shake the voice from his head. She had spurned

him. *This* was his path now. The path he had wanted.

Resolutely, Khyven bathed, but even when he emerged, he still didn't feel clean. He ate, but the food tasted bland. He slept, but fitfully.

When the sun rose and roosters crowed in the distance, he let out a breath and dressed himself. He paced the room half a dozen times and had just decided to walk down to the Night Ring when a knock sounded upon his door.

Outside, the king's elites waited for him. No spearmen this time. Khyven started to bow but stopped at the last second and inclined his head instead. After his meeting with Vamreth, after Khyven became a baron, he would outrank these Knights of the Sun.

"Please come with us," the first of the knights said. "His Majesty would like to break his fast with you."

Khyven followed them into the foyer, up the two flights of steps and into the room where Khyven had first met the king. This time, there were no dancers. Instead, Vamreth sat at the head of the table, Vex the Victorious stood impassively behind him, and five other places were set. A noble sat to the king's left and next to him sat a woman Khyven assumed was the noble's wife. It took Khyven a second, but he realized he recognized the lord. He was Duke Derinhalt, one of Vamreth's most powerful nobles. To Vamreth's right sat the young mage, Slayter. Next to him was an empty seat that had been clearly reserved for Khyven, and in the next seat…

Shalure turned to face him, her face bright with that alluring smile. She was dressed in exquisite finery, a blue dress with white down the front and embroidered silver piping starting at each shoulder and following the curve of her body to her hips. The dress's sleeves were long and wide. Compared to Shalure's usually evocative clothing, this was demure.

She stood as he entered, as did everyone else.

"Khyven the Unkillable," King Vamreth said, both hands held apart as though he would embrace Khyven, despite standing twenty feet away. "You have certainly earned the name."

"Your Majesty is kind," Khyven said.

"Sit down, eat," King Vamreth said. "Did you receive the gifts I sent last night?"

"I did, Your Majesty. Thank you."

"It wasn't nearly the reception a hero deserves, but it was the most I could scrape together at midnight. You faced the noktum, did you?"

"Yes, Your Majesty."

"And returned alive. I can barely believe it. You have stories to tell, I can see it on your face."

"Yes, Your Majesty."

"Well, there will be plenty of time for that. For now, let us eat."

A dozen servants brought trays bearing curved loaves of bread and crocks of fresh honey. Khyven sampled the bread and his mouth began watering. It was light, buttery, and flaky. He had never tasted anything like it.

Course after course came, including eggs, rashers of bacon, and two roasted pheasants. Khyven ate until his stomach felt like it would burst.

This is what it is to be a noble, he thought. *To eat like this every day. To have the respect of knights and powerful nobles like Duke Derinhalt.*

King Vamreth kept the conversation going. He talked of how pitiful the past few bouts in the Night Ring had been, that the winners didn't have half the showmanship Khyven possessed. Vamreth talked about the weather. There had been two legendary thunderstorms while Khyven had been away. Lightning had actually struck the palace. He talked of anything and everything except the Queen-in-Exile, and with every story Khyven felt the anticipation, like the skin across his back was stretching tighter and tighter.

Finally, as Vamreth's servants cleared the many plates from the table, the king brought his conversation with Duke Derinhalt—who was talking about the training of his new

Knights of the Steel—to an abrupt finish.

"That is interesting," he said, "but it's time for Khyven to regale us with his tale." Vamreth sat back in his chair. "You went into the noktum and returned, which no one else has ever done. You followed that little demon into the black, and on the other side found the traitor's nest?"

Khyven felt the cold cloak settle over him again and he hesitated. Warm fingers touched his forearm, and he glanced at Shalure. Her eager eyes, her eager smile told him that she felt abundantly satisfied with herself and with the choice she had made, the gamble she had taken, in attaching herself to him.

"I did," Khyven said.

Vamreth's grin practically split his face. "That"—he exhaled, like he had been holding his breath—"is fantastic news. Where is she?"

Khyven thought of the circuitous path through the forest, and he hesitated. "It's… She's southwest," he said. "In the forest."

"Southwest?" Vamreth's grin faded to a curious expression. "The noktum is southwest. She is in the noktum?"

"Not exactly. There isn't a landmark near her camp that I can relay, but I can show you."

"Ah," Vamreth said. "So, you will take us there."

"Yes, Your Majesty."

"What do you think?" He glanced at Slayter, who hadn't said a word during breakfast. "A complement of four hundred?" Vamreth said.

"Splendid, Your Majesty. You'll need two full days to muster them," Slayter said.

"One day," Vamreth insisted. "We can put that together in one day."

Slayter hesitated, then nodded. "Will you send a scout to ensure the location is accurate?"

He shook his head. "No. No scouts. I don't want to risk warning her before we are ready to crush her. No, I trust Khyven. We will quietly arm four hundred knights and footmen, then we will march. We will destroy her and her pitiful little band. Inform Sir Cantoy at once."

"At once, Your Majesty." Slayter stood from the table and bowed.

"No fanfare," Vamreth said. "I want us to move quietly. By the time the sun sets tomorrow, little Rhenn's rebellion will be dead and we'll hear no more about it."

He turned to Khyven. "Well done, Khyven. Or should I say Lord Khyven?" He waved his hand. "We will have your ceremony the morning after we return from the forest."

"Thank you, Your Majesty."

"Yes, yes. Now, I'm sure you'd like to spend some time getting reacquainted with your lady." He nodded to Shalure, who looked down at the table and blushed. "Away with you, both of you. We will make all the preparations. Ready yourselves for tomorrow. I'll send my knights to collect you when the sun reaches its zenith. Until then, the day is yours, and the night." He winked.

"Thank you, Your Majesty." Khyven stood and turned when Shalure coughed to get his attention. She looked significantly at the arm of her chair.

"Ah, apologies," he said and pulled her chair out for her. "My lady."

"Isn't young love wonderful?" King Vamreth said to Duke Derinhalt. He grumbled something and barely nodded.

Shalure took Khyven's hand and led him toward the door.

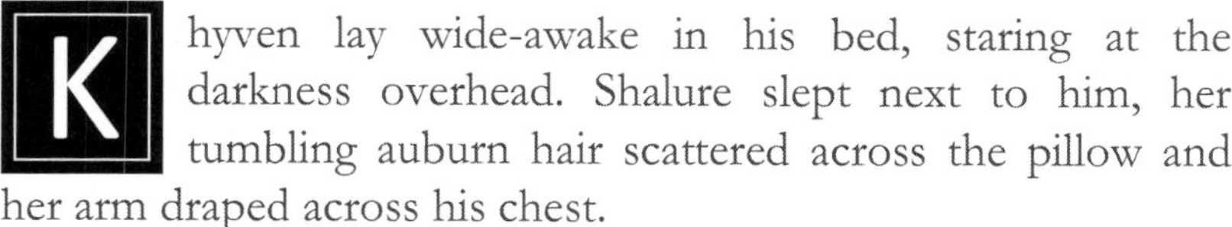

Chapter Twenty-seven

Khyven

Khyven lay wide-awake in his bed, staring at the darkness overhead. Shalure slept next to him, her tumbling auburn hair scattered across the pillow and her arm draped across his chest.

They had spent the day together, and with every passing moment, Khyven had felt worse.

He and Shalure had talked about their future, the holdings the king would give them, the type of house they would build. They had lunched and supped, and she'd finally taken him to bed. She had fulfilled every desire she'd promised with that first kiss.

After they had finished and she had fallen asleep, a foreboding grew within him, like a terrible lightning storm gathering on the horizon, coming ever closer. Now he lay next to the woman he had once wanted so badly and he felt like beetles were crawling all over his skin. He kept thinking of Rhenn's camp. He kept thinking about Lorelle and Vohn. Basant and the musicians. Even Lord Harpinjur and the two mute knights who protected the queen. He thought of them all, over and over, and the same phrase repeated in his head.

What have I done?

He shouldn't care. He'd done what he needed to do. He had protected himself, secured the most power, ensured that he would survive and rise. This was what he had wanted. Power was the only thing that mattered, and now he had a place in the palace. A seat at the right hand of the king. Land. Holdings. Money. The lovely, desirable Shalure—a baron's daughter!—as his betrothed.

Those accomplishments, so important only a month ago, suddenly seemed like chunks of floating garbage. Contemplating his future with Shalure and Vamreth suddenly filled him with loathing.

He kept thinking about how he'd felt fighting Txomin. The terror of going blind. Digging deep within himself, expanding his abilities to meet the challenge. His impossible victory.

Khyven had faced challenges before, perhaps even challenges as great as Txomin, nothing had changed there. It was the aftermath that had changed. After his previous trials in the Night Ring, he'd been thrown into a cage, alone and reviled by those around him. This time, he'd been laid protectively on a bed, surrounded by Rhenn and her people. He'd woken, half-blind, to Vohn's quiet companionship and Lorelle's gentle ministrations. Respect and gratitude had shone in their eyes.

They had valued him, not just for his swordsmanship, but for the person he was.

Or rather, for the person he might have been.

An aching thought settled into his heart and grew. What if Rhenn's friendship hadn't been a ploy? What if she was exactly what she claimed, a queen who cared for her people? What if she hadn't been manipulating him? What if she had just been… honest?

What if Rhenn and Lorelle and Vohn had, for a moment, become family?

The foreboding in his soul thickened, bunching into a dark and ugly knot.

He hadn't been looking for family, but what if he'd found one anyway?

And what if he'd thrown it away to spend his life beside a woman who wanted to use him like a bag of gold, to serve a man who wanted to use him like a sword to cut apart more families like Rhenn's, like Lorelle's…

Like the old man and Nhevaz…

What have I done?

Cold sweat broke out on Khyven's forehead and his heart pounded in his chest. He felt no euphoria this time, only the sense that he was falling and that he would never stop falling for the rest of his life.

He gently removed Shalure's arm and placed it back on the bed. She mumbled in her sleep but did not wake.

He got up, gathered his clothes, and went to the other room. The warm air seemed frigid, and he shook in silence as he dressed. He buckled on his sword and went to the doorway for one last look at the slumbering Shalure.

Without another sound, he left.

CHAPTER TWENTY-EIGHT

VAMRETH

King Vamreth sat in his study, lanterns burning, as he went over maps of the Royal Forest. It had once been called the Laochodon Forest, but he had eliminated that name in his first year as king.

A knock sounded on the door.

"Yes?" Vamreth said.

The door opened and Sir Cantoy entered. He dropped to a knee, his plate and chain mail rattling, then rose to his feet as though his seventy pounds of armor weighed nothing. Sir Cantoy didn't have Vex's size, but he was deceptively fast and a better swordsman could not be found outside of Vex himself…

… and possibly Khyven the Unkillable.

Sir Cantoy stood straight, waiting for Vamreth's permission to speak.

Vamreth waved a hand. "Tell me."

"You were correct, Your Majesty. He just left through the front gate."

Vamreth *tsked* and shook his head. "So, the lovely Lady Shalure's charms weren't enough after all. I am not surprised."

Sir Cantoy said nothing to that.

"And the guards let him through?" Vamreth asked.

"As ordered, Your Majesty."

Vamreth took a deep breath and sighed. "That is disappointing, Khyven," he said to himself. "So extremely disappointing."

"I crave the honor of slaying the bastard when we take the camp," Cantoy said.

"No slaying. I want him alive. I want to talk to him about his poor choices."

"I will bring him to you," Sir Cantoy said.

"It will have to be you or Vex," Vamreth said. "I am not confident any of the others could manage it. You two can fight over the privilege. Or better yet, attack him at the same time. Have your elites surround him. Be certain."

"Yes, Your Majesty."

"A bag of gold to split between you if you can bring him alive."

"It shall be done, Your Majesty."

Vamreth allowed himself a moment of pique and slammed his fist on the table. His rage flowed through his arm and out of his body. He couldn't afford to make decisions with anger, so it helped to release that anger ahead of time.

"Damn him," Vamreth said. "I had plans for him."

"He wasn't worthy of you, Your Majesty."

Vamreth didn't answer that. The truth was, Khyven was well worthy. Though Cantoy craved the honor of killing Khyven, and Vamreth had humored his ego, the leader of the Knights of the Sun wasn't capable of such a feat. Vex, yes, but Khyven was astoundingly good with a blade, and he was… somewhat miraculous as well, beyond his fighting skill. He had a knack for surviving when no one else could. Vamreth had desperately wanted to put that talent to use.

He'd dared to hope that Khyven was telling the truth. He seemed loyal, even though Vamreth had reports that someone named Khyven the Unkillable had killed the Sandrunners'

Champion of the Sun at the Burzagi Tor and had commanded that three hundred Lantzas be brought north for some mysterious purpose. He'd dared to believe it was some other using Khyven's name, but Vamreth was now sure that it had been Khyven himself.

Rhenn needed an army and Khyven had won her one. He was working with the bitch.

Of course, Vamreth had suspected Khyven the moment he'd returned, but he had hoped that somehow Khyven had, instead, come to his senses, or he'd maybe been forced to serve Rhenn and fight the Sandrunner bout. Now, though, it was clear the boy had been won over.

Cantoy had begged Vamreth for the privilege of killing Khyven the moment he showed his face, but Vamreth wasn't king because he swung wildly at shadows. No. If Khyven wasn't going to serve willingly, then Vamreth would make him useful in other ways.

Khyven was tough. Moving straight to torture would have been risky. He might have tightened his lips and taken whatever information he had to the grave. But given freedom, well… he might lead them straight to Rhenn's camp anyway.

"Do you believe he is the spy?" Cantoy asked.

Vamreth rose from his reverie. "The spy? No, of course not. We were leaking information before Khyven came to the palace. The spy is one of the nobles, or perhaps some servant." Vamreth and Cantoy alone knew there was a spy in the palace, and Vamreth had tried to root the bastard out, but he'd had no luck so far. His frustration had been mounting for months. Some little traitor had been feeding information to Rhenn. She knew things she shouldn't.

It could be Lord Derinhalt, or one of Vamreth's lovely dancers, or one of the damned servants who brought dessert.

But Vamreth's latest plan, with Khyven's unwitting assistance, would bring the spy to the surface and crush the rebellion in one sweep. Vamreth had announced at breakfast that they would attack with four hundred troops tomorrow at noon. But unbeknownst to anyone except Vamreth and Cantoy, they had assembled a force of fifty knights in secret, as well as three mages Vamreth never included in matters of state. He was reasonably sure none of them could be the spy.

In addition, Vamreth's four best scouts were, even now, following Khyven into the woods. Within an hour, they would know the camp's location. The Royal Forest would burn, and anyone who fled the conflagration would run into the swords of the awaiting knights.

A second knock sounded on the door. Cantoy's visored helmet turned, the sudden movement revealing his surprise.

It was after midnight and Vamreth wasn't expecting anyone. His anger rose. Who would dare to come to him at this hour? He wondered if it could be the spy, somehow trying to learn of Vamreth's ploy.

"Yes?" Vamreth said.

The door opened. It was Sir Ehvron. "My apologies, Your Majesty."

Vamreth narrowed his eyes. Could one of his elites be a traitor? It seemed impossible. He had investigated each of them thoroughly before choosing them as personal guards, but things changed. Things always changed. Even the most loyal could flip with the right pressure.

Vamreth did nothing to hide his annoyance. "What could it possibly be?"

"Lady Chadrone has come. She claims to have urgent information. About Khyven," Ehvron said.

Vamreth's suspicions and his anger settled. "Shalure has information, does she?"

"That is what she claims, Your Majesty," Ehvron said.

Vamreth grinned. "By all means, bring her in."

Ehvron nodded and vanished. A moment later, a disheveled Shalure entered in an embroidered linen night dress. She curtseyed and bowed her head.

"Your Majesty, thank you for seeing me at such a late hour."

"It is always a pleasure to see you, Lady Chadrone," Vamreth said.

"Please accept my apologies. I realize I am not dressed for an audience."

"You would look a duchess in a burlap sack, my dear. What can I do for you? Ehvron says you have urgent information about Khyven the Unkillable."

"Yes, Your Majesty. I knew if I wasted even a moment it might be too late."

"Mightn't it?" he said.

"Yes."

"Then do not wait, my dear. What is this urgent news?"

The girl hesitated and drew herself up a little straighter. "I would… barter with you, Your Majesty."

Cantoy, who had far more experience with diplomacy, stood stock still, but Ehvron turned his helmeted head to look at the girl.

Vamreth chuckled. "You would barter with me? For this information?"

"Yes, Your Majesty. As you know, once Khyven was bestowed with titles… That is to say, I was to marry him once he had the rank Your Majesty saw fit to give him."

"But you began your marriage a bit early, did you?" Vamreth said.

She swallowed and a blush crept into her pale cheeks. "Yes, Your Majesty."

"Good," he said. "And now you have information you wish to sell me."

"B-Barter, Your Majesty. I would like assurances. Perhaps… another suitor that you would approve for me."

"A noble husband."

Her blush increased. "Yes, Your Majesty."

"Because you no longer wish to marry Khyven."

Her blush became a deep red and her voice came out quieter. "No, Your Majesty."

"What an odd conundrum to bring to me at this late hour. Did you leave Khyven sleeping in his bed?"

"I—Your Majesty… I will tell you all. But first—"

"Your assurances."

"Yes, Your Majesty."

"Of course, my dear. I promise you I shall find a suitor for you. One who matches your station and your loyalty to the crown."

The tension drained from the girl. She let out a breath and curtseyed again. "Thank you, Your Majesty. You must move with all haste. Khyven has left."

"He has left, has he? Where has he gone?"

"I think… I think he has gone back to *her*, Your Majesty."

"Her, is it? That sounds so nefarious. To whom do you refer?"

"The Queen-in—" Shalure stopped herself from uttering the last bit and she paled. "I mean, the traitor in the woods, Your Majesty. The one who plots against you."

"That *is* urgent news, Shalure. Do you know where he goes to meet her?"

"I—No, Your Majesty. I—I could not possibly know—"

"For *that* would be truly valuable information," Vamreth said. "Are you sure he did not let slip this urgent information while you rode him?"

She glanced at Cantoy and Ehvron, embarrassed, and her blush increased. "He…" She swallowed. "Your Majesty, he did not."

"So, he is a traitor, is what you're saying?"

"Yes, Your Majesty. This is why I have no desire to marry him."

"Did you know that keeping the secret of a traitor is treason itself?" Vamreth said.

Shalure opened her mouth to say something, but nothing came out. She flicked a confused glance at him, then at Sir Cantoy and Sir Ehvron on either side of her. "What… do you mean, Your Majesty?"

"It is the obligation of every loyal subject to root out traitors and provide all information about them to the crown. Immediately." He stood and came to stand before her.

"I—Yes, Your Majesty. That is why I came to you immediately."

"To report your information."

"Yes."

"To extort me for payment," he said darkly.

"No," Shalure said, her attempt at a regal posture now desperately shabby. A wayward girl in a linen night dress. "To serve you. I live to serve you, as you know, Your Majesty. I came to you with all haste." She waved at her clothing, but Vamreth was beyond bored with her.

He towered over her and he spoke in a whisper. "You should have run to me stark naked with the urgency of this news, Shalure. You should have fallen to your knees and blurted it before I could greet you. But what did you do? You made me wait so you could squeeze me for a new husband."

"I—"

"Do you really think I need a trollop to feed me information? Do you think me so pitiful as that?"

"Your Majesty, please! Of course, I don't think that—"

"Your news comes late, Shalure. Too late to help me in any way except, of course, to show me what you really are."

Fear washed over her and he reveled to see her composure fail. She stepped away from him.

"B-But, Your Majesty…" she stammered. "I have served you. I have done everything you have asked of me. I even—I came to your—"

"As a whore, you are adequate," he said. "To that I will attest, but your charms have paled. For me and, it seems, for Khyven as well. So, I ask you, in what way can you serve me now?"

"In any way you wish, Your Majesty. Of course, I will."

"And why would I trust you, now that I know you are a traitor?"

"A traitor?" She looked lost, scared, just a little girl. She shook her head. "Your Majesty, I-I came to you."

"And you need never go anywhere else."

"Please!" she said, stricken. "Your Majesty! I-I only wanted to help."

"Indeed." Vamreth turned away. "Take her."

"Tybris, please." She dared use his first name, a privilege he'd allowed on that first night when she was fresh and brazen and standing naked before him. Her audacity had been like a drug then, but it enraged him now. He signaled to Sir Ehvron.

The knight cracked Shalure across the jaw with his mailed fist. She sprawled to the ground with a grunt. Blood dripped down her beautiful chin. She lifted her head shakily and looked in wide-eyed horror at Vamreth as he seated himself behind his desk.

She reached out a hand to him and gave a guttural wail, but Ehvron dragged her from the room and closed the door.

"Now," Vamreth turned back to Cantoy, "where were we?"

Chapter Twenty-Nine

KHYVEN

Khyven stood in the shadows of the woods outside Rhenn's camp for half an hour trying to think of how to explain where he'd been. He'd been gone a full day, plenty of time to do many things, including betray them to Vamreth.

As he watched the midnight tentacles wave lazily at the edge of the noktum hiding Rhenn's camp, he considered many things. He thought about lying, of course, about simply telling Rhenn that he had gone exploring in the noktum—gone to test the immunity Rauvelos had implied.

Then Khyven had thought about telling the truth. Ever since he had considered the notion that Rhenn might be exactly what she'd claimed, he thought she might understand what had driven him to Vamreth again, and what had driven him back. She might understand his change of heart. She might even celebrate it.

Then again, she might simply kill him. That was what Vamreth would do. Khyven had gone to sell her, and her subjects, to Vamreth for a title and a baron's daughter.

Once Khyven had looked at his actions straight on, a dam

had burst inside him. He loathed what he had done, and if he could go back and undo it, he would.

But I didn't betray them, he told himself. *Not yet, anyway. I meant to, but I didn't. Vamreth doesn't know where the camp is. I never showed him. I—*

Someone emerged from the noktum at the thin exit point. Khyven shrank into the shadows behind the tree. The tentacles reached toward the man leaving the camp, then backed away as they sensed his amulet.

Another man emerged, looking determined and walking fast. He headed in a different direction than the first. Close behind, Lord Harpinjur emerged on his horse along with two Knights of the Steel, mounted and ready for a fight.

The lord and his retainers galloped northward, toward the main road.

What's happening?

Khyven crept sideways toward the noktum. The tentacles avoided grabbing him and he walked between them into the dark. The odd black light filled the world. Khyven walked southwest over the charcoal-colored heather and between the dark trees until he reached the edge of the camp. He took a breath and pushed through.

The normal nighttime light of the stars and the moon washed over him and he looked at the scene.

Everyone was bustling about the camp. The pallets under the open sky had been rolled up and stacked in a pile. The pots had been removed from the cooking fires. The makeshift stage had been dismantled, leaving only the trampled grass where Rhenn's followers had danced. The eating tables had been dismantled as well, and everything was being loaded on carts.

They were packing it all up. They were leaving—

"Intruder!" a voice went up and Khyven spun. Two of Rhenn's peasant knights came at Khyven from the left, crossbows leveled at him.

"It's Khyven," Khyven said, putting his hands in the air, well away from his weapons.

Rather than put their weapons away, the guards stopped,

knelt, and steadied their aim.

"Khyven!" one of them, a woman, yelled. "Khyven the Unkillable has returned!"

Everyone within shouting distance stopped what they were doing. Hammering and hitching stopped. Tasks were dropped and heads turned his way. As one, the crowd moved up the hill.

Khyven got a sinking feeling. There were no smiles in that crowd. It was as though each of them knew exactly where he'd been. Those with hammers, knives, and other implements gripped them tighter, as though they were weapons.

Khyven's hand drifted toward his sword and he backed toward the noktum.

"No, milord," the woman holding the crossbow said. "Not another step."

The crowd thickened. Khyven's heart began to pound.

"Make a path!" a voice boomed from behind the crowd. People milled and moved out of the way. Rhenn, wearing a sword and dressed in plate mail, except for a helm, strode between the milling crowd, her blue cape trailing behind her. Lorelle glided quietly at her side, her blonde hair braided into a tight, single queue behind her head, blowgun in hand. Vohn came behind her, stomping quickly to keep up, his white horns prominent in the dark. Both of Rhenn's mute knights flanked her, swords drawn.

Rhenn and her retinue stopped ten feet from Khyven and the tight expression on her face told Khyven that he only had one path now, the truth, because somehow, she already knew.

"Rhenn—" he began.

"Your sword, Khyven," she said. "Two fingers on the pommel. Pull it from its sheath and toss it away. Any more than two fingers and we make you a porcupine. Understand?"

He glanced at the two crossbowmen and saw there were two more archers with long bows, arrows nocked and pulled. He glanced to his right. Five more archers emerged from the woods, all with longbows, all ready to feather him.

Slowly, carefully, he pinched the pommel of his sword, lifted it out of its sheath, and tossed it away. Everyone seemed to relax a little.

"Take his amulet," Rhenn commanded. Vohn moved forward cautiously. If Khyven was going to take a hostage, this was his moment.

He reached up, removed the amulet, and gave it to Vohn. The Shadowvar snatched it and quickly backed away.

Rhenn stared daggers at Khyven. "I'll give you this," she said. "You never cease to amaze." Her smile was flat. There was no mirth in it this time. "I never believed you'd come back. The only question is why?"

"Rhenn, I don't know what you heard, but—"

"Senji's Spear, Khyven," she interrupted, speaking through clenched teeth like she could barely hold her rage in check. "If you're preparing to lie, don't. You will be afforded a fair trial for what you've done, but if you lie to me now..." She clenched her fist so hard it shook. "I'll order them to shoot and be done with it."

How did she know? Did she just assume he would return to Vamreth the moment she didn't know where he was? And then he remembered what she'd said earlier.

"Vamreth isn't the only one with spies..."

Somebody knew! Somebody had told Rhenn that Khyven had gone back to Vamreth. Was it the guards at the front gate? Duke Derinhalt or his wife? Could it have been Shalure...?

Khyven put his hands in front of himself in a pacifying gesture. "It's not what you think."

"You have exactly as long as my patience lasts to explain how it isn't what I think."

Khyven swallowed. He glanced at Lorelle, but her impassive mask was back in place. He couldn't tell what she was thinking, but he could probably guess. Rhenn mattered to Lorelle more than anything in the world, and if Rhenn believed Khyven was a traitor, Lorelle believed it, too.

"I did," he said. "I did it."

"Did what, Khyven? Be specific. Did you go to Vamreth to

reveal the location of our camp so he could come here and kill us? Is that what you did?" Rhenn said through her teeth.

Khyven's heart raced and flickers of blue wind swirled around Rhenn's ankles, around the forms of the archers, but he knew no matter how fast he was, no matter how many weaknesses the blue wind might show him, he couldn't win this fight. He was dead, here and now, unless he could convince Rhenn of…

Of the truth.

"I did go back to Vamreth," he said. "I came with Vohn in the first place for that reason. I promised Vamreth I would find the location of your camp and bring it to him. And yes, I went back to do that."

"You bastard," Rhenn spat. Her eyes blazed.

"But I didn't do it," he said quickly. "I had breakfast with him. Yes, I told him I would lead him here at midday tomorrow, but I didn't do it. I didn't tell him where you were. I…" he trailed off.

Suddenly, the revelations he'd had in the quiet of his own mind seemed ridiculous. What was he going to say?

Rhenn, I realized you were family, and I couldn't do such a murderous thing? I realized I made a mistake and I wanted to undo it so you'd still… What? Include me in the dancing and the drinking? Clap me on the back like we're friends…

Everything he might say sounded pitiful.

"You what?" Rhenn demanded.

"I have no excuse for you. I left intending to do exactly what you think, but I… stopped. What I thought I wanted, I actually don't. I left the moment I realized it and I came back to find out if…" He hesitated, then shook his head. "I came back to find out if you're the woman you claim to be, the leader you portrayed to me. I came back to see if—if you're my queen."

"That," Lorelle finally said in her smooth, dusky voice, "is a pretty speech. We opened our home to you and you betrayed us. Now you ask us to believe these words when every other word out of your mouth has been a lie?"

"Not every word," he said, his heart hurting.

"You have no idea what loyalty is." Lorelle's hair began to glow. "I cannot believe I ever thought you might. I cannot believe we ever gave you a chance, Khyven."

"And we gave you many," Vohn snarled. They both glanced at Rhenn. The queen's gaze had not softened.

"We don't have time for this," Rhenn said. "Khyven, you are accused of treason against the crown. You will be clapped in irons until your trial. If you are found guilty, you will be executed."

Lorelle gazed down on Khyven with cool appraisal. Vohn glared with outright fury.

"Approach him carefully," Rhenn said, drawing her sword. "Khyven, don't make a fight of it. If you mean what you say, we'll give you full opportunity to voice your side and try to prove it. But if you fight now, we will—"

One of the trees in the little glade burst into flames. The explosive cracking sound filled the camp and gasps went up from the crowd.

Another tree burst into flame with a boom, as though lightning had struck it. Then another, and another. The flames and the heat washed through the camp. More trees caught fire.

"It's an attack!" Vohn shouted. "Magic attack!"

Rhenn shouted orders and the crowd leapt to action as though they were all parts of one huge creature. People dragged the carts away from trees. Others ran to get buckets of water. Still others ran toward the thin wall of the noktum, weapons drawn, ready for a physical attack. The archers ran to brace the entrance.

In the sudden conflagration, everyone seemed to have forgotten about Khyven.

All save Lorelle.

Khyven turned to see the Luminent standing, blowgun lifted to her lips.

"No!" He held up his hands. "Lorelle, please. Let me help you."

"You have helped quite enough," she said through her teeth. "They are here because of you."

"No, I didn't. I didn't give you up. I swear on my mother's

grave."

"You do not even remember your mother, or was that another lie?"

"I swear on Nhevaz's grave," Khyven said. "I'm sorry. I'm so sorry. Please!"

"You don't understand," Lorelle shouted. "It doesn't matter if you're sorry! This was our home, and our home is burning because of you!"

"Let me make it right," Khyven said fervently. "Let me stand with you. Let me die with you. If you clap me in irons, you take me from the arena."

"This is not the Night Ring, damn you!"

"Put a sword in my hands and I will show you how like the Night Ring it is, except this time, I'm on your side." He stared into her huge brown eyes, and he prayed that she could see his heart.

The tips of her hair began to glow. The shouts and cries of Rhenn's followers rose behind her. Her eyes misted.

"By all the gods, I hate you, Khyven," she whispered.

"Then we are of one mind."

The cries turned to screams. A shout went up. "They're in! They've breached the noktum!"

Lorelle's head whipped around. Knights of the Dark rode through the thin shield of the noktum, trampling Rhenn's followers under hoof, slashing at them with swords.

"No!" Khyven yelled.

Lorelle spun back to him, tears in her eyes. She kicked his sword toward him. "Take it, Khyven. Fight for your queen, and may the gods curse you if you fail!"

Khyven snatched up the blade and ran past Lorelle toward the attackers. His heart thundered and tears burned his eyes.

They were supposed to attack tomorrow! What were they doing here tonight?

Swirls of blue wind whipped through the carnage and Khyven rushed down the slope, nearly falling over with the speed of his stride. He reached a knight just as the man turned his visored head to face him. Khyven launched himself into the air with all his speed and strength.

His knees slammed into the knight's chest. Knight and horse slammed into the ground and the horse screamed as Khyven rolled clear. The horse thrashed, crushing the knight in its panic to regain its feet.

Swishes of blue wind charged at Khyven from two directions and he dodged them both. A moment later, a lance stabbed the air where he had been and a sword chopped at the ground. Blue funnels opened up; Khyven chopped the closest man's arm off with one mighty swing.

He spun away as another horse reared in front of him, lashing out. Swirls of blue wind preceded the horse's hooves. Khyven rolled under them, popped up, and hacked off the rider's leg. The knight screamed. Khyven kept moving. Desperation drove him and the euphoria sang through him. He had to stop this, had to drive these bastards back.

May the gods curse you if you fail…

Spikes of blue wind stabbed toward him and he danced between them. Two knights on foot closed and swung their swords. Khyven batted the first blade away and stabbed the knight through the neck. He dodged another spike of blue and turned, bringing himself face to face with the second knight.

Khyven's dagger was in his hand though he didn't remember drawing it. He shoved it under the man's helmet.

Both knights fell, gurgling, and Khyven charged the next, a mounted knight who was hacking at something on the ground.

Three fighters, not knights, charged him as one, poking spears at him. Khyven batted them aside, getting inside their range. He chopped the first fighter's arm, the second's leg, and ran the third through the chest. All three screamed and fell to the ground.

A Knight of the Sun rose before Khyven, mounted and gleaming, sword glimmering red in the firelight.

"You die!" Khyven yelled.

"It's him!" the knight shouted. "It's Khyven the Unkillable!

Take him!"

Blue funnels opened up all over the mounted knight as he turned in his saddle, bringing his sword around. He was fast, but not fast enough. Khyven skewered him through the gap in his armor, just beneath his arm. The knight screamed and tumbled off his horse.

Because of the blue wind, Khyven felt his enemies close in before he saw them. He spun, and spikes of blue wind came at him from every angle, so thick he couldn't avoid them all. He dodged to one side, evading a sword aimed for his heart and blocked a second blade.

Someone shouted, "No blades! His Majesty wants him alive!"

Blurs of blue assailed him and he barely ducked beneath a steel mace that whistled over his head.

When he came up, three of a dozen blue tendrils touched him, too fast to avoid. A second later, a club came down on his thigh. Pain burst through him. A fist crashed into the side of his head, and he staggered. A wooden cudgel came down on his forearm so hard his arm went numb and he dropped his sword.

Then they were on him. Rough hands grabbed his arms, pinning them, forcing him to the ground. Fists smashed into his face, into his ribs. Feet kicked his belly and legs.

Khyven tried to throw them off, but there were too many. With a mighty roar, he raised his head—

In time to see a man standing before him, club raised high before it came down on his head with a crack.

The world went black.

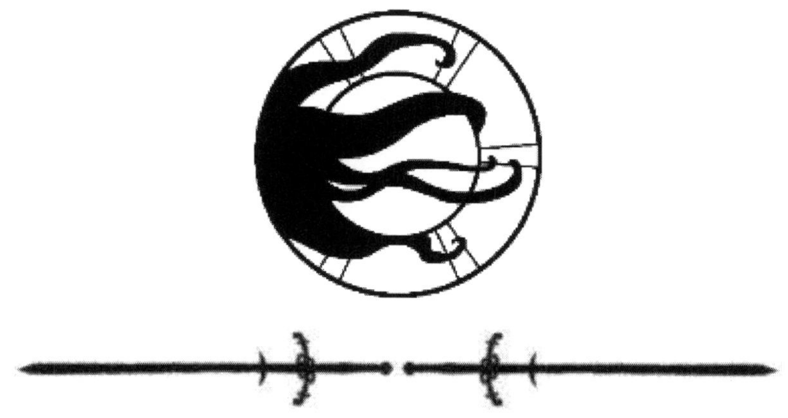

Chapter Thirty

KHYVEN

The pain came first, like thunder coming closer. *Thump-boom.... Thump-boom... THUMP-BOOM!*

The pain dragged him up from somewhere deep underground, and he rose toward the thunder. Each *thump-BOOM* pounded through his whole body like his heart was pushing too much blood through his veins. With every beat it felt like his head would burst.

There was light, a flicker of orange on his eyelids and then he felt the agonizing pain in his arm. It felt like someone had placed it on a rock and was slowly lowering a boulder onto it. It squeezed and squeezed until he thought the rock would squish his arm to paste.

He gasped and opened his eyes. Firelight flickered on black stone walls. The room was roughly twenty feet across, with walls that angled from a wider wall on one side to a smaller wall on the other, just like the antechambers of the Night Ring. In the Night Ring, all of the rooms narrowed as they neared the arena in the center.

Khyven had never been in this antechamber before, but he'd

heard the screams from ringers who *had* visited the torture room.

The torture room was for those who had no talent for fighting. They were used for a different kind of spectacle. They would be mutilated or experimented upon to make them look less Human just before the fight. Then they would be thrown into the arena as a grotesquerie, as fodder for better ringers.

It was also widely known that the torture room was used as punishment for those against whom the king held a particular grudge.

Some who went into the torture room never emerged. And those who did never lived long.

Khyven clenched his teeth and looked down at his sword arm. It was swollen, though it wasn't bent at any unnatural angle. His right thigh hurt badly, but Khyven had endured enough deep bruises to recognize that neither his arm nor his leg was broken.

Thank Senji for that at least.

Next, he peered around the room. There were four hanging cages large enough to hold a man, but not so large that a person could stretch out. Two of them were empty, but the third held a lump in a dirty sheet. Khyven squinted in the flickering torchlight. No, not a sheet, a nightgown draped over the curve of a female hip.

"Hey," Khyven whispered. Speaking brought a fresh crop of pain from swollen eyes, bruised cheeks, and a split lip. He grunted and tried to push the pain to the back of his mind. "Are you alive?"

The figure stirred and she rose shakily on her elbow. Wavy auburn hair fell away from her pale face.

"Shalure!"

She had a black eye, a swollen cheek, and for a moment he thought she had no chin because it was bathed in dark blood, from her bottom lip all the way to her chest, staining her nightgown in a V-shape between her breasts.

"Senji's Spear…" Khyven said, dumbstruck. "What did they do?"

She opened her mouth to speak, but only a guttural sound

emerged. The sound of an animal.

"Ah-en..." she said weakly, then squeezed her eyes shut. It sounded like she was trying to say his name, but she couldn't because...

They had cut out her tongue.

"Shalure..." he whispered. He clenched the bars so hard lightning jolted through his right arm. "No, no... Oh no..."

"Ah-en..." she said again. She scooted closer to him, causing her cage to rock on its chain. She pushed one slender hand through the bars and reached for him. Tears welled in her eyes and streaked down her dirt-smeared cheeks.

Khyven's eyes blurred with his own tears. "I'm sorry, Shalure," he said. "I'm so sorry—"

Keys turned in the iron lock and the door opened dramatically, slamming into the wall.

King Vamreth, the hulking Vex the Victorious, Sir Cantoy, another of the king's elites, and a fifth man with a large leather satchel slung over his shoulder, entered. The fifth man was smaller and older, with wispy white hair. He immediately moved to the only table in the room, dark with stains that looked suspiciously like blood, and thumped his satchel on top of it.

Sir Cantoy and the other elite held bright lanterns high overhead, illuminating the dark room.

Vamreth stepped into the light. Shalure shrank back in her cage with a pitiful sound and began shaking. Vex, impassive in his full suit of plate mail, took up a position behind Khyven's cage.

"Oh, well done," Vamreth said to Sir Cantoy. "Is he very broken?"

"Only bruised, Your Majesty," Sir Cantoy said.

"That's perfect," Vamreth said. "Just perfect. And the girl?"

"As ordered, Your Majesty."

"No more selling secrets for you, eh my dear?" Vamreth said.

Shalure began to cry. She pulled her arms and legs into her body and cringed at the furthest edge of her cage.

Khyven managed to unclench his teeth long enough to

growl. "I'm going to kill you, Vamreth."

Vamreth chuckled. "Are you now? You're going to do this how? From your cage? With no weapons?"

"Why…?" Khyven said. "Why did you do have to do that to her?" He looked at the shuddering Shalure and it felt like his heart was tearing in two. "How can that possibly help you?"

Vamreth drew his sword in a flash and swung at Khyven's hands. He barely pulled them back in time. The blade smashed into the bars and sparked, ringing loudly in the small room.

"Because I'm king!" Vamreth growled. "Because that bitch had the temerity to give me terms. Because I wanted to. That's why, you damned traitor."

Vamreth showed his teeth, the mean-spirited smile of a mad dog. "I should have seen through you from the first moment. I wasted so much time and effort shaping you, all for nothing."

The rage in Khyven's belly spread to his whole body, and for a moment he couldn't feel any pain through his overwhelming hatred for this man.

"See here?" Vamreth said, putting a hand on the white-haired man. "This is Santor-Veth. He does exactly what you would imagine. He hurts people. A cross, you might say, between a sawbones and a blacksmith. He can create a work of art from a Human body. Just about anything you can imagine. And he keeps his creations alive. At least… long enough to be useful."

"By Senji, I'm going to kill you," Khyven said so low it didn't even sound like his own voice.

"No," Vamreth said. "Here's what you're going to do. Santor-Veth is going to remove your right arm, your sword arm. He's going to cut it off and then we're going to throw you into a fight against a nobody. Today, in fact. The entire kingdom is going to see Khyven the Unkillable slain by some unknown ringer. Perhaps the one with the limp who came in yesterday." He glanced at Shalure. "She'll join you. That's what you're going to do. That is my final order for you."

Shalure sobbed.

"Figure out what you'll need," Vamreth said to Santor-Veth, who nodded with an eager gleam in his eyes. "I'll send Vex, Cantoy, and a half dozen others to take him out of the cage and strap him down so you can work."

"Yes, Your Majesty," Santor-Veth's voice creaked like an unoiled hinge. He rubbed his hands together and approached the cage.

"He's fast, Santor," Vamreth warned. "You get too close, he'll kill you."

"I will be careful," Santor-Veth creaked as he approached Khyven's cage with a gleam in his eyes. "Oh, so careful. We will dance, you and I. We will make art together."

Vamreth turned when he reached the door. "I want you to remember, Khyven, when you're dying in the Night Ring, that you could have had everything." He gestured at Shalure. "You could have had a beautiful wife. You could have had a place at my side. A barony. Lands. Respect. Power. And you gave it up. For what? For some bitch in the woods? What did she promise you? Did she hike her skirts for you? What made you change sides?"

Khyven glared balefully at Vamreth and didn't answer.

"Feh." Vamreth waved a hand in the air. "I wash my hands of you. I look forward to seeing you die." He turned and went through the door. His retinue followed, slamming and locking the door behind him, leaving Santor-Veth alone in the room with them.

Khyven grabbed the door of the cage and shook it, but it was solid, the lock well-made. He looked for some way out while Santor-Veth hummed to himself, opened his bag, and began inspecting the various steel tools within. He laid out a few hooked and serrated blades, along with an ominous-looking saw. None were weapons Khyven had ever seen, and they struck fear into his heart. The idea that one—or all—of those would be working their way into his flesh made him turn his gaze away.

"Very well..." Santor-Veth finally said softly, patting his tools like beloved pets. "I think we are ready." He looked at Khyven with those eager eyes, still rubbing his hands like he was washing them. "I will see you soon, beautiful man. We will have such a time, you and I. I can see your strength. Before we are done, you will know exactly how strong you are."

He turned to Shalure and she huddled even harder into herself, shrinking into a bony ball. "And you, my dear, perhaps a shorter dance for us—"

"Don't you talk to her," Khyven roared. "Don't even look at her!"

The white-haired man didn't seem to hear Khyven. He just nodded to himself and turned toward the door. "Oh, yes," he murmured. "A short but exquisite dance…"

He unlocked the door, vanished into the dark, and closed it behind him, leaving Khyven and Shalure in silence, save for her soft, muffled sobbing.

The pain that coursed through Khyven's body was suddenly minor compared to the pain in his heart. He had done this. He had brought himself and Shalure to ruin, to be hacked up by that butcher and served as a final amusement to Vamreth and his horde.

How could I have been so blind? Khyven thought. *How could I have, even for a moment, served a man who could do this?*

But Khyven had known, hadn't he? He'd seen Vamreth's cruelty in the Night Ring, in the very existence of this place. He'd known and he'd gone along anyway.

Every bit of this was his fault.

"Ah-en…" Shalure said.

He turned his aching body so he could see her. She sat up, blood and tears making horrific tracks down her dirty face.

"Shalure, don't try to speak. I'm going to free us. I promise you."

"Ah-en…" She shook her head and said, her eyes full of pain, "Ah ohg eng."

She was trying to tell him something. He squinted, focusing on her lips.

"Ah"—she pointed at her chest, "ohg"—she pointed at her bloody mouth, "eng"—she gestured at the door. "abah ooo"—She pointed at him. She bowed her head, still watching him through her lashes. More tears welled up in her eyes. She pointed a shaky finger at him again. "Ah ohg eng abah ooo." *I told them about you.*

"Shalure, no. It's all right."

"Ah ahrry," she cried. "Ah oh ahrry." *I'm sorry. I'm so sorry.*

"Listen to me." Khyven clenched the bars, forcing the words past the lump in his throat. "Nothing you've done—nothing you could ever do—would warrant what he did to you. Nothing. I'm going to get you out of here. I swear I'm going to stab that man through the heart."

"Ah ahrry, Ah-en," she murmured, hanging her head. She slumped back in her cage and it rocked softly, the great chain squeaking in the ring set in the ceiling.

Gods damn it!

Khyven shook the cage with all his strength. Lightning bolts of pain shot up his right arm, but he didn't care. He thrashed and pulled at the door and the cage began to rock. He used its momentum, trying to swing the cage so hard he might reach something. Maybe those tools on the table.

The cage swung wider and wider, the chain making great, grinding squeaks, but its arc took the cage high above the table. No matter how hard Khyven strained, how hard he pushed his good arm between the bars, the tips of his fingers were still two feet from the table.

Breathing hard, exhausted, he fell back, and the cage settled into a gentle rocking, then stilled altogether.

I have to wait, Khyven thought. *Stay sharp. Wait for my chance. When those bastards come for me, when they take me out of this cage, that's when it will happen. I'll have to fight like I've never fought before.*

They would be ready for him to try something like that, but he would bet they wouldn't be ready for his fury—

"Well," a voice came out of the darkness.

Khyven jolted upright. Shalure did the same, and both cages rocked. He peered into the flickering darkness, toward the door. It stood ajar.

Vohn emerged from the shadows, orange torchlight

flickering off his black skin and dancing across an amorphous black hat he had pulled over his head to hide his horns.

"Vohn!" Khyven whispered in disbelief. "How did you…?"

"There is no dark place where I cannot hide, Khyven the Unkillable," Vohn said. "I thought you knew that."

"Is Lorelle—Is Rhenn—" he began, then found he could not ask the question. He couldn't make the words "Are they dead?" come out of his mouth.

"They live," he said, and relief swept through Khyven like a flood.

"Thank Senji…" he murmured.

"But so many did not," Vohn said. "Vamreth's knights killed them. Cut them down, left and right. Twenty of us survived, the twenty who had amulets and could escape into the noktum."

"No…" Khyven said, and his momentary relief twisted into thorns. Twenty… out of two hundred.

Vohn stared at Khyven with his black eyes, full of rage and accusation. Suddenly, Khyven realized Vohn was here to kill him, not to help him. He'd come to ensure Khyven didn't get a second chance to serve Vamreth.

"Did… Rhenn send you?" Khyven asked, wondering what he would do if Vohn tried to stab him. Would he fight? Or would he simply accept what was rightly his?

"Rhenn doesn't know I'm here," Vohn said. "She is… broken. She trusted you, and you stabbed her in the heart."

Khyven's throat tightened, and he couldn't form words. He suddenly knew if Vohn drew a weapon to slay him, he wouldn't raise a hand to stop it.

"But I saw you…" Vohn said, his voice shaky with emotion. He clenched a trembling fist in front of his face. "I saw you fight them. You fought like a rabid Kyolar for my queen. You killed ten of them. Ten knights, and not just Knights of the Steel, but Knights of the Dark and a Knight of the Sun; Vamreth's best. You hewed through them like stalks of wheat. If we'd had even a half dozen of you, Khyven, we'd have won that battle. And you"—Vohn swallowed—"you gave her the time to escape. If not for your fierce attack, Rhenn would be dead."

Vohn bowed his head, then raised it again, and his dark gaze was like a spear. "There are few I've hated more than you, Khyven the Unkillable. I led you to my queen's camp and you destroyed us. But… for that single moment at the Burzagi Tor, when you defeated Txomin… and again last night when you took on Vamreth's entire army, you made me believe. I see you doing the impossible, again and again, and I think"—he hesitated, and he clenched his fist as though the words pained him—"and I keep thinking, if you were just on our side, we could win this war."

Khyven said nothing.

"So, here we are," Vohn said. "Back where we started, our positions reversed, but I find myself desperate to make the same demand of you. This time for real. This time for the last time. Swear to my queen, Khyven. Fight for us like you fought last night. Fight for us for the rest of your life, and make the impossible possible again."

Khyven felt the tears slide down his cheeks and he whispered, "Just give me that chance."

Vohn produced the key, shoved it in the lock, and turned it. The cage door swung open and Khyven climbed out, landed next to the small Shadowvar.

"I'm gambling everything on you," Vohn said, opening his clenched fist. In his palm was Khyven's amulet.

"I know." Khyven put it over his head.

Vohn nodded once, tersely, then headed toward the door. "They'll be coming soon. Hurry."

Khyven went to Shalure's cage and unlocked it.

Vohn spun around. "What are you doing?"

"I can't leave her here."

"Khyven… no," Vohn said. "We can't take her. You can't blend with the shadows, which means we have to go through the noktum. She doesn't have an amulet. She won't survive."

"I can't leave her, Vohn. They'll torture her to death. Look at her."

Vohn turned to Shalure, his gaze going to the blood on the

front of her night dress, the blood on her chin. His stern face softened. He glanced at Khyven and something changed in his eyes. "Yes." He nodded. "You are right, of course. Come girl. Shalure, is it?"

She nodded.

Vohn led them through the halls to the next antechamber and unlocked the door. A guard lay crumpled on the floor next to the door, as though Vohn had already been here.

They went into the antechamber, lined with cages containing a dozen sleeping ringers. Some awoke and sat up as they entered.

"Get yourself a weapon," Vohn said, striding between the cages toward the stacks of weapons… and the gate leading to the arena.

"Wait." Khyven stopped in the midst of the cages. A hopeful naïf came forward, grabbing the bars.

"Let me out," he said. "Please, for the love of Senji, let me out."

Khyven glanced at Vohn, then back at the naïf, and he smiled. "Yes. I think we will."

"We will?" Vohn said incredulously.

"Take Shalure. We're going through the Night Door?"

Vohn nodded.

"Then give me those keys and we'll leave Vamreth a present."

Vohn understood what Khyven meant at last. With a smile that mirrored Khyven's own, he tossed the keys, and Khyven snatched them out of the air.

"We will wait for you," Vohn said. "Don't be late."

Khyven chuckled and began unlocking cages. The ringers milled into the room. Khyven went to the weapon racks, chose a longsword and a practice sword. He slid them both through his belt.

"You want your freedom?" he announced to the freed ringers. "Arm yourselves. Make for the front gate. Fight your way out. Tonight is your night. Make it count."

A whooping cry went up from the crowd and Khyven

hissed. "Idiots! Quietly. Get as close to the gate as you can before alerting the whole city."

Khyven ran from the room, down the hallway to the next antechamber, released its prisoners, gave the same speech, and ran to the next antechamber.

By the time he had reached the sixth antechamber, he passed the keys to one of the ringers. "Release them all," he said. "Form up together, head for the gate. Escape into the forest."

Khyven went to the arena gate next, opened it, and slipped inside.

As promised, Vohn and Shalure were waiting by the Night Door, which gaped open. The rest of the huge noktum doors were shut, but Vohn had done his work.

Out of breath, Khyven ran up to them. Shalure looked terrified.

She pointed at the lazy tentacles deep within the archway. "Ih ere?" *In there?*

Khyven took the Amulet of Noksonon off and put it around Shalure's neck.

"Trust me," he said.

Vohn shook his head, then said tightly, "Ready?"

"Let's go," Khyven replied.

Shalure made an indistinguishable noise of terror and gripped Khyven's arm with both hands.

They plunged into the noktum.

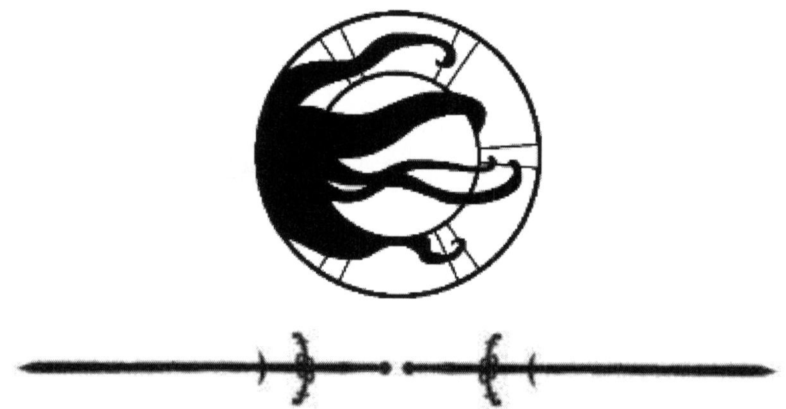

CHAPTER THIRTY-ONE

KHYVEN

he darkness enveloped them and Shalure clung to him so hard he stumbled.

"You have to walk, Shalure," he whispered. "We have to move quickly."

She whimpered and staggered alongside him. Dark light glowed from Vohn's amulet and it seemed to spread all the way to the horizon. Slowly, Khyven's eyes adjusted to that dark twilight. Shalure's gasp told him that she could see now, too.

In the distance, a Kyolar stood on the ridge of a hill, its ears perked, its feline muzzle pointed toward him. Khyven drew his sword with his left hand, sparing his throbbing right arm. He was better with his right, but Khyven had trained with his left hand as well.

"They're coming," Vohn said. "This isn't going to work, Khyven. Rhenn tried it before and people died! Three people, three amulets. They'll get to you—"

"I'm not leaving her behind."

"You don't have a choice. She cannot help my queen's cause, but you can."

"She's one of us now."

"*You're* not even one of us anymore!" Vohn said.

The Kyolar sprinted down the hill toward them. Another loped out of the dark woods to their left. A giant shape appeared, moving through the forest, its top rising, spherical, with segmented legs pushing it above the treetops. Khyven realized with horror that it was an enormous spider of some kind. Shadows flitted overhead. Khyven looked up and saw a swarm of the giant, fanged otters slithering across the sky, shooting past them and wheeling around, as though inspecting their prey.

"Put on the amulet, Khyven!"

"She'll die—"

Shalure screamed. The otters dove. Three of them hammered into Khyven so fast he didn't have time to raise his sword. They ripped him from Shalure's grasp so violently she stumbled and sprawled onto her face.

"Khyven!" Vohn shouted, reaching hopelessly into the air as the otters pulled him up—

Something huge slammed into Khyven and the otters, scattering them. The otters hissed, dropping Khyven and slithering through the air in every direction. The world whirled as Khyven fell. He slammed into the ground and his injured arm screamed as he tumbled to a stop.

A giant Kyolar landed next to him. The thing had obviously leapt into the mass of giant otters, scattering them and stealing their prey.

Clenching his teeth, Khyven rolled to his knees. He'd dropped his sword in the fall, so he pulled out the practice sword and staggered to his feet.

The Kyolar faced him, massive paws wide and head low. Its slanted eyes glowed darkly, and it hissed, showing teeth as long as Khyven's fingers.

It didn't attack.

Khyven spared a look behind him, sure that another Kyolar was closing in, or that enormous spider.

And he was right. Three other Kyolars appeared, padding silently toward him. The flying otters overhead went insane, flying this way and that like black banners in a storm.

Fifty feet away, Vohn and Shalure watched helplessly.

Khyven gripped the practice sword, facing the closest Kyolar even as he tried to grow eyes in the back of his head. The giant spider loomed off to his right, slowly moving through the trees toward him.

"Well, what are you waiting for?" Khyven shouted.

One of the otters dove straight for Khyven, breaking from the pack, talons out. He brought his sword up, but the Kyolar leapt for Khyven at the same time and he threw himself sideways, knowing he wouldn't be able to avoid those jaws—

The Kyolar snapped the otter in half. The top of its bloody body landed in front of Khyven. The Kyolar shook its head, flinging the other half a dozen feet away, where it tumbled across the black grass.

The otters continued their frenzy of movement above, but no more attacked. The Kyolar turned to Khyven, black blood dripping from its furry lips and it bowed its head. The three other Kyolars did the same.

What the…?

"Khyven, what's happening?" Vohn said.

"I… don't know."

Then the answer hit him like a lightning bolt. Rauvelos. The giant raven had told Khyven that he would always be safe in the noktum as long as he wore his amulet, but somehow these Kyolars recognized him without it, even if the otters did not.

Khyven looked around. The Kyolars—now there were six of them—stood about him in a circle, bowing their heads.

"Senji's Boots…" he murmured. He glanced at the giant spider. It had stopped moving, still towering over the woods.

Tentatively, Khyven started toward the Kyolar that had killed the otter. He walked with his wooden sword before him, and as he neared the Kyolar gave way without attacking. Khyven continued toward the astounded Vohn and Shalure, stopping only to pick up the sword he had dropped.

The Kyolars fell into line, three on a side, and flanked Khyven as he walked.

"Khyven…" Vohn said incredulously as Khyven rejoined them.

"Let's go," Khyven said.

"Khyven—"

"Quickly."

Vohn stopped talking and they strode swiftly up the path that had been created by Rhenn's followers.

They walked in silence for half an hour. The Kyolars continued pacing them and Khyven began to get the impression that the Kyolars had become a sort of honor guard, protecting Khyven and the others against anything in the noktum that might choose to hurt them. Even the flying otters had vanished, no longer circling overhead.

"We're not going back to the camp," Khyven said.

"No," Vohn said.

"Where did… the survivors go?"

"Into the mountains, a cave. It's temporary. Rhenn was just contemplating going to Triada when I slipped away."

"Triada?"

"She has lost her army. Even with the Sandrunners, she won't have enough fighters to unseat Vamreth. She has to come up with another solution."

"So, she's going to Triada for what? To ask them for troops?"

"To marry Alfric."

"Marry—?"

"If she marries Alfric, the king of Triada will give her the troops she needs."

"And after the war, five hundred Triadan fighters will be sitting in the middle of Usara," Khyven said. "Why wouldn't they just kill Rhenn and claim the kingdom as their own?"

"I have made that argument," Vohn said. "She believes she can ask for the right number of troops, enough to bolster the Sandrunners, but not enough that Triada will have the upper hand."

"That's ridiculous."

"You didn't leave her many choices, did you?" he said scathingly. "I'm hoping you can come up with a better idea."

"Me?"

"Yes."

"I'm not a strategist, or a diplomat."

"But you have a knack for making the impossible happen. Think of something, damn you."

Khyven went silent. "Two hundred and fifty Sandrunners might be enough to take the palace, if we came in stealth."

"Maybe, but Rhenn plans to set out for Triada immediately if she hasn't already."

"Let's walk faster."

They tried, but Shalure's bare feet had already been cut in half a dozen places. Her pace had slowed until she was limping. She didn't complain, but tears streamed down her face as she tried to keep up.

"Wait, Vohn," Khyven said, and stopped. Shalure stopped with him and she looked miserable, like she had stepped into her own personal nightmare. Beaten, mutilated, exhausted, and probably starving, she was now walking through this benighted land on lacerated feet, shadowed by monsters. "I'm sorry, Shalure, it's just a little farther."

She nodded, blinking back tears and limping past him. In her guttural tone, she said, "I'm ah aigh." *I'm all right.*

But she wasn't all right. He suspected she was terrified that if she couldn't keep up, they'd leave her.

"Shalure," he said. "I'm not going to leave you. I promise. Here"—he gently took her wrist and stopped her—"I will carry you." He patted his shoulder.

She looked at him gratefully. With a boost, she climbed onto his back with a sigh. He hooked one hand under each of her thighs and hiked her a little higher. His bruised right arm voiced its protest, but he ignored it.

"Ank ooo," she whispered gratefully into his ear. *Thank you.*

He strode forward and caught up with Vohn. When Khyven surmised they'd been in the noktum about an hour, mostly because the Kyolars began looking at both Shalure and Vohn hungrily, Vohn left the path, veered right, and stepped through the veil of the noktum into the bright sunlight of a new day. The morning rays filtered through the trees of the Royal Forest, almost blinding them as they stepped away from the questing tentacles that oozed out of the noktum.

Shalure gasped in relief, and she wiggled to be let off Khyven's back. He set her down and she whimpered as her feet touched the ground. Immediately, she took off the amulet and pushed it into his hands like it was a poisonous snake.

"How much farther?" Khyven asked as he put the amulet around his neck.

Vohn pointed through the trees where the land started upward. "A hike."

Shalure squeezed her eyes shut, like she wanted to cry, but she didn't.

"Let's get to it." Khyven motioned to her and she climbed onto his back again.

They hiked into the woods for what seemed like another half an hour, and finally they crested a rise that led to a cave. Lord Harpinjur sat on top of a knee-high rock with two other knights flanking the cave's opening.

"Senji's Spear!" Lord Harpinjur leapt to his feet and drew his sword. "You!"

Khyven gently put Shalure on the ground.

"Sheath your sword, my lord," Vohn said. "I brought him."

"I can see that," Lord Harpinjur roared. "The question is why. This traitor slaughtered two hundred—!"

"It wasn't him," Vohn said.

"He brought Vamreth!"

"I brought him because we need him," Vohn said.

"By all the hells, we do not. We kill traitors here—"

"What's going on?" Rhenn's voice rose from the cave, full of command. She appeared, and her gaze fell upon Khyven.

Her reaction wasn't what he'd hoped for. Her eyes hardened and her jaw clenched. Lorelle appeared from the shadows behind her, and behind her was the handsome prince of Triada, Alfric.

"What," Rhenn said through her teeth, "is he doing here?"

"I brought him," Vohn said. "I went into the city."

"You what?"

"Your Majesty, we need him. You know I wouldn't have gone after him if I didn't think that—"

Rhenn marched toward Khyven, baring her teeth. Lord Harpinjur tried to put a hand on her shoulder to stop her from getting too close to Khyven, but she batted the lord's hand away.

Khyven saw the dagger slip into Rhenn's hand from a spring-loaded forearm sheath. One second it wasn't there and the next it was. It was so subtle and well done that another might have missed it, but Khyven had spent too long in the Night Ring.

She brought the dagger up to his throat and Khyven forced himself to stay still. He had no choices anymore. Either Rhenn would accept him, or she wouldn't.

The dagger pressed against his neck, quivering.

"I should kill you, you bastard," Rhenn hissed. Lorelle stood behind Rhenn, her chin high. Her face was impassive, but the tips of her hair glowed.

Then Vohn was there, his hand on Rhenn's arm.

"Your Majesty, he fought for you. He leapt into the middle of the knights at the camp. If Khyven hadn't distracted them, they would have killed you. He slew ten of Vamreth's knights—"

"And he slew two hundred of mine!" She pushed the dagger against his throat. The line of steel burned against Khyven's skin, and he felt a rivulet of blood trickle down his neck.

"Aren't you going to save yourself?" Rhenn demanded. "That's what you do best, isn't it? Fight for yourself? Show me those miraculous fighting skills, now. Let's have it out."

"The games are over," Khyven said hoarsely. "I won't fight you. Not ever again. My life is yours. If you wish to take it, I won't stop you."

"O!" Shalure shouted. *No!* She grabbed Khyven's arm like she would somehow protect him.

Rhenn turned her furrowed brow in Shalure's direction. "Who is this?"

"I don't know," Vohn said.

"Lady Shalure Chadrone," Khyven said. "Daughter of the Baron of Turnic."

Rhenn looked back at Khyven. "Her tongue, your handiwork?"

"It's my fault, if that's what you mean," Khyven said.

"Khyven the Cruel. Khyven the Traitor. Khyven the Backstabbing—"

"Please, Your Majesty," Vohn pleaded. "The Sandrunners. I know he said they should listen to anyone who has an amulet, but if we have him here, it will be that much stronger of a position—"

"The Sandrunners aren't coming," Rhenn said.

Vohn's mouth, open to speak, hung there. "Not coming?" he said, mystified.

"Our stunt at Burzagi Tor failed."

"Wha—Why?"

"Apparently the Hareazko Clan refused to enforce the rules that would give Khyven the right to lead them. They retained the throne. The Ilunsenti Clan declared war. The Urdina and Griza Clans sided with Ilunsenti. The Nabarra with Hareazko. Civil war rages in the Eternal Desert. We will see no Lantzas from them."

"No..." Vohn said.

"So, we are going to Triada. Thank Senji Alfric survived the attack. If he hadn't, every kingdom in a thousand miles would kill us on sight."

"Your Majesty—"

Rhenn sliced a hand through the air. "Enough, Vohn! You brought this traitor back for nothing." She sneered at Khyven. "Unless you can fight Vamreth's entire army by yourself, Khyven the Useless, then you have no purpose here."

Khyven swallowed.

"Go," Rhenn whispered lethally, lowering the dagger. "If I ever see you again, I *will* kill you. We won't bother with a duel.

You'll never get this close to me again. We will shoot you down with arrows. Go seek your fortune with King Vamreth. He will be kinder to you than I will."

Khyven's heart pounded. Vohn looked stricken, but didn't say anything.

Khyven looked to Lorelle. Her eyes seemed sorrowful, but she said nothing.

"I will go." Khyven swallowed. "But I would beg a favor—"

"Would you now?" Rhenn chuckled; it was a thin, mean sound. "Well, I am fresh out of favors, Khyven."

"Please," Khyven said. "Take Lady Shalure. She has—she won't survive if you don't. Turn me out. Kill me if you must, but shelter her, I beg you."

"You've destroyed everything I built," Rhenn said, her voice thick with emotion. "Get out of my sight." She turned, her cloak furling about her as she stalked toward the cave. Alfric followed close behind, but Lorelle hesitated, watching Khyven without expression. Finally, she turned and followed.

Vohn came forward, his eyes downcast. He took Shalure's arm, and only then did he look up at Khyven.

"I'll take care of her," Vohn said softly. "But… you should go."

Khyven's heart ached. "She—You don't think she'll change her mind? About me? I could help."

Vohn hesitated, like he wanted to give Khyven hope, but then he shook his head. "If it was up to me…. But it's not."

"I could help, Vohn. I-I know which side I'm on now. I could help her!"

"That's why I came back for you. But…" He shook his head. "It doesn't matter anymore. You should just go."

Khyven couldn't believe it had come to this. When Vohn had opened his cage, he thought he'd get another chance. Just one more chance. He had planned to show Rhenn he believed in her, believed in her cause.

His throat tightened.

Shalure clung to him and made a series of guttural sounds that even Khyven couldn't understand, but the meaning was clear. She wanted to go with him.

Slowly but firmly, he disengaged her arms. "You can't. You're hurt, Shalure. Vohn will look after you."

"Ah-en…" she said, broken-hearted.

"I'm sorry," he said. "Tell Rhenn I'm sorry," he said to Vohn. "When she calms down, tell her, and tell Lorelle I wanted…"

But he couldn't finish the sentence. He turned and started down the hill.

Chapter Thirty-Two

KHYVEN

Khyven walked down the slope in a daze. He didn't know how long he meandered through the woods. His stomach began to growl. He had no place to go, and for the first time in his life, he didn't know what he should do. He didn't have an old man telling him to train with this or work at that. He didn't have the dire, life-threatening Night Ring to define his actions. He had no ambition to rise through Vamreth's court.

He had nothing.

He reached the edge of the old camp, the swelling of the noktum reaching out like a hand, encircling the spot that used to be safe.

He considered going inside, but he envisioned bodies lying there, people he had met, who had danced in front of Rhenn's stage.

Sickened, he turned and faced the tentacles of the noktum, lazily reaching out to him. He walked into them. They avoided him because of his amulet, but as he passed through the wall, the darkness swallowed him, nonetheless.

He stood there in blessed, absolute blackness. He hoped one of the fanged otters would descend and kill him before he could move, before a Kyolar could come to his rescue.

He let out a sigh and encircled the amulet with his finger. The bleak landscape appeared in the black light, the castle of the nuraghi in the distance.

The flying, fanged otters had noticed him, but they kept their distance in frustration because a Kyolar remained at the spot where Khyven, Shalure, and Vohn had exited. It padded toward him, its great head glancing upward at the otters.

Khyven gave a rueful bark of a laugh.

"So, this is the only place I'm welcome," he said as he walked along. "The only place I belong. The land of death and monsters—"

His foot kicked something hard, and he looked down.

Gohver's Mavric iron sword lay on the grass a hundred feet from the noktum wall. He'd almost tripped over it, and now he stopped. He stared at the thing, thinking of Gohver's last, horrible moments. At the time, he couldn't have imagined a worse fate, but that was exactly how his insides felt now. Gohver, who had clung to that sword even as it killed him. He remembered one of Gohver's last excited statements about the blade.

In my hands, that sword could cut through a dozen o' the false king's men.

A dozen…

An idea formed in Khyven's mind. Khyven had slain nearly a dozen men with normal steel. With that sword in hand, how many might he kill?

Unless you can fight Vamreth's entire army by yourself, Khyven the Useless, then you have no purpose here….

Rhenn's words. But even with the sword, Khyven couldn't kill an entire army, could he?

The idea expanded and Khyven imagined himself breaking into the palace, a lightning attack, slaying anyone who got in his way as he cut a path to the king.

It was a slender thread. Any of a hundred things could go wrong. As Vohn had said, if Khyven only had a half dozen of himself, then he could make that happen.

A half dozen monsters like me, all charging into the palace. We could…

Khyven's thought trailed off and he looked at the Kyolars—now there were four of them—surrounding him protectively.

A half dozen monsters like me…

He looked at the nuraghi in the distance, then broke into a run. The Kyolars paced him, loping easily alongside him until he reached the gates. The giant cats peeled off left and right, and stood outside the gate, but they clearly were not going to enter.

Khyven looked overhead, but he didn't see any of the enterprising fanged otters. He sprinted across the long, wide courtyard filled with statues. Apparently, the Kyolars knew that Rauvelos didn't want Khyven harmed and the otters did not. He couldn't be sure there weren't a hundred other species of monsters inside the nuraghi that agreed with the otters. But he reached the gates without incident and slipped into the grand foyer with the Giant skeletons. Out of breath, he jogged to the first room, the room where Gohver had first taken up the sword. Khyven stood in the middle of the room and peered into the darkness high overhead.

"Rauvelos!" he boomed. His voice echoed into the darkness and back. He called the giant bird's name again, and a third time.

Shadows moved overhead. A great darkness unfurled, dropping down from above, and Khyven leapt backward. The *whoosh* of giant wings drove air downward and Khyven squinted as Rauvelos landed, his thick talons clicking on the dark stone. His giant wings folded against his huge body.

"Well," the enormous raven said with his beak, once again forming impossibly articulate words, "you have returned, Khyven the Unkillable. I am glad. It gets so lonely here."

"I need a favor."

"Ah," Rauvelos said, "a favor."

"I need an army."

"My dear, delectable Human. An army?"

"I heard a legend about the creatures of the noktum emerging into the world of Humans. In the night, long ago. Can they do that?"

Rauvelos didn't respond.

"Can they do that?" Khyven pressed.

"Those who live here will venture into the world of mortals briefly. For food, perhaps, but not for any other purpose," Rauvelos said. "Unless the master of the nuraghi commanded them to."

"*You* are the master here," Khyven said.

"No. I am only a steward," Rauvelos said. "Nhevalos is our master."

"But I am protected by Nhevalos."

Rauvelos narrowed his bird eyes. "Protected, yes. But you are not Nhevalos himself."

"But he gave me his symbol. You said so yourself. Maybe he knew I would come. Maybe he knew I would need this very thing from you."

"And maybe he left me here to kill someone like you who had the audacity to ask for such a thing."

"How do I do it?" Khyven demanded.

"You cannot. The Helm of Darkness was made for the Eldroi, those your kind call the Giants," Rauvelos said.

"Helm of Darkness? What's the Helm of Darkness?" Khyven asked. Then he recalled something Rauvelos had said during that first, terrifying moment Khyven had met him.

… every time I remove the helm, they just do what they want to anyway….

"It controls them," Khyven said. "You have a helm that controls them."

"The helm calls to the children of the noktum," Rauvelos said. "It opens the wielder's mind to their minds, but the wielder must be strong enough to take hold."

"It calls to all of them?"

"As many as you can imagine," Rauvelos said. "But it would kill you, as I'm sure you know by now." The raven's eyes glinted knowingly. "Mavric iron kills Humans."

Khyven thought of Gohver, and he swallowed hard.

"How long would it take?" Khyven asked.

Rauvelos cocked his great head. "How long until it killed you?"

"How many hours?"

"A few hours; less than a day. It depends on how strong you are, Khyven the Unkillable, but the end result would be the same."

"But for that day, I might wield it?"

Rauvelos chuckled. It was a low, dark sound. "You think your will would be strong enough to wield it?" He shook his head. "Humans are so arrogant."

Lorelle's words echoed in his head.

What you did requires more than training. It requires magic.

"I have magic. Will you give me the helm?" Khyven asked.

Rauvelos's bird eyes blinked once, twice. "When the masters still lived in their noktums do you know what they did to Humans who made demands of them?"

Khyven heard a noise, and he turned to see a dozen bat-things descending from the dark all around. A Kyolar slunk into the room, followed by another, and another. The hairs on the back of Khyven's neck stood on end.

"Rauvelos—"

"You have tempted fate," Rauvelos said. He unfurled his wings. "I gave you the freedom to move through the noktum without harm, but I cannot save you any longer. Your fate shall have you." He jumped into the air and flapped mightily, lifting his huge body upward.

"Rauvelos!" Khyven demanded. "Help me!"

The bird vanished into the darkness overhead.

"RAUVELOS!"

The denizens of the noktum closed in.

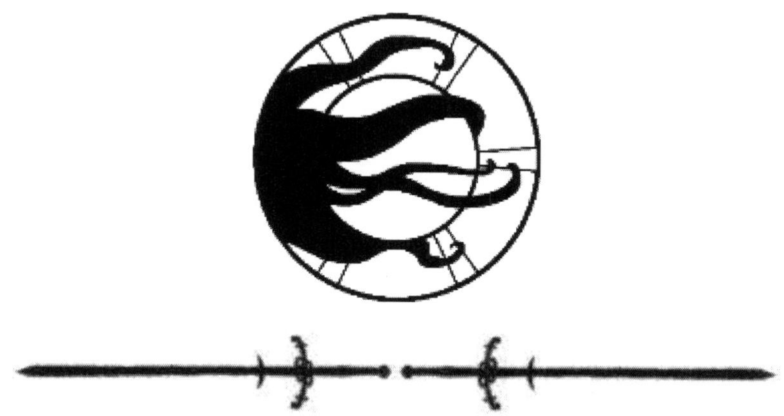

Chapter Thirty-Three

LORELLE

Lorelle didn't understand why she cared about Khyven, but his banishment weighed heavily on her.

She sat on the edge of the promontory beside the cave, just out of view of the small band that was all that remained of Rhenn's rebellion. The oranges and yellows of the sunset were fading to purple, but the beauty of it did nothing to cheer her or uncloud her thoughts. Even the smell of the pines, something she'd always loved about Usara, failed to enliven her.

Rhenn's little group had organized their belongings, put together their party, and they would set out for Triada in the morning.

Khyven had made his own bed, and she should despise him for it, but she felt sorry for him.

Rhenn collected broken people, fixed them up, made them believe in themselves again, and she had given Khyven everything she had. He'd been given chance after chance, and he had lied to them all.

And yet…

She had looked into his eyes when Vamreth's knights had

attacked the camp. She had believed him. He hadn't meant for the attack to happen. He'd taken up the sword and leapt into the fray. Vohn was right. If it hadn't been for Khyven, Rhenn would have been captured or killed. Khyven had fought like a man possessed. He'd attacked like he intended to drive back the entire force, and for a brilliant moment it seemed like he actually might.

So many of Vamreth's knights had been forced to concentrate on Khyven that it had given Lorelle and Vohn the time to evacuate Rhenn from the camp through the noktum, against her vociferous protests. At the edge of the black, Lorelle had turned for a precious moment, watched them beat Khyven unconscious, watched them bind him and haul him away.

Her heart had lurched and she had almost turned back for him. She'd had to forcefully remind herself that Rhenn was her primary concern. But she couldn't shake the guilty feeling that they had, literally, left Khyven to die at Vamreth's hands when he had fought to save them.

Then the impossible had happened. Khyven had returned. Again. Vohn, who had as much reason to hate Khyven as anyone, had risked his life to go back and pry Khyven out of Vamreth's grip. It was almost as if the god Lotura were talking to Lorelle, telling her that Khyven was somehow necessary to Rhenn's rebellion. How many times had he done the impossible now? How many times had she written him off, and yet he had resurfaced?

Khyven the Unkillable, indeed…

But Rhenn had closed the door on him and that was that. Lorelle had never seen her so angry. She blamed Khyven for everything. The loss of the camp. The deaths of her friends and followers. There was no coming back from that. People *had* died. Khyven *had* brought the enemy, indirectly at the very least. There was no possibility of redemption short of bringing back the dead.

Lorelle understood that. What she couldn't understand was why it bothered her so much. Was it that she detested the idea of her friend having to marry Alfric? Going to Triada as beggars undermined everything she and Rhenn had built. There was no guarantee that allowing the king of Triada into Usara wouldn't be trading one Vamreth for another.

Lorelle turned her head as Vohn navigated his way onto the promontory. He was about as stealthy a person as there was, but he wasn't trying very hard, and her tall Luminent ears didn't miss much. He sat down next to her.

"You're thinking about Khyven," he said.

"I'm thinking I'm probably going to be hungry tonight." They hadn't taken any food with them when they escaped the attack. Two of Rhenn's knights had gone hunting, but they hadn't yet returned.

"No, you weren't," Vohn said, pulling his knees up and putting his chin on them.

"Why did you go get him?" she asked.

"Because I felt the same thing you're feeling now," he said.

"And what am I feeling?"

He raised an eyebrow.

She sighed. "It's illogical," she said. "He can't do anything for us. Not now."

"And see? I believe the opposite," Vohn said.

"What can he do, Vohn?"

"I don't know. I suppose if I knew, we wouldn't need him."

"You're saying Rhenn was wrong to banish him?"

Vohn paused. "That isn't the question. Yes, he deserves banishment for what he did. Maybe even worse. The real question is whether can we afford to lose him."

"Rhenn has to have people she can trust. In the end, what can one untrustworthy man, even one as exceptional as Khyven, do?"

"Don't tell me you didn't feel it. What he did at the Burzagi Tor? Libur's Sparks, Lorelle, he has something. When he's around, it seems that anything is possible, and that is what we need right now."

"You want to believe. That's all. We all want to believe. But all you really know is that he's a talented swordsman. He dazzled us at Burzagi Tor, won us an army, and we've loved him ever since. But he was planning to betray us all along. Think about that, Vohn. No matter what he *can* do for us, how could we ever trust him again?"

Vohn fell silent and they watched the darkening horizon.

"Then why are you here?" he asked. "Out here? Thinking?" The sun was gone, and the forest sank into soft twilight.

"Getting rid of unneeded baggage," she said.

Vohn sighed and stood up. "I don't like it when you lie to me," he said. "But it's worse when you lie to yourself."

Anger flickered in Lorelle's heart. Vohn was so relentless sometimes.

"You're annoying me," she said.

"I hear that a lot."

She turned to face him. "Khyven is not our salvation. Rhenn is. And if Rhenn says our next move is Triada, then it is Triada."

"We've overlooked something with Khyven," Vohn said, ignoring her words like he did sometimes. "Yes, he did wrong, but we've cast him out because we're angry, not because we're right."

"Tread lightly, Shadowvar," Lorelle said. "We didn't turn him out in a fit of pique. His actions brought Rhenn's rebellion to ruin."

"What if he could bring it back from ruin?"

"You think too highly of him. He can't bring it back. People are dead—"

The scout's horn sounded, deep and mournful.

Lorelle cursed, leaping to her feet. "What now?"

Had Vamreth found them? Had he tracked them somehow? Was their final battle upon them?

She ran to the front of the cave just as Rhenn, Lord Harpinjur, and the dozen others emerged.

Sir Chellit, who had obviously sounded the alarm, ran up the hill as though being chased by his worst nightmare, the horn bouncing about from its shoulder strap. Lorelle peered past him into the darkness of the failing light.

Chellit gave a guttural cry, trying to shape his warning

without a tongue. The more Lorelle concentrated, the more she could see. The shadows moved, flitted through the trees. Men and horses and…

No, not horses. They weren't moving like horses.

Her gaze flicked up to some enormous, winged creature soaring over the tops of the trees bearing a Human rider. Below it, a writhing mass of darkness burst from the trees. Hundreds of Kyolars churned the dirt as they ran up the slope toward Rhenn's hideout.

"Lotura preserve us…." Lorelle murmured, stepping back and gripping her blowgun as though it could possibly do anything against that horde.

The monsters of the noktum had broken into the world of mortals.

The Kyolars churned up the slope directly toward the cave, mewling at the sky. Giant, fanged otters slithered overhead, circling their very spot. Lord Harpinjur, Rhenn, Vohn, and all the rest gripped their weapons and looked up in stunned silence.

But none of the creatures attacked.

The Kyolars slowed to a walk, then sat on their haunches, putting their butts to the ground and looking up the hill.

Shalure screamed, and every person in the group drew weapons and backed up as an enormous bat beat its wings overhead, then landed on the flat ground before Rhenn's cave, right in front of what remained of Rhenn's band. The rider, who wore a huge metal helm that shadowed his face, jumped to the ground. As he walked forward, he reached up and removed the helm.

"Khyven!" Rhenn blurted.

"You said I could return if I could fight Vamreth's entire army by myself," Khyven said. "Did you mean it?"

Chapter Thirty-Four

LORELLE

No one spoke for what seemed like an eternity. Finally, it was Lord Harpinjur who broke the silence.

"Senji's Teeth!" The old knight blurted. "What did you do?"

"We needed an army," Khyven said, holding the huge helm beneath his arm. "I found one."

"Khyven…" Rhenn finally found her tongue. "How did you… Is this…"

"It's a story," he said. "Perhaps better told later. But suffice it to say that as long as I hold this"—he indicated the helm—"they'll do what I ask. Even attack Vamreth."

Lorelle looked at the black, rough iron of the helm, then at the sword on Khyven's back. That was Gohver's sword. The blade that had killed him. Lorelle looked closer at Khyven's face and saw a blister the size of a fingernail on his forehead.

"Khyven, that's Mavric iron," Lorelle said.

"I know." He patted the huge blade slung across his back.

"It'll kill you…" Lorelle said.

"Not before we unseat Vamreth," he said. "Not if we move

quickly."

"Khyven, I—"

"Take it off," Rhenn interrupted. "Put it—Put them back. We'll find another way."

Khyven fell silent and a small smile crossed his face. "Thank you for that… Your Majesty."

"You can—You can help us some other way," Rhenn said. "We will find another way."

"There is no other way, Your Majesty. Not that I'm certain would work. This is the way. Either you come with me, or I go without you. You are clearly the leader Usara needs and I'm going to make sure you have the chance to be."

"Then follow my command, Khyven," Rhenn said. "Take that abomination back. Now."

He shook his head. "With respect, Your Majesty, no. I spent my whole life trying to gain power and I never gave a thought to what I should use it for if I got it, other than my own survival." He glanced over his shoulder at the unholy horde crouching down the slope. "I know now. We're going to put you on the throne."

"This is insane," Lord Harpinjur murmured.

Prince Alfric was clearly thunderstruck, but he finally stepped forward. "Take your monsters back to the abyss from whence they came," he said. "My father will retake Usara for her."

"I'm sure he will," Khyven said. "And Rhenn will lose a lot more than one turncloak ringer."

"How dare you?" Alfric said.

Rhenn put a hand on Alfric's chest. "Quiet please, Your Highness."

"Rhenn, this traitor—"

"I said be quiet, Alfric," she snapped and turned back to Khyven. "I won't sacrifice your life," she said.

"Three hours ago, you wanted to kill me."

"You saw what happened to Gohver. I wouldn't wish that on anyone."

"You're wasting time, Your Majesty," Khyven said. "This is

the path. You could be on your throne tonight, but not if we waste time. Vamreth isn't expecting this. We'll take the whole city by surprise. But we must go. Now."

Rhenn's eyes were wide, and she furrowed her brows. Lorelle had never seen her friend at such a loss for what to do.

"I'm going to tear down the gates and every Vamreth loyalist who stands in my way," Khyven said. "If you'd like to come with me, I welcome you. If you'd like to come after I've done, that is fine as well."

Rhenn folded her arms across her chest. "You're a stubborn ass."

"Who is finally on the right side of this war," he said.

"At what cost?" she said.

"Rhenn—" Alfric said, but Rhenn raised her hand. His face turned red with anger, but he finished his sentence. "That army is evil."

"Yes," she said, surveying the horde. Her eyes narrowed, and she let out a breath. Her chin tilted down ever so slightly. "But it is *our* army."

Khyven smiled and started back for the giant bat. "To the front gates," he said. "Mount up and try to *keep* up—"

"Sir Khyven!" Rhenn's voice cracked like a whip. He turned, eyebrows raised at the command in Rhenn's voice.

He hesitated, then bowed. "Yes, Your Majesty."

"I gave no such order. We will move out according to a plan that we all understand. We aren't going to run pell-mell at the front gates."

"The plan is a straightforward attack," Khyven said. "We have the force. We have the surprise. We move now."

"We attack when and where I say we attack, Sir Khyven. If we go through the front gates, the casualties will be immense. Innocent people will be killed. I won't harm any more of my people than necessary."

"Harm your—They killed your friends yesterday. Anyone who stands in our way is loyal to Vamreth. Anyone who's not, can run. We have to—"

"Two days ago, *you* were loyal to Vamreth," Rhenn said.

Khyven's mouth hung open.

"We save lives, Khyven the Unkillable. We don't waste them. We do this my way."

"And which way is that?" Khyven asked.

"We end it as it began," she said, glancing at Lorelle.

A thrill of irrational fear went through Lorelle as she realized what Rhenn was saying. "Rhenn, are you sure?"

"We reclaim what is ours, one step at a time."

Oh, sister of my heart.... Lorelle thought.

"All very well and good, but what does that mean?" Khyven asked.

Rhenn turned from Lorelle back to Khyven. "It means we go through the noktum."

Chapter Thirty-Five

KHYVEN

Khyven, Rhenn, Lorelle, and Vohn flew across the noktum's midnight landscape on the backs of Gylarns—the name of the giant bat-things, according to Rauvelos. The rest of Khyven's army of noktum denizens either flew behind them or sprinted across the charcoal-colored heather below.

The remainder of Rhenn's band had stayed behind. Of course, Lord Harpinjur had railed against that decision, but Rhenn had said that with the might of a thousand Kyolars at their backs, a dozen more Human fighters wouldn't make a difference. All they could do was get themselves killed.

"I need you to stay, Lord Harpinjur," she'd told him. "If we fail, I need you to take care of the rest of us." She had indicated the ragged remains of her band, standing atop that rocky promontory, still watching with wide eyes.

Harpinjur had reluctantly agreed, but when Rhenn, Lorelle, and Khyven had mounted the Gylarns, Vohn had climbed onto the back of another without saying anything.

"You're not going," Rhenn had said.

Vohn glanced at Rhenn in defiance, then at Khyven. Khyven smiled back, then ordered all four Gylarns into the air.

Rhenn spat curses at Khyven for several minutes after that, and he derived a deep satisfaction from it, but his amusement had since faded. Time was running out. He could feel it in his body.

As the Gylarn beat its wings, the helm shifted back and forth on Khyven's head, and everywhere it rubbed burned like Khyven had touched a torch to those spots. He tried to ignore the pain, but he could feel his body softening, succumbing to the power of the Mavric iron. He had no idea how much longer he could endure this. They had to get to the palace, unleash this horde, and destroy Vamreth. And they had to do it soon.

Rauvelos had abandoned Khyven in such a dramatic fashion that Khyven had been certain he was about to die at the hands of the noktum horde. But the Kyolars, Sleeths—the giant, fanged otters—and the Gylarns hadn't attacked him. They'd simply waited, watching, until Rauvelos had swooped back down, landed with the big iron helm in his beak, and set it gently into Khyven's hand.

Khyven had felt that same compelling pull and revulsion he'd felt near Gohver's sword. It was like the helm was a succulent, roasted chicken leg that made his mouth water and his stomach twist at the same time.

"Put it on and you will feel them," Rauvelos had said. "But once you feel them, you must master them."

"What if I can't?"

"Then your mind will unravel and your body will fall as if in sleep. You will waste away here until you starve, staring at the darkness as your scattered mind tumbles though an endless night."

Khyven stared at Rauvelos. "So… that's bad, is what you're saying."

"These magics were not made for Humans, Khyven the Unkillable."

But Khyven hadn't hesitated. He had destroyed Rhenn's

rebellion, and if his life—or death—could resurrect it, he would take that chance.

He'd lowered the helm onto his head, plunging his mind into its dark depths. Khyven would never have described his mind in any particular way. He didn't "see" himself in his own mind when he thought about things, he just thought about things.

Suddenly, with the helm, it was as though his mind became an enormous dark room and he was standing in the center of it. Most importantly, he wasn't alone. It wasn't just him and his thoughts. He had sensed a thousand other creatures in that room, though he couldn't see them.

Each of those unseen creatures had their own desires that Khyven could feel, and the fiercer the desire, the "closer" they seemed to be to him.

And they'd sensed him, too.

Those faceless creatures had clustered close, pushed up against him, hot and muscled and suffocating.

He had shouted inside his mind, panicked.

"Get back!"

They had scattered like leaves in a storm wind. His command had flung them back.

For one breathless moment, he felt alone in his mind again, but then, slowly, the presences crept back, this time with fear and respect.

"You must tell them what to do," Rauvelos had said in the real world, of which Khyven was still vaguely aware. "Like wolves in a pack," Rauvelos had continued. "If you do not tell them what to do, they will become agitated, uncertain, and one of them will try to take control."

Within his mind, Khyven had told the closest presence to approach him and sit down. In the outside world, the nearest Kyolar had padded forward and sat down on the marble floor next to him.

"This is going to work," Khyven had breathed to Rauvelos, who simply watched him with those cold, bird eyes.

It was the last thing Khyven had said to Rauvelos before

taking his army to Rhenn.

Now, the helm was melting his body, inside and out, just as it had melted Gohver's. Khyven was beginning to feel a tenderness on the top of his shoulder now as well, beneath his tunic.

It's in my blood, he thought. *It's moving through me.*

"There!" Rhenn and Lorelle shouted over the wind at the same time. They both pointed down at the long line of stones they had been following from above, and the mouth of a cave where the line abruptly ended. Khyven peered down, trying to see past the wide cowl of the helm. Every other path Rhenn and her crew had made through the noktum had two lines, bordering the space where a traveler should walk. This was just a single line of stones, as though it had been made long ago before Rhenn and Lorelle had decided how to shape their noktum paths.

Khyven let his focus on the real world fade and retreated into the helm, into that room in his mind.

The Kyolars were the easiest to command, as it turned out. He gave them an order, there was a notable resistance, but soon they capitulated. Once cowed, though, they stayed true to Khyven's mandates without reinforcement for a long time. The Sleeths, by contrast, had been amazingly easy to cow. There was barely any resistance at all before they did Khyven's bidding, but they were flighty, as though their brains weren't large enough to hold a thought long. If he didn't reinforce the command every few minutes, they would begin to fly away. One of them had even dived at Vohn and almost bit him before Khyven had brought the creature back under control.

The Gylarns were flat-out the worst. It took tremendous effort to get them to bend in the first place, and they kept trying to break free of Khyven's control. Part of his attention had been on them constantly since they'd begun their journey, and it was the reason he'd only commanded five of them to come on this quest. He wasn't sure he could handle any more than that.

The bat creatures dove toward the cave, then pulled up at the last moment, settling more or less gently on the ground. Everyone dismounted gratefully, with Khyven last.

The moment Khyven's feet hit the grassy turf, the Gylarns leapt into the air and flapped high into the sky.

"What's happening?" Rhenn asked, watching the Gylarns wing away even as the Sleeths clustered in a writhing mass overhead, blotting out the Gylarns and the sky. The hundreds of Kyolars arrived moments later, lining up in row upon row that seemed to go back forever.

"I let the Gylarns go," Khyven gasped at the relief of not having to control them anymore. "I think the Kyolars and the Sleeths will be more than enough to do the job."

Rhenn looked wistfully at the sky as though she didn't want to waste a single resource.

"Do you think we'll need them?" Khyven asked, and he steeled himself to call the great bats back.

"No," Lorelle answered for Rhenn. "She just doesn't want to go in there."

Rhenn flashed an angry look at Lorelle.

"It's killing him, Rhenn," Lorelle said. "You could see the strain on his face. The Gylarns were harder to master than the others. Is that not correct, Khyven?"

"I'll call them back, if you like," he said.

Rhenn waved a hand. "No. As usual, Lorelle is correct."

Rhenn turned and faced the cave opening. She took a deep breath and murmured to Lorelle, "We were girls when we came out of there."

"We are not girls any longer," Lorelle replied.

"What's in there?" Khyven asked.

"When we came through the tunnel the first time, we battled one of those." She looked overhead. "What did you call them? Sleeths?"

"Yes."

"A Sleeth attacked us when we came out," Lorelle said. "We had to fight it and we had no weapons. We almost died."

"Lorelle saved me," Rhenn said.

"We saved each other," Lorelle murmured.

"Well, it appears as though the Sleeths are on our side this time," Vohn said. "Is there any other reason we should wait?"

"No," Rhenn said, starting forward, but slowly.

"And the other side? It leads into the palace?" Vohn asked.

"Into the lowest room of the palace, some secret place my father kept hidden my whole life," Rhenn said.

"An open doorway to the noktum inside the palace? That seems unwise," Vohn said.

"It was always closed and locked behind a gate." Rhenn pulled an old, iron key out of her tunic. "But I have the key."

"And Vamreth doesn't know about it?" Khyven asked.

"Oh, he knows about it, but he would never imagine we'd use it like this. Come back through it, bringing an army with us. He'll be surprised."

"To say the least," Vohn murmured, looking nervously back at the frenetic Sleeths and the horde of chill inducing Kyolars.

Khyven started toward the cave's entrance. His muscles felt weak, his bones soft, and his skin had begun to bubble down the length of his arm.

A fierce stab lanced through his thigh and he gasped. Before he could stop himself, he fell hard, landing on his side. His head smacked a rock outcropping and the helm tumbled away.

"Khyven!" Lorelle leapt toward him. She crossed ten feet effortlessly, landed in a graceful crouch, and knelt at his side. She gasped when she saw his face.

"That bad, is it?" he said wryly.

Her delicate eyebrows came together in concern and the tips of her hair began to glow, adding pink to her cheeks in this land of black and gray. She rummaged through her satchel and came out with a small box.

"My helm," he said. "I need to put it back on. The Sleeths…"

Rhenn and Vohn stayed respectfully behind Lorelle and let her work. She opened the box, hesitated as she looked inside, then selected two vials.

"Open your mouth," she said.

"The helm—"

"Stop talking and open your mouth. You can have the Senji-be-damned helm back in a moment," Lorelle snapped. Rhenn and Vohn exchanged a look, eyebrows raised. Khyven chuckled, then opened his mouth.

"Just… keep it turned up and stay like that," Lorelle said as she uncorked each of the vials. She held them poised over his mouth with a look of intense concentration, then she poured a little from the right-hand vial and more than half from the left. After a second, she poured a little more from the right. "Swish it," she said. He did.

She shook her head like she was disappointed in something none of them could see, and she sat back. "Okay, swallow it." He did.

Lorelle glanced over her shoulder at Rhenn, who looked on gravely.

"I need that helm or the Sleeths are going to start diving at us—" As he spoke, something wet flecked his chin. He reached up and touched. Dark and sticky. It looked dark gray, just like every other thing in the noktum, but he knew what blood felt like.

Lorelle stood up, facing away without looking at him, as though she didn't want to show him her face.

He turned gingerly, picked up the helm, and set it back on his head. It seemed far heavier this time, but there was also a sense of relief. Its power flooded through him and he immediately felt the presence of all the Sleeths and Kyolars in his mind. The Kyolars were fine, but the Sleeths were restless, as expected. He reinforced his command for them to hover over them, awaiting his next order. They capitulated.

"We have to hurry," he said. He rolled to his knees, ready to stand, and every movement hurt. Vohn and Rhenn helped him up, and even their hands on him seemed to burn. He gritted his teeth.

"What happens if…" Rhenn began, then she steeled herself and finished. "If you… lose control before we're finished."

"I don't know," he said. "I think most of them will flee back to the noktum if they know which way to go. Even at night, they don't like being out in our world. They'll probably try to eat anything they can on the way. Your necklaces should protect you. So, we get in, make a run through the palace, and I send them away."

"How many stairs do you think you can climb like this?" Rhenn said.

"As many as it takes," he replied.

Rhenn pressed her lips into a line, then nodded.

Together, they started into the tunnel, and Khyven commanded his army to wait at the entrance. Rhenn had insisted their attack be focused and precise. He wanted to be on the far side of the tunnel, into the palace so he could see the lay of the land before he let the beasts wreak havoc.

His forehead seared, his bruised right arm throbbed, and his leg now felt like someone had stuck a spike in it. He had no idea what that was, but it didn't bode well. He limped harder into the dark.

Just let me see Vamreth's face, Khyven thought. *Just give me a glimpse and I'll send the entire horde at him. Senji, if I can do nothing else, at least let me kill that bastard.*

The passage went steadily down, deeper and deeper into the earth. Khyven stumbled forward, most of his attention on ensuring that his army stayed where it was, waiting eagerly for the attack order.

The ground evened out, and that's when Khyven saw orange light ahead. Torchlight. It flickered far ahead like a little round mouth.

"That's it," Rhenn said, pulling the key from her tunic.

Khyven's right leg gave way again, and he pitched forward—

Lorelle's strong hand caught his arm, held him upright. "Easy steps, Khyven," she said, her hair softly glowing about her face. She kept her stoic expression in place, so he couldn't deduce what she was feeling. "You'll be fine. You just—" Her voice broke and she cleared her throat. "You stay with us and I'll take care of you."

"Going to give me that kiss at last?" he asked. He wanted it to sound jaunty, but his voice came out a rasp.

The light of her hair glinted off her watering eyes and she forced a smile. "You just stay with us."

"Don't worry about that," he rasped. "I failed my family once. I'm not going to do it twice."

"No…" Rhenn's despairing voice came from ahead of them, and Lorelle's head snapped up. She wrapped Khyven's arm around her neck and practically carried him to the gate.

Except it wasn't a gate. It was two. The old gate Rhenn had mentioned was there, and she'd jammed the iron key into the lock, but a foot beyond it, larger and thicker, was a second steel gate. A steel frame had been fashioned for it, bolted into the floor and the wall. Rhenn twisted the key and threw open the first gate, thick and black and iron, and she threw herself at the bars of the second.

"No!" she shouted.

"He built a second one," Lorelle said breathlessly.

"I never… imagined," Rhenn said, her teeth clenched. "I should have known."

"How could you have known?" Lorelle asked, inspecting the gate. Khyven did the same. The second lock, thick and formidable, was set off to the side so that it would be impossible to hit it with any kind of force with a ram or a hammer. Not that they had either of those things.

"We go back," Khyven said. "We go through the city's front gate."

"You won't make it," Lorelle said.

Vohn had slithered between them to look at the lock closely, and he mumbled something.

"Well, we don't have any other choice!" Rhenn said.

"She's right. I can make it," Khyven said.

"I can pick it," Vohn said softly.

"I'm telling you he can't—" Lorelle shouted, then cut herself off in mid-sentence. Everyone looked at Vohn.

"What?" they all said at once.

Vohn pulled a little pouch from his tunic, opened it, and

shook it out onto the floor. Buttons and beads bounced across the stone, as well as lengths of wire, the broken point of a dirk, a coil of wire, a coil of twine, a miniature wine skin, and a smattering of needles.

"I think I can pick it," Vohn said.

"When did you become a picklock?" Rhenn asked.

"Tonight," he said, choosing the lines of wire, the dirk point, the coil of wire. He handed the coil to Rhenn. "Unwind that," he said.

She tried to pull it apart, but it snapped back into shape, slipped from her fingers, and fell onto the floor.

"What is this?" she asked.

"Something I'm trying. Pull it apart!" Vohn demanded, going to the lock with his pieces of wire.

"Well, isn't this familiar," a dark voice said from the other side of the gate.

Everyone's head snapped up.

Vamreth entered the room from the wooden door in the wide, circular pillar beyond the gate. Several of his thugs followed him: Vex the Victorious, four of Vamreth's Knights of the Sun and his royal mage, Slayter. In addition, four Knights of the Steel filled the room, crossbows loaded and pointed at Rhenn's group.

"If the Shadowvar tries to pick that lock," Vamreth said to his butcher knights. "Shoot him."

Chapter Thirty-six

KHYVEN

hyven's heart dropped. Even if Vohn was a burglar of the first order, he wouldn't be faster than a crossbow bolt.

No… No!

They could retreat. If they faded back into the noktum quickly enough, Vamreth might try to follow them to get the kill. He didn't know there was an army of Kyolars and Sleeths a hundred yards down that tunnel. If they could just get him to open that gate—

"Khyven," Lorelle said, touching his shoulder.

He followed her gaze to Vamreth, and his blood froze. Underneath Vamreth's arm was an enormous iron helm, a helm that looked just like Khyven's.

A Helm of Darkness.

"Spotted that, did you?" Vamreth said, his hawk's gaze on Lorelle and Khyven. "A gift from my patron. Did you think you were the only one with allies in the noktum? He told me what you were planning and he gave me this." Slowly, deliberately, Vamreth lifted the helm and set it on his head.

Khyven gasped. The world around him faded as he was slammed into that dark room inside his mind. The presences of the Kyolars and Sleeths were still there, but now he felt Vamreth's presence as well, and it wasn't like the others. Every Kyolar and Sleeth was like a tiny flame in a dark room. Vamreth was like a bonfire.

"Out!" Khyven yelled in that private place, but unlike the denizens of the noktum, Vamreth didn't budge.

"You don't even know what you're doing," Vamreth said quietly and forcefully, filling the dark room with throaty amusement.

A searing pain slammed into Khyven's head, a hot cleaver that tried to cut his skull in two. In the distance, he heard screaming coming closer and closer. Finally, the scream reached him, piercing his ears, and he realized it was his scream.

Vaguely, he was aware of arms around him.

"Khyven!" Lorelle shouted.

He stopped screaming, but the echo reverberated in his mind. His mind…

He was no longer in the dark room, no longer felt the presence of the creatures of the noktum, and he looked up at Lorelle without the shadow of the dark helm hovering over his eyes.

"The helm!" he gasped.

"I took it off. Khyven—"

"He's got them. He has the Kyolars, the Sleeths—They're coming."

Lorelle looked sharply at Rhenn.

"They are indeed," Vamreth said. He approached the gate, his retinue fanning out behind him, crossbows trained on them. "You see, little Laochodon," he said to Rhenn, "this was how it was destined to be. This should have happened ten years ago, but you cheated fate." He shook his head like he would at a recalcitrant child. "Fate doesn't like cheaters."

Rhenn slowly drew her sword, her eyes flinty. "The Fates don't want my blood. They want yours. You're going to die screaming."

A breeze picked up, blowing from the dark of the tunnel. Khyven could hear them, the hunting screams of the Kyolars. The Sleeths filling the passage, slithering through the air. They only had seconds.

Vamreth chuckled. "Am I now? I should like to see that."

"That is the one thing we have in common."

"You were so eager to flee the first time," Vamreth said.

"I was ten."

"Yet now, so eager to fight," Vamreth said, then shook his head. "No, I think I'll deny you that little satisfaction. Unless you're going to try to stab me through the gate?"

There was a *clunk* and the gate swung open.

"What?" Vamreth roared. His overlarge helm slipped askew as he jumped backward.

A sudden strength flooded into Khyven, filling his body. It was like a good night's rest, Shalure's electrifying kiss, and three shots of Triadan whiskey all at once. He leapt to his feet, strength vibrating in his arms and legs.

Pandemonium broke loose.

Rhenn leapt straight at Vamreth, her sword missing him by inches as he stumbled backward. Vamreth's Knights of the Sun leapt at Rhenn. Lorelle blew a dart from her blowgun. Crossbow strings sang and bolts filled the air, impacting the stone next to Khyven's head and his leg. Vohn threw himself to the ground.

Khyven's heart raced, the euphoria filled him, and the blue wind swirled around his enemies. With a cry, he drew the Mavric iron sword with his left hand and leapt at the elites, deflecting a blade that would have cut Rhenn's leg off.

A Knight of the Sun went down, a dart sticking through the gap between visor and breastplate.

With a cry, Khyven spun, avoiding a slash at his arm, and ran a second elite through the side. The man gurgled and died, his blade an inch from Rhenn's neck.

Rhenn pushed Vamreth back, swinging again as the king scrambled to get away from her.

"The mage!" Vamreth screamed. "Slayter is the spy! Kill him!" Two of the butcher knights whirled on Slayter.

Suddenly, it made sense. The gate opening. Khyven's sudden burst of strength. Magic. *Slayter's* magic! He was Rhenn's spy in the palace!

Slayter held one of his clay coins before him, a grim expression on his face. A butcher knight leapt at him, and Slayter gripped the coin. White lightning crackled around his fist. The butcher knight swung at Slayter but missed. His swing continued, spinning the knight in a circle, a full revolution. And then the knight spun again. And again. He continued, faster and faster, like he was caught in a tornado.

The second butcher knight closed in on Slayter. Khyven wanted to help, but he had his hands full. One elite and two butcher knights sliced at him, and it was all he could do to keep ahead of the spears of blue wind that poked at him. He would have died right then if not for the Mavric iron sword. The thing seemed to know what Khyven wanted before even he knew. It danced in his hand, blocking, deflecting, counterattacking, and it seemed to weigh nothing at all now.

Sir Cantoy attacked Rhenn, but she'd finally come to her senses. She'd stopped her all-out assault on Vamreth and was fighting smart, putting her skill with the sword to use. Cantoy appeared to be her match, though, and their deadlock gave Vamreth time to regain his footing, his breath, and his confidence. He drew his sword.

"Push!" Lorelle shouted, and Khyven spared a precious second to glance back at his comrades. Sleeths poured into the room, slithering through the open gate. A single Kyolar forced its way through even as Lorelle and Vohn tried to shove the gate shut.

With a roar, Khyven attacked his three antagonists, the Mavric iron sword sheared through one blade and knocked the other two opponents back. Khyven turned and leapt at the gate, throwing his weight against it, but two Sleeths were caught between the gate and the casing. Beyond, barely twenty feet away, the rest of the horde barreled down the tunnel. Once they hit the gate, nothing would hold it shut.

With a cry, Khyven brought the Mavric iron sword down on the two Sleeths, shearing them in half. The gate clanged shut, and the lock clicked just as the Kyolars slammed into it, rattling the steel so hard Khyven thought it would rip free from of its moorings.

Sleeths dived at him, and he hacked left and right. The two otter-like creatures fell to the ground, writhing and biting the air. Lorelle screamed, and he spun to find a Sleeth with its claws in her shoulder. Two more lifted a struggling Vohn into the air.

Khyven switched his sword from left to right, wincing at the pain, drew his dagger and threw it in one motion. It stuck into one of Vohn's Sleeths, high on its left side. The thing shrieked and dropped him. The second Sleeth couldn't hold Vohn by itself. Together, they crashed into the ground, and Vohn rolled free.

Khyven reached Lorelle, threw the sword into his left hand again just as Lorelle stabbed her Sleeth through the neck with a dirk nearly as thin as a needle.

"Rhenn!" Lorelle snapped at Khyven. Her hair blazed about her face, lighting up the wall and the bloody Sleeth in a bright golden light. "Protect the queen, Khyven!"

Khyven whirled to see Vamreth and Cantoy pressing Rhenn hard, swords slashing. She was holding them off for now, barely keeping herself alive.

The Kyolar that had made it into the room stalked Slayter, who had managed to stop the second butcher knight, but blood soaked his robes from the knee down. He'd been hit, and by the way he was dragging his foot, it was bad.

And Vex was…

Khyven suddenly realized Vex hadn't entered the fight. Where was—

"Khyven!"

Lorelle's cry and the whirl of blue wind gave Khyven a split second's warning. He threw himself to the side as Vex's longsword sparked on the stones.

Khyven recovered his feet and threw up his blade, barely blocking Vex's second strike.

"You're better than when I last saw you," Vex said, his voice chillingly familiar.

The blue wind spears came again and again, and Khyven let the euphoria sing through him. He danced left, avoiding a blade, blocked right, deflecting another of Vex's attacks.

"I'll be even better when I finally kill you," Khyven answered, seeing the first funnel open up on Vex. It flickered, there and gone, and Khyven couldn't quite get his sword to it in time. It clanged off Vex's blade.

Vex chuckled… but it wasn't the laughter Khyven remembered from that fateful day two years ago. Vex's laughter had been gravelly. Still, Khyven knew that laugh.

The momentary memory cost Khyven. Seven blue spears lanced at him, all from Vex. Khyven spun and blocked, but only barely.

Vex leapt back, climbing the steps of a dais that stood before a giant archway filled with colorful, magic lights. Questions abounded in Khyven's mind. What was that arch? Was it some other door into the noktum?

He thrust his questions aside and followed Vex. At first glance, the giant arch looked like one of the archways in the Night Ring, but in the center, rather a mass of black, reaching tentacles, were shifting colors: blue to amber to green to red to charcoal black.

Vex paused before the archway. "You learned well, Khyven. I couldn't be more proud." He reached up and pulled his helm off.

The breath rushed out of Khyven's lungs and he forgot about the arch. He gaped. His arms suddenly felt like lead. The point of his Mavric iron sword clinked against the stone.

The man beneath that visor wasn't Vex. It was Nhevaz.

"Sorry, brother," Nhevaz said. "There are stories to tell. Maybe someday we'll even have the time."

Khyven still couldn't breathe, couldn't think.

"A parting gift for you." In a blur, Nhevaz raised his arms overhead and hurled his sword. Khyven flinched, but the throw wasn't aimed at him. The blade spun around and around, unerringly true, and struck the Helm of Darkness from Vamreth's head. Vamreth staggered under the powerful strike, dropping his sword, and falling to one knee. The thick, heavy helm clanged to the floor and rolled away.

"If it is meant to be, we'll see each other again." Nhevaz gave Khyven a half-smile. He said several thick, foreign words and held up a large coin pinched between two fingers.

"Nhevaz!" Khyven screamed, forcing himself to snap out of his reverie, to make his body move. He leapt up the dais.

Nhevaz stepped into the swirling lights and vanished.

Khyven dove after him—

—and smashed his face and chest against the colored lights, bouncing off them like they were made of stone. He dropped his sword and fell onto his butt.

Head ringing, nose broken, Khyven growled and scrambled to his feet. He staggered toward the lights and, this time, tentatively reached out to touch them. They were as hard as a rock. The colors swirled beneath his hand but touching them was like touching polished stone.

"Nhevaz!" But his brother was gone. Gone again, but alive! A dozen questions swirled through Khyven's befuddled mind....

Until clanging steel brought his attention back.

They were in the middle of a battle. He couldn't let Nhevaz's stunning appearance cause him to lose sight of why he was here.

He whirled around just as Rhenn drove her sword through Cantoy's neck. The knight gurgled, tried to stagger back, but he was stuck on the end of her blade. She lifted a leg and kicked him in the chest. The blade came free and Cantoy crashed to the ground in a clatter of plate mail.

Vohn huddled against the wall holding his arm, a dead Sleeth next to him. Slayter lay, unconscious or dead, beneath the claw of a Kyolar that looked like it had taken a bite out of his leg. The Kyolar's focus was now on Lorelle, who had put three darts into its neck. She loaded a fourth. The cat screamed at her and took a step toward her. Lorelle fired her fourth dart. The Kyolar wobbled, gave a querulous mewling sound, then collapsed.

The elites were down. The butcher knights were down.

Except for the Kyolar, Vamreth was alone.

The king lunged for his helm, even got his hand on it before Rhenn's boot came down with a crunch, breaking his fingers.

Vamreth wailed, tried to draw his hand back, but she stepped harder. More bones broke. With a whimper, he gazed up at her in terror.

"Rhenn!" he said. "Don't!" He shook his head, looking back and forth between her face and her bloody blade. "You don't want to kill me. If you do the—the nobles won't follow you. I'll...." His eyes rolled wildly as he searched for the right words to say.

Khyven went down the steps of the dais, picked up his Mavric iron sword and approached Vamreth.

As though she had eyes in the back of her head, Rhenn held up her hand, indicating he should stop. He did.

"Let me live," Vamreth babbled. "I'll tell them to follow you. I'll step down. I'll tell them you're the queen. I'll leave Usara and never return."

Rhenn cocked her head, took her foot off his mangled left hand, and stepped back. With the toe of her boot, she kicked Vamreth's sword toward him.

"Pick it up."

Vamreth glanced at the sword, then back at her. "Rhenn, be smart. You want the kingdom. I want to live. It's a simple exchange."

"I don't need you to tell me what I want. And I don't need you to give me what is mine," Rhenn said, her voice low and full of hate. "There is only one thing you can give me."

He glanced at the sword again, hesitated.

"I tell you what," Rhenn said, for a moment sounding like her usual self. "If you best me, my friends will let you go." She gave a significant look at Lorelle, Vohn, and Khyven. Slowly, they all nodded, though Lorelle was the last and most reluctant.

"You beat me. You win. The rebellion is over and you get to return to your insidious little life," she said. "Or... I just kill you right now. Your choice."

Vamreth's gaze flicked left and right, from Khyven's face to Lorelle to Vohn, and finally back to Rhenn. His good right hand, shaking, picked up the sword. He stood.

"Are you ready, Vamreth the Usurper?" she asked.

"Rhenn, be smart—"

"Are you ready," Rhenn repeated. "Vamreth the Usurper?"

Vamreth growled. "Fine, you little bitch." His sword came up.

"Oh yes…" Rhenn breathed, and she smiled wide. "That's the Vamreth I know. Now… Remember what I told you? That you'd die screaming?"

Vamreth roared and tried a quick thrust, tried to take her by surprise. He was fast.

Rhenn was faster.

Vamreth died screaming.

Chapter Thirty-seven

KHYVEN

Vamreth lay dead on the floor. Rhenn watched him for a long moment, then looked up as though she had performed a necessary task and was ready for the next. Lorelle, Vohn, and Khyven gathered close.

"We have three things to do now, and four people to do them," Rhenn said. "First, we need Lord Harpinjur and my remaining knights to come to the front gates. Vohn, do you feel up to going back through the noktum and getting word to him?"

He gripped his limp left arm, but he nodded. "Yes, Your Majesty." He got the key from Vamreth's belt, went to the gate, and opened it. The Kyolars and Sleeths had milled about for a moment, then fled back into the noktum the moment the Helm of Darkness had been knocked from Vamreth's head. Without a moment's hesitation, Vohn brushed his finger around the rim of his amulet and plunged into the noktum.

"Lorelle, see to Slayter," she said. "If he's still alive, make sure he stays that way."

Lorelle looked from Rhenn to Khyven, then back again. "Rhenn—"

"Just do it, Lor. We're going to need him, and he served us well. We can't let him die if you can save him."

"Khyven cannot—"

"Lor," Rhenn said tersely. "Please. Stay focused. This isn't over, and it won't be unless..." Rhenn's voice trailed off, and she avoided looking at Khyven. "Unless we finish this."

Lorelle stared at Rhenn, her brow creased. Her hair glimmered like sunlight flashing off a gold coin, but she gave one terse nod and moved quickly to Slayter's side.

Rhenn turned to Khyven. "Nothing went to plan," she said. "Yet we have prevailed. Vamreth is dead. That was our toughest battle, but—"

"But what's to stop another Vamreth from rising among the nobility if you have only a dozen knights to keep the kingdom?"

"I need a show of strength, Khyven," she explained, "and I need a showman to pull it off."

"So you *do* need a ringer after all."

She smiled, but it was a sad smile. "I do." She put her mailed hands gently on his burned cheeks, and the cool metal felt good. "Thank the gods for you, Khyven. I'm sorry. I'm sorry to even ask, but—"

"I'll do it," he said. "To the end of the job. But we should be quick. Whatever your mage did for me, it's starting to fade. Once it does..." He shrugged.

She nodded. "I understand. Here's what I want..."

Donning the Helm of Darkness again, Khyven brought back two hundred Kyolars and the swarm of Sleeths to the tunnel. He sent a different direction to one hundred Kyolars, commanding them to follow and protect Vohn from any and all harm during his journey, then serve as Lord Harpinjur's retinue.

Once Khyven's army of night returned to the room under the palace, he and Rhenn marched up the winding stair into the palace proper. They encountered a few bastions of Vamreth loyalists who fought, and quickly lost, but most swore fealty to the rightful Queen of Usara on the spot. In fact, Khyven was happy to see that many seemed grateful for her return.

Vamreth was not as beloved as, perhaps, he had thought.

By the time Rhenn's noktum army left the palace, at a stately pace so everyone could get a good look at the muscled Kyolars and frantic Sleeths swirling overhead, word had spread ahead of them. People woke and filled the streets to see the spectacle.

Once her audience had gathered, Queen Rhennaria Laochodon made her speech from the wall of a grandiose fountain in front of the Night Ring.

"Many of you know who I am," she said. "Some have called me the Queen-in-Exile, the Lost Laochodon Princess, or perhaps other, more colorful names. Whatever names you have used for me, I am the daughter of King Behniran Laochodon and I have returned. No longer lost. No longer in exile, but the rightful Queen of Usara. The usurper Tybris Vamreth has been slain and his reign of tyranny is over!"

A cheer went up from the crowd.

"You will no longer have to fear for your lives, to fear being thrown into the Night Ring if the angry gaze of some butcher knight falls upon you. The gods sent this army from their noktum to aid me in my righteous quest to bring peace and prosperity to my people. The gods have judged Vamreth, and this is their answer!" Rhenn stared at the gathered crowd.

The Kyolars screamed at the sky in unison. Even Rhenn was startled by that, but she didn't show it except to give Khyven a sidelong glance.

"I ask you now to go back to the warmth of your hearths and homes. The nightmare is over. Justice has been served. The days of peace are coming."

Another cheer, louder than the first.

"Guards!" she shouted up the main street. "Throw open the gates!"

The hapless spearmen who held the gates hesitated only a second with the eyes of all the Kyolars on them, and with the Sleeths circling over their heads, threw the gates wide open.

Outside, Lord Harpinjur and Vohn, with Rhenn's twelve remaining knights, rode into the city with the hundred Kyolars padding along silently behind them, looking this way and that.

Lord Harpinjur and the knights' horses clopped majestically up the main road and joined Queen Rhennaria before the Night Ring.

"Long live the queen!" Harpinjur shouted, thrusting his fist in the air. A cheer went up, and just as it began to die down, Khyven made the Kyolars scream at the sky again.

"Join me now, citizens of Usara, in a peace guarded by the gods themselves."

Another cheer. Another scream by the Kyolars.

Rhenn held her hands up in the air, nodding to the crowd for a long time. As the cheering began to die down, she turned to Khyven, "All right, my friend," she said, her voice thick with emotion. "Let them go."

Khyven closed his eyes and commanded Rhenn's noktum army to run through the front gate and back to the noktum. The Kyolars charged away, muscles bunching as they sprinted. The Sleeths swarmed in a horizontal column, spinning around each other as they shot like a giant arrow into the night. In moments, the army of night was gone, and Usara was filled with her stunned citizenry.

Everyone cheered for Queen Rhennaria, and no one noticed Khyven as he pushed the Helm of Darkness from his head. He turned, intending to set it on the ground, but it fell from his nerveless fingers.

The world spun. He heard Rhenn call his name as he hit the ground. His entire body felt like it was melting. But he'd done what he'd come to do.

Rhenn was queen.

Vamreth was dead.

Somehow, the pain didn't feel so bad. A cloak of satisfaction covered it over.

Senji be blessed, he'd done it.

"Khyven…" Rhenn's stricken face hovered over his, and he felt her hands on his shoulders, clinging tightly. She began to blur. "Hold on," she said, crying. "Just hold on…"

CHAPTER THIRTY-EIGHT

KHYVEN

e's a fighter."

The words warbled into Khyven's ears, not sounding quite right. A man's voice.

"Are you being funny? He's a ringer." A woman this time.

"Something nobody knows about me. I'm quite funny."

A dusky laugh. Lorelle's laugh. A happy laugh.

"Ah. See? He's waking," the man said.

"I'll get her." Vohn's voice this time. Footsteps moving away.

Khyven blinked. Warm sunlight made dust motes sparkle in the air. Tall, arched windows lined the wall to his right. White marble. The palace.

Lorelle's beautiful face came into sight, leaning over him. She didn't say anything, just smiled like she'd been longing to see him for a week.

Senji's Boots, she had such a beautiful smile.

The youthful looking Slayter, with his copper curls in disarray around his face, sat in a chair behind Lorelle with his leg on a high stool, elevated. Khyven blinked and realized that the lower part of the mage's leg was missing, and the stump was wrapped tightly in bandages.

"Slayter…" Khyven croaked, and his voice was rusty with disuse.

"Ah, he remembers my name," Slayter said. "I'm flattered. Though I question your mental soundness. A beautiful Luminent leans over you, and you say *my* name?" He looked at Lorelle. "Maybe he's dying after all."

"Stop," Lorelle said fondly, and Slayter leaned back in his chair and smiled lazily, like a man who had done a good job and was regarding his handiwork.

"I'm alive," Khyven said. "How did you cure me? You couldn't cure Gohver…"

"No," Lorelle said softly, touching his forehead like she was checking for a fever. "But then, I didn't have a mage's help, either."

"Slayter… healed me?" Khyven said.

"I had an idea," Slayter said. "It worked. We weren't sure. You were very weak when you fell. It was a rough road back. You almost left us several times, but you didn't."

Khyven looked at the bright windows. "How—How long have I been asleep?"

Lorelle and Slayter exchanged a glance, as though they didn't want to tell him.

"Lorelle—" Khyven began, preparing to insist.

"It's been two months," she said.

"Two months!" he exclaimed.

"Khyven, you are alive. That's what matters," she said.

"Senji's Boots…"

"Your insides were melting," Slayter said, then shrugged. "And also your outsides. And your face—"

"Slayter," Lorelle said.

"Apologies," Slayter said. "In short, it's a miracle you came back at all. I wouldn't have thought there was that much strength in a Human body, but you rallied. I doubted, but Lorelle… well, she wouldn't let you go. Some say death is the one inevitable force. But whoever said that never met a

Luminent on a mission before."

A cloud passed over Lorelle's expression, there and gone, but Khyven saw it. She smiled again, and the smile was genuine.

"I'm grateful," Khyven said. "But you two are dancing around my original question." He was more fully awake now. "*How* did you heal me?"

Slayter glanced at Lorelle, almost as though asking permission.

"Very well." Lorelle nodded.

"Giant's blood," Slayter said proudly, holding up a thick, short bottle. It was corked, but the bottle was empty as far as Khyven could tell. "We gave you a Giant's blood."

Khyven swallowed down a dry throat. "You did what?" He pushed himself upright, and Lorelle caught his arms. She seemed about to force him back down, but instead, she helped him sit up. A dizziness took him, and he closed his eyes.

The dizziness passed.

He opened his eyes and looked down at his arms. His right arm was splinted and wrapped in clean white cloth. His left arm had a scab in the crook of his elbow.

"You put Giant's blood into me?" he asked.

"Do you understand how Mavric iron works?" Slayter asked.

"It's… magical," Khyven said.

Slayter chuckled. "Yes, it is that."

"Well?"

"What about pitchblende? Do you know what pitchblende is?"

"Just tell me—"

"I'm trying, but there are several levels to it."

"I don't need the levels. Can't you simplify it?"

Slayter pursed his lips like he'd bitten into a lemon. "Fine. Giants can wield Mavric iron; Humans cannot."

"Rauvelos told me as much," Khyven said. He had withheld his first meeting with the giant bird from Rhenn and the others, but he was done withholding from them.

"Rauvelos?" Slayter perked up, like he recognized the name.

"Slayter," Lorelle said.

"Apologies, I just—" He pointed a finger at Khyven. "You

met Rauvelos?"

"Slayter," Lorelle warned, more insistently.

"Very well. Very well. But we are going to talk, you and I. I'm very curious about your adventures. The Helm of Darkness. Rauvelos. Do you know that he—"

"Slayter!" Lorelle said.

The young mage cleared his throat. "Right. Apologies. In short, your blood is too thin. Because you're Human. The power in the Mavric iron, once activated, saturates your body with magic it is not strong enough to handle. Giants were, apparently, made of sterner stuff. So, the Mavric iron allows you to wield great power for a short time, and then it pulls your body apart."

"That shows as burns?"

"It does," Slayter said. "And growths, and mushy flesh, and—"

Lorelle glared at Slayter, and he stopped speaking.

He cleared his throat again. "I had a theory, that if we put a Giant's blood into your body, it might—just might—mingle." He fanned his fingers and interlaced them. "Join with your blood and strengthen it. And if it did, the blood would spread throughout your body, soak up the magic and bolster your natural healing enough to overcome the Mavric iron sickness. And I was right." He turned to Lorelle with a satisfied look on his face. "There. Fast enough for you?"

"It will do."

Slayter smiled and sat back, adjusted his stump.

"Your leg," Khyven said.

"Yes," Slayter said. "Kyolar got hold of it. Just couldn't save what was left." He didn't seem upset about it.

"I'm sorry," Khyven said.

Slayter chuckled. "For what? For saving the kingdom and returning the queen to us? You bastard."

"I just…"

"Many others suffered worse under Vamreth's heel," Slayter said solemnly. "For ten years. You are to be commended. Part of my leg is a small price to pay for that."

Khyven suddenly realized this mage was far more complex

than he had initially appeared. What must it have been like to stand next to Vamreth day after day, to witness what he was doing, to smile and nod along—perhaps even to do horrible things in his name? All in order to preserve his facade so that, when the time came, Slayter could act when it mattered the most. The pressure of such a mission staggered Khyven. The fear of being discovered at any moment. The uncertainty of waiting, wondering if that one critical opportunity was ever going to come.

Despite all the difficult things Khyven had overcome, he couldn't imagine doing what Slayter had done.

"Like you," Slayter said, "I would have given my life for her." His smile returned. "I call this a bargain." He gestured flamboyantly at his missing leg.

Khyven reached out a hand and Slayter took it, gripped it with a strength that belied his skinny frame.

"Thank you, Slayter," Khyven said.

"You are welcome," Slayter said, and his smile turned wry. "Khyven the Unkillable."

"I suppose that name is never going away now," Khyven said.

"Was there ever a man more deserving of the title?" Slayter asked.

The door swung open and slammed into the wall as Rhenn burst into the room. Her wild hair had been tamed, swept back behind her ears and restrained by two intricate braids encircling the top of her head. The rest of her hair fell in a tumbling mass behind her back, and a golden crown perched atop it all, big emeralds glimmering.

Her green dress had a modest, flat neckline of green velvet overlaid with a thick gold and green brocade. It was tied tightly around her waist, then flared as it fell all the way to the floor. The sleeves, likewise, were tight around her arms and dagged at the cuffs.

She looked every inch the queen.

Except, of course, for her unabashed grin and the flush of

her cheeks.

"Khyven!" she cried.

"Easy," Lorelle warned, but Rhenn flung herself on him.

"Ooof!"

Half laying on top of him, she squeezed him in a crushing hug. He coughed and laughed at the same time, and then hugged her back.

"Senji be praised..." she whispered in his ear. "You are the luckiest man alive." Her voice became hoarse. "I-I'm just so happy," she whispered, still not letting him go.

She finally did let him go, scooting back on his bed. One of her meticulous braids had come undone, loosing half her mass of hair to tumble over one shoulder. Tears stained her face, but she was smiling.

"Well, that was an uphill battle," she said, regaining some of her composure. She wiped at her eyes, then reached out and touched his cheek as though appraising him. Her fingers left a cool trace of wet. "And you've got some nice scars to show for it. And a broken nose."

"Do I?" he asked.

She traced a finger from his hairline to his right eyebrow, then from his left ear to his cheek. "Khyven the Scarred. Oh, it's a tragedy."

Lorelle sighed and shook her head at her friend.

"You always were too pretty anyway," Rhenn continued. "But not anymore. Now you're rugged and...." She paused as though struck by a realization, and then threw up her hands. "Oh, but that's even worse! No maiden in the entire kingdom will be safe. They'll get one look at you and fall flat on their backs and—"

"That is enough, Rhenn," Lorelle interrupted.

Rhenn laid the back of her hand across her forehead in a mock faint. "Oh Khyven, you're so manly and scarred—"

"Rhenn," Lorelle warned, but she, too, was smiling.

Rhenn ceased her act and took Khyven's hands in hers, gripping them warmly. "Thank you, Khyven," she said seriously. She spoke in her queen voice now, that vibrant, compelling tone she'd used during her speech outside the Night Ring. "You saved my kingdom. You deserved to live and I'm glad you did."

"I cost you over a hundred and fifty lives, Your Majesty. One single life isn't enough to balance those scales."

"You didn't kill them. Vamreth did," Rhenn said somberly.

Khyven didn't agree with her. He knew what he'd done, and he thought he'd balanced those scales with his death. But here he was, alive again against all reason, and he silently swore he would spend this next lifetime in service to those with worthier souls. Those like Rhenn and Lorelle. Like everyone in this room.

"So, it seems like there is a lot I need to catch up on," he said hoarsely, changing the subject.

Rhenn grinned, seeming only too happy to move on. "They told you, did they? Two months," she said. "There is, in truth, much to tell, but there is no hurry. No battles that need fighting right now. You've earned your rest and then some. Walk in the garden. Work on getting Lorelle to smile."

"That sounds… divine," he said.

"Or you could just lay here day after day and let Slayter tell you stories. He has a thousand of them, and he won't stop boring us with them. Usaran history or Triadan history. Or Imprevar and Lumyn. Tales of Giants and the formation of the noktum and—Ye gods. It's your turn."

"In point of fact," Slayter said. "I should like Khyven to tell *me* a story."

"Well," Rhenn said as she stood up, still looking at Khyven. "Tell *him* stories, then."

Khyven nodded, and Rhenn stood there, seeming to enjoy the look of him being alive and awake. Vohn slipped past her and stood by Khyven's bed. His dark face reflected the emotions everyone in the room shared, and he wore his spectacles, just as Khyven had envisioned the first time he'd met the Shadowvar.

Vohn took his hand and patted it. "I knew you would make it," he said. "They doubted, but I knew." He released Khyven's hand and stepped away, taking his place behind Rhenn.

Khyven looked at them each in turn, and warmth flowed

through him, a feeling he dimly recalled from his buried, forgotten childhood. No one spoke, he just let the warmth spread through him.

The world, for so long a cold, frightening place, was suddenly warmer. It was suddenly safe for the first time because he was surrounded by those he trusted, by his new family.

"All right," Lorelle finally said. "I believe I will put my foot down now. Get out. All of you."

"I as well?" Slayter said.

"Especially you. Story time later."

"Oh, very well. My crutches, if you please," he said to Vohn, but Rhenn had them in hand, passed them to him, and helped him to stand. The three of them headed toward the door, with Vohn and Slayter talking about something called a "prosthetic." They shut the door and the room was quiet.

"Now, you sleep," Lorelle said softly to Khyven.

He realized she was right. The excitement had buoyed him up, but it was as though he only had a thimble full of vitality to spare, and suddenly he was exhausted.

She helped him lay back down, then adjusted the coverlet over him.

"Welcome back," she murmured.

"Thank you. It's good to be back."

"I believe I owe you something," she said.

"Do you?"

She leaned over and pressed her lips to his. The kiss was long, soft, and meaningful, as though Lorelle wanted to push into him how much she had missed him. She withdrew.

"Lorelle—" he said, stunned.

"For you. For being… more than I imagined you could be." She smiled, and the smile seemed a little sad.

The lump in his throat stopped him from speaking.

"Sweet dreams," she said.

"But I—"

"Stories are for later. For now, sleep." She stood, went to the door, gave him one last glance, then closed it behind her.

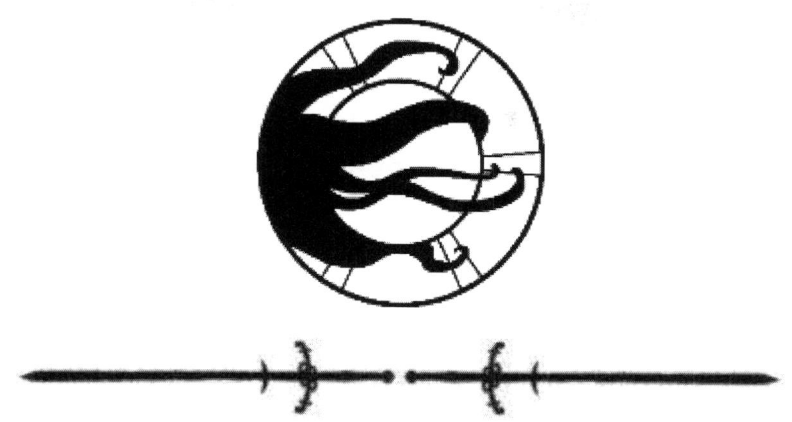

Epilogue

RHENN

Rhenn looked at herself in the mirror, her white night dress glowing in the moonlight that shone through the window. Everything had come together. The kingdom had rallied under her banner. There had been some pockets of resistance, of course. Duke Derinhalt had fled to his holdings in the south and refused to respond to her entreaties to talk, but the rest of the nobility had seemed grateful for her return. In the end, Vamreth had not been a popular ruler.

It was as though the ten years of strife and bad luck had suddenly reversed, as though the gods felt remorse for all the suffering Vamreth had created and sought to make restitution. She kept waiting for something awful to happen, but it didn't.

Rhenn was settling into her new life. She addressed problems. She made commands. It was what she was good at, and she loved doing it. She thrived being the center of attention, being where people constantly needed her. She always had.

Of course, there were downsides as well. She glanced at the ornate green dress draped over the changing screen. She had thought she would enjoy dressing in finery again, but every time her maid laced her up in one of those damned queenly dresses, she thought she would suffocate. More and more, she longed for her woodsman's garb.

Her gaze went from the changing screen to the bed, and then slowly to the rest of the room.

This had once been her father's and her mother's room, the room in which Vamreth had cut them down. He had, of course, changed it around, but Rhenn had disposed of every one of Vamreth's personal effects once she reclaimed the palace. She'd burned most of Vamreth's things, sold the rest, had this room scrubbed top to bottom, and re-outfitted it with a new bed, a new wardrobe, chest of drawers, and two full-length mirrors. It was a start. She had washed the stain of Vamreth away as best she could. The only specter of his presence lingered in her memories.

She had thought of putting the room back together exactly as her parents had made it, but she'd known that was the wrong choice. Let her parents become legends, not ghosts. Rhenn was here for her people to start a new age, not to lament the tragedies of the past.

A light knock came on the door, and Rhenn smiled.

"Come in," she said.

Lorelle entered. "Are you ready?" she asked.

"In a moment," Rhenn said.

Lorelle closed the door behind her and walked quietly across the room. She kept her gaze on the floor as she approached, and that told Rhenn all she needed to know.

"You didn't tell him, did you?" Rhenn asked.

"Not yet, no."

Rhenn let out a little sigh.

"He carries enough without having to carry that as well," Lorelle said. "Let him heal."

"He is healing, and he might like to carry it."

Lorelle drew a long, quiet breath. She didn't let it out, and she nodded.

"I'm sorry it frightens you," Rhenn said.

"Yes," Lorelle said. Her hair began to glow softly and tears welled in her eyes.

"He wouldn't have survived without it," Rhenn said.

"I know." She gave a sad smile and the tears spilled down her cheeks. Rhenn went to her friend and hugged her. "I thought I would…" Lorelle said, barely able to speak. "I simply didn't see it happening that way."

"It's going to be all right," Rhenn whispered in Lorelle's ear.

"At least now I don't have to go back to Lumyn." Lorelle gave a pitiful little laugh.

"Have faith," Rhenn said.

"I'm scared," Lorelle said, hugging her tighter.

"I know. And we go through our fear to the other side. We always have. He will surprise you. He has surprised us time and again."

Lorelle said nothing.

"It will work out," Rhenn murmured. "You'll see."

Lorelle released Rhenn and wiped at her eyes. She let out a little breath as she looked at her wet sleeve. "Tears. By the gods, it's been forever."

Rhenn gripped her arms and held her friend's gaze. "You have to tell him."

"I didn't ask him. I just—"

"You gave him half your soul and it saved his life, Lorelle." Rhenn touched her sister's cheek. "You think he's going to be angry with you for that?"

"He will feel obligated. A Soulbond must be free, Rhenn."

"Maybe he wants to feel obligated."

Lorelle broke the gaze and looked down again. Finally, she nodded. "I'll tell him," Lorelle said. "Perhaps tomorrow."

"Very well," Rhenn said, and she let it drop.

Rhenn looked at the room and let out a breath. "Are you ready, or should we wait a moment?" she asked.

"Lotura knows I'd rather do anything else." Lorelle flicked away her tears and her sad tone changed to her usual neutral one. "I am ready."

"Tonight, we banish the evil," Rhenn said. "We reclaim what

was ours."

Lorelle took Rhenn's hand as they both faced the room, their fingers interlaced.

Slowly, carefully, they retraced their steps from that horrible night ten years ago. They visited every room in the royal wing. They bid goodbye to their parents, to Rhenn's siblings, to all the servants and guards who were slain the night of Vamreth's bloody coup.

When they were done, they went to her father's study, now her study, and entered the hidden doorway. They wound down through the tight corridor of the spiral staircase until they emerged into the circular room at the bottom. The bodies from Rhenn's countercoup had been removed and the blood cleaned the day after the battle. The gates to the noktum had been re-locked, and the room was as empty as it had been that night two frightened children had raced down here, trying to escape Vamreth's bloody knife.

Rhenn felt the culmination of everything, felt the circle coming together, joining that first moment to this one, with all the wounds and scabs and scars in between.

"Let it be complete," Lorelle intoned.

"Let it be complete," Rhenn echoed. "We move forward from this point."

The colors of the Thuros—the name of the ancient Giant gateway, Slayter had informed her—swirled within its stone archway atop its dais.

The new path forward had its challenges and plenty of them. There were mysteries aplenty, and Rhenn wasn't going to uncover them without putting the ghosts of the past to bed.

She drew a deep breath, let it out. Lorelle did the same. Rhenn let her father and her mother go, and she intentionally thought of the new things that needed her attention, not the least of which was learning more about this mystic Thuros.

Rhenn and Slayter had been meeting frequently, and they had talked about the Thuros a great deal. The mage knew a staggering amount of history and, despite how Rhenn had joked about it, she was hungry for those stories.

One of the standing mysteries was Khyven's adopted brother, of course. Lorelle had revealed to Rhenn everything Khyven had told her about his adopted brothers, and questions had sprung up like weeds in the wake of Nhevaz's surprise appearance in Vex the Victorious's armor the night of the battle.

How long had he been an impostor in Vamreth's court, posing as Vex the Victorious, and why? That seemed like a fleck of gold on a rock face, indicating a rich vein of mystery beneath.

But an even more important question was how in the thousand noktums had Nhevaz stepped through the Thuros?

According to Slayter, no one could use a Thuros—*no one.* Not since the great wars of the Giants at the beginning of recorded time. Slayter said only Giants could use the mystical gateways, and the Giants had been dead for nearly two thousand years.

Slayter had practically vibrated out of his chair with excitement when Rhenn had mentioned the name Nhevaz. Apparently, there had once been a Giant named Nhevalos who had been the Lord of the Noktum in this region before the kingdom of Usara had even existed.

That seemed far too great a coincidence. She and Slayter had gone back and forth, asking a thousand questions. Could Nhevaz be descended from Giants? Could Nhevaz actually be a Giant himself? According to Slayter, Giants could live thousands of years. But if Nhevaz was a Giant—or of Giant's blood—why wasn't he… giant? Could Giants shrink to Human size?

But for all their questions, Slayter and Rhenn could produce no answers.

Rhenn shivered. She was barefoot, clad only in a night dress, and it was cold in the bowels of the castle. It was time to go.

"You are fascinated by it," Lorelle said as she came up next to Rhenn and they considered the Thuros together.

"You're not?"

"We came to put the past to bed," Lorelle said. "Perhaps we leave this artifact alone."

"He stepped through it, Lorelle. Stepped through it and

vanished. That suddenly makes it our future, not the past. How did he do that? Who is he really? Why was he here? We have to know."

Lorelle said nothing.

The colors in the archway swirled faster, agitated, as though responding to Rhenn's words.

"Senji's Eyes..." Rhenn breathed. Both she and Lorelle stepped cautiously back.

"What is happening?" Lorelle asked.

Rhenn reached for her sword and realized it wasn't there.

Like a body rising from rainbow water, a figure emerged from the Thuros.

It was Nhevaz! And he was no longer dressed as Vex the Victorious in plate mail armor but rather in plain, brown leathers. He stepped onto the dais.

Vex the Victorious had always been a big man, but when she looked at Nhevaz—with all the thoughts on Giants rushing through her head—he seemed enormous now. She felt for all the world like she should run, but she was overwhelmed by the need to *know*. Lorelle gripped her hand, as though to pull her away, but she too, hesitated.

"I'm sorry," Nhevaz said. "I would have liked for this to have gone differently, but I see no other option. He lived, and that means things will move quickly now."

"Who are you?" Rhenn blurted. "Are you Nhevalos? Are you a Giant?"

Nhevaz flung a coin at their feet, and too late Rhenn tried to back up. She knew what it was. Slayter's spells looked just like that. The metal coin had an elaborate, symmetrical symbol on it. White lightning flashed.

Rhenn couldn't move. It felt like stiff rods had been stuck in her arms and legs and along her spine, like she was nothing but a garment on a clothes hanger. Even her eyes wouldn't move, but in her peripheral vision, she saw Lorelle was also frozen.

Nhevaz stepped down from the dais and walked toward them.

"This is the only way." He picked up Rhenn and put her on

his shoulder like a piece of cord wood. She tried to scream, but nothing came out. Nhevaz walked back up the dais and turned.

"Tell him not to follow. Not to even try," he said to Lorelle. "It isn't time yet, and they will kill him."

Nhevaz turned again, carrying Rhenn closer to the swirling colors. She screamed inside her own mind.

The Thuros engulfed them.

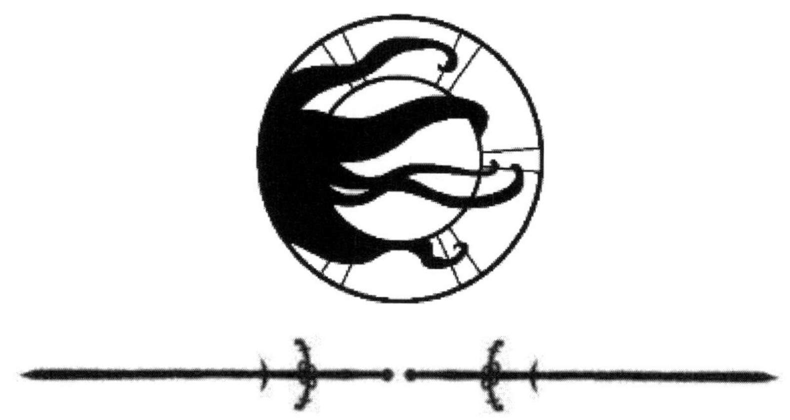

Interlude

ELEGATHE VENTINE, HIGH MASTER OF NOKSONON

Elegathe stood at the base of the dais before the glowing, multi-colored swirl of the Thuros. She felt like a young apprentice again: uncertain, vulnerable, immersed in a world she knew nothing about, like she was when Darjhen first took her in. She hated that feeling.

Her High Master's black velvet robes, custom fit by the Order's tailors, hugged her body and gave a stylish window of her cleavage while her black cloak hung from her shoulders to the floor, completing the mysterious silhouette of a Reader.

The air smelled stale, ancient, but she took a long breath of it anyway to steady herself, quietly so Darjhen wouldn't notice.

He noticed anyway. The old man never seemed to miss anything.

"Don't be nervous," he said. "I'll do the talking."

She turned a cool glance on him, a look she had mastered over the past decade. "You," she said coldly, "do not tell me what to do anymore. You're not my master. Remember that. If the others knew you were alive, you wouldn't be for long."

He chuckled drily.

"Are you laughing at me?" she asked, then snapped her mouth shut and turned her head away, mentally berating herself. That was something an apprentice would do, something the emotionally volatile young woman she had once been would say.

Damn it. And damn Darjhen! Damn him to Senji's third abyss.

Elegathe, the newly anointed High Master of the Readers, would never have blurted such a thing. Not for a decade. She was known on the Council for being cool and in control. Immovable. Unflappable. She always seemed to know what to say, what to do. It was why *she* was the High Master of the Council of Noksonon now, rather than any of a cadre of older Readers, and all at the unprecedented age of twenty-nine. The Reader next closest in age was two decades her senior.

In the last ten years, Elegathe had cunningly built her power base, both magically and politically, among the Readers. She had become apprentice to High Master Lengstrom two years ago over the favored choice, a man thirty years her senior. Now she was the youngest High Master in history because she kept them guessing and she knew how to move every single one of them where she wanted them to go.

With the recent death of High Master Lengstrom, Elegathe had jockeyed her way into his spot, and she now held the key, the Plunnos, given only to a High Master. The Plunnos opened the Thuros, the gateway that swirled before her, which would take the High Master to the secret Hand of Fate Conclave—a gathering of the High Masters from each of the other continents in the world.

The people of Noksonon didn't even know there *were* other continents besides Noksonon. They certainly didn't know there were other Readers on those continents. By Senji, most of them weren't even aware of the Readers of Noksonon, who quietly kept the knowledge of all things within their great libraries and their highly trained minds.

But while the general populace of Noksonon was, in Elegathe's estimation, ignorant and her Order highly educated, even the Readers didn't know about the Hand of Fate Conclave.

Only Lengstrom had—Lengstrom and his apprentice, of course.

And well… Darjhen. He had been High Master in his day, before his "death." He'd trained her, starting at age sixteen, embroiled her in his convoluted plot, he'd said, to uphold the essence of what the Readers really stood for, rather than the ever-restrictive dictates of the Order.

And she had believed him.

She'd believed anything Darjhen told her back then. She'd been a starry-eyed apprentice who adored him, imagined him as a grumpy-but-loving grandfather.

She knew now she'd been moved like a piece on a game board that only Darjhen saw in its entirety. She knew now he'd chosen her specifically because she was an orphan, because she would emotionally bind herself to him. She understood that sort of thing quite well now.

Back then, he'd asked her to follow him blindly and she had. He'd asked her to stab him with a dagger. He'd asked her to lie to her fellow Readers, to manipulate them by any means necessary and build a power base within the Council. She'd done it all, anything for her beloved grandfather, the only one who'd ever loved and cared for her.

It had been ten years since Darjhen's great spell, his faked death, and his abandonment of her. He'd not contacted her once—not once—until he showed up yesterday with his demands, as though she would simply drop her life to carry out his orders.

He was a rogue reader now, not her master. He had broken his oath and used his powers for his own ends rather than following the proscribed protocols of the Council.

He was no longer High Master to sling edicts. He was a villain, in fact, in the Council's eyes. If she hadn't helped him by faking his death, by "executing the rogue Reader," they'd have hunted him.

Elegathe's entire reputation was built upon that deception and now its architect had returned. Her solid foundation might as well be built on sand. One glimpse of Darjhen and every

Reader on the Noksonon Council would know the truth: she'd lied to them. The life she'd meticulously built would crumble. They'd both be put to death.

Certainly, Darjhen realized this, but it was obvious he didn't care. He resumed their relationship like she was still his apprentice—fresh-faced, gullible, and hanging on his every word.

Elegathe pinched the bridge of her nose and closed her eyes. She couldn't afford this turmoil. These were dangerous waters and she had to pay close attention to what she was doing, not to what she *wished* she had done. The fact was, she'd made her decision. He'd returned and, rather than casting him out or dragging him before the Noksonon Council, she'd agreed to help him. That was that.

The truth was, deep down a part of her believed in Darjhen. Senji help her, she *wanted* to believe in him....

She cleared her throat, feeling heat in her cheeks as she realized she didn't know how to operate the Thuros. The one time she'd gone through, High Master Lengstrom had brought her into the room only after he'd activated the Thuros. She barely had time to wrap her mind around the idea of Darjhen's return, let alone everything she needed to know to summon the High Masters of the other continents.

"I just touch it to the surface?" she asked Darjhen tightly, holding up the Plunnos, which looked like a large coin with the symbol of Noksonon embossed upon it.

"Touch it. Flip it. Throw it," Darjhen said. "It doesn't matter. It just needs to contact the surface, then it will bounce back to your hand."

"Bounce back to my hand?"

He didn't respond and she felt a flash of embarrassment. Darjhen never responded to extraneous questions, and she knew that. She was acting the apprentice again.

She had to calm herself, remind herself who was in charge here. Darjhen had come to her because *he* needed *her* help. Because *she* was the one who could open the Thuros, because *she* had put herself in that position through her own cunning and hard work—

A realization struck her, and her thoughts fluttered away. All but one…

What if she *hadn't* put herself here? What if she was High Master because Darjhen *wanted* it that way?

Impossible…

But Darjhen had read the kairoi ten years ago to see the future of Noksonon. Why not also look at her future as well, see what she could become?

She clenched her fist at her side, hidden within the folds of her cloak. Of *course*, he'd looked into her future. And if he'd done that, he would have positioned her to provide him this key at exactly this moment.

Senji's Teeth…

Ten years! It had been ten years… How could he possibly know how events would turn? But according to Darjhen, that was exactly what Readers were supposed to do. The Readers of old, at least. They manipulated events that were years, decades, even centuries in the future.

If she was still that young apprentice, she might have voiced her anger, but the woman who had become High Master marveled at Darjhen's mastery.

Darjhen pulled the cowl of his black Reader's cloak over his bald head and shadowed his face. His calm confidence supported her realization.

The confidence had to be an act, though, didn't it? The members of the Hand of Fate Conclave on the other side of the Thuros would respond to Darjhen like the Noksonon Council would. Kill him first, investigate how he'd escaped his fate later.

He couldn't possibly manipulate all the High Masters from the other continents, each of whom was as powerful a Lore Magician as he.

"What if I'd turned you away?" she asked him.

He glanced at her. Did his shadowed face show a flicker of pity? She couldn't tell. "But you didn't."

And she wouldn't now, either, and he knew it. They were in

this together.

She took a breath and followed his lead, pulling up her cowl and shadowing her face.

Despite his advanced age, Darjhen mounted the steps quickly and gracefully, with an eerie vigor. He moved like a man of thirty, not a hundred. She'd only seen him act his age once before, that night he'd cast his grand spell, the night he'd saved that boy from the burning manor, the night she'd stabbed him. It was as though Darjhen's body was kept young by his magic, but when he turned that magic upon something else he became almost debilitated.

She flipped the coin at the Thuros. It struck those swirling rainbow lights and bounced back, right into her hand, just as he'd said.

"Now walk through," Darjhen prompted.

"I've done this before," she said curtly. *Once before.*

She walked forward warily. The one time she'd gone through she'd held High Master Lengstrom's hand. Despite that previous experience, she was certain she was going to bounce off just like the coin, but the swirling lights gave way like oil. She pressed her face and body into it and the colored lights oozed over her. The oily feeling slithered through her hair and over her skin like she was naked. With a gasp, she emerged, expecting to be stripped and covered in slime…

But she was dry. She was clothed. She resisted the urge to pat herself…

And realized she wasn't alone.

The smell of the sea pervaded the room, humid and salty. Eight robed figures stood around a stone table with three concentric circles carved in its center. They clustered in pairs, each pair wearing the color which designated their continent: blue, gold, green, and red. They all looked up as she and the cowled Darjhen entered.

Elegathe gathered her wits in an instant. She knew the effects of presence and how important it was to cast an initial impression that served her needs. She had plenty of practice setting people off balance, misdirecting attention, creating pockets of indecision in which she could seize control of a situation. It was why she had cultivated her cool stare. It was why she had the tailors fashion form-fitting robes that accentuated her figure.

And it was why she now waited three heartbeats cloaked in mystery to let these waiting masters fill their minds with their own personal notions.

A beautiful red-robed young woman, even younger in appearance than Elegathe, turned a keen-eyed look upon her. Her gaze was sharp enough to cut glass and Elegathe thought the woman would pierce the shadows of her cowl and see that she was not, in fact, High Master Lengstrom. This was Jekka, High Master of Pyranon. She looked nineteen years old, but based on Lengstrom's notes, she'd been on the Conclave forever, at least three generations. The old High Master hadn't known exactly how old Jekka was, only that she was ancient.

"Lengstrom," Jekka said to Elegathe, obviously *not* seeing through the shadows of her cowl. "Why have you called us?"

"Not Lengstrom," Elegathe said. She flipped her cowl back and swept her cloak over her shoulders. "*I* summoned you."

Eyes widened. Glances flicked left and right, then all turned back to her.

"And who are you, a lowly apprentice, to summon us?" asked Talliah, the High Master of Daemanon. The tall, elegant old woman stood on the far side of the table in her Daemanon green robes, the fingertips of her hand touching the polished surface like she was posing for a portrait.

The smiling man to her right, and half a step behind, was her Vice Master, Abissar. Lengstrom's notes had lauded the Vice Master of Daemanon, indicating he was a model Reader, everything a true Reader should be. According to Lengstrom, Abissar was a staunch proponent of rules and order, a man who deferred to his High Master in all things.

Abissar's gaze dropped almost imperceptibly from Elegathe's face to the curve of her breasts and hips. His left eyebrow lifted a hair's breadth, and there was no mistaking his intentions.

Model Reader indeed. Good to know.

She made a few mental notes of her own about the man.

"Lengstrom…" the crazy-looking Te'zla, the man to Elegathe's left, began, speaking to the cowled Darjhen as though thinking he was Lengstrom because, of course, Elegathe herself couldn't possibly be the new High Master. She checked her ire and maintained a cool façade.

"Why did you allow your apprentice to break protocol?" Te'zla continued. His wild gray hair stuck out in all directions, and he wore ill-fitting gold robes that looked made for someone larger. "*She* summoned us? Only the High Master can activate the Aurora."

The Aurora was an emergency pulse of magic that somehow reached all five continents, drawing the members of the Conclave to this place. Typically, the Hand of Fate Conclave met only once every twelve months, on the cusp of the New Year.

"Lengstrom is dead," Elegathe said. "I am High Master of Noksonon now."

"What?" Abissar blurted, sounding both astonished and appalled. Talliah reached back and, without looking, put a quieting hand on his arm. For a flickering moment, his smile faded to an expression of subtle disappointment, perhaps even frustration. Elegathe suspected Lengstrom had been important to Abissar somehow, but half a heartbeat later, a grim, calculating smile replaced the friendly one he'd worn a moment before.

"It is as I feared," said Ulient, the blue-robed High Master of Shijuren. His quiet demeanor and steady gaze were exactly as Lengstrom had delineated in his notes, as was his cryptic response. He didn't elaborate on *what* it was he feared.

"I told you!" Te'zla gesticulated, the gravity-defying fronds of his white hair shaking back and forth. "The Giants killed him."

"Calm yourself," Talliah said in a distasteful voice. "It's far too soon to draw conclusions." Her calculating eyes flicked to Te'zla and then focused squarely on Elegathe.

Jekka narrowed her eyes and stabbed two long-nailed fingers at Darjhen, still hidden by his cowl. "This is your new apprentice?" she asked Elegathe.

Elegathe took a deep breath. Her part was over. It was time

to give control of the meeting to Darjhen. It was a terrible risk, but if he had orchestrated all of this then he truly was the only one who could navigate the meeting properly.

She stepped back and Darjhen stepped forward. She only hoped the young apprentice she'd once been hadn't been wrong about him.

"In a manner of speaking," Darjhen said and threw back his cowl, revealing his bare scalp and piercing blue gaze.

Jekka hissed.

"What is *that* doing here?" Talliah pointed, her voice cool, frosting the room with a regal authority one would expect from an angered monarch. Elegathe actually flinched. "*That* was supposed to be dead. And if it is *not* dead, it should be executed immediately."

Jekka pulled a long dagger from her belt. "I can make that happen."

Ulient held up a calm hand. "Wait. Let's hear what the oathbreaker says first."

"No!" Anya, Te'zla's Vice Master, spoke up for the first time. Lengstrom's notes hadn't mentioned anything about Anya, almost as though he didn't consider her relevant. She wore her straight brown hair pulled back into a ponytail so tight it made her pointed nose seem even longer than it was. She flicked an angry glance at Elegathe, as though this was all *her* fault, before centering on Darjhen. "He has forfeited the right to *live* much less speak."

"He is an oathbreaker," said Bakhar, Ulient's blue-robed Vice Master, "but Wyrd demands that we follow Her, not our own passions."

"We must hear his warning," Te'zla intoned prophetically, like he was reciting scripture.

"Forgive me, High Master," Abissar said to Talliah, letting his voice carry over the room.

Elegathe narrowed her eyes. Despite Lengstrom's glowing praise of this man, just the sound of his voice made the hairs on the back of her neck prickle.

"Perhaps we should hear him out and *then* kill him," he said in a smooth, reasonable tone. "Knowledge, after all, is the root of our power."

Talliah seemed to consider that, then nodded once. "Very well. If it is the will of the Hand of Fate, I shall listen to his lies." She glanced at Jekka. "I trust your blade is sharp."

Jekka continued to stare at Darjhen. She made no acknowledgement of Talliah or her comment, and Elegathe got the impression it had been rhetorical. Jekka's blade would *always* be sharp.

The frightening woman started toward Darjhen, but her Vice Master, Traemic, put a soft hand on her arm.

"Hold," he said.

Traemic was a handsome young man, and though he had been quiet this entire time—almost as though he preferred to remain in the background—he had a presence about him, something that made him seem… more important than he should be. Elegathe studied him, trying to understand the feeling.

Traemic's gesture calmed Jekka and stopped her advance, which surprised Elegathe. She would have assumed that any attempts to pacify the volatile Jekka would have driven her into a rage. Again, Traemic had… a way about him. He turned to face Darjhen. "Speak your truth and know it may not be Fate's."

Darjhen nodded, but his lip curled almost imperceptibly. Elegathe wondered if anyone noticed, but to her that expression was as loud as a snarl. Darjhen clearly felt that some in this room, if not all, were fools. "My truth. Fate's truth. Soon enough, nothing we think or want will matter anymore. Not unless we do something right now."

He flipped a large, heavy metal disk onto the table. It spun toward the center, then rolled loudly on its edge, getting lower and lower, louder and louder, until it flattened on the table with a final ring that echoed in the silence. The coin was significantly larger than the Plunnos Elegathe carried, which bore the symbol of Noksonon—a sun slowly being devoured by tentacles of darkness.

Each continent had a similar symbol: an open tome with five

lines of copy for Shijuren, a golden dragon with five spines for Drakanon, a green demon with five horns for Daemanon, and a mighty castle with five towers engulfed in flames for Pyranon. Elegathe would guess that each of the other High Masters's Plunnoi bore the individual symbols of their own continents, just as Elegathe's did.

The larger coin bore them all.

"It holds all of our symbols, not just our own," Ulient noted as though he had read Elegathe's mind. Each of the High Masters and Vice Masters seemed to draw in breath at the same time. Elegathe could feel the power of the huge coin, but she didn't know what it meant. The others, apparently, did.

"The Giants have returned," Darjhen said.

Fate's Dagger

BONUS SHORT STORY

Darjhen lowered his old body to a sitting position, wincing at the pain in his joints. Before him, Elegathe's slender silhouette cut a hole in the orange glow as she watched the manor burn. They stood on a promontory, a good vantage point for what Darjhen needed, but the wind blew uphill toward them. Smoke obscured the scent of fresh pine, and he took a deep breath before it got too thick. In moments, it would be difficult to breathe. He bowed his head and closed his eyes, shutting out the fire. He couldn't afford to be distracted. The kairoi was coming, and he couldn't make a mistake. He invoked his magic and opened his eyes.

In his vision, a veil of translucent blue spread over the sky, the trees, the smoke, and even Elegathe's dark silhouette. With it came… so many possibilities. But none were the kairoi he sought, so he waited, his magic ready like water behind a dam.

The magic leapt to do Darjhen's bidding these days. He'd practiced Lore Magic for more than a lifetime, but the important kairoi—the strongest confluences that could move future events—were still often elusive. It was so easy to misread the indicators, to make a mistake. A Reader had to be certain. He not only had to be willing to give his life for his certainty…but the lives of all people.

Of course, it was Fate's own curse that as Darjhen's arcane skill reached its peak, his body had begun to fail. He was running out of time. So was the world. He only prayed he could stay alive long enough to reach the cataclysm he'd seen coming… and do something about it.

He glanced at Elegathe and felt a swift pang of remorse at what he was about to do to her. She stood so strong at the top of the promontory, legs spaced equally apart, fists at her side like an intrepid child about to embark on an adventure. She didn't know how true that actually was.

She was so young for a Reader—barely twenty years old—but it was her youth he needed. Darjhen had searched the hearts of the Readers on the Council, and he didn't trust them. They had become too certain of their place in this world. They refused to see that the end of days was upon them.

But Elegathe had new eyes, a keen intelligence that attacked mysteries, and a mind that never forgot anything. He only hoped her loyalty to him would match her natural talents. That was the one possible flaw in his plan. He had chosen her so carefully….

But would it be enough?

"You are using magic," she said, sensing it. She was barely twenty, and already she could feel when he was casting.

He didn't answer her. When the answer was obvious, he never answered her.

"You aren't supposed to interfere," Elegathe continued. "Readers don't interfere with human events."

That was a lie the Council told the junior Readers. Unfortunately, the Council had come to believe it themselves. Except the Readers had come together thousands of years ago to do just that: to interfere, to move events at the exact right moments.

The enemies of humanity—Darjhen's enemies—were moving events. He had seen it. The continent of Noksonon was vulnerable, disconnected, ripe to be conquered. When the bloody, savage metamorphosis came, humanity would be enslaved. Or they would emerge triumphant. There were no other options. Noksonon needed heroes.

And Darjhen was going to make one.

A window shattered in the manor below as a boy crashed through it. He hit the ground, tumbling awkwardly. He clawed to his feet like a wild animal, eyes wide and full of primal fear, hands scrabbling with the dirt as he pushed himself to escape the fire. He raced into the trees.

Now Darjhen's magic came to life. The kairoi was at hand.

The magical blue tinge birthed darker strands, and they angled toward the boy. It was as though he had just burst through a gossamer blue spiderweb and the wind of his passing pulled the fluttering strands after him. They stretched out from everywhere: the manor, the trees, the sky itself. As they neared him, the strands coiled about each other, creating a larger, thicker, woven thread.

A kairoi.

Darjhen drew a swift breath. Fates be kind, he had never seen one so large!

The kairoi pursued the boy through the trees like a giant, slithering snake. It followed, and Darjhen waited…waited until it attached itself to the boy. He couldn't afford to be wrong. He had to be sure.

The thick, woven rope of strands hit the boy's back and sank in. Of course, he didn't feel anything, didn't notice that the world had just pointed its finger at him, shouting to Darjhen: This is the boy! This is the one!

"Come," Darjhen said to Elegathe. "We have to catch him. You have to catch him. My old legs are too feeble."

She turned, looking at him curiously. "We're chasing the boy?"

"Now, Elegathe!"

She twisted her Reader robes into a fist to free her bare legs, then leapt after the boy. Nimble as a squirrel, she dodged between the trunks, hopped a deadfall, and vanished into the underbrush.

Darjhen levered himself to his feet. His back creaked, his knees popped, and a small groan escaped his tight lips. He stood there until he was sure of his balance, unsteady as the pain receded. Once he felt he could walk without stabbing pain in his hips, he hobbled after Elegathe. He used the wispy blue threads to follow her, and soon came across her standing over the boy. He was sprawled, unconscious, next to a tall pine tree.

"He saw me chasing him," she said. "And he just…collapsed."

Darjhen nodded as though he had expected that, though he had not.

"Why did he fall down?" she asked.

He ignored the question.

"What will you do with him?" She tried another.

"Teach him," Darjhen said.

"Lore magic?"

"Yes."

"He's too young," she blurted. "He can't be more than ten." Elegathe was the youngest reader Noksonon had ever seen, and her training had begun at age eighteen.

"I do not intend for him to become a Reader," Darjhen said.

That stopped her. "Are you…can you do that?"

"I do not intend to consult the Council."

"I didn't mean that," she said. "Can you even teach Lore magic to someone who is not to become a Reader?"

"A limited kind, yes."

"Limited?"

"He will only be able to see a short time into the future," Darjhen said as he painstakingly knelt next to the boy, felt for a pulse. It was steady and strong. Perhaps the boy had simply passed out from sheer fright. "A second. Maybe two."

"What will that do?"

"It will keep him alive."

"For what?"

"For what is coming."

She knew about his cryptic statements about the future, and she didn't rail against them. Instead, she often went quiet. He imagined her keen intellect attacking the puzzle in her mind like a lion ravaging a deer. Elegathe craved the knowledge Darjhen possessed. And he wanted her to know. But he had taught many apprentices before her, and he'd made plenty of mistakes, which was probably why the Council was what it was today. He didn't want to train another Reader who simply learned what she was taught and did what she was told. He wanted her to figure it out herself, to make her own choices. She was smart enough. She was independent enough. He had chosen her for both of those qualities.

"He is a key piece," she finally said. "This boy. To...whatever you have seen. The dire future ahead."

"Yes."

"When?"

"Fate willing, not for decades," he said.

"But you don't think it will be that long."

"No." Darjhen looked sadly down at the boy. "No, I don't."

Elegathe went silent again, and he could practically hear the roaring lion in her mind, still attacking the puzzle.

"We are not telling the Council," she said.

It wasn't a question, so he didn't answer.

"Then where will we go?" she pressed. She knew he couldn't use this level of magic without telling the Council. Someone would find out. There would be consequences. And even Darjhen couldn't withstand the entire Council if they decided he was a rogue Reader.

"I will vanish," he said. "And you will return to the Council."

"Return to the..." Her head came up like he'd stuck her in the butt with a dagger. "I will not!" she exclaimed. "I serve you—"

"Then I have failed as your mentor!" He cut her off and

grabbed her slender hand with his gnarled, veined claw, gripping so tightly she winced. "You serve Noksonon, Elegathe. You serve humanity."

"But the Council—"

"Has forgotten that. Don't you forget as well."

"So we are rogue," she murmured, looking down at the boy again, but this time with rage, as though he was at fault for this sudden turn of events.

"I am," Darjhen said. "You will return to the Council. You will give me up. You will tell them exactly what happened here—"

"I will not!"

"You will, and you will be convincing or the best you can expect is expulsion from the Order. The worst? Death. You will tell them you killed me when you witnessed me affecting events without the Council's approval, breaking the rules for my own hidden agenda."

Darjhen withdrew a long dirk from his robes. It was thin and as sharp as a razor. Elegathe's eyes widened.

"What are you doing?" she whispered. "I'm not actually going to kill you."

"They have to believe it." The magic hovered around him, the immense kairoi pulsing, still connected to the boy. Darjhen focused on what he wanted, and the magic responded. A blue strand lazily drifted up and attached itself to his side, just under his ribcage. He put the tip of the dirk there.

"Wait!" Elegathe held up both her hands as though calming a skittish colt.

"This is what you will do," he said, calming her with the softness of his voice. "You will tell them you stabbed me, and that I died here. You will tell them I was working a great magic on one of the people in the burned manor. That person burst through the window, and ran to this spot, where they fell."

"That is what happened," she said.

"Exactly. There will be truth in your voice when you say it because it will be true."

She hesitated, thinking. Lions tearing into the puzzle. "But you're not leaving the boy. You're going to use one of the burned bodies within the manor, leave it in this spot," she guessed. "And you're going to take the boy away."

He said nothing. When she knew the right answer, he always said nothing.

"You're going to stab yourself and then give me the knife to show them," she said. "They'll test it. They'll know its your blood."

Again, he said nothing.

"Darjhen..." she said. "What if...the dirk... You are old, what if it does kill you?"

He ignored the question. "Keep your own counsel, Elegathe. Keep your thoughts within your head. The other Readers are not..." He shook his head. "Well, you must make up your own mind about them. I do not trust them because they do not look far enough into the future, but you may...find use for them. You are far more clever than I ever was."

"I don't want you to leave," she said in a small voice.

"If I am able, I will come back for you. If not, then you must make your own decisions."

"When? When will you come for me?" she asked.

"A decade, if we are lucky."

She drew a quick breath, and he could see she was fighting tears. "Then...I am alone?" she said, her voice breaking.

"You are strong enough to do what needs doing, else I would not have chosen you."

Her gaze flicked down to the unconscious boy. "How will you carry him...?" she began, then trailed off as the answer came to her. "You have help. A friend is coming to help you."

"The time for talking is done." He turned his focus inward and gripped the dagger. "Go," he murmured. "Be a Reader. Grow up. Learn. Hold your wisdom close. We will meet again." He tensed to drive the dagger in.

Her hands closed over his, pulling the point away from him.

He glanced up at her, ready to reprimand her. This was no

time to be soft-hearted—

"I'll do it," she whispered. "It will be more convincing if I do it."

He raised his eyebrows, stunned.

"If they employ Life Magic," she said. "They might be able to tell who was holding the dagger when you… When it goes into…" She trailed off. "Let me do it."

She was thinking, planning, looking to the future. The sign of a true Reader. He had chosen her well.

Her lip trembled as she gripped the hilt and put the tip of the dirk back where he'd had it.

"Guide me," she whispered hoarsely.

He put his hands over hers, adjusted her slightly according to the blue line that showed the way to make the dagger enter deep without killing him, and he prepared himself for the pain.

"Darjhen…" she whispered reluctantly, a final plea for some other course of action, but there was none. This was the way.

Her small voice showed her anguish, but it was the only thing that did. Her lip stopped trembling, and her hands steadied. Her eyes glittered with resolve.

Together, they shoved the dagger into his chest.

He gasped at the searing agony, and for a moment he couldn't breathe. For a moment, he thought he'd miscalculated and the dagger into his heart, rather than next to it. He fell onto his side.

She pulled out the dagger with a sob and stood. His blood dripped down its length, dotting the ground next to his head.

Elegathe's entire body trembled. Tears streamed down her face. "Darjhen…" She seemed to want to reach out to him, to help him.

"Stop crying," he rasped, bloody hands pressed over his wound. "Go now."

She turned and ran into the woods.

He waited, taking little gasps, trying to control the pain with the strength of his will. Elegathe's words hovered in his mind as all sound of her faded away.

A friend is coming to help you…

No. Not a friend. An enemy, Darjhen thought. An enemy who is going to save Noksonon.

A long shadow fell across him, the dark head, shoulders and torso unnaturally tall and thin as they laid across Darjhen. The enemy had come.

And no one knows what you really are, Darjhen thought. None save me and your unnatural shadow.

"Let's get you healed," the enemy said. "We have work to do."

About the Author

Todd Fahnestock is a writer of fantasy for all ages and winner of the New York Public Library's Books for the Teen Age Award. *Threadweavers* and *The Whisper Prince Trilogy* are two of his bestselling epic fantasy series. He is a 2021 finalist for the Colorado Book Award and winner of the Colorado Authors League Award for Writing Excellence for Tower of the Four: The Champions Academy. His passions are fantasy and his quirky, fun-loving family. When he's not writing, he teaches Taekwondo, swaps middle grade humor with his son, plays Ticket to Ride with his wife, plots creative stories with his daughter, and plays vigorously with Galahad the Weimaraner. Visit Todd at toddfahnestock.com.

Author's Note

What a whirlwind this project has been. *Khyven the Unkillable* is arguably the best book I've ever written, and it's an inspiration born of a writerly threshold I reached at the beginning of 2021.

Let me explain. I started out writing for myself, to explore my ideas, create my heroes, and manifest my dreams on the page. In short, I wrote to create a catharsis for my own psyche. I'm not the only writer who does this. In fact, I'd bet all the best books start this way. But I believe stories can only become amazing by finishing with the intended audience in mind, by intentionally bringing readers into my world.

This was a revelation for me. I'd always thought the best way to write a book was to pour my heart on the page and hope other people got into it. But what if I intentionally tried to serve the readers? What if I made a list of story elements I logically thought my readers would love? What if I kept checking off those elements as I included them in the book, "baking them into the pie" as it were. What kind of book would that produce?

Well, *Khyven the Unkillable* is the answer. That's the book you're holding in your hands.

What was my "intended audience," you might ask? D&D players. Readers who loved Dragonlance growing up, who geeked out over Forgotten Realms. Readers who followed the adventures of Tanis Half-Elven and Raistlin Majere. People who felt that thrill when Drizzt Do'Urden drew his sword. Readers who loved monsters and action and dire situations. Readers who like a touch of romance in their fantasy.

But the original idea—the idea that sparked this whole journey—wasn't even mine. It belonged to four other people I had no idea were going to become such an important part of my life.

Here's how it started…

It was a blustery day in late January, and I was pacing my office, which I do to sort through thinky issues. I'd just gotten off the phone with a group of friends, frustrated about a potential collaboration that had slid sideways.

About three weeks earlier—after a lonely year of COVID

quarantine—I was primed to collaborate on a project. I was so primed that I roped three friends into it, even though none of them wrote high fantasy. We had just finished a brainstorming session where we all picked five characters, five plot possibilities, then narrowed them down by voting.

The result was a half-warmed microwave burrito, this Machiavellian thriller self-help book about fighting for social justice with swords. My scalp had begun sweating halfway through the well-meaning, egalitarian exercise, and by the time I hung up, I felt that horrible drop in my stomach. I'd had the feeling before, and it always accompanied the expenditure of great energy toward an endeavor I knew was doomed to failure.

That's when the phone rang.

"Hello?" I picked up, glad for someone to distract me from my gloomy thoughts.

"What's up, Wild Man?" Mark Stallings said. He always greets me by calling me Wild Man. It's an intentional mispronunciation of Wildmane, the title character of the first book in my *Threadweavers* series. I had once told Mark that the character was based on an idealized fantasy superhero of myself back in college. So, he teases me by calling me Wild Man. I still don't understand the mispronunciation, but I get the teasing. Guys raised in the 1980s do that. Not sure why, but it's a sign of affection. In the beginning, I corrected him, but he persisted, so I understood it was a thing. It amused him. It's an inside joke.

I think.

"Hey Mark," I said.

"I have a proposal for you," he said.

"Oh?"

"We are forming a shared fantasy IP. We want five people. We just had our fifth bow out, and I was wondering if you were interested."

That was a lot to absorb in five seconds. Mark's good at that.

"What's an IP?" I said, playing for time.

"You call yourself an author?" I could envision him shaking his head. "Intellectual Property, Wild Man."

"Okay," I said. "You're making a shared fantasy world."

"Yes."

"Then why didn't you just say that?"

"I did say that."

"And you want me to write in it?"

"We want you to become a founding partner."

I paused.

"Really?" I asked. My longing for a collaboration reared its head, turning its dragon eyes from the warmed-over microwave burrito to this new bauble.

"We just lost our fifth," Mark said. "Rob asked if we knew someone who writes fantasy that we might get to replace the guy. Marie suggested you. I seconded. What do you think?"

"Wow," I said. "I'd… Wow. Y'all thought of me?"

"Immediately," he said. "Marie and I said 'You gotta get Todd Fahnestock.'"

Mark's really good at the flattery, too.

"Well… Wow. I'd be honored. What's involved?"

"Let's get on a call with the others…"

For me, that's how the Eldros Legacy began. After a few introductory Zoom calls and individual brainstorming sessions with the individual founders—Quincy J. Allen, Marie Whitaker, Rob Howell, and, of course, Mark—we all agreed on a D&D style fantasy in the vein of Forgotten Realms and Dragonlance, two series I had devoured as a teenager.

Late January gave way to early February, and ideas exploded in my mind. Those of you who know me know that when the muse comes to sit in my office, I can't turn away from the keyboard. My book wasn't due until September, but I couldn't hold back. I put my other two projects on hold and started writing on the manuscript that would become *Khyven the Unkillable.*

At this point, I need to give a nod to Jessica Brody, author extraordinaire who wrote *Save the Cat Writes a Novel*, an essential bit of writing know-how for someone trying to do exactly what I was now trying to do: make a story for the readers that's going to capture them and keep them on the edge of their seats until the end. In Jessica's book, she lays out a flexible structure for novel writing based on Blake Snyder's original and game-changing *Save the Cat* (a screenplay writing how-to).

Jessica talks about how, after she adopted Blake Snyder's premises, her books immediately got better and she began to get book and movie deals. I'd had a similar experience of success recently. In my previous fantasy story, *Tower of the Four*, I had used elements of Save the Cat, and the book garnered a wealth of positive attention, not the least of which was becoming a finalist in The Colorado Book Award and winning the Colorado Authors League Award for Writing Excellence.

With *Khyven the Unkillable*, I decided to make sure I hit all the Save the Cat story beats as an experiment. So, for the first time, I plotted out my book before I wrote it, then I sat down and got to work.

In a month, I had the first draft done. I went back, adjusting and tweaking, highlighting the emotional content, making sure it did exactly what I wanted. Or… so I hoped.

I sat back, swallowed, feeling that elated and frightened feeling I always feel when I finish a story. Getting to the end of a novel is always an accomplishment, a Herculean effort worthy of celebration every time. And at the same time, I'm always terrified I've created something flawed and uninteresting, that is going to completely fall flat.

It was early in the morning when I finished, and I wandered from my office into my wife Lara's and my bedroom to find her working on her computer in bed.

"I'm done," I said.

She looked up from her work and beamed. "Yay! Congratulations."

"I think maybe it sucks," I said.

Her smile kind of froze, like it had started genuine and was now forced.

"I think maybe I completely screwed everything up by—"

She sighed and interrupted me. "I'm sorry, Todd."

I stopped. "What?"

"I'm sorry, but I actually have a meeting early this morning. I have to do this email, then I have to get ready. I don't have time for this right now."

"Time for what?"

"For you to talk about how horrible your book is when it's not. You do this every time you finish a novel."

"I don't do this every time..." I said. *Do I?* I thought.

"You do," she said. "And I'd be happy to help you out tonight, when I have time, and be your backboard. But I literally don't have time to get into it with you right now."

"I don't do that every time, do I?" I said.

"*Tower of the Four*," she said, ticking off a finger. "*Ordinary Magic*." She ticked off another finger. "*Summer of the Fetch*. Every time, you go through this. And I totally get it. You're doing your process, and that's fine, but I'm telling you I don't have time to dance this dance with you right now. Celebrate. Have a milkshake. Shake it off. Call Chris. Give the manuscript to someone to read and give you feedback. You'll feel better."

As she spoke, memory flashes of Tower of the Four, Episode 6 came to me. God, she was right. I had worried it was crap, an unworthy follow-up to the first three episodes, which had won all those previously mentioned awards. I'd only calmed down after the rave reviews began coming in.

"I *do* do that!" I said, like someone had opened the curtains to the sunshine. "Why do I do that?"

She got up, kissed me long and lingering, then pulled back. "I have to get into the shower. You're amazing. The book is amazing." And she strode to the bathroom and closed the door.

I smiled, mollified. I do that when pretty girls kiss me. Damn, did I *ever* marry up.

So I did exactly what she said. I called Chris Mandeville (my writing co-worker), I sent the book to the Eldros Team. I shoved my nattering monkey mind back in its cage and let the book stand on its own.

And now here it is. I hope you enjoyed Khyven and all of his colorful companions. I hope you're strapped in for an epic journey, because my fellow Eldrosians and I are going to give you one whale of a story. You've only touched the surface.

Welcome to The Eldros Legacy. This one was written just for you.

Also By Todd Fahnestock

Eldros Legacy (Legacy of Shadows Series)

Khyven the Unkillable
Lorelle of the Dark
Rhenn the Traveler
Slayter and the Dragon (forthcoming)
Bane of Giants (forthcoming)

Tower of the Four

Episode 1 – The Quad
Episode 2 – The Tower
Episode 3 – The Test
The Champions Academy (Episodes 1-3 compilation)
Episode 4 – The Nightmare
Episode 5 – The Resurrection
Episode 6 – The Reunion
The Dragon's War (Episodes 4-6 compilation)

Threadweavers

Wildmane
The GodSpill
Threads of Amarion
God of Dragons

The Whisper Prince

Fairmist
The Undying Man
The Slate Wizards

Standalone Novels

Charlie Fiction
Summer of the Fetch

Non-fiction

Ordinary Magic

Tower of the Four Short Stories

"Urchin"
"Royal"
"Princess"

Other Short Stories

Parallel Worlds Anthology — "Threshold"
Dragonlance: The Cataclysm — "Seekers"
Dragonlance: Heroes & Fools — "Songsayer"
Dragonlance: The History of Krynn —
"The Letters of Trayn Minaas"

Want More Eldros Legacy?

If you enjoyed this story and the world it's set in, then the creators of the Eldros Legacy would like to encourage you to don thy traveling pack and journey deeper into the mysteries of the world Eldros and all the myriad adventures set therein.

The mortal world of Eldros is coming apart. The Giants, who once ruled its five continents with draconian malice have set their mighty designs on a return to power. Mortals across the globe must be victorious against insurmountable odds or die.

Come join us as the Eldros Legacy unfolds in a growing library of novels and short stories.

More Novels in Noksonon

Relics of Noksonon Series by Kendra Merritt
The Pain Bearer
The Truth Stealer (Forthcoming)

Worldbreaker by Becca Lee Gardner (Forthcoming)
The Beacon by Rebecca K. Busch (Forthcoming)

Founder Series in Eldros Legacy

Legacy of Deceit by Quincy J. Allen
Seeds of Dominion
Demons of Veynkal (Forthcoming)

Legacy of Dragons by Mark Stallings
The Forgotten King

Legacy of Queens by Marie Whittaker
Embers & Ash
Cinder & Stone (Forthcoming)

Other Eldros Legacy Novels

A Murder of Wolves by Jamie Ibson
Deadly Fortune by Aaron Rosenberg
Stealing the Storm by Aaron Rosenberg
Dark and Secret Paths: Warrior Mages of Pyranon by C.A. Farrell
Stonewhisper: Crimson Fang by H.Y. Gregor

Other Eldros Legacy Short Stories

Here There Be Giants by The Founders
The Darkest Door by Todd Fahnestock
Fistful of Silver by Quincy J. Allen
Electrum by Marie Whittaker
Dawn of the Lightbringer by Mark Stallings
What the Eye Sees by Quincy J. Allen
Trust Not the Trickster by Jamie Ibson
A Rhakha for the Tokonn by Quincy J. Allen